PENGUIN BOOKS

2086

THE HEART OF LONDON

MONICA DICKENS

The great-granddaughter of Charles Dickens, Miss Monica Dickens was educated at St Paul's School for Girls. She has been writing novels and autobiographical books since she was twenty-two, when she wrote *One Pair of Hands* about her experiences as a cook-general, the only job that her upbringing as a debutante had fitted her for.

During the war, Miss Dickens worked as a nurse in a hospital and subsequently took a job in a munitions factory, turning out Spitfires. During the latter part of the war she was again working in a hospital. 'I would like to make it clear,' she says, 'that I did not take these jobs in order to write books. The books just came out of the experiences.'

After the war Miss Dickens gave up nursing to concentrate on her writing, and has published several novels, of which the latest is *Cobbler's Dream*. Apart from her books, she writes a weekly column in a well-known woman's magazine. She is married to Commander Roy Stratton of the U.S. Navy, and has two daughters.

A list of other Penguin titles by Monica Dickens is to be found at the end of the book.

Monica Dickens

THE HEART OF
LONDON

PENGUIN BOOKS
IN ASSOCIATION WITH
MICHAEL JOSEPH

Penguin Books Ltd, Harmondsworth, Middlesex
AUSTRALIA: Penguin Books Pty Ltd, 762 Whitehorse Road,
Mitcham, Victoria

—

First published by Michael Joseph 1961
Published in Penguin Books 1964

—

Copyright © Monica Dickens, 1961

—

Made and printed in Great Britain
by Cox and Wyman Limited,
London, Reading and Fakenham
Set in Monotype Times

TO ROY

Part One

ARTHUR SEARS came out of the telephone box with a sliding twist, and looked quickly from side to side without moving his head.

Coast clear. Smart boy, Arthur. He had known when the other girl's voice came on the line that she was supposed to keep him talking while they traced the call.

So Miss Gasp-and-giggle had squealed. Ah well. Arthur ducked down into the Underground, slipping sideways down the ironclad stairs as if they were a ship's ladder, and in the acrid seclusion of the Gents, he took out a soft black notebook and crossed through a telephone number. Plenty more where she came from.

He lay low for a while, wondering whether anyone else had gone into the box right after him and been nabbed. What a laugh. He saw his mild face, with the loose skin weathered almost as brown as his gardener's hands, grinning in the silvered mirror. Wetting his hands, he smoothed them over his fluffy hair, exaggerating the narrowness of the top of his head, which sloped quite sharply inwards above the temples and looked like a turnip, he sometimes thought.

He rubbed his shoes on the backs of his trousers and retied his tie to hide the frayed part. That made the lower end hang down too far, so he pushed it down inside the waist of his trousers and went jauntily up the stairs and out on to the crowded pavement of Park Road. He wheeled on his heel and turned sharp right. Arthur liked to move sharply, so that people should think he had been in the Army.

'I'm sorry.' A woman coming out of the Underground in some kind of who-does-she-think-she-is hat stepped back as he turned across her. Sorry wasn't the half of what she would be if she knew that the front of her coat had just brushed the sleeve of the Beast of Cottingham Park.

Martha wondered why she had said that she was sorry, when it was the man's fault. No one said Sorry any more. They pushed and glared and schemed how to get on a bus ahead of you and how to get served before you in shops. In the Underground, a girl had trodden on her toe, and when Martha gasped, the girl had bent to examine her sharp heel, as if it were her shoe that had complained.

Turning right past the legless matchseller on his trolley, she gave him sixpence without taking any matches and began to count her steps from years of habit. Thirteen to the low vent in the wall where the sound of a wireless calypso and the smell of doughnuts frying in rancid fat came from the bakery cellar. When Martha was a child, it had been eighteen steps to the bakery vent, and the smell had been of steaming crusty bread, still hot to the hand when you bought it uncovered.

Twenty-three steps, past the dairy and the post office, to the sad little nameless shop: 'Second Hand Clothes. Misfits. Uniforms. Waiters. Weddings. Riding Clothes Bought and Sold.'

*

Walking briskly, the slight, innocent figure of Arthur Sears threaded its way through the crowds going home, or going out, or going somewhere. Going somewhere with girls. Arthur had never had a girl. Too dangerous. The Wilsons would like to get him for May, no doubt. Ma Wilson hadn't given him that new folkweave bedspread out of the kindness of her heart. She had no heart. But even old May with her broad moon face and her ugly hands would be dangerous. Too big anyway. You could suffocate under a woman like that. In his imaginary encounters with women, Arthur always saw himself as underneath.

Turning the corner into West Hill, he slowed his pace, so that he could come to a casual stop in front of the newsagent's glass case with the advertisements. Mr Angel, who owned the glass case, pushed his reptile head out over the counter which was open to the street.

'Still looking for that flat, cock?' He winked, a lizard's lid descending.

Arthur met his eye solemnly. 'That's right,' he said. 'Still looking.' He managed a little breathy whistle, though his insides were harp strings of fear that Mr Angel might know which of the advertisement cards he was reading.

'Second Hand Clothes. Misfits. Uniforms. Waiters. Weddings. Riding Clothes Bought and Sold.'

When Martha was a child, the dingy shop, with its window full of out-of-date clothes and hopeless shoes trodden over by forgotten feet, had been a blot on the respectable shopping street.

Now that Park Road was not so respectable, with many of the better traders moved away and those who remained gone gradually downhill with the district, the second-hand clothes shop was no worse than many. No worse than the snack bar with the sticky stools and stained linoleum counter burned into little ruts, the cheap lingerie store where a girl with black matador pants and dirty bare feet knelt in the narrow window to arrange the cone-shaped falsies and black and scarlet nightgowns.

These, like the Abracadabra Espresso, into which Martha had once wandered innocently for a cup of coffee and been scared away without it by the bleak existentialist stares of its ageless young occupants, were comparative newcomers to Park Road. They had sprung up like inedible mushrooms as the courteous grocers and the old-established chemists and butchers gradually moved away because their customers were gradually abandoning their unpractical Victorian houses to be chopped up for furnished rooms and odd-shaped little flats and basement clubs for occult sects.

Surrounded by the tawdry new growths of the changing district, the older shops, like the bakery and the dairy which smelled of babies and the old clothes shop, now had a certain charm of antiquity. Had it for Martha, at least. She had lived here all her life, and taken this walk from the station uncountable times, and the clothes in the window seemed to have been here as long as she had.

The mess uniform of the Sixteenth Lancers, faded scarlet and blue with all its tarnished gilt buttons but one, had been there for at least thirty years, for who in Cottingham Park would want it? Any more than they would ever want the black side-saddle habit on the headless dummy, or the pair of cracked brown hunting boots which leaned sideways away from each other behind the dirty glass, as if Jorrocks had pulled them off when he was drunk.

But Martha had wanted them once. When she was twelve, and hungry for horses, the boots had called to her every time she passed them. At last, in a state of hollow hypnosis, she had walked into the sour-smelling shop and asked the price.

The man with the cigarette wetly on his lip had laughed at her. They were men's boots, ten sizes too big. Confused with shame and disappointment, Martha had managed to say: 'Thank you, but I was asking for my father. He's going to ride in a steeple-chase.'

Although he could not know that her father was dead, the man did not believe her. He had laughed again and tried to sell Martha a walking stick with a handle like a shrunken human head, and she had stumbled out in a panic. The riding boots were still there, twenty-six years later.

The traffic from central London came down Park Road like an army, bearing the red banners of its buses. At the corner lights where West Hill came in with three other bus routes, and a press of traffic from the north, Martha waited to cross. Girls coming home from work with short crisp haircuts and Italian baskets waited with her. Men in grey belted raincoats. A girl with flat slippers and a shadow of a moustache holding hands with a bearded man in a vast black sweater like a tarpaulin. Two coloured women dressed gaudily for a party as far as to their feet, which were in quilted bedroom slippers. A schoolgirl from Martha's old school, the hideous hat unchanged through the years. The mass rebellion of Martha and all but the smuggest of Form Seven when they threw the black felt buckets into the river at Hammersmith had been in vain.

Martha thought of saying: 'I went to Queen Adelaide's too.' But the child would only stare, unable to conceive that a woman of thirty-eight with a flower-pot hat and a svelte umbrella which she dared not unroll in the rain for fear of not getting it so svelte again could ever have been a schoolgirl anywhere.

The girl's blunt shoes turning up slightly at the toes looked like Terry's, so Martha had to say it. The child did stare, uncomprehendingly, as if she had never heard of Queen Adelaide's.

The child went on staring. Martha looked away, like an embarrassed dog trying to be invisible. She could not escape, because although the lights had changed at last, the traffic was jammed across the corner in one of Park Road's Gordian tangles.

This section of Park Road was going to be widened eventually. The rumour of it had been around Cottingham Park for a long time. Martha would believe it when she saw it, the same as she would believe it when she saw all the slum streets of the Rise which dragged upwards towards the railway converted into sanitary housing estates, and the brothels of Carbine Road curetted clean of their unphotogenic 'models'.

She crossed with the crowd and turned downhill into the long deteriorated road that led to home. Released from the frustrations of Park Road, the buses thundered down West Hill, picking up speed on their way to the railway bridges and the far northern suburbs. Farther down where the road levelled out at the crossing of Armstrong Avenue, where Martha had lived all her life, it was all houses and flats and small private hotels with names like Cavendish and Excelsior; but at this end, near the junction of the main road, it was a clutter of second-rate commerce. A twenty-four-hour cleaner where the clothes hanging on racks to go looked as dingy as when they came in. A hairdresser with two red wigs and a contemptuous cat in the window. A delicatessen whose display of provisions was an accurate survey of the district's myriad nationalities.

The old flower woman with the shorn eyebrows and the bunches of flowers stuck into cooking-fat tins sat under what had once been the courtyard archway of the Rising Sun in the days when it had been a livery stable. Beyond her was the newspaper and cigarette shop, little more than a kiosk with a narrow space behind for cheap plastic toys and packets of envelopes that fitted no size of paper. Beyond that, where the pavement widened, was Zlotnik's secondhand store, with a mountain of junk piled up inside against the door and grimy windows, and a derelict array of tables and chairs and commodes out on the pavement with Zlotnik and son sitting on them.

As Martha stopped at the open counter for cigarettes, a young man in a duffel coat with a red, uncomfortable-looking face and a tripod under his arm counted his change and moved away.

'See him?' Mrs Angel leaned her negligible bosom out over the magazines to watch him go. 'Been hanging about here off and on these last several months. Him and some other fellows. Smokes Churchman's. Not my smoke, but it takes all kinds.'

To Mrs Angel, pale as paper with etiolated hair that had once been yellow, tobacco was not only bread and butter but the breath of life itself. You never saw her light a cigarette or stub one out, but there it always was in the middle of her face, always the same length with the same length of ash.

'Yes, Mrs Banting, hanging about in the wind all day with those sticking-out ears and that thing, that three oddy – trodilla –' Mrs Angel gave up and served a coloured man with a packet of Weights carelessly, without looking at him.

'Theodolite,' said Martha. She was anxious to go, but Mrs Angel was holding on to her change because she wanted to talk.

'Measuring, Mrs Banting.' Martha's name was Banning, but since Mrs Angel had been writing it wrong on bills for newspapers and magazines for the last ten years, there was no longer any point in trying to straighten her out.

'There's something up.' Mrs Angel's eyes were screwed up and watery from the rising smoke. 'And I don't care who hears me say it.'

Martha resisted the impulse to say: 'Why should you care?' She had known Mrs Angel for years with her vehement statements about nothing, and she had learned that it made no difference what you said, because her ears were turned inwards to herself. So instead she suggested, holding out a hand for her change: 'Perhaps they are really going to widen the road at last.'

'Don't you believe it.' Belying her bold statement that she did not care who heard her, Mrs Angel lowered her head and her voice and swung her smoke-pickled eyes from side to side. 'They're going to tear this whole lot down. Erase it to the ground and build a bloody great mental institution, criminal lunatics and all, right here in Cottingham Park. Watch your daughters, Mrs Banting.'

'Oh, I doubt it. Not here.'

'That's your opinion. That is the opinion you hold. All right, you're entitled to it, but I'm entitled to mine, and I don't care who says I'm not.' Mrs Angel always made such an issue of everything that you often regretted the most conventional remark. She dogmatized on, continuing to take coppers for newspapers and hand out cigarettes and give change automatically. 'I wouldn't be surprised to see them turn this whole area into one of these housing estates – supermarkets and picture palaces and the Queen Mother down cutting ribbons all over the place. There's some say it's to be a heliport. Of course, you wouldn't have heard about that, living down there in the Valley as you do.'

To the older inhabitants of Cottingham Park, the pattern of residential roads at the bottom of the gentle slope of West Hill, before it rose to twist its disenchanted way through the mean streets of The Rise, where policemen patrolled in pairs or not at all, was always 'the Valley'.

Once, there had been a small river there, and water meadows

12

and tilted willows between the folds of the green hills. That memory was perpetuated in its name through the tongues of generations, even long after the only relics of meadowland were the trodden lawns of the Squares and the sour tufts of grass which sprouted among the soot-spindled flowers in tiny front gardens.

''Copters, Mrs Banting, flying in and out all hours of the day and night and taking the top off your TV aerial. How will you like that?'

Martha took a step backwards and said: 'Oh, well –'

'It won't be Oh well,' Mrs Angel hammered at her. 'It will be Oh bloody awful. But I shan't be here to see it. We shall be gone, lock, stock and barrel, swept off the face of the earth like so much dust. That right, dear?'

'That's right.' Mr Angel had not heard, but he had lived with her for thirty years and knew where his best chances lay. He took a florin from a man in a heavy brown overcoat like a bear and laid it at the side of the cash register.

The man looked at his change. 'I gave you half a crown.'

'Don't try that here,' Mr Angel said sharply. 'I wasn't born yesterday.' He raised the two-shilling piece triumphantly.

'Never put a florin in the drawer,' Mrs Angel instructed Martha, 'until you've given change. Never do that.'

There was a man looking at the advertisements in the glass case beyond the shop. Shameless and fascinating the advertisements were. Martha and Guy stopped to read them sometimes. A woman alone could hardly be seen looking at them with serious interest. Or a man either for that matter; although this man was. He was not looking at the cards at the top of the case, which touted Furnished Rooms. Conveniences. No Children . . . Utility Van for Hire. Are you Moving? We can Help you. . . . Bedroom Suite for Sale at Loss. Never Used. (Bought for Bride.)

He was looking at the lower half of the case, which was full of cards of varyingly crude artistry. Some of them bore photographs of girls with burgeoning breasts half covered, usually sitting with the thigh furthest from the camera drawn up to show its inner flesh. One girl was smiling right out of the case at you with her forearm along the back of a chair and one bosom hanging over the arm like a pumpkin in a sack.

The cards said things like: 'Sheila. Famous model. Welcomes friends old and new.'

'Beautiful model offers her services. Anything considered. Bust 40. Waist 20. Hips 37.'

'Exciting French model just arrived. Genuine redhead. Exotic temperament.'

The small man who was looking at the cards with his back half turned towards the Angels to hide what he was reading was the man who had pushed past Martha outside the Underground. She recognized the colour of his jacket, that unlikely shade of bice green not often seen outside children's paint boxes. He turned away from the showcase as she passed, and wrote something down with a stub of a pencil in a black book.

A telephone number? He did not look like the kind of man who would venture to Carbine Road, where many of the 'models' hired their business premises by the hour. But what did a man look like who would telephone to Sheila or the exciting redhead or the girl with the forty-inch bust?

Fascinating. A fascinating neighbourhood. Nothing like it in London. Cottingham Park had struggled through the Blitz and been patched up and rebuilt and even prodded here and there into the shape of Council estates without losing any of its complicated individuality. In Martha's lifetime it had grown and changed, coming up in the world in spots and going downhill in others; but it was still The Park. The Cottie. Cotters. Gotting-ham Puk. Home of a kind for a motley of people from every class and every nation.

If Mrs Angel's extravagant prophecies of destruction could possibly be true, an irreplaceable part of London's character would be lost. Leave us alone. Tear down London somewhere else, Martha thought. Anywhere else but here.

But then she did not live in Glidden Road. Edgar Biggs did, and Frankie Bott, who walked home with him from Boy Scouts against the strict orders of his mother, who in the southern United States would have decked herself in a bed sheet and burned the fiery cross, ran quickly away down the street when Edgar went into his house.

Edgar was a coloured boy from Trinidad with a head like a nugget of coal and brilliant eyes, who lived with his parents in two rooms on the top floor of a terrace house that seethed with half a dozen other families. There were about eighteen people in the house. Even Edgar, who had lived there for two years, did

14

not know how many, because relations and homeless friends came and went, and the mothers of some of the shrieking children did not always have the same men coming home to them at night.

Billy, who lived in the worse half of the basement, had had at least three fathers, not counting the one responsible for his birth, who had disappeared before Billy was old enough to notice. Edgar Biggs had never had more than one father, and he knew that he was married to his mother, because Edgar had gone to the church with them when they did it.

Mr Biggs was a bus conductor. He and his wife prided themselves on being a respectable family and living in one of the better houses in the street. Eighteen people was nothing. The house on one side had twenty-six or more, and the tall corner house on the other side had twenty, not counting the unnumbered members of the Conga Club on the ground floor and basement.

Mr and Mrs Biggs were always going to the police station to complain about the noise from the club, which sometimes went on all night. They got no satisfaction, because you had to have a form signed in duplicate by three householders before you could lodge a formal complaint, and no one else seemed to mind the noise, and no one was a householder except the Jamaican landlord who lived in Kilburn and was never seen.

Displaced Europeans, and the more enterprising West Indians who were not too discouraged by the reality of the Mother Country Utopia in which they had been taught to believe to be able to make a good thing of it now that they were here, had bought up the property in streets like Glidden Road cheaply, when it was condemned. The Council would not get round to demolishing it for several years, and meanwhile they could cram it greedily with tenants who could not find a better place to live.

All along Glidden Road the houses were stuffed to bursting, and some of the residents had always spilled outside, whatever the weather. On hot days in the summer, they brought sagging sofas out on to the pavement, and the boys sat on chairs the wrong way round with their arms on the back and their legs spread, and called out to passing women. Even on a chilly day like this, there were women out on the steps or leaning on the area railings in headscarves and two or three torn sweaters, with their babies wrapped like bundles of dirty laundry. And there were always the boys and the men lounging on the corner by the Conga Club.

The club had once been a shoe repair shop decaying over the years. The old shoe-mender had moved out long ago when the street was first condemned, believing that the crusaders of the Borough Council, to whom he listened hand to ear in the public gallery of the Town Hall, meant it literally when they thumped the table and proclaimed that they would tolerate the slums no longer.

The shop had stood empty, its dark recessed doorway a place for urinating or making love, until three flash characters from Guiana had bought it for a 'social club', paid the magistrate five shillings for a drinking licence, and boarded up the windows so that no one could see what was going on inside.

At any time of day, even when the club was not open, there were always men hanging about outside: doing nothing; saying nothing; chewing on matches; waiting for something to happen. If it did happen, as it had happened on other corners of other streets like this, and it was not just a routine fight between members of the club, but a real murderous rumble with the whites, Glidden Road would be front page news. There would be television vans and reporters down questioning everybody, and the West Indians would get the chance to say what they thought of England and English democracy, and Edgar's mother would read it aloud from the paper and say: 'See. Like I always say. We been tricked. We had ought to went home.'

Because of the boys on the corner near his house, Edgar ducked into the public convenience at the other end of the street and took off the Scout uniform which he wore over a pair of sawn-off jeans and a T-shirt. He was the only boy in Glidden Road who went to the Scout meetings at the Recreation Centre, and he was the only coloured boy in the troop. He was trying to better himself. That was why he went to Scouts, because it was an extra chance to learn something outside the school hours which were too short and too chaotic for his eager mind.

He was older than Frankie, but they had made friends, because they were both somewhat misfits in the group, whose leader did not like either of them, and was too enervated by the disillusionments of Scouting in Cottingham Park to disguise it. Moreover, Frankie's mother hated the Spades, so being friendly with Edgar behind her back made him feel that he had put one over on her.

For the same reason, although it was out of his way, he deliberately walked three-quarters of the way up Glidden Road with Edgar before the coloured boy ran on ahead and up the splitting stone steps of his house, and Frankie turned and ran back along the littered pavement towards the safety of the Council estate,

When he had turned the corner, and another corner, and reached a district which was equally shabby, but mainly white, he slowed down. He was not anxious to get home, and he wanted a little peace and quiet, before he entered the domination of his mother's voice, to think about the woman he loved.

Frankie was twelve. The woman he loved was twenty-three and she was his teacher in Form 1B at Abbot's Road Secondary Modern School. Her name was Grace Peel. She had bright hair the colour of the bay pony which pulled the knife-grinding cart of Louie Maule's grandfather, a smiling voice, and eyes which jumped with light, like sun on water. If Form 1B got too far out of hand, trying their chances, drunk with their own noise, the eyes could cloud with tears.

She would not let the class see her cry, but once when the bell had rung just in time, and they had gone roaring and stamping out, Frankie had found some excuse to come back into the room and seen that the tears had spilled over.

She was standing at the blackboard with her hands dangling at her sides. She was crying, not as Frankie had seen drunken women or his mother in a rage cry, with shrieks and gulps and ugly gapings of the mouth; but 'like a lady', as Frankie told Edgar afterwards, with no noise, and nothing changed in her face except the redding tip of her nose. Because she was doing nothing about wiping the tears, he had given her his handkerchief. He had never ceased to thank his luck that he had a handkerchief that day.

Miss Peel was his Queen, his Grace Darling, his Lady of the Lake. All the heroines of all the soppy poems through which the class had stumbled and giggled their way, while Louie Maule, who would never read or write, sat grinning over a jigsaw puzzle at the corner desk.

The other boys liked her well enough, but they said things behind her back like: 'Who slipped on the orange peel?' and 'Peel me some of that', because to them she was only a teacher.

The other boys said dirty things to the girls in school and made rude gestures with their fingers; and a lot of the girls let them do much more than that behind the bicycle sheds, or on the

17

bombed sites, or in the alleys and doorways, or any of the dozens of places where you could take a girl for a feel.

Frankie would never need to have that kind of girl. He had Miss Peel, and today he had waited for her outside the high brown playground wall and walked with her to the bus stop, and she had told him that she liked Abbot's Road Secondary and that she was glad that she had chosen to become a teacher.

'Glad you got our class, Miss?' Frankie pressed her. 'With me in it and all?' he added casually, and she had laughed and said: 'Yes, Frankie. With you in it.' In a dream of romance, Frankie Bott took his round blue eyes and his sticky porcupine hair up in the lift to the top floor of Collingwood House, which was one of the blocks of red brick Council flats that made up the estate of Nelson Court. All the blocks were named after famous admirals, although there was nothing remotely seafaring about either the neighbourhood or the architecture. Or the smell in the lift. It smelled of urine, as usual. When the porter complained, and someone from the Council came sniffing round with a stoical slumming face, the residents declared that it was outside drunks who did it at night. But Frankie knew who did it, just as he knew who spat all over the little glass window in the door, because he had been in the lift with some of the kids when they were bent on messing it up.

The front doors of each flat opened on to the stone balconies which ran in tiers along one side of the building. On the other side, each flat had another little square balcony off the sitting-room, designed for such amenities as window boxes and sitting out for a breath of the fresh air which generations of slum dwellers on this site had never known.

Some of the balconies did indeed have window boxes and potted plants, but on most of them, anyone who had tried to sit out would have been quickly smothered by a forest of slapping wet washing. The architect had provided drying cupboards in each flat, but the gas heaters in them smelled, and so as soon as the housewives discovered how to turn them off, up went the lines and out went the washing on the balconies, just where the Council did not want it.

Mooning along the balcony, Frankie scared his stomach by leaning over the parapet and looking down five storeys to the play yard where foreshortened children scuttled and fought and screamed. The parapet was wide, but it was much too low.

Everyone said so, and they said that the architect had not only obviously never had a wife who did her own washing, but had never had children either.

The Nelson Court Community Association, of which Frankie's mother had been made a committee member to stop her sniping from the sidelines, had been demanding railings on the parapets for a year now, to no avail. When one of the daft boys who sometimes walked along the edge for a dare finally fell off and was smashed like an egg, then the railings would go up, people said. Talk about shutting the stable door after the horse has escaped, Frankie's mother said. They make me sick. Everyone automatically reviled the Council, because although they had provided the homes, they also sent round the rent collectors.

The view from the balcony high over the slate roofs and chimneys and television aerials, fading into the vapours above the railway terminus, was enchanting to Frankie. If Miss Peel were standing here at his side with her hair blowing in the breeze, he would point out all the sights to her. The big stone lion striding atop the roof of the old pub away up on the other hill. The gasometer which went up and down so slyly that you never saw it move; one minute it was just an empty cage, and the next time you looked, its insides had swollen up like a boil above the factory sheds. The water tower, the spires of all the churches, the beautiful steel arc of the railway bridge, and in the distance, proud as a lance, the quivering television transmitter mast, which meant rain coming if you couldn't see it.

The front door of his flat was ajar, not only to save his mother the trouble of letting him in, but so that she could hear anything interesting that might be said on the balcony. Even before he was properly inside, she began to scream at him.

Where've you been? ... Why are you so late? ... I'll do you ... I'll flay you alive. ... I'll ave your liver. ... The threats of Mrs Bott were extravagantly cannibalistic. Frankie had heard them a thousand times before. They passed through his head like water.

'Scouts, Mum.' She was in the kitchen. Frankie did not go in to her. He had not kissed his mother for years, nor she him. He went into the sitting-room where Kenny with his big bony head and his little useless legs wrapped in a blanket was sitting in his chair watching television.

Kenny was a spastic. He had never walked and he never

19

would, and he was entirely at the mercy of his mother. She doted on him with a fearful tyranny, giving lavishly of her time and care, but souring the giving into martyrdom. With some sort of sloppy, half-formed belief in reincarnation, she declared that she must have been a vile sinner in the world before this to have merited such a judgement. What Kenny might have been to have deserved his crippled imprisonment, she did not speculate, since she never thought of him as the victim of his disease, but only herself.

Like all true martyrs, she clung fiercely to her cross, and was currently engaged in a battle with a doctor at the clinic who wanted to try an operation that might give Kenny the partial use of one of his rigid hands. Two years ago, Frankie had got the idea that Kenny could walk like other boys if only his mother would let him. One day when she was out, he had hauled him out of the chair, propped him as upright as possible on his trembling, crooked legs, and given him a push to set him going.

Kenny had fallen at once and struck his head on a table. He was unconscious for two days, and when he woke and burst into tears at the sight of his mother sitting by the ward cot with a mammoth plastic handbag on her wide knees, Mrs Bott had announced that he would never be the same again.

This was not true, but Mrs Bott continued to say it to remind Frankie of his guilt. Kenny had always been and still was perfectly sensible, although he knew nothing beyond what he picked up from Frankie and the television, because at eight years old he had never been to school. He was supposed to go to a special school for handicapped children, but Mrs Bott was fighting it as fiercely as if the harassed woman who came to talk with her about it were trying to send Kenny to the gas ovens.

Gross and uncorseted, the front of her hair in pins and the rest bundled into a pink net, she stood at the kitchen door and yelled at Frankie to run three different errands at once and not to do four different things which he was not doing.

'Just wait till your Dad gets home. He won't half give it to you, you little bastard,' she shouted without thought. Her abuse was no more than idle conversation.

Frankie laughed. His father, a hollow-chested man beaten by his marriage and a wretched job in a hotel kitchen, had never given it to anybody. Although he must have given it to Mum at least twice, or he and Kenny would not be here. Better perhaps,

Kenny had whispered to Frankie once in their bedroom in the dark, if he never had.

*

The road where Martha Banning turned off for home was at the bottom of West Hill, before it climbed into the purlieus of the Rise, where Glidden Road was only one of many decaying streets, and the Nelson Court Estate was an island of so-called decency in the huge stinking puddle of squalor and junk and juke boxes and railway grime that no Family Bagwash at three-and-three-pence the twelve-pound bundle could ever cleanse entirely away.

Armstrong Avenue, where Martha lived with her husband and her two children in the house where she herself had been born, was the farthest of the comparatively respectable streets in the Valley, the last frontier of decent living before the ascent to the railway where the real rot set in.

When Martha's mother was first married, the square plastered houses with their broad front steps, not too far from the Park and the shops, were still solid with bourgeois respectability. To the Victorians who had built them, Armstrong Avenue was an excellent address, designed for people with three or four hapless servants, which accounted for the inconvenience of the basement kitchens, with their pantries and sculleries and larders half a day's walk apart down cold stone passages.

When Martha was a child, the families were gradually beginning to move away. By the time she was grown up, there were no longer any servants who would put up with the grim basements and closet bedrooms under the roof. Her mother's house, with its pair of loyal old sisters in the kitchen, was almost the only one in the Avenue that was not cut up into flats and maisonettes and furnished rooms. Failures and revolutionaries and penniless students and strange, potty people began to live there. It was now far from an excellent address, and there had been times of youthful snobbery when Martha had caught herself feeling ashamed of her enduring affection for the shabby old district.

Guy had been so poor when he married Martha, struggling to get the business going after the war, that they had lived in the Armstrong Avenue house, with Martha's mother fighting emphysema in the bedroom where Martha was born. Guy beat his business doggedly into shape, and when Martha's mother died, she thought that he would want to move; but he chose to

21

stay on in the house. He said that the neighbourhood would come up again, and so it had.

Armstrong Avenue never went back to being prosperous family dwellings, but the awkward, high-ceilinged flats began to be modernized and to have less hopeless people in them. Some of the bigger houses were taken over for kindergartens and secretarial colleges and career girl hostels. They were smartened up with paint, and the cats and blown newspapers were chased out of the front gardens to make way for optimistic little trees and tubs of flowers.

Guy painted their house and put in another bath and let the basement flat to Martha's young cousin, a teacher of physical culture, who wore tight blue shorts when she was working and long wide skirts like floral bells when she was not.

The old sedate inhabitants had nearly all gone long ago, but a new kind of population began to drift into odd pockets of Cottingham Park, the people for whom the suburbs were too suburban and the better parts of town too expensive. In the old heaving lifts of the Underground, bowler hats began to be seen standing next to beards and duffel coats. Corpse-white girls with seaweed hair, no lipstick and six layers of mascara rubbed shoulders at the ticket window with trim young wives in suits from fashion house boutiques. The children who went through the side streets to the Park once again began to have names like Jeremy and Sarah, and some of them had nannies, although they were not the kind of nanny that Martha's had been, with a moustache and a round grey felt hat; but foreign girls who met their lovers on benches while the children played.

The slums and the shabby shops and lodging houses and the Teddy Boys and the lurching men who were sick outside the gloomy pubs on Saturday night were still there; but mixed up with them, integrating colourfully with the old squalor, some of the mews houses and the tiny back street cottages were converted into 'amusing' little painted places, where it was reasonably chic to live. A ballerina moved in. A gaunt Method actress came with a car like an alligator and a great white dog like a mountain bear. Well-spoken homosexuals were arrested occasionally for importuning. The Beatnik generation dolefully sat out their time in coffee bars. Imperceptibly, Cottingham Park was becoming the poor man's Chelsea.

The address was once again nothing to be ashamed of, although if you gave it in a police court where you were answering a charge of rape or assault, heads would nod and lips tighten to indicate: I might have known it.

That was the thing about Cottingham Park. It could be all right to live there, or all wrong. Anyone might be found there. Anything might happen.

When Martha went into her house, what happened was what she had been fearing all the way down the street. The baby sitter, a Mrs Pellew, was sitting on the hall chest, fully dressed in her hat and coat with her umbrella laid across her lap like a rifle.

Martha was afraid of Mrs Pellew, with the same sort of grovelling deference inspired by butchers in the days of meat rationing. She wished that she had the nerve to say to her: 'Would it kill you to carry the tea things to the kitchen?' But then Mrs Pellew, who was always looking for belittlement, might not come any more, and who else was there to rely on?

You could say that for Mrs Pellew. She and the children disliked each other, but she was always available. She lived on a Merchant Navy pension, some of which was drained away to a daughter who had married a beast in human shape, and so she needed the extra money badly. She knew that Martha knew this, because she had broken down once when she had flu coming on and told her about her daughter and the beast. She still pretended, however, that she came only as a favour, to release Martha and Guy for the orgiastic excesses of which Mrs Pellew's face when they returned from a party showed that she suspected them.

Her refusal to regard herself as a businesswoman made paying her very embarrassing. 'How much do I owe you?' Martha would ask, and Mrs Pellew would close her eyes as if a naked man had stepped into the hall, and murmur: 'That's entirely up to you, Mrs Banning,' knowing that this would fluster Martha into paying too much.

Her habit of being found waiting fully dressed in the hall was equally unnerving. It was an effective condemnation of the dissolute hours some people liked to keep at the expense of those good souls who sacrificed their time to minding the abandoned children.

'Well, Mrs Pellew.' Martha took off her hat and forced a bright smile into the hall mirror. At five in the afternoon, at least the woman could not make that face which spoiled the homecoming from every evening out, as if she feared to get intoxicated on Martha's breath. 'How were the girls?'

A question that should never be asked, any more than a hypochondriac should ever be asked: 'How are you?' Mrs Pellew made the face she always used for speaking about Terry. 'We had a little trouble over Madam's tea. I knew you wouldn't want her to have peanut butter and chocolate spread in the same sandwich.'

In heaven's name, why not? 'Oh dear,' Martha said. 'Was she rude to you?'

The banging on the piano stopped, and Terry came out of the drawing-room with a sullen look. Mrs Pellew glanced at her and then glanced away as if it hurt. 'I don't tell tales out of school, Mother,' she said, managing to reprove both mother and daughter at one blow.

'Where's Bernie?'

'Bernadette is downstairs with Miss Myers. She came home early and your girls just begged and begged me, so I said they could go down just for ten minutes. Bernadette has been there all afternoon. The rascal.' Mrs Pellew added unconvincingly.

'But I didn't want – Oh well. Thank you so much for taking care of everything,' Martha said. 'I've forgotten what time I went out. How much do I owe you?'

Mrs Pellew rose and turned slightly away. 'That's entirely up to you, Mrs Banning.'

When Martha had found the money, Mrs Pellew hovered about by the front door for some reason – but surely she had been paid enough? – then finally opened the door, shivered theatrically and put her hand in a martyred way to her hat, as if Martha had deliberately built the house so that the February wind should strike Mrs Pellew on the front steps, and went haltingly down.

That was the winning shot in her locker. She was slightly lame. That was the final accusation.

'Why do you always give her too much?' Terry asked. 'Look at the time. She should have had exactly eight and ninepence.'

'I'm sorry for her.'

'Why?'

'Because you are so vile to her.'

'She's vile to us. Daddy's home.'

'Did she know? Oh dear. That was what she was hovering for. She thought he ought to drive her home.'

'Get the car out of the garage just for that? She's got a bleeding nerve.'

'That's mews talk.'

'I'm sorry.' Theresa bowed coolly. 'I forgot where I was.' Then her round face split in a conciliatory smile, with gaps in the teeth. Her sister could keep up an attitude, but Terry could never remain cool with her mother for longer than it took to frighten herself that she was jeopardizing love. 'Are you angry?'

'Never.' Martha hugged her. The child needed constantly to be hugged and kissed. Martha had read a book which told her that this was due to lack of love in the first year of life, or even before birth. She knew that she had not neglected Theresa as a baby, so it must be the perilous pre-natal influence on which the book harped so distressingly. And so belatedly, for who would buy such a book unless the baby was already born?

Some women, perhaps. The enlightened, gynaecological ones who were so desperately maternal that they were able no doubt to project love into the one-celled baby even at the hilarious moment of conception. Martha visualized them sitting about afterwards for nine months with an inturned smile, patting their swelling stomachs to assure the uncomfortable foetus of its welcome.

If the book was right, then Martha should feel guilty that after two years of marriage she had still been so much more in love with Guy than with the unborn baby. Could a foetus feel jealous? The book hinted that it could, and made some presumptuous suggestions about continence. When she was expecting her second child, Martha had thought of writing to the author and asking him – or her, for it was one of those unlikely names that might be either – how you were supposed to get this idea across to your husband.

When Bernadette, with the same pre-natal influences as Terry, had turned out to be as self-assured and independent as her sister was dependent and insecure, Martha had thrown the book away.

Downstairs in the basement flat of Miss Bessie Myers, Bernadette was drinking wine with Bessie and her friend James Donahue.

Bernadette was sitting on James Donahue's knee. He was a florid man of about fifty, with a shock of white hair and the kind of deliberately roguish round eye that the Irish feel they have to cultivate if Nature has not already wished it on them.

Bessie Myers, with a hair-cut that looked, quite truthfully, as if she had shorn it herself, was sitting slackly on the sofa with her legs spread wide and a pile of gramophone records in the lap of her heavy bright skirt. Bessie was flat-chested and got thicker as she went down. She had haunches like a Percheron and legs like oak trees, massive enough in her wide skirts, but overpowering when she wore the brief shiny shorts in which she and the girls from her physical culture school sprinted about the neighbourhood like a herd of buffalo.

She said ''Lo, Mar,' and stared. She had a disconcerting way of boldly staring, as if she were waiting for you to make a fool of yourself.

Martha smiled and said something, but her eyes were on her daughter and the wine glass she was holding, and the boiled beef hand that was clutching round the child's waist.

'Come on, Bernie,' she said. 'Time to go upstairs.'

The child did not move. She turned towards James Donahue's wide tweed chest, but Martha knew from her back view what her face would be like.

'She can stay if she wants,' Bessie said. 'I don't care.'

'That's not the point. I mean it, Bernie,' Martha said more firmly. 'I want you upstairs at once.'

'Ah, you shouldn't talk to the little angel like that,' said James Donahue in a maudlin way. All over his face, patches of veins had burst open under the skin, extravasating like spilled wine on a tablecloth.

Bernadette looked from him to her mother, weighing her chances. She decided in favour of her mother, and stuck out her lip, but changed the grimace to a smirk of affected flirtation for James Donahue as she slid slowly off his knee.

'She's a darling. She's my little angel,' he babbled. Putting his hands on either side of her face, he kissed Bernadette wetly, right on the mouth, with his own soft, slobbery lips apart.

Martha went storming in to Guy. 'She'll have to go. That girl will have to get out of here. That disgusting old man!'

'Uncle James? What's the old cocksmith done now?'

Elements of crudeness still clung to Guy, although he had made himself into a gentleman since his business and his marriage required it. He had been brought up in a Children's Home, because his mother, who had only come once a year to cry over

26

him because he did not love her, had refused to consent to adoption.

When she died in an alcoholics ward, Guy was twelve and too old for anyone to adopt. He had lived on at the Home until he was eighteen, joined the Army as a private, and come out of it as a sergeant at the end of the war to put his intelligence into business with another man's money. When they began to succeed, his partner sold out, and the business was Guy's.

'Local bastard makes good,' he had said to Martha. He still reminded her occasionally of his unfavourable history, with a sort of spuriously gleeful bravado, to make sure that she did not think it mattered.

It did not matter. It had never mattered. She had loved him always.

Martha told Guy about the kiss, and he stopped typing and pulled a disgusted face. Under his thick sandy hair, which was receding but not thinning, he had one of those lively, rapidly negotiable faces that are less a composition of features than a vehicle for changing expressions.

He was small and nimble, but muscular, with powerful hands. When people were showing off after a few drinks, Guy would break an apple or tear a telephone book in two, and some woman would look at him with a visible genesis of interest, and Martha would think that if he had not been hers already, she would have looked at him that way too.

She looked now at his hands waiting on the typewriter, as he said: 'The filthy old devil. Shall I go down and kill him?'

The hands remained relaxed, so Martha said: 'If you like. If you want to do that to my cousin. He's the only man she'll ever get.'

'Don't kid yourself. Old Bessie does all right.' Guy quite liked Bessie, who was the kind of completely unfeminine girl who nevertheless appealed more to men than to women. What had they got, these unpowdered, pale-lipped mares with their ragged hair and unsubtle conversation?

'Well, I wish she would go,' Martha said. 'I don't like to have her here. I wish the basement was ours again, and I could turn her sitting-room back into the big kitchen like it used to be, and the girls could do their homework down there while I cooked.'

'Just like I did when I was a child.' Guy mimicked the words which she tried to remember not to use now, because she had

27

overdone it and sickened him of her comfortable childhood, which was so different from his.

'If Mrs Angel could possibly be right about what she told me today,' Martha said, 'Bessie will have to go before long, and so will we.'

'Mrs Angel has never been right about anything, especially about what we owe her. What did she tell you?'

'That they're going to tear down all that part of Park Road and West Hill by the Underground and where the shops are, to make a heliport or a housing estate. Or a criminal lunatic asylum, she said, but I don't think she meant that bit. That was just to shock me, because she thinks I let the girls go out alone too much.'

'Who tells her all this?'

'She saw a young man with one of those surveying instruments.'

'Road widening, probably. About time.'

'I hope it's only that. It wouldn't be much fun living here with a taxi service to London airport raging over our heads and commuting executives whizzing in from Herts and Bucks. Suppose we had to go. Where would we go?'

'Back to Clapham Common, and then I could tell you all about when I was a boy and how they used to boil the cabbage in with the nappies. Don't worry, Martha. Nothing's going to happen to the Cottie.' That was what people like Guy called Cottingham Park. 'Though I sometimes think it might be a good idea to blow the whole mess up and start again.'

'Don't you like it here?'

'I can be happy anywhere. You know that. Learned to be long ago.'

'That wasn't what I wanted you to say.'

'As long as I'm with you. Was that it?'

That was not it, but Martha said: 'Yes, that's better,' and kissed his hair and went away.

*

When he had put the small black book in his inside breast pocket and patted it to make sure that it was safe, Arthur Sears walked half way down West Hill and down one of the side streets on the right to the tall brown house where he rented a furnished room from the Wilsons.

It was not a bad house, except that the Underground ran

almost underneath, but you could not feel the thunder of it in the top room where Arthur was. It was not a bad room either, for the price, and the district was all right. He could get out to the greenhouses in thirty-two minutes flat if he was lucky with the trains and ran from the station the other end with his head flung high and his hands clenched, so that people should think he was a training runner, holding corks. And there was always something going on round here. The neighbourhood was always in the newspapers. It was a pleasant thrill to open the paper and see the name Cottingham Park, which the papers were now using as an eye-catching headline, like Mayfair or East End, and read some tale about someone being cut up or robbed or assaulted, or some nigger being done by the Teddy Boys.

Arthur did not object to the coloured people who were scattered all about him in the shabby mongrel area between Park Road and The Valley. He rather liked them, because they were easy and joked a lot and hung about and were not going anywhere special, and their girls would sometimes answer him if he said Good Evening. A white girl would not answer unless she was that type, and with all their bosoms sticking out high up and their lips painted a funny sweet colour not like lips, Arthur could not always tell which type was which. He had got his face mashed in by a handbag once on the corner of Faulkner Road. A plastic handbag that felt as if it was full of lead shot.

There was a coloured man working at the greenhouses, and he was better tempered and cleaner mouthed than any of the other men. He worked with Arthur sometimes on the wreaths or wedding orders and it was peaceful, because he did not grumble all the time, but enjoyed the flowers and the things his hands could do with them, and made up stories about the people who were going to be married or buried.

The Wilsons did not mind coloured people either. It was not always easy for a Spade to get a room in a decent house, but they had one, a medical student, living with them, and Mrs Wilson had tacked up a picture of the Queen in his room and was always talking to him about the Commonwealth. He had one of the best rooms, the one with the big wardrobe, next to May's bedroom. It was a good thing poor old May was such a baboon. Even a black man would think twice before he forced his way into that room.

The medical student was leaving the house as Arthur went in.

He raised his hat and said 'Hello, Mr Sears,' in that molasses voice. Arthur did not have a hat, but he flipped his hand briskly by his head and said: 'Cheerio, Mr Porter.' Mr Porter's christian name was Constantine, but nobody ever used it.

May's bicycle, with its carrier for her midwife's bag, was leaning against the area railings. In the hall, May in her nurse's uniform with the round blue hat was standing by the shelf of the coat-stand looking through the letters. Her hands were red and always rather swollen, like bundles of uncooked beef sausages. Disinfectants and too much scrubbing and sluicing in her training hospital had started their ruin, and seven years of district nursing had completed it.

'Anything for me?' Arthur asked.

There never was. Arthur had no family, and no friends who would keep him enough in mind to write to him. There had been a man for whom he worked in Wales after he came out of the hospital. He had written several times to Arthur, but that was only to demand the return of the suitcase he had lent him for the trip to London.

May said kindly: 'Not today. You can have this if you like.' She gave him a pamphlet from Sir Oswald Mosley, which had headlines about the H-bomb and about terrible things the coloured people were supposed to have done. Arthur did not worry about the H-bomb any more than he worried about the Spades, although he had thought of joining the next march to Aldermaston, because it would make a nice break and get him out into the country.

May had gathered up the small pile of letters and bills, but she waited, smiling uncertainly, to see if Arthur had anything to say. She was a plain girl with hopeless hair and a face like moulded dough. Her shape under the blue gabardine overcoat was comfortable, that was the best you could say for it. Moving away from her, Arthur stayed for a moment with one arm hugging the brown varnished top of the banister post and asked her: 'Have a good day?'

'Not too bad, thanks.' May put her hand with the letters and the other hand into the pockets of her coat, an instinctive gesture when she talked to anybody. If she had been in a chair, she would have sat on her hands, or hidden them in the folds of her skirt. 'Mrs Mahoney had her baby early this morning. I had to get her into the hospital. That's taken half my day, getting the ambulance and persuading the sister on Casualty to admit her.'

'Something wrong then?' Arthur liked to hear about the obstetrical crises of May's trade.

'Retained placenta.'

'That's bad.' Arthur shook his head sagely. This was one of the reasons why May liked him. He was interested in hearing about her work, and she could talk to him and use the right words. Nobody else was interested, not her parents nor even her best friend Veronica, and if she did tell her parents anything, she had to hedge around the details. If she had used a word like placenta, her mother would have winced; but Arthur Sears, who had spent several weeks of his life in hospital with nervous colitis, said in a professional voice: 'D and C then, I suppose.'

'That's right. Poor soul, I hope they don't keep her in long, because her husband is looking after the other kiddies and I think he takes a drop too much.' May sighed. 'It's hard on these women. They marry some fellow and they think it's going to be like the tales in the magazines, happy ever after, and that. And then it turns out this way.'

For years and years May had wanted a baby. Not especially a husband, but you had to have him to go with it. She knew that if she could give birth to a child, she would not mind any of the pain. That was why she was sometimes brusque with women who became hysterical in labour and shrieked out that they could not stand it. She would never fuss. And afterwards, when she held the baby within the tender circle of her arm, she would have that radiant, enchanted look on her face, like you saw in newspaper pictures of famous mothers in expensive nursing homes.

Very few of the dozens of women she had delivered in her years as a midwife had looked like that. With the first baby sometimes, especially if they were older and had almost given up hope; but after that, each new baby was just one more thing to drag you down.

'Like Mrs Mahoney,' she told Arthur. 'I've seen so many of my young mothers let themselves go. There's the wedding photo on the bureau just as pretty as a picture, but two babies and on goes the headscarf and slippers and never come off.'

'Put you off marriage, eh?' Arthur asked with less interest. He was not concerned about the emotional problems of women. Everything that happened to them was their own fault.

May blushed. She could say Yes, as an excuse for the shame of spinsterhood at thirty-three; but odd as he was, Arthur was the only single man she knew.

Confused, she pretended not to have heard, and asked him brightly: 'And how did your day go today?'

'Nothing extra. Been with the carnations most of the time. Thinning seedlings. Heard a bit of news though, on my way home. The lady at the newspaper shop. I heard her telling that they're going to pull down all this part of the Park.' That was what people like Arthur called Cottingham Park.

'Whatever for?'

'Build a landing place for helicopters, she said. You know, them things that go up and down with the big fan on top.' Arthur whirled one hand round his head. 'So it seems we'll all be out on the street before we know it. Only there won't be any street left either.' Arthur chuckled. He had made a joke.

'Well, fancy that. Mum, did you hear that?' May turned excitedly to the small nosey woman who had just come round the top of the basement stairs like a fieldmouse coming out of its hole, wiping her hands on a grey dishtowel. 'It'll be like the Blitz, only worse. Remember the night Fletchers got it and Dad went running out with all the silver, because he thought ours was coming down too?' Since the war, there had not been much excitement. Here was excitement indeed. May would not mind seeing her home wiped out. If they had to move, something might happen. You never knew. Perhaps this was what she had been waiting for, keeping cheery, because she knew that in the end something was bound to happen.

'Hear what?' asked Mrs Wilson suspiciously. She was usually prepared to disbelieve anything her daughter might say.

May looked at Arthur, but he hardly ever talked when her mother was there, so she told the news herself.

'I don't believe it,' her mother said. 'They can't do that, not here in Cottingham Park. Wherever do you get such daft ideas from, May? That's her,' she said to Arthur. 'Always fanciful. Goes about in a day dream half the time. It's a miracle to me how any of her patients live to tell the tale.'

She smiled as she spoke. She spoke pleasantly enough, and people said that she and her husband were kindly souls who wouldn't hurt a fly, and yet daily they practised on their daughter the fake honesty of speech that goes beyond tactlessness into brutality. 'I speak as I find,' they boasted, and from May's earliest childhood they had been finding her slow and clumsy and something of a buffoon, and obligingly telling her so.

Arthur went on up the stairs without saying anything. He did not mind talking to old May, but the combination of the mother and daughter together was a bit much. Up in his room, he lay down on the folkweave cover of the low narrow bed and thought about the girl with the giggly voice and how she'd shrieked 'Oh!' Suppose he ever said something like that to old May. She'd die, wouldn't she? Might be almost worth trying, just to see. Through the door of her room, perhaps, when she was in there at night with the little wireless going. If Arthur lowered his voice and got some spittle up to make it treacly, she might think it was Mr Porter.

*

Martha was having tea with Miss Sutcliffe and Mrs Vulliamy, the two elderly sisters with whom she had been having tea off and on ever since she could remember. Their motherless niece, whom they had partly brought up, had been Martha's childhood friend; but even when Anne was not staying with them, Martha had had to go with her mother and eat cress sandwiches and marble cake and play with the soldier who shot pennies into the bear's mouth, just as listlessly as her own two children were now doing with the same toy.

An unbroken thread of dull, oppressive habit; prison visiting those who had committed the crime of growing old. But when Terry and Bernie were grown up, the old ladies would be dead, so they would not have to take their children to tea.

Mrs Vulliamy was soft and well-intentioned and could have been all right on her own. You could have made easy chatter, telling her of the astonishing world that was carrying on without her, beyond her steamed-up windows, and she would have listened and said Yes yes, and What an exciting life you have, Martha dear. But with Miss Sutcliffe there, dominating the scene, as she had dominated everything in an impotent way since she was a protesting baby, things were more strenuous. Miss Sutcliffe did not say Yes yes to conversational efforts. She argued. She argued with Martha, with her sister, who argued back, even with Martha's children and with the old servant who could only hear a quarter of it.

Park Lodge, where the sisters lived, was a large old red brick house on the 'better' side of Park Road, away from West Hill and the slums and the council estates. Known as 'The Scotneys', because many of its streets and lanes and avenues were named after the rich family whose deer and cattle herds had once grazed here, it had its mean and dirty corners, but it also had some attractive Georgian houses and some good imitations filling in the gaps knocked out by the war. It was the southern edge of Cottingham Park, from where the streets dropped gradually downhill into a greener, less polyglot borough whose squares were kept trim and free of dogs and ragged children, and where it was neither quaint nor questionable to live, but perfectly normal.

In the days when Cottingham Park had been the big estate and the few houses of Cottingham no more than a hamlet clustered beseechingly at its gate, Park Lodge was the Dower House, built for somebody's mother-in-law who could not be tolerated up at the big house and had been put at the bottom of the garden with the compost heap.

In those days, nearly three centuries ago, what was now the clamorous thoroughfare of Park Road had been the broad tree-lined avenue leading to the big house. West Hill was no more than a cart track meandering down to the river in the valley through common land on which the peasants might 'graze their cattel, cut turfes, or dig sand, gravel, clay or loom for their own use'.

Long after Cottingham had ceased to be an outlying village and had become a part of urban London, there were still gipsies to be found here and there on the pieces of waste-land that still remained. There was no waste-land now, except the few torn open gaps of junk and rubble that had not been built up again since the war, but there were still a few descendants of the gipsies, holed up somewhere in the warren of alleys and grimy courtyards on The Rise, intermarrying, living somehow without jobs.

Dark and outlandish even in modern clothes, they appeared occasionally at back doors with clothes pegs for sale or a basketful of odd-coloured puppies. Sometimes, but never when you wanted it, a small cross pony weaved down the street with a knife grinding machine and an old gnome crying for custom in a strange tongue.

The big house of Cottingham Park, built so arrogantly in

defiance of the seventeenth-century Plague Law which prohibited building within ten miles of the city, was gone long ago, the victim of a bureaucracy grown as arrogant as the landed gentry had ever been. All that remained of its large and beautiful estate was the Dower House, now called Park Lodge and almost unrecognizable under its load of Victorian additions and embellishments, and a piece of walled garden that surrounded it. It was only an infinitesimal part of the original garden, but it was spacious compared to the little back-yards and narrow strips of the other houses round about.

When Martha was a child going to tea at Park Lodge, or to parties there, or to play with Anne under the cautious eyes of her aunts, the garden had been well kept. During the war, it had been taken over by Civil Defence. Vans and ambulances and canteens had turned the lawn into a patch of beaten mud. A public shelter was built by the wall where the fruit trees used to spread their tenderly crucified arms, and Light Rescue squads practised light rescue in the corner where half the house next door had buried the greenhouse in a mountain of bricks and timber.

The gap in the high wall where the A.R.P. vans drove in and out had since been boarded over, but the garden remained a jungle of rubble and firewood, marauded by children and soured by cats. The Council had had their eye on this dismal space for years. It fretted them to see a quarter of an acre of building space unbuilt. Miss Sutcliffe and Mrs Vulliamy, who never went out into the garden and seldom looked at it through the muslined windows, would give it up over their dead bodies. Park Lodge had been their grandfather's house, then their father's. They had lived there all their lives, not counting a brief and unromantic interval which Mrs Vulliamy had spent with an impotent husband until he died of heart failure and left her free to come thankfully back home.

Martha and her children and the two old ladies were having tea in what was still known as 'father's den', which was now the centre of living for Miss Sutcliffe and Mrs Vulliamy because it was the only warm room in the house. They had moved in pieces of their favourite furniture until there was scarcely room for people. The fire blazed high and the window was never opened and there was a smell of musty clothes, and Terry and Bernadette were yawning and so fidgety that Miss Sutcliffe asked them sharply: 'Do you want to go somewhere?'

They shook their heads. They were afraid of the bathroom at Park Lodge, which was big enough to hold a meeting in, with twin basins enclosed in a sodden wooden box, a wicker armchair over the lavatory, and a bathtub cased in like a coffin. To reach it, you had to penetrate down dark passages, past shut up haunted rooms.

From the depths of one of these passages, moving black-mottled lips in a wordless murmur, came Pringle creeping with a tarnished silver teapot in one hand and slopping milk jug in the other. She could not trust herself to carry anything on a tray. Waiting on Miss Sutcliffe and Mrs Vulliamy and battling with the stone-floored kitchen and pantry and larder which were miles apart and infested with metallic insects, had killed off or discouraged all other maids. Only old Pringle, who had always been there in the party days, serving jellies, scooping out ice cream, muttering and a little senile even then, had remained.

Instead of saying Thank you, or accepting the coming of the teapot in silence, Miss Sutcliffe had to say: 'I must say, I was getting rather thirsty.' That was the way she talked. Impossible to please.

If you asked kindly after her bad leg, she was liable to say: 'I was wondering whether you were going to notice I was in pain.' Today Martha had brought the sisters a present of a little lustre jug which she knew they would like. Mrs Vulliamy had exclaimed: 'How beautiful! Such a kind thought, dear.' But Miss Sutcliffe had said: 'You shouldn't have spent your money. We've got dozens of those.' She did not mean to be rude. It was just the way she talked.

As she argued sharply with her sister about where they had bought the cake, the children, wondering why they could not get away with insults like that, stared at her over cups of milk, sweetened by Mrs Vulliamy with lumps of sugar dropped in with a splash. Miss Sutcliffe was the neat precise one. Mrs Vulliamy, whose blouse would never stay buttoned over the place where her bosom and stomach merged, was the sloppy, slapdash one who trod on the cat and knocked over lamps and could never find her glasses.

When the children passed their cups obediently for more milk which they did not want, her sister made an ostentatious show of pouring the splashed milk from the saucers into the slop basin. 'You're always so messy, Celia,' she nagged. 'The girls shouldn't have all that sugar anyway. It's bad for their teeth.'

'Don't talk nonsense,' answered Mrs Vulliamy. 'I've taken sugar all my life and I'm the only person I know of my age who's still got all her teeth.'

'There aren't many people of your age *left*,' said Miss Sutcliffe rudely, although she was the elder. 'And what about that tooth that man put in for you two years ago?'

'That's only a bridge. That doesn't count.'

'Well, it shows. It's twice as long as all the others. I always said you were a fool to pay that dentist's bill.'

A stranger might not have guessed how devoted the old ladies were to each other. Their vituperation was in some way an expression, not a denial of their love. Martha, who had been listening to it for too many years, sighed and closed her ears as they went on about Mrs Vulliamy's teeth. The children looked from one to the other and giggled. The uncivil cross-talk was the only thing that enlivened these visits.

Celia Vulliamy, childless and unfulfilled, had always been attracted to children, but nervously, as if they had landed in a flying saucer. She kept trying to make Martha's daughters eat, but Miss Sutcliffe had stopped up their stomachs with a forced load of potted meat sandwiches at the start.

'Not a bit like your mother,' Mrs Vulliamy said, shaking her large head which was crowned with a nest of pin-scattering brindle hair. 'The human dustbin, we used to call her. What do you think of that?'

The children did not think much of it. Theresa, who was old enough to feel stirrings of pity for other people besides herself, smiled politely, but Bernie scowled and flopped her short thick dark hair forward so that the sides swung over her face like scimitars. They were not interested in their mother's far-off eating habits. They were afraid that she would start to reminisce, as she always did at Park Lodge.

Although she felt their apprehensive eyes on her, Martha could not help going ahead with: 'Do you remember . . .?' and: 'I'll never forget the time when . . .' There was not much else to talk about, and it was a way to get back to what she had come for – some information about Anne. Every time she had mentioned her, the old ladies had changed the subject. There was something wrong.

37

'Do you remember,' she said, 'that party after the Lord Mayor's Show when Anne had an acute appendix and everyone thought it was the walnut cake? Then the father of that boy who used to bite people came and he was a doctor and he –'

'Can Bernie and I go in the garden?' Theresa interrupted.

Martha was beginning to say Yes, for it was not yet dark, although Pringle was creaking about by the window with her corsets sticking out behind like a shelf, endeavouring to shut out the approaching night; but Miss Sutcliffe said quickly: 'Not today. I think there are some *children* there.'

When she said *children* like that, she meant the wild grubby youngsters who came from the other side of Park Road and the less dignified corners of the Scotneys and climbed her garden wall.

'Yes. There are some *children* there,' Terry said, imitating Miss Sutcliffe's tone. 'That's why we want to go out.'

'Not now.' Martha frowned.

'Why not?' Terry put on her blank arguing face. 'One of them is Billy Few. I can see him.'

'Martha dear,' said Miss Sutcliffe, picking over the words as if they were questionable apples, 'do you let your girls play with the *street* children?'

'Why not? They meet them in the streets at the back of our house. The girls play cricket in the mews with them. I don't see that it matters.'

'How *very* democratic,' said Miss Sutcliffe damningly. She was silent for a while. She disapproved. Mrs Vulliamy kept silent too because she did not disapprove and did not want to have her head bitten off for saying so.

The sisters usually filled the room with voices. When they were mute, Father's den had a thick muffled air, as if all their words had collected in a padding on the walls. 'Please tell me something about Anne, Aunt Jessie.' Martha tried to sound casual, but her voice broke so strange and high into the silence that her children turned round from the window to look at her. 'I haven't heard from her for so long. Has she written to you?'

Mrs Vulliamy looked at her sister, and Miss Sutcliffe stirred out of her disapproving position and said to Pringle: 'You'd better go and see what the boiler is doing.' They had used an electric water heater for years, but the boiler was a time-honoured excuse to get Pringle out of the room. They had no secrets from her, but it did not look well to talk in front of her; and so she would go, provided someone would tell her afterwards what she had missed.

Miss Sutcliffe again offered the children the bathroom, but again they declined. Since she could not retract her veto of the garden and there was no other way to get them out of the room, she gave them some more pennies for the soldier toy to shoot and said in one of her austere voices: 'We had a letter last week. She is still in New York.'

Anne had married a gentle loving man who had taken her to America, failed in his business and died falling asleep at seventy miles an hour while he was driving through the night to an interview for a job. His legacy to Anne was debts. Instead of allowing her aunts to pay her fare to England, she had found work in New York and stayed there.

'Is she still at the same address?' Martha asked. 'I've written to her several times, but she hasn't answered.'

'She's moved. A much bigger flat, she says. I don't see how she can afford it, but she never bothers to explain anything. The address is something East Something Street. I can't remember those stupid numbers. So unimaginative. As if they couldn't think of enough names.' She went to her desk, but could not find the letter, although the desk was in perfect order.

'I have it, Jessie, I think. I was reading it again.' Mrs Vulliamy got up, knocking a plate of biscuits off the cakestand, and went to her desk on the other side of the room, which was littered with papers and pamphlets and unposted letters which she started to write to societies and newspapers and authors whose books she admired.

Flushed and losing hairpins, she found the letter at last and gave it to Martha to copy the address.

'May I read it?' Martha knew them well enough to ask that. She had been Anne's best friend. Before the old ladies began to be so mysterious, they had always shown her the letters, and argued about what Anne had meant by this or that.

'If I say No,' Miss Sutcliffe said, with down-to-earth candour, 'you will think we have something to hide. So I'll say Yes, and hope that you can make more of it than we can. We don't quite understand. She used to write so pleasantly. You know our loving girl.'

How Anne had hated to be called Our Girl! Her grandparents, up to the time of their death when Miss Sutcliffe and Mrs

Vulliamy were well into middle age, had consistently referred to them as The Girls. Anne had always been scared of being forty and being still Our Girl. Perhaps that was one reason why she had not come back to England when her husband died.

'But she didn't write to us for three months!' Mrs Vulliamy blurted out, pushing a mess of escaped hair out of her eye. 'And now she sounds so strange. Not like our girl at all. And there's this name that keeps cropping up – Alex this and Alex that. We don't know who it is.'

'She's going to marry again, is that what you mean? Oh, I hope so.'

'I haven't said that.' Miss Sutcliffe was standing in her flat brown dress with her hands on the back of her chair, looking the way the headmistress of Queen Adelaide's used to look when she doubted your story. 'I didn't say she wrote that.' She looked over to the corner where the children were quietly bickering. 'That's right, dear!' she cried, in a high bright voice calculated to warn all but the stupidest child not to be fobbed off from listening. 'Press the handle down hard and the penny will go right in the bear's mouth!'

Martha was reading the letter. It was quite clear. Anne was living with a married man whose wife had gone away with someone else. She did not set it down as clearly as that for her aunts, but she hinted at it broadly, with a strange note of defiance. Aunt Celia was right. The letter did not sound like Anne. In one part, where the sentences began not to have any nouns, it sounded as if she were a little tight when she wrote it.

But Anne had always been the sober one when she and Martha went out together before they were married. Her quiet, mild-mannered husband had not taught her to drink. What had happened to her?

'This isn't Anne,' she said quickly, looking up.

'I know,' Miss Sutcliffe said tautly, gripping the back of the chair with her bony freckled hands. 'That's what we don't understand.'

Martha looked at them both and saw their unhappiness. 'But you do understand, don't you?' she said, for she saw that they did. 'She's living with this Alex person, and he doesn't sound as if he were any good for her.'

'*Pas devant les enfants*,' Miss Sutcliffe said.

Martha shrugged her shoulders. She and Guy did not bother

much what they said in front of the children, believing that if they could understand it, it would not hurt them, and if it was too bad, they would not understand.

'If only we could get her home.' Mrs Vulliamy took off her glasses because she was afraid that she was going to cry. 'If only we could go out there to her. But look at us –' She brushed her large slipped chest disgustedly. 'A pair of old fools. A pair of old crocks. What can we do?'

'We can keep our dignity, Celia,' Miss Sutcliffe said astringently, 'at least.'

'Can't Anne's father help?' Martha asked.

'Oh Harold. Oh him.' Miss Sutcliffe dismissed her younger brother impatiently. 'He's quite hopeless. You know that. No, there is nothing to be done. Anne has made her –' she turned away from the word bed and substituted 'her choice. And she will have to take what comes. Celia and I are finished with her.'

'We're not!' her sister cried.

'Don't shout at me. We are.'

'You don't mean that,' Martha said. 'You would never be finished with Anne.'

'Why should I not mean it? I've said so, haven't I? What are you crying for Celie, you foolish old woman? Go and help the little girls on with their coats. Martha wants to go. It is written all over her.'

The children dropped the lead toy with a rattle of pennies and went thankfully into the twilit hall for their coats.

'I hate to go,' Martha said, 'and leave you so unhappy about this.'

'Who is unhappy?' No one was going to catch Aunt Jessie out in vulnerable sentiment. 'My sister and I are all right. We have our dear house and all our Things. Our life goes on in the same way. If we could just be left alone. Don't you see, don't you see, Martha?' She put her hand on Martha's arm and looked up at her, and her eyes showed that the hardness was only a defence of pride. 'We're too old. You think I'm unkind about Anne, but it's just that when you're so old, you can't face being involved in all these messy troubles. You just want to be left alone.'

Why had Anne told them as much as she had? The old aunts did not have to know. It seemed so deliberately, unnecessarily unkind. A sudden mean impulse perhaps, out of her own unhappiness, to hurt them. To take a swing at their ostrich conviction that nothing in their lives could ever change, ever go wrong; nothing happen to them except death.

The same kind of sudden mean impulse that made Martha, who was not unhappy in herself, but only for Anne, say in the hall: 'Did you hear the rumour about them pulling down all this part of Cottingham Park, both sides of the main road, to build a housing estate, or a heliport or something?'

'Don't be silly, Martha.' Miss Sutcliffe looked at her craggily in the sombre polychrome light which filtered through the stained glass in the top half of the front door. 'Some of the houses in the Scotneys are period pieces. Even the Government wouldn't be so deranged as that.'

'It's progress though,' Terry said, standing on tiptoe to make sure of a place in the conversation.

'But Theresa.' Mrs Vulliamy assumed an instructing voice. 'Parts of this house go back to the seventeenth century. A gentleman came once to photograph that piece of cornice in the dining-room. He thought it was Grinling Gibbons. Mr Davenport says No, but he admits it is a fine piece of carving.'

Mr Davenport was a retired civil servant who occasionally persuaded the borough newspaper to print his esoteric little articles about quaint old corners of Cottingham Park, especially the Scotneys where he lived. He was known as Our Local Antiquarian, and had written a book, privately printed, about the old houses in the neighbourhood, which had enjoyed a small but appreciative sale among people like Miss Sutcliffe and Mrs Vulliamy.

'I thought we were going,' Bernadette said ungraciously, kicking the front door, and Martha raised her voice to cover this.

'Well, it's just what I heard,' she said, wishing she had not brought it up, for if the old ladies' house were really doomed, they would want to go with it, like Parsee brides. 'It probably isn't true.'

'Of course not.' Miss Sutcliffe squared her shoulders. 'Mr Davenport would never allow it. And neither should I. The Council has been trying to get their hands on this place for years to put up shoebox flats for irresponsible hooligans who won't work hard enough to pay a decent rent. I wish you wouldn't stand about in the draughty hall, Martha, if you mean to go. Good-bye, Theresa. No, with the glove off. Where is Bernadette?'

'I'm here.' Bernie presented a theatrically smiling innocence at the door of Father's den. She had sneaked back to get the pennies out of the soldier toy when she thought no one was looking. Terry had seen, but she would say nothing if her sister shared.

'I wish I hadn't told them,' Martha said to Guy. 'It's only a rumour, after all. They pretend not to believe it, but really they were upset. Jessie practically threw us out. They're worried sick over poor Anne as it is, only they won't let on.'

Guy grunted. He had listened unwillingly to ten minutes of Martha's fear that Anne was mixed up with a married man who was either teaching her or driving her to drink. Anne was one of the elements of Martha's past, or pre-marital life, which he could do without.

Anne and Martha had secrets. They had done things and shared jokes and experiences and known other men long before Guy appeared. Why not? Martha was nearly thirty when she married. There had to have been other men. Guy would never let her tell him about them, although she sometimes wanted to, in a burst of masochistic confession which he recognized as purely egotistical. He did not want to know himself, and yet he resented the fact that Anne knew, and resented Anne for knowing.

Anne had not liked him when he came into Martha's life. He had not liked Anne. He did not even think her attractive. He was irritated by the long pale face and sleek black hair and cool laugh which Martha had always envied. At first Martha had been unhappy with torn loyalties. Then Anne had married and gone away and Guy was glad; but Martha was sad, because Anne had been her best friend, and you did not make deep friendships after you were married. You were not supposed to need them.

Guy and Martha were in the Lion having a drink before dinner. They usually preferred to come here rather than to one of the tricky little cramped Italian and Spanish and Czech restaurants which had sprung up to meet the changing demands of the neighbourhood, so that people said, untruthfully, that it was just like Soho. At the Lion you could spread your elbows. The two waitresses had dirt under their chipped magenta nail varnish, but they were quick both to serve you and to learn your name. The roast beef and chops in the dark dining-room beyond the bar were excellent, and the treacle tart was a matter of local pride.

People had been known to come from all over London just for the treacle tart.

The Lion was a large old public house which, like the Elephant & Castle and the Royal Oak, had for years been a landmark even for those who never saw it, because it was a fare stage whose name was printed on the rolling blinds at the front and back of buses.

Outside it was unprepossessing. Brown plaster pillars divided the narrow windows, which were painted black and tarnished gold half-way up to hide the unspeakable orgies which had never taken place. Above was grey peeling stucco and arched windows with drawn blinds where nameless, faceless people eked out solitary lives in furnished rooms, and on the plaster parapet of the roof, the ill-executed stone lion with the curl of his tail broken off.

Inside, the saloon bar was semi-circular, with a high back drop of bottles and lettered mirrors and twirled mahogany pillars. The seats round the walls were cushioned with black leather, splitting and torn, and the round tables had been hideously stained with brews of all colours and mutilated with pocket knives and forgotten cigarettes over the years.

The dated drabness of the ornate bar and the ugly marble fireplace with the tiny grate and the pictures on the walls of low-waisted girls peering through their hair at brands of port and sherry long since unobtainable, had been deliberately preserved. It was what the customers expected. No funny business about the Lion. No juke boxes or pin tables or chrome stools in the saloon bar. Not even a dartboard. And yet it was the most popular public house in Cottingham Park. You might find anyone there. Mackintoshed men dawdling away the hour of going home. Middle-aged women in turban hats, who drank gin with strange diluents by themselves, and were unplaceable of background or destination. Itinerants and regulars. Soaks and half-pinters. Men with dirty collars and rubbed elbows and men like Guy in good suits and the combination of striped shirt and stiff white collar which Martha hated, but which Guy assured her gave him the air of having been to the right school.

Incongruously, over the whole dull, mid-Victorian kingdom of the dining-room and the saloon bar and the beer-washed Public, reigned a healthy modern couple called Jack and Nancy.

Nancy had been a dancer, and Jack a professional athlete.

44

When Nancy's left knee went, and with it, Jack's metatarsal arches, they turned, as many people do whose development has been more physical than mental, to public houses, abandoning their dream of a timbered country hostel with horse brasses when they were offered the shabby but prosperous old Lion.

Tonight, in a flaring red skirt with a tight black sleeveless sweater over her small muscular breasts, Nancy joked with Guy as she passed him on her nimble flights up and down the bar.

'You are a quiet one tonight, Martha,' she said accusingly. 'What's the matter? Had a fight with lover boy?' When she laughed, she flung back her cropped head and showed all her teeth. Her teeth were perfect. Her skin glowed. Her unreflective eyes were clear and bright. Her hands were graceful. Her body was firm and lithe. Everything about her, except her left knee, was perfect with the perfection of cheerful, healthy youth. To Martha, who did not often worry about being nearly forty, she was irritatingly young. Exhaustingly healthy. It would take someone like Jack, who was full of muscle and stamina, to keep up with her. Sometimes, when she was weary of the Lion, and enervated by Nancy's bounding good fellowship behind the bar, Martha wondered morosely whether Guy ever thought about trying.

'Martha is depressed tonight,' Guy told Nancy, leaning on the bar in a way which made it a link rather than a barrier between them, 'because she went to tea with two old ladies.'

'The Queen bees?' Nancy jerked her head in the approximate direction of Park Lodge. 'Mustn't let them get you down, love. They're good sports. One of them, the sweet woolly one, was in here the other night after a bottle of gin. Medicinal. "Give me the kind in the black bottle," she tells Jack. "Then no one will know what's in it." Yes, dear. Same again?' She answered the flicking gesture of the man on the other side of Martha, who had a deep black moustache which looked as if for some reason he had dyed it a darker colour than his hair.

'The way I hear it,' Guy said, 'the old girls may soon have to go and be good sports somewhere else.'

Nancy went away to pull beer. 'How so?' she asked as she passed on the return journey.

'Going to pull the whole ruddy lot down,' Guy said, 'and build a temple of arts and culture.'

Nancy had gone without waiting for the answer, but the man

with the black moustache had looked up from his newspaper and raised his eyebrows, which were short and stiffly thick, like little nail brushes.

'Is that a fact?' he asked Guy. 'Excuse my butting in.' He smiled at Martha as he leaned forward to talk across her.

'Fact,' said Guy. 'My wife heard it from the highest source.'

'Oh no, I didn't. It's just local gossip. People have been surveying round here. They're probably going to widen the road, but of course a silly rumour starts right away that they're going to pull everything down and start again.'

'Interesting,' the man said, and Martha smiled briefly and turned back to Guy. The man was a stranger, talked to for a moment, noticed only casually, forgotten already as she began to ask Guy to finish his drink so that they could have dinner. And then with a jolt somewhere in the middle of her inside, time stopped.

Motion stopped, and processes of thought. For an instant, there was no past, and the future had dropped away into an abyss. There was only this moment, suspended like a lantern slide. The ridge of muscle in Nancy's bare armpit as she reached for a bottle of rum, Jack's white shirtsleeve stretched towards the cash register, wet rings on the scarred old bar and the sour smell of alcohol, the olive like a dead fish at the bottom of Guy's glass, his strong fingers round the stem, and the man's voice behind her back saying for ever: 'Odd, isn't it, how the silliest rumours invariably turn out to be true?'

The cash register pinged and rang up two-and-seven, and everything began to move and happen again. Guy's fingers picked out the olive quite normally; but Martha felt very strange. She had a shaken, unreasoned feeling that that suspended moment would stay with her all her life. When she was very old she would remember the tableau and the man's quiet voice and think: 'That was when it all began.'

When what began? Nothing probably. Nothing personal. It was not going to affect them personally. The man said that. He said: 'If your house is half-way down Armstrong Avenue, it should be safe, according to the plan as I recall it.'

'Oh wonderful,' Martha said starkly. 'Nothing to worry about. Just everything I've ever known, every bit of pavement I've ever walked on, every shop I've been going to since

46

I was too little to see over the counter – gone, disappeared, bulldozed under the earth.'

'Steady with the dramatics,' Guy said. 'It probably won't come to anything.'

'Steady yourself,' the man said. 'We're usually the last to hear anything in the Press Bureau, but this I do know. Everyone at County Hall does. Even the women who wash the teapots. It's Development Plan Four-O-Two Q Stroke Eight Four. That's the general plan for the whole project, as submitted to the Ministry. Now that they've agreed to put up the cash for property purchase and rehousing – that's about half the cost of the whole caboodle – the story can be told. Everyone all over London, all these types here' – he flicked a long scrubbed finger backwards at the crowded saloon bar – 'anyone who can read a notice or a newspaper will know about it in a few days. That's why I'm down here. When the news breaks, I'll have all the papers on my neck asking questions, and I'll be feeding out titbits to bored reporters for years to stop the public thinking we've gone to sleep on the job. So I thought I'd come down and have a look at Cottingham Park as it stands today in all its decaying glory before the 'dozers come and flatten it without a trace.'

He smiled, a twitched, one-sided smile, as if the inky moustache had been grown to hide a defect or a nerve injury of his upper lip.

'Look here,' Guy said, not smiling, 'is this some sort of rotten joke?'

'Are you making it up?' Perhaps he was. Hope flickered in Martha again. Perhaps for some futile reason he was pulling their legs.

'I wish I were, if it upsets you,' the man said gallantly, 'but it's the naked truth. In all its glory.' He tacked on his favourite phrase like an amen.

They had moved over to a small table in the corner. 'It doesn't matter my telling you,' said the man, who had revealed, on a card to each of them, that his name was Robert P. V. Peregrine, 'since you're going to know anyway in a day or so; but I don't especially want to leak it to our two muscular young friends behind the bar before the brewery has been officially informed. It will probably take a chap half a day to draft out the formal notice. I don't want to spoil his fun. They're touchy about that kind of thing in Valuation.'

'Notice to Quit you mean?'

'Don't put it so harshly, Mrs Banning. An offer to purchase by agreement, let's call it. Compulsory purchase is the last resort.'

'It comes to the same thing. They're going to pull down The Lion.'

'In a nutshell. Another Lion will be built, of course. Probably near the underpass where the buses will run. Must have another Lion because of the bus stop. Nice red brick, formica bar, stainless steel beer handles, good clean atmosphere and so on.'

'State owned?'

'Unfortunately, no.' Robert P. V. Peregrine winked briefly. Sometimes it seemed surprising that he had stuck this job for ten years. 'But it will probably be one of the first things to go up. We aim to please. Get the pubs up first. Then the council flats. The Council' – he paused to take a pull of his beer – 'looks after its own. We always try to remember that we are dealing with ratepayers.'

The beer had left a little edging of foam along the moustache. Martha had an impulse to say: 'Wipe your mouth' in the laconic tone she used for the children, and get up and walk out. But she stayed. Like a squeamish person too fascinated to walk out of a horror film, she stayed to hear the grisly details of Development Plan Four-O-Two Q Stroke Eight Four.

The Transurban Expressway, 'to name it in all its glory'. A super-highway linking central London with the northern arteries. Branches scything through the streets and houses and shops and modest squares to the western approaches. Flyovers and underpasses. A comprehensive redevelopment of marginal sites to provide for flats and office space and shopping concourses.

'It's ghastly,' Martha said, and Guy went to the bar to get them all another drink.

'Why ghastly?' Robert P. V. affected to look hurt. 'I think it's neat. Don't you think it's about time somebody did something about getting traffic in and out of London?'

'Yes, but – why here? Why through here?'

He shrugged one narrow shoulder. 'That's what everybody says: "I'm all for progress, but just don't do it here." Two miles, approximately, of this triumphal avenue, slap through the anthill of Cottingham Park and other desirable districts, and all along the way, the ants crying out: "Why must you put it here?" '

'What if the ants object?' Guy set down the drinks and leaned

48

the slightly convex tin tray against the table leg, whence it fell with an oscillating clatter. Martha was begining to have a headache.

'Oh, they'll get a chance, of course. There will be a Minister's public hearing, an inquiry on objections to the authority for compulsory purchase, right of appeal to the Lands Tribunal, and so on. Must strain every nerve to give at least the illusion that there is still some liberty of the subject.' Mr Peregrine let out a grisly chuckle. 'God bless,' he said, and lifted the tankard.

'For a public relations man, you don't talk very good propaganda,' Guy told him.

'Bear with me. I'm off duty now, and I like you people. I wouldn't cod you, not in a pub with your drink in my hand. If we were in my office now, I'd give you the line. You ought to come up there some day and hear me do it.'

'No thanks,' Guy said. 'I can vomit by sticking my finger down my throat at home without coming all the way to County Hall to do it. Where are they going to start on this bloody thing? You said two miles, so at the rate they build roads, I suppose we'll have a few years reprieve before they get this far.'

'It won't be started at the beginning. Nor yet at the end. It will be attacked first from the middle and spread both ways from there.'

'In the middle?' Guy and Martha looked at him, and Robert P. V. looked at them, his eyes under the crew-cut brows a little sad.

'Just so,' he said. 'In Cottingham Park. In all its –'

'But why, why? Oh, it's so unfair!' Suddenly Martha felt afraid, small and vulnerable, as if the grab of a giant crane were already hovering above her like the talons of a vulture, to snatch away her world. 'Why pick on us?'

'It's the obvious thing. This is a decaying neighbourhood. Much of it is under the chopper anyway, and here's a chance to get cracking on the slum clearance that should have been done years ago.'

'But it isn't all slums. A lot of people love living here, and all kinds of new people move in all the time, and spend a lot of money on their houses too.'

'Oh, I know. Your street is all right. Well naturally – excuse me – or you wouldn't be living here.' He lifted the moustache to bare one side of his teeth. 'A lot of the old houses that have been

49

done up are very charming. And many of them will stay, of course. This isn't going to be an atomic blast, you know. Strip demolition, that's all it is.'

'A strip how wide?' asked Guy, his elbows on the table, his small bony chin on the knuckles of his thumbs.

'Oh' – Mr Peregrine spread his hands out vaguely, frowned at them, brought them closer together – 'well, if you include the marginal sites the Town Planning Committee has earmarked for redevelopment' – he inched them farther apart. 'But there is plenty of slum property along that strip, and some frightful, anachronistic horrors. That's one reason you've got a crime problem and a colour problem here. Undesirables will always come to a decaying area and make it worse. The coloured people crowd into those filthy little streets up on the hill towards the railway because its one of the few places they can get in. The district is so bad that they're not excluded.'

Guy laughed shortly. 'Motto of the mother country. Welcome to the West Indians. This is your home, but you'll have to bed down in the cesspool, because it's the only place that's dirty enough. So now you're going to flush them out of the cesspool.'

'Into something better. If you're racially tolerant, you should be glad to see these poor devils have this chance to get out of the stews. They'll all be rehoused. Everybody will.'

'That's a laugh. With the poor devils already sleeping thirty in a house and six in a bed, and waiting lists as long as your arm for the council flats. What are you going to do – rehouse them like Hitler did the Jews, in pits full of lime?'

Shocked and angry at Mr Peregrine's news and his bland assumption that she would not mind the rape of her own little corner of the city, Martha was grateful to Guy for trying to bait him. He was a pleasant enough man, if one had met him under any other circumstances; but under these circumstances, he represented the planners, the statisticians who figured out small lives on paper, the tyrants who could say Pay Up, or Get Out, or Go Here or There without anyone ever telling them to go to hell.

But Mr Peregrine, like his masters, was impossible to bait, although for a different reason. Guy was steaming up for an argument, but he could not argue with a man who dropped his official voice into his beer and agreed with him.

'That's going to be the big headache. We'll build like mad,

50

of course, if we can find any space to build. We'll shovel a lot of them out into the suburbs, protesting bitterly, and we'll get some of them out to the New Towns. But they can't get those houses unless they've got a job out there, and a lot of the types in town these days are almost unemployable, and from what I've seen, you've got 'em all here. Fairies, tarts, coffee-bar weirdies, unwashed geniuses, juvenile delinquents, old ladies living and dying under sheets of newspapers on the benches by the playgrounds. Drunks and thugs and Maltese pimps, all living cheek by jowl with people like you who are madly normal, and people who are madly chic in ballet slippers and paint up mews houses in Italian pastel washes. One half of this extraordinary place is going up, and the other half is plunging downhill like the Gadarene swine. Incredible state of affairs.'

'But that,' said Martha sadly, 'is what makes it such a fascinating place to live in. Why here?' she asked again helplessly. 'Oh why do they have to do it here?'

Nancy was with them all at once, exploding with vitality over Martha's left shoulder. 'Glad to see you found friends.' She beamed at Mr Peregrine. 'I never like to see a man drinking alone, however good for business. When Guy drops in here by himself, I always try to hurry him along home to you, Martha.'

'To settle any doubt in your mind,' Martha said wearily, 'I know that Guy comes in here sometimes on his way home, and I fail to see any reason to object.'

'Oh well, that's nice.' Nancy remained bright, though disappointed to find that there had been no point in sneaking. 'I came to say that if you want dinner, you'd better go in now.'

'I don't know that I feel like dinner', Martha said bleakly.

'Too many Martinis.' Nancy laughed briskly. 'I know how it is. But that's when you need the food. It acts like blotting paper, they tell me, though I wouldn't know.' Nancy had never taken a drink in her life. She did not need it.

When she had gone, scooping up the fallen tray like a diving gull, Mr Peregrine put his hand comfortingly, sexlessly, over Martha's. 'Don't worry,' he said kindly. 'Nothing will happen yet. What with all the thousands of negotiations that make the head reel merely to guess at, it will be a long time before they even get started. The whole Expressway may take years to complete. By which time, I shouldn't doubt, all the trunk roads out of London will be obsolete and we shall be going everywhere by monorail.'

After Guy had driven Mrs Pellew home, and she had gone through the farce of waiting in the front seat to see if he was going to get out to open the door for her, and when he did, to get rid of her, of clambering awkwardly out by herself before he could get round the car, he drove to his lock-up garage in the mews near his house.

It was a narrow cobbled mews that had once been stables, with quarters for grooms and coachmen above. Now, since it had been officially condemned as a slum and so had not been taken over by the philodendron and unmatched wallpaper brigade, it was dark little flats over private garages with ill-hung doors, some of them used for cars and some for storing barrow and market stalls.

In the narrow tunnel of garage opposite Guy's, a man with pale eyes crossed over one of those eaten-away noses that hint at congenital syphilis, kept a stack of junk and a lopsided barrow on which he pushed a selection of it each Friday to the Caledonian Market and each Saturday to the Portobello Road.

This man, referred to as That Commie by the other residents of the Armstrong Mews who were in the main old-world and respectable, had a habit of leaving his barrow in such a place that Guy could not make the turn into his garage.

It was there today. Guy sighed and put his finger on the horn, and the window over the man's junk store shot up and emitted the Medusa-like head of the woman who did not bother to pretend she was his wife, mouthing abuse.

When no one came out to move the barrow, Guy got out of the car and knocked on the narrow slip of front door. It was opened immediately, for the Commie had been waiting on the other side for the ritual exchange of hostilities.

Guy had learned to control his temper. Once he had almost struck the man, and the woman had screamed: 'Assault!' from the window. The man had gone running off down the mews to fetch a policeman, and by the time he returned, without one, for he had merely run round the block, Guy had moved the barrow. He had learned not to do this either, for the woman was screaming: 'Private property!' and beginning to throw down potato peelings, and half the mews was out with folded arms to watch.

Squinting down his gruesome nose, the man stood at the foot

52

of the steep wooden stairs which started just inside the door. Guy merely jerked his thumb towards the barrow and said nothing. This was the ritual.

'Think you own the whole bleeding town,' grunted the man. This was part of the ritual too, and so was the woman urging him on from above: 'Don't take no crap from 'im,' with the empty bladders of her bosoms draped across the sill.

Guy jerked his thumb again, and went back to wait in the car. The performance was no longer irritating, but very tedious, and Guy would have abandoned it long ago if he had not paid five years' rent on the garage in order to secure it.

Taking his time, and leering across his nose and making rude gestures with his fingers, the man eventually pushed the barrow aside, not one inch farther than necessary. Then he banged back inside the tiny door, while the woman watched, malevolent-eyed, to see if Guy would scrape the barrow with his bumper so that she could yell: 'Damage!'

When Guy had put the car away and locked the door, he turned and raised his hat to her as she slammed down the window. 'One day,' he said to Mrs Saithe, who had come out of her front door next to the garage, 'I'll machine-gun them both, right from here, right through that window. But not until my lease is up.'

'Bloody reds,' said Mrs Saithe. 'They bring this whole place down.'

Tiny and neat, with hair the colour of unwashed sheets dragged back into a small tight lump at the back of her head, Mrs Saithe had lived in the mews for forty years, ever since Mr Saithe had carried her, shrieking with glee, over the threshold of the flat beneath which he stabled his Beardmore taxi. When the lady from the borough Housing Department came to talk tentatively about slum clearance, Mrs Saithe, whose teeth were in the gravy boat that morning, had set her fierce little jaw below the sunken gums and repeated stoutly: 'They'd ought to let us alone. We're not complaining.'

The surprised visitor from the Housing Department, a girl in her mid-twenties who had taken a six months' course and thought she knew it all, found Mrs Saithe's attitude corroborated at door after door.

The mews was odorous and primitive. It saw the sun for a brief ten minutes each day at the height of summer, and not even then if the washing lines which stretched across it were filled. The rooms were tiny and airless and there were bugs under the damp wallpaper. The plumbing in the noisome little lean-to sheds at the back alternated between running all over the floor or not at all.

The younger ones fretted, and moved away when they could, but most of the other residents had lived in the cramped upper storey flats for many years, and they tolerated the mews because it was their home. They did more than tolerate it. They actively liked it, and the young Housing visitor, writing her report, threw page after page in the wastebasket trying to explain why, and finally gave up, because it was impossible to explain in the kind of language that could be turned in at the Town Hall.

Cut off from the world at one end by the high brown wall where the children chalked their stumps in the cricket season, the mews had generated in itself a village atmosphere of gossip and vendettas and everyone's business intimately known and discussed. In flatlets and wretched back rooms all over London, old ladies and trembling old men died alone and lay there stiff and purple and undiscovered for days until the half-pint bottles of milk piled up; but this could never happen in the mews. A sickness or a death or a childbirth were common property, and the low-ceilinged bedroom in which someone was entering or leaving life was usually so full of both practical and theorizing neighbours that the doctor or the nurse could hardly get in.

Even the Commie's woman, when she had her miscarriage, had been busily attended during the time that she was in extremis. When she recovered, the women shunned her again, but as long as there was a chance of her bleeding to death, they were all in there in plastic aprons with their sleeves rolled up.

Impossible to describe this in officialese, so the baffled young visitor had merely stated that the residents were actively opposed to displacement. They had no legal right to object or to obstruct the demolition of their dingy pleasaunce, but since the Council had already more slum clearance on their plate than they could manage, they decided to shelve the mews for a while and let the people alone.

'But they'll get you in the end,' Guy was telling Mrs Saithe. 'If they really go ahead with this new road, you'll find yourself thirty miles out in a New Town before you know it.'

'Bugger that,' said Mrs Saithe, who had never been farther out of London than Canvey Island. 'They're not shifting me. They'll never pull this place down. We all been 'ere too long.'

'They don't care. They can't put curves and loops in the road to accommodate everyone who doesn't want to move. If this chap I was talking to is right, the road will cut slap through here. Like a scythe, Mrs Saithe.'

He realized that he had said: 'Like a saithe, Mrs Scythe,' but she was too indignant to notice. 'I'll object,' she said. 'All of us will. We'll bring pressure to bear. They'll be sorry they ever tried to muck us about. You'll see.'

'Probably I will.' Guy smiled. He and the taut little woman had developed a cheerful friendship through their many brief encounters when he was locking or unlocking the garage and she stood in her doorway with her toes in grey gym shoes planted exactly at the edge of the sill. 'But don't say I didn't warn you. I thought you'd be glad to hear the news, so you can be the first to pass it on.'

High heels clattered clumsily down the stairs behind her, and her lodger, Eileen Kelly, appeared, going out to work. From her appearance, which was ordinary enough except for a gold charm bracelet round one thick ankle and lumpy mascara weighting her pale eyes, it was not readily apparent what her work was; but Guy had seen her once in the section of Park Road where most of this kind of business was done, or at least initiated.

She was a thick-set girl with dull blonde hair turned under at the ends, accentuating the potato shape of her face with its heavy adenoidal lips and jaw. With her on a leash she had a ratty little mongrel with a fancy collar, who had come to her as a stray one night, begging for acceptance, and not been refused. Eileen often took him out with her when it was fine. She had seen the girls round Burlington Street with their poodles, and thought it chic.

'One of these days,' she told Guy, 'I'm going to have this dog dyed mauve and get a costume to match. I suit mauve.'

'That's true.' Mrs Saithe sucked in the place where her teeth should have been, in recognition of fashion talk. 'That's a pretty scarf, dear. I haven't seen that one.'

'C & A Modes. I'm surprised you've not seen it in my drawer.' Eileen knew that Mrs Saithe rustled through her possessions when she was out. Nothing could be done about it, with rooms so hard to come by now that every black man and his brother had moved in; but she took all her money out with her in her red handbag.

Mrs Saithe would not have stolen the money, but she would have liked to count it. 'I wonder you don't sew it in your corsets,' she said once sarcastically, and Eileen had said: 'I would, if there was a chance of keeping them on.'

Mrs Saithe was not embarrassed by Eileen knowing that she went through her things and read her letters. If there was to be any talk about morals, she was one up on the girl from the start. Not that she minded particularly what her lodger did for a living. Since her daughter had married and gone away and she had buried Mr Saithe at Gunnersbury, she had needed to let the other bedroom, and Eileen was a nice-spoken girl and paid the rent, and conducted her business elsewhere: in the Park, or in one of the rooms in Carbine Road, which she referred to as 'my office'.

'You got your cardigan, dear?' Mrs Saithe asked. 'It's draughty out. Not half as draughty as it's going to be if Mr Banning is right, what he just told me. Tell Eileen, then. Tell her the tale.'

Guy told it again briefly, and the girl's jaw sagged open as she listened, showing a bulge of bluish tongue behind her black raspberry lips. 'I never,' she said, moving her head from side to side with the eyes fixed.

'I'll believe it when I see it. You don't want to take every rumour you hear as Gospel truth,' said Mrs Saithe, although she was shortly going all round the mews to spread the tale as a fact.

'You'll believe it all right,' Guy said, 'when the bulldozer comes nosing up to your door like a man-eating buffalo. Well, I'm off.' He winked at Eileen. 'My wife will think I've been picked up.'

Eileen laughed, a thickened neigh when she brought her chin out of the fur collar of her coat to perform. She liked that sort of joke. She had never been the kind to make pretences with any man. That was why she was popular in her line of work.

'Fat chance I've got with you,' she said. 'If you wanted to go with a girl, you'd go up West. I know your sort.'

'Oh, I don't know,' Guy said. 'I haven't seen anything in the West End that looks as good as you.'

'Sod off,' Eileen said cheerily. 'You're not my type.'

Wish he were though. Wish I could find a decent clean fellow like that. That kind take you up sometimes, they say. I mean, really take you up. Keep you in luxury, and that.

Eileen walked up the mews, her spindle heels slipping between the rough cobbles, and turned into the wind for the walk up to

Park Road. If Rhona's chest was still keeping her at home, she'd take her corner on the other side of the street, out of the wind. Or perhaps try the Brass Monkey, if there weren't too many girls there already. Si Robbins did not mind a few of them in his bar as long as they bought at least one drink and paid him something now and then, but if there were more than three or four, he would throw the last comer out.

That was not dignified. Eileen thought quite a lot about dignity, and keeping up her standards. There were things at which she drew the line, although if the fellow would pay the extra, she might stretch a point, to give pleasure.

Some girls did not mind being thrown out of the Brass Monkey and other bars, but Eileen disliked it. If you were asked to leave, and you made a bit of a stir, the fellows noticed you all right; but not one of them ever followed you out, even if he had been looking at you while you were inside. There was no loyalty left in the world. No chivalry.

And so now she and Toodie could be turned out of their nice little room, if Mr Banning was right. And he might be. That kind had a way of knowing things. She'd have to start looking for another place. With her job and a dog who shed stiff ginger hairs on the furniture, it was not going to be easy to get in with someone as respectable as Mrs Saithe. Might be she could move in with one of the other girls, if she could find one who wasn't tied up with a Maltese or a Cypriot or a nigger ponce. Tramps. Eileen wanted no part of that. A decent chap of her own, yes thank you, but although she was willing to go with a black man – well, you had to these days, if you didn't want to starve – she was buggered if she was going to work for one.

A young, edgy-looking boy, walking towards her with his knees high, looked at her and smiled nervously. 'Hullo, dear,' Eileen said, and the boy dropped the smile in fright and quickened his pace to walk past her.

Not for several months, Mr Banning had said. A year, two years perhaps, before they would pull down the mews. Might be she'd find a man by then. Might be – Eileen daydreamed, walking with short steps in her narrow skirt up the dark streets with Toodie on the leash beside her, pulling her back and forth across the pavement as he veered between smells on lamp posts and walls – she would not even be in London. To go back to Ireland married. That would show them. That would stop their mouths.

Back to her dear sister. Back to Olive, who sorrowed for her and was the only one who understood. *Better not come home*, she had written last Christmas, when Eileen had saved enough for the trip over. *Mam and Dad still won't hear your name. I want you, Eily, but I don't want to see you hurt.*

Rhona was not there, so Eileen took her corner, which had a nice deep doorway for shelter and conversation. There were not many people about in Park Road: not many on business. Apart from a few coloured fellows coasting a lime, as they called it, and not really looking seriously for cat, everyone was going somewhere briskly.

After a while, Eileen turned her collar up higher and took a few steps back and forth to keep warm. When Toodie began to shiver and drag at his blue plastic leash, she picked him up and put him inside her coat, where he snuggled warm, like it must be to hold a baby.

He was a great comfort to her. A church worker, who had tried to talk to Eileen once after she had been in court for her fine, had suggested to her that she had only taken up the streets because she needed love.

'I'm in it for the money,' Eileen had said indignantly. She didn't want the old cow to think that she was one of *those*. Some of them would do it for nothing, just as long as they got it.

But perhaps the cow had something at that. She did need love. For two pins, she might have kept the baby, only since she had signed him away before he was born, nobody at the hospital had asked her. Well, she had Toodie. He loved her. She brought his gruff brown head out of her coat and laid her chin on it so that she would make a nice picture for a man across the road who had slowed down and looked as if he might come over.

The dog was useful to start a conversation if fellows were a bit shy. And when they were through wasting Eileen's time with conversation, Toodie was as good as gold. Went to sleep and never bothered anyone. Though there had been that man – 'He's looking at me,' he kept saying. 'For Christ's sake, can't you stop him looking at me?' Eileen had to smile at the memory of his hapless face.

The man across the road caught the smile and stopped dithering and came over, looking relieved. Bloody idiot. Had he thought she was waiting for a bus?

*

58

In the staff room of Abbot's Road Secondary Modern School, Grace Peel ate her sandwiches while she corrected the essays of Form 1B. When she was not on duty in the lunch room, she seldom ate the school dinners, except on Fridays when it was hot treacle roll. At twenty-three, Grace was still enough of a child to enjoy hot treacle roll. Miss Bowden, who had been eating hot treacle roll at Abbot's Road Secondary for twenty years because she could not be bothered to make sandwiches, assured her that she would grow out of it.

Miss Bowden also told her that she would grow out of her optimistic enthusiasm for teaching, and the tenderness which made her patient in finding excuses for the more squalid antics of the rough, dirty children in her care; but she did not expect to. The treacle roll, perhaps. Not the children.

They were her despair, and then suddenly her joy. She could be utterly defeated, exhausted by the impossible struggle to force knowledge into minds that were stockaded against learning. Then all at once the class was quiet, listening to what she read, and some shabby twelve-year-old who had not said a sensible word all week jumped up with flailing hand and asked a beautifully imaginative question.

Mrs Dormer came in with the tea trays and looked in disgust at the long trestle table in the middle of the room littered with books and papers and attaché cases and Mrs Purdie's knitting. She pushed the tray on at one end, knocking off a dictionary, which fell upside down agape. John Ferris, who was in the staff room with Grace, got up with a groan for his spine to pick up the dictionary, and smoothed out the crumpled leaves. He took up the teapot to pour for Grace.

'Don't you ever wash the cups, Mrs Dormer?' The lines in his long grey indoor face all ran downwards. The deep suffering clefts of the gastric between nose and chin embittered his mouth and spoiled it for smiling.

'You know I do,' said Mrs Dormer, 'but the soot is everywhere.' She rubbed the corner of her apron briefly round inside one cup and handed it to him. 'Take this one, my Lord.'

'Thanks. If I have a cup of milk, there won't be enough. Could you get some more?'

'Can't be done. I've got my floors to finish. Where do you think you are – Eton College? It's a dream, my sister tells me, how they wait on them hand and foot there.' Mrs Dormer's sister, married to a porter at Windsor Hospital, was a maid at Eton, and was frequently produced in marvelling quotes.

'Even the boys, she says, live in the lap of luxury. The little ones have to wait on the bigger ones, you see. When they want anything, they open the door, my sister says, and shout: "Hey Hammerstein?" Don't ask me why, because the boy's name is more likely to be Jones.'

'Hay, Hammersley,' Mr Ferris said, pouring Grace's tea. 'They were the first fags at Eton. It's a very old tradition.'

'You know a lot about it,' said Mrs Dormer, affronted by a piece of information unknown to her sister.

'I ought to. I was there for five years.'

'Oh, very likely. And end up in a dump like this.'

'Well, perhaps you're right.' John Ferris looked at the broad slatternly woman, looked round at the shabby room with its patches of damp on the distempered walls, its battered electric fire, its chairs that had needed for years to be restuffed or re-covered or thrown away. 'Perhaps I never was.'

Mrs Dormer went out, smiling into her chins, glad to have put him in his place, and Mr Ferris ambled his long legs down to the other end of the table and set down the cup before Grace, slopping some of the tea into the saucer.

'Thanks, Mr Ferris.' Grace called the younger masters by their christian names, but Mr Ferris, who was the senior assistant, was too old for her to do it unless he asked her, and he had not asked her. She gave him one of her nicest smiles. She was sorry for him because his life seemed to have gone wrong somewhere, while hers seemed to be going ahead in the way she had planned it, even down to having a job instead of marrying Brian, which, although everyone had assumed them to be made for each other since they were ten, she had always known in her heart was what would happen.

'You are too pretty to be so industrious,' Mr Ferris said. He brought out the word pretty in a creaking sort of way, as if it was difficult to him to say words like that. 'You won't catch me correcting essays in the lunch hour. I flick through 'em in class while the flower of Commonwealth youth is copying down the dates of kings. Where should we be without the dates of kings? You're even *reading* those abominations, aren't you?'

'But I really enjoy reading them.' He was standing behind her, his hand on the back of her chair. Grace turned and looked up at him, expecting to find him staring at nothing with a disgruntled face; but to her surprise, he was looking down at her hair, and his mouth was doing the best it could for a smile. 'It's so exciting when they improve, even just a little bit, or when they suddenly put in something, with the grammar and spelling all wrong, but some really original twist of imagination. Listen to this.' She turned back to the mutilated exercise book on the table in front of her. 'Terry Raines. He lives in one of those awful streets behind the Baths and he thinks Hampstead Heath is the country, but he's written here: "I am looking forward to the spring because the leaves curl out of the buds like a hand opening." '

'Oh, for God's sake.' Mr Ferris took his hands off her chair. 'And do you know,' he said, as he went to pour himself most of the milk that was for the other members of the staff, 'that however enthusiastic you are, however hard you work on him, or encourage him, or waste your pretty youth on him, Terry Raines will go on spelling Because Becuas for the rest of his life?'

Grace took another sandwich, gave Terry an A mark, although the bottom half of his one page essay was almost obliterated by blots and a smear of blood, and took the next open book from the pile.

There were only two lines on the page, cramped up at the top underneath a heading elaborately embellished with curlicues and tassels. 'Wy I lik Spring. It is a seson after Winter. Not so Cold.'

The next composition was longer. It covered three pages. It may have contained some startling thoughts, but it was completely illegible. Darlene Archer could not write at all, but she copied handwriting, as a very young child scrawls rapidly over a page and tells its mother: 'Look, I've written a letter.'

The class which had been Grace's for the year since she had finished her probation at Abbot's Road and moved on to the staff as a qualified teacher, was in some respects the most difficult group in the school. They were the first-year children who had moved on from the primary school two streets away, not in the excitement of progress, but in the dullness of disappointment.

These were the boys and girls who had failed their eleven-plus examination and could not go on to Grammar School. They might have another chance for it when they were thirteen or fourteen, but at this point they did not even want that. They had given up, and it was Grace's gargantuan task to get them going again.

Before they took the examination, the more literate among them had known ambition. Since they failed they had lost interest and in most cases their parents had lost whatever interest they may have had in their children's schooling. When Grace had organized a short, scrappy play at Christmas, with costumes made by herself and the class, very few of the parents had bothered to come.

Some of the boys were 'latchkey kids', whose mothers could not have come even if they wanted to. They had jobs which kept them away longer than the school hours, so that the boys either went round to 'my Nan's', or home to an empty flat, or out casting for trouble on the streets.

The lack of audience had not mattered, because the children's enjoyment of the play did not depend on it. Acting, which was not a lesson, was their favourite lesson, and Grace quite often let them perform impromptu sketches of bloodshed and torture as a means of keeping them eager. For some of them, it was the only piece of the school day, apart from dinner and recreation, in which they could take part. After five years at elementary school, they were almost completely illiterate. Next year, they would go into the Remove, and break the heart of poor Denzil Raymond; but this first year, until those who could learn something were sorted out from those who would never learn, they were with Grace.

'You can help them,' the headmaster had told her. 'You can help the thick ones by making them feel secure at school and – what's the word I want? – necessary, I suppose. Wanted in a way that most of them aren't wanted at home. And you can help the others by making them feel that this is the beginning of their school life, not the end. Any of them who were doing more than just coasting at elementary school have been scared to death of the eleven-plus ever since they were old enough to understand what it meant. And then they understood it wrong, as an all-or-nothing deal which could make or break them.

'Thanks to our educators, who have dangled the carrot of higher education before the noses of those who can't ever have it, there's a mistaken idea that Grammar School is everything that matters. But we can give them just as much here. More, for some of them. You ever seen a boy from a really degraded family

62

trying to hold his own in Grammar School when his mother can't or won't give him a clean shirt and he either can't or won't improve his accent? We've got some of 'em. They get sent here because they can't make the grade at Grammar School. Or because they fight or steal or run away. They settle down here like a fish getting back into water. I won't say they never fight or steal or play truant again, but they do it for different reasons; not because they are ashamed of themselves or afraid of the school.'

Mr Rawlings, the headmaster, was a man who had retained his humanity and his ideals as well as his common sense under circumstances that do away with all three in lesser men. For ten years at Abbot's Road Secondary he had been in charge of the minds and bodies of adolescent children of all colours, all races, all varieties of morals from the teeming streets of The Rise and the red brick jungles of the council flats.

Poor and shabby as it was, he was very proud of his school. A widower for many years, and childless, Abbot's Road was his whole life. He might be called a dedicated man, although he would have jumped on anyone who said it.

He did not consider that being the arbiter of the development and destiny of some hundred and fifty of Cottingham Park's least privileged children was difficult enough to call for dedication. To him it was engrossing. Each child was a challenge, to be met as far as possible on his own level; not thrown into a common jurisdiction of regulations and set standards.

Teachers who had not stayed at Abbot's Road had labelled Mr Rawlings 'progressive'. They meant this as an insult, but it was a word he liked in its simplest sense. The children had to progress. They must get somewhere, and it did not matter if their goal was not an educationally conventional one. He wanted them to get somewhere as human beings.

Because of Mr Rawlings and the way the school was run, Grace was very happy at Abbot's Road. Her mother, far away in Cumberland, put panicking paragraphs in her letters whenever the newspapers told her of some disturbance or crime in Cottingham Park. She said that Grace was too young, the district was too dangerous. If she did not want to come home, she should at least find a post in some nice respectable girls' school in the suburbs or the country.

But in a nice respectable girls' school, Grace would have to stick to the rules and teach them what she was instructed to teach in the way she was told to teach it. At Abbot's Road she did not have to be rigid in her lessons. If she could capture the attention of the class and teach them something, the Head did not mind if she veered miles away from the curriculum. She could spend all day reading them Treasure Island if she liked, or taking them down the river on a boat to Hampton Court.

Of the rest of the staff, those who called Mr Rawlings too progressive did not stay, and those who remained were able to work together in a common purpose to run the school for the pupils, and not the pupils for the school. Even Mr Ferris and Mrs Bowden, Grace knew, had not despaired of the children and of their job as completely as they pretended.

It was a shabby, old-fashioned school with small rooms and narrow windows, many of them ecclesiastically shaped so that the arched top half would not open. The classrooms and their furniture were inadequate. The large central hall had to serve for everything from Assembly through gymnastics and school dinners to recreation on a wet day. The lavatories, too antique and too few, were outside at one end of the playground of cracked concrete. This was separated from the street by a high brown wall, crowned with broken glass. The three narrow doors labelled in stone: BOYS, GIRLS, and INFANTS dated from the days when Abbot's Road had been for all ages, a kind of village school among the unassuming terrace homes of those who worked to build and serve the spacious Victorian houses on the other side of the Valley.

And oddly, in spite of what it had now become, and what the neighbourhood had become, the school retained a sort of family spirit and as much of its parochial tradition as was possible among the conglomerate, shifting population.

Best school in the district, people said, with a mild local pride. Although the children reviled it as much as other children in other schools, most of them were contented at Abbot's Road after their fashion. Sometimes a sixteen-year-old would come back, arriving suddenly in his old classroom with an embarrassed grin in the middle of a lesson. He had come ostensibly to give news of his triumphal adventures in the outside world, but it seemed more as if he were finding the outside world a chill mystery, and was groping back to the place where he had felt that he belonged.

When the rest of the staff came in for their tea, Grace put aside her pile of exercise books, because she knew that after last night, she must say at least something to Denzil Raymond. If she went on working, he would not think that she was merely correcting essays, but that she was deliberately trying to snub him.

The teachers were a motley group, with a variety of ages, backgrounds and teaching ability. Mrs Purdie, for instance, could not teach at all. She would never have taken it up if her parents could have thought of anything else she could do; and she would not have gone back to it after marriage when her husband's income began to go down in inverse ratio to the cost of living if it had not been the only job which would fit in with her children's school hours. She had been put on Art this year. Art and Handicrafts, which were the safest subjects to palm off on someone who was hard to fit in anywhere else.

Mr Ferris was an intelligent teacher, educated far beyond Abbot's Road requirements, and fettered beneath his abilities by a fourth-year class which contained a few bright souls, but many whose brains appeared to be lodged in the two-inch soles of their 'creeper' shoes. Mr Ferris's boys were almost ready for the world, but some of them, as he informed them when they told him gleefully of the night's episodes – for no teacher at Abbot's Road would ever turn copper's nark – would get no farther in it than the first penal institution that would accept them.

Geoffrey Savage, who had one of the third-year groups, was a muscular young man with a beard and a cockney accent, both thick. He was an enthusiastic teacher, and a believer in homeo-pathic remedies for insolence. If a boy cursed him, he would join in a slanging match. If a boy hit him, as some of the bold rougher ones did occasionally, he would violate the teacher's unwritten code and hit back. If a classroom fight broke out, he would get in among it to break it up, and do as much damage as anyone. The boys liked that. They could understand that. They preferred his methods to the sarcasm of Mr Ferris, which they could not understand. Because of his name and his beard and his be-haviour, Geoffrey Savage was known as the Wild Beast, frequently portrayed on blackboards as an unidentifiable animal behind bars, with a balloon coming out of his mouth, saying 'il kill you'.

Mrs Bowden, who wore a coarse wedding ring, but was otherwise not noticeably married – 'Has anybody ever *seen* Mr

Bowden?' Miss O'Leary cavilled – may have taken the married title as high-class cooks once did, to enhance her status. She was rugged and square, with a slight moustache and a hockey-stick manner which caused her class to show more obedience but less respect than they did to teachers who were recognizable as women, like Grace and Mrs Purdie.

Miss O'Leary, with her artificial foot, had been accepted at first with the children's queer, unpredictable sympathy which made them treat tenderly one deaf or handicapped or backward boy, but bait another half to death. She had lost favour very quickly when it was seen that she would not accept the accept-ance, but wished to remain at bitter war with her class. She was one of those who could not condone Mr Rawlings' principle of letting the children say whatever came into their heads in the middle of a lesson on the chance that it might be worthwhile. She was on her way out, just as quickly as she could obtain her transfer. She was already gone in spirit, and merely stumped through her days giving set lessons to which nobody listened, since as far as her class were concerned, she was gone already.

Denzil Raymond, who got stuck with the Remove class of thick-headed second-year children, was too young and in-genuous for his job at Abbot's Road. Uncle Oswald Bartlett was much too old, and could not hear a riot breaking out in class as long as the boys sat still and did not shout. Burns and Goslett, spectacled bachelors who roomed together and were reputed to be queer – which they were not – were able enough men, who had meant to get far in their profession, but had somehow got stuck in the cheerful slough of Abbot's Road.

With the exception of Miss O'Leary, who viewed her col-leagues with a distant pity because she was going and they were not, the ill-assorted staff were friendly with each other, better integrated than most teachers in this kind of school. All of them except Grace and Denzil Raymond had been there for several years. This was unusual in the world of Secondary Modern schools, where bedevilled teachers come and go like travellers in a commercial hotel.

Denzil Raymond got landed with the job of pouring tea for everyone. By the time he got to his own, even after adding all the hot water Mrs Dormer had thought fit to bring, he had only half a cup, with no milk, thanks to John Ferris and his grumbling ulcer. Holding the cup limply, so that it slid across the saucer,

66

he looked uncertainly round the room, his forehead wrinkling up into his low-growing crew cut. The chairs were all taken. He started for the sooty window seat, which offered a view of grey roofs crowding away to the gasometer and an off-white cat crouched under a chimney cowl with its eyes malevolently on the staff room window.

'Come and sit here.' Grace lifted a pile of books from the chair beside her.

'Oh, let me.' Denzil was too late, as always. By the time he had stumbled over the cord of the electric fire and put down his cup precariously on the littered table, Grace had set all the books neatly on the floor.

'Thanks.' He sat down and looked at her. 'I suppose you're furious with me.'

'Furious?' Grace's heart sank. Here we go. Why must he always torture himself with post mortems? 'Why should I be?'

'About last night, I mean.'

She had gone with Denzil to the cinema, as she did occasionally, for want of better male company. Half way through the main feature, she had allowed him to hold her hand, as she did occasionally, for want of better male contact. When he took her home, he had held shut the gate of the villa where she had her flat on the top floor, breathed heavily and said: 'May I kiss you?'

Now in the staff room, she tried to explain to him why she had said No and lifted his small hand from the latch so that she could go through into the gravelled garden. 'You must never ask. Just go ahead and do it.'

'Would you let me?' His brown eyes were industriously baffled, like a member of his own class trying to master subtraction.

'I don't know.'

'Could I try again?'

She shrugged. Geoffrey Savage was listening, and enjoying it.

'Tonight? Shall I try tonight?'

'Oh Denzil –' Grace laughed and sighed together. 'You're so naïve. Making matter-of-fact plans for it, as if you were going to take up billiards.'

'It's the only way to go about it, don't you see? Lay your plans beforehand. I'd planned since the day before, ever since you said you'd come to the cinema, how I'd ask if I could kiss you, what words I would use, and so on. My brother found me practising in front of the hall mirror, as a matter of fact. I had to pretend it was for amateur dramatics. Well, I got it wrong, last night. Now I must try again, the way you say. You know about these things.'

'You think I'm so experienced?'

'Well, I mean, after all, you've had boy-friends. It stands to reason you didn't shake hands with them. You must show me how its done the way girls like it.'

'Oh, Denzil, you're so – so –' he had winced when she said naïve, so she said 'cold-blooded.'

He liked that better. 'Cold-blooded. Yes. Ruthless. All males are ruthless. Where shall we go tonight?'

'I've got to wash my hair.'

'You said that two days ago.'

Denzil put on his hurt airedale look, and Grace was glad when the door opened and Mr Rawlings the headmaster came in. He shut the door and stood against it, looking round at them with the pebble pupils of his eyes behind the thick glasses.

He did not often come into the staff room, for he was too busy to gossip during the tea break. He also thought that if his staff wanted to talk about him or about things he should not know, they should have a chance to do it.

Mrs Purdie got up, fluttering a little. She was not in love with Rawlings, nor afraid of him, but she had that kind of ineradicable underdog attitude which causes flutters or giggles in the presence of the boss. 'Quite a pleasure, Mr Rawlings.' She looked into the teapot and the cracked hot water jug. 'Oh dear, there isn't any. Do you suppose we dare ask Mrs Dormer for a fresh pot?'

'I've had mine. I didn't come here for tea. I came to tell you all something. And I'm afraid, Mrs Purdie, that when you've heard it, you'll be sorry you said Quite a pleasure.'

Margaret Purdie blushed. Had she said a platitude again then? Mr Rawlings had warned her once or twice about teaching platitudes to her class. She tried hard, but she was not always sure when she was doing it.

Denzil Raymond and Burns and Goslett had all got up to offer their chairs. Mr Rawlings told them to sit down, and walked heavily over to the fireplace which was blanked off with a piece of wallboard, scrawled over with messages and telephone numbers and various ways of spelling Buonaparte, which had been an argument last term between Denzil and Mr Ferris. He stood beside the electric fire, his shoulders against the mantelpiece, and looked round at them all, his long dark face unusually solemn.

'What's up?' John Ferris asked. 'Is there a Black Maria at the gates to pick up the whole of my class? I suppose it was they who did that job over at the fur warehouse.'

'I wish it were as simple as that,' the Head said. 'We could cope with that. We've been through that kind of thing. We –' He bit his lip. Grace had never seen him at a loss for words like this. Usually when he came in to tell them something, he was loquacious, incisive, holding the floor with a breezy speech that left no room for interruptions. His badly shaven jaw was as dark as usual at this time of day, but the rest of his face was oddly pale and strained.

'The chairman of the governors was in to see me this morning. He'd just come from the Ministry. He brought a – a rather big piece of news.'

Mr Rawlings took off his glasses and rubbed at his eyes, the heavy, dark-rimmed glasses dangling from one hand.

'They're going to build us a new school,' Denzil piped up. 'How absolutely smashing. I knew they would some day. After all the terrific work you've done here, they ought to give you the finest school in Cottingham Park. Socking great plate glass windows and strip lighting. Shall we have a lab? When are they going to start tearing down this ruin?'

'Ruin. Yes. Quite soon, young Raymond.' But he should be smiling, if it was true. He had always dreamed of a modern, airy school. He had been badgering the Ministry for years about the conditions under which he struggled to give his children an idea that life could be better than it appeared in their corner of Cottingham Park. He swayed a little and put out one foot to steady himself. Grace found that she was sitting on the edge of her chair, ready to jump up. She thought he might be going to have a heart attack.

'They are going to tear down our school,' he said slowly, and all the staff were watching him, as if their eyes were on strings leading to his face, 'and they are never going to build it up again. There will be no more Abbot's Road.'

'I don't believe a word of it.' The string from Mrs Bowden's eyes snapped, and she shook her shaggy bobbed head like a dog with water in its ears.

'I didn't hear you right.' Uncle Oswald cupped a veined hand behind his ear. 'Did you say they were going to pull this school down?'

'That's it.' The fire was burning the Head's leg. He kicked the switch off impatiently. 'They're building a new road, from somewhere to somewhere – I've forgotten exactly what he said – and this place is right in the line of fire. They're releasing the story officially at the end of the week. You'll read all about it in the local press. Don't ask me the details, because frankly, I stopped listening after the first blow. It sort of' – he smiled for the first time – 'took me below the belt. Odd thing, I've actually got stomach cramps. Psychosomatic manifestation. You got any of those chalk tablets, John?'

He went over to Mr Ferris. When he left his position at the end of the room, the eyes left him, and immediately a clamour of talk broke out among the staff. Everyone was thinking: What will happen to me? but since unity rather than egotism was the custom among them, they disguised their personal anxiety by saying: 'What will they offer us? Where will the children go?'

Sucking his tablets with a wry face, Mr Rawlings sat down on the window sill and looked out over the ugly mountain range of slate roofs among which he had kept his little kingdom for so long. 'The kids will be spread round among various schools, wherever places can be found. Some of them will have to go to Green Lane, I'm afraid.'

The Green Lane school on the edge of the borough was notorious. People who had seen jungle schools in the worst districts of London and Glasgow said that they had nothing on Green Lane, which was a turbulent anarchy of junior savages and adolescent gangsters.

'Under that man?' Denzil Raymond asked. The Green Lane headmaster was notorious too. 'I say, they couldn't make any of *us* go there, could they?'

'They couldn't *make* you. Though you might have to take it on Supply for a while if you didn't get an appointment anywhere else. Of course I'll do everything I can to help you get what you want.'

'But we won't be together.' Grace realized suddenly just how fond she was of this odd collection of people, how much she depended on them.

'Do you see the authorities throwing out the whole staff of a school so that our little lot could move in? They wouldn't do it if they could, Grace. We're too close an outfit. We work too well together. There may be people at the Min. of Ed. rubbing their hands at this very moment at the thought of breaking us up.'

'Honestly?' Denzil Raymond was exasperatingly literal.

'There's a plan though, I understand, to build a big comprehensive school – grammar, technical and modern, the whole lot together – somewhere the other side of Park Road, if they can get the land. If we apply early enough, some of us may eventually come together again there.'

'With you as Head?'

'Dear Grace.' Mr Rawlings had always liked to say her name. She was tall and long-legged and sometimes immaturely clumsy in her movements. He claimed that by reiterating her name caressingly, he could make her graceful. 'Assistant junior physics master, more likely. I haven't got the right kind of degrees. Or teaching methods.'

'Oh damn, they've worked well enough here.' Geoffrey Savage got up with a jerk and began to pace the floor like the caged beast which so frequently caricatured him on blackboards. When he was aroused, his cockney grew cruder and he could not sit still. He was estimated to cover three miles in the classroom when Form 3A was giving him a bad day. 'It don't make sense, to do away with Abbot's Road, of all schools. It's a dirty trick. A rotten, lousy trick. Why can't we fight it?' He stopped before the Head with his mutton fists clenched. 'We'll stand behind you, and so would the kids, for what that would be worth. And most of the parents too. They – they –' His eyes bulged, his ginger brown beard was aflame over his working jaw. 'Well, listen, they love this lousy place. So do we.'

Geoffrey was not trying to flatter. He was saying what they all believed. But suddenly the Head was sick of the discussion, the speculation, the useless protests. 'Who do you suppose cares? A dog might as well stand and bark because the new road ran right through his kennel. They'll do it. We're finished. I've told you that.' His voice rose harshly. 'Let's not talk about it any more. Not now. It will be months before anything happens. I'll discuss all your futures with you later. Not now. I've got a line of boys outside my office waiting to see me. Shut up about it, can't you all?'

He plunged out, banging the flimsy door so that the

reproduction of *The Boyhood of Raleigh* trembled on its worn string. There was a moment's silence, then: 'He's really upset, isn't he?' Miss O'Leary said with a smirk.

John Ferris, who was usually polite to people he disliked, rounded on her. 'Don't try to make us think *you* care!'

'No. Why should I?' She patted her uninteresting hair which was wound in a sausage round an old nylon stocking all round her head. '*I'm* not going to Supply to Green Lane. I have my job already settled at Putney, thank you very much.'

They hated her. The bell cut into their hatred and stirred them into the activity of putting out cigarettes and collecting books. Grace automatically piled the dirty tea cups into the tray, because it annoyed Mrs Dormer if someone did not do it.

'Do we tell the children?' asked Miss O'Leary, unsquashed by their antagonism.

'No,' snapped John Ferris. 'That's *his* job. Leave him something, can't you?'

In her classroom all that afternoon, Grace felt uncomfortable, because she could not tell the children what she knew. It seemed unfair to let them go on accepting her as a stable part of their Abbot's Road world which they thought was going on for another three years. She felt like an impostor. When Archie Roper actually got two sums right out of eight and crowed: 'You'll be proud of me yet, Miss!' she could have cried.

She had been unfair to Archie Roper in the past. She had badgered him because he was lazy, although she knew from his sluggish shape and his skin that he was a hypothyroid. She had been guilty of making him the scapegoat in a general riot because his voice was the loudest and his appearance the least attractive.

She should have been nicer to Archie. She wished that she had been nicer to them all, wished that she had shown them that she did love them, however rude or wild or stupid they were; but until now, she had not really known it herself.

One more term, the Head had said, one more term might be all that was left to them. The summer term, with its unruly crocodiles to the public playground, and always one or two boys sneaking away off home. The drowsy, fly-buzzed afternoons when almost every boy had his moth-holed bathing trunks rolled up in a grubby towel in the cloakroom and could think of nothing else but the Baths. The sour perspiration of Mrs Purdie – how did

72

her husband stand it, or did he never get near enough to notice? The beetroot salads, the pathetic interest in Grace's holiday in Guernsey from boys who had never seen the sea. The end of term exams with tongues half bitten off and someone always having to go out to be sick. The straggled bunches of flowers on her desk, which you pretended not to know were stolen from squares and private gardens. The offerings of fruit and tomatoes from Dad's stall up the market.

One more summer term and then these children would be gone from her, separated from each other; and the younger brothers – 'My nipper, be here next year, 'e'll never do is eleven-plus. I 'ope 'e gets you, Miss' – would know Abbot's Road only as a blank wall and three closed doors with chalk crosses, marked for demolition.

About half the boys would be all right. They were bright enough or hardened enough to make their world wherever they found it, even if it had to be Green Lane. But what would happen to the others? The loons and the rogues and the misfits and the deprived children whose first piece of luck in life had been to find themselves at Mr Rawlings' school, where chances were given instead of kicks.

Ted Jelks, for instance, the product of a black father and a white mother, would go completely to pot. The half-caste children were usually problems. There was an innate lawlessness in them, because even at this age, they sensed that they belonged nowhere. As often as not the mother had left the father – if she had ever been with him for longer than it took to conceive – and was living with a white man who had no time for a nigger's coffee-coloured brat.

Grace had tried so hard with Ted, and he had broken her heart for her time and again. For the first four months he had been a non-participant, one of those who sit with folded arms and look out of the window while the rest of the class bends to a task. It was only recently that she had broken him down by the chance discovery that he could tell stories. From his Caribbean ancestors, tale-spinning had come to him, the weaving of strange stories, which were his own, yet flavoured with the old mysteries of the islands.

Would they let him tell stories at Green Lane? Would they let him tell the one about the dragon who came up from the sea and swallowed whole towns, to spew them up intact centuries later? Would they let Louie Maule do jigsaw puzzles? While the rest of the class were torturing their brains with sums and torturing their bodies into screws and humps over the double desks, legs twisted around chairs, feet splayed along the aisles, Louie sat placidly at a table by the door, fitting pieces into a large and complicated puzzle. As he worked he whistled softly through the gap where his front teeth should have been. His second front teeth, already gone through neglect. His grandmother had pulled them out when they went bad.

His father, who peddled necklaces from a suitcase in Oxford Street, was the son of the swarthy old man who drove the pony in the knife-grinding cart, crying his trade in an unintelligible wail. The family all lived together in a sort of converted stable at the back of a reeking courtyard. The stable was not really converted. It was still more a stable than a home. The bad-tempered pony lived at one end of it, and in the winter the smaller children slept in the straw with the pony for warmth. The Maules were gipsies. Gipsies in the heart of London who were descendants of those same Romany families who had camped on the common land below the gates of Cottingham Park, three centuries ago.

And what would happen to Frankie Bott? He sat at the front too. Not because he was backward enough to need supervision, nor, like the earnest Cypriot Stefi, because he wanted to miss nothing and be the first to answer, nor yet because he was almost completely deaf, like Gloria Noonan, whose faulty hearing aid was worn by almost everyone in the class except her. Frankie Bott sat in the middle of the front row because he had fought Stefi at the beginning of term for the seat immediately below Grace's desk.

'Don't make favourites,' the Head had warned her; but when a boy was so devoted, and so appealing too, with his round blue eyes and his hair always in a spike at the cowlick, it was hard not to make a pet of him. Grace had seen his mother. Mrs Bott never came to the school, because she was not interested, but Grace had seen her once in the street, a mountainous, vulgar woman pushing a little wheelchair with Frankie's spastic brother in it, the big-headed prisoner who got from her all the love and care that Frankie missed.

Frankie was not jealous of his crippled brother. He was devoted to him, and even proud of him. But the fact that at school his only mention of his home was what our Kenny had done or said, or what present had been bought for our Kenny, indicated

74

that the household revolved round the spastic child, with Frankie at the outside of the circle, on sufferance.

Don't make favourites. But it was all right for Grace to love Frankie, because he needed love so badly. But didn't the others need it too? the Head had asked her. Even the stubborn, unloveable, incorrigible ones had only become like that through lack of love, and could only be cured by its generous bestowal. That was Mr Rawlings' theory about all the bad children in the school, and Grace agreed with it. Mrs Bowden laughed at her for embracing a theory with which many of them had started when they were green, but had overcome, like a disease. Mrs Bowden had been teaching for twenty years. If she had tried to give love to every impossible child who set its dirty cheeky face before her, she would have been taken off feet first to the asylum long ago. That was what Mrs Bowden said.

After the boys and girls had gone home, Grace stayed on in the classroom to balance her lunch money and bring her registers up to date. Jobs like these were usually done during class, but today she had not been able to withdraw her mind from the active, restless presence of the children. In the half hour when they were supposed to read to themselves – what was laughingly called the Quiet Period – she had allowed Billy Glover to play his mouth organ, which came as naturally to him as speech, and they had all sung together. Not schooly songs, like *Hearts of Oak* or *Richmond Hill*, but the cruder ditties of love and rhythm which were the overamplified background of their lives at home. Miss O'Leary had sent a boy in from across the corridor to ask for quiet, so they had sung *Rock Me Lullaby*, but not quietly.

As Grace sat alone in the classroom with the chairs piled on to the desks, for it was sweeping day, she looked up and saw a shadow watching her through the opaque glass panel in the top half of the door.

She made a face at the door and bent to work again. When she took another look, without raising her head, the shadow was still there. She called out: 'Denzil, I wish you'd either come in or go away.'

He put his bristly head round the door.

'I'm trying to work. Why do you spy on me?'

'I like to. I've never really known a pretty girl like you. At the training college they were all bags. I like to watch you. See what you do when you're alone.'

'You're the kind of man who'd hide in a bush to watch a woman's shadow on a bathroom blind.'

'I might,' he said complacently. 'Oh – not for what you think. But just out of interest. I like to know what girls do. What they wear. What kind of girdle do you wear?'

'Honestly, Denzil –'

'Don't be outraged. My interest is purely clinical. You see, when I first – well, go with a girl, I want to know what to expect. I don't want to be taken by surprise. That puts one at a disadvantage.'

'I wish you'd go with a girl and get it over with and stop bothering me.' Grace could not help smiling. 'Go up to Park Road tonight and pick something up.'

'Don't be a cheese,' Denzil said. 'I wish you'd take me seriously. How –' He put a foot up on the low platform and leaned his arms on her desk, looking thoughtfully at his small clean hands. 'How does a man get a girl to take him seriously?'

'Oh, don't let's start all that again. Not now.'

He stood up. 'Can I see you home, ma'am?' He was suddenly brisk.

'No. I want to do some shopping.'

'Right you are.' He saluted, turned neatly about, marched to the door and wheeled out of it like a toy soldier, hands to his side.

To get to the locker where she kept her coat, Grace had to walk through the basement cloakroom with its rows of pegs and its inadequate washbasins which dripped water brown, brown, brown on to the ancient stains. A small figure was sitting on a bench under a torn brown coat. It was Frankie Bott. He got up and took his coat off the peg. 'Could I walk with you to the bus, Miss?'

'Oh, Frankie. Well, I suppose so. But you should have gone home long ago. Your mother will wonder where you are.'

'Not home,' he said laconically. 'It's her afternoon for taking our Kenny to the clinic.'

'The clinic's open all day. Why doesn't she take him during the time you're at school?'

Frankie stared uncomprehendingly. To him there was nothing wrong, but Grace could never get used to the idea that almost half the children at the school were latchkey kids, or had to play in the streets until one of their family came home.

When she came back from her locker, Frankie was waiting in his short, lopsided coat, picking pieces of plaster from the crumbling wall. 'This old place is falling to bits, ain't it?' he said affectionately. 'If Mr Rawlings would give us some paint and brushes and stuff, us boys could fix it up. Why don't you ask him, Miss? We could do it in the holidays. Nothing much else to do. Be a lark.'

Yes, it would be a lark for them. They would really enjoy it, and probably do a reasonable job as well. If they had thought of it last week, the head might have said Yes. As it was – 'I don't think he'd let you, Frankie,' she said. 'Better forget about it.'

'Why? Why wouldn't he let us?' He kept on at her, trotting beside her up the stone stairs and out into the playground, cold with the smell of a grey March evening. 'It's the sort of thing 'e might jump at. We been making plans for it, me and Joey and Bill and them. We're all dead keen on it. It's just a question of asking 'im the right way, see? And we all thought you'd be the best one to do it.'

They went out into the street. Frankie shut the old door in the wall behind them under the stone that said INFANTS, and as he turned back to Grace, his round face was bright with confidence. 'Will you do it, Miss?' he asked. 'Will you do it for us?'

She had to tell him. It would not matter telling just one boy. 'You must keep this to yourself, Frankie,' she said. 'Mr Rawlings will announce it at Assembly. Perhaps tomorrow. He wants to –'

A motor-cycle raced by with its exhaust open, and the rider sounded a klaxon at the sight of Grace standing by the high brown wall in her red coat and thick fur gloves. When the noise had gone by, she said: 'There wouldn't be any point redecorating the school, you see, because it's going to be pulled down. Come, let's walk. It's cold.'

As they walked, she explained to him about the road. He walked beside her with his collar turned up and his eyes on the littered pavement, hunched in the thin coat. He did not say anything. When they reached the bus stop at the corner of the main road, Grace looked down and saw that tears had silted dirt into the corners of his mouth. She reached out the fur paw of her hand to him, but he ducked and ran zig-zagging away across the traffic.

77

Cold and unhappy, Frankie hung about the courtyards of the Flats, vaguely looking for something to do, but not really wanting to do anything. He looked with disgust at some of the younger children in woollen hats shrieking on the swings in the wired-in playground, going back and back like robots up the steps and down the slide, polished by a thousand bottoms, fighting and yelling round the concrete tunnels and terraces built for them by an indulgent Council.

Walt Peters, who went to Abbot's Road, joined him at the wire. 'Know what the Wild Beast did today?' Out of his mouth came a pink bladder of bubble gum. He sucked it back and chewed rapidly to get it into condition for blowing out again. 'E takes a swipe at Oakie, and Oakie ducks, see, and the Beast socks is 'and on the bookcase. Language? It was a treat.' He laughed and blew out another rubbery bubble.

Frankie looked at him pityingly. Silly bastard didn't know the score. Well, he would know soon enough. Frankie wasn't going to tell him. Miss Peel had said not to. It wouldn't matter telling his mother though. He had to tell someone. And perhaps this time Mum would be decent about it, make over him like she did with Kenny when he cried.

Hands in his pockets with his fingers coming through the holes at the bottom, he wandered out into the street to watch for her. Dick Plesser from the flat below theirs was out fiddling with his motor-bike. When the men and boys were home, there were dozens of scooters and motor-cycles parked in the roads all round the Council estate. Quite a few little cars too, in defiance of Frankie's mother's edict that if you could afford a car you didn't ought to have a subsidized flat. 'What about the taxpayer?' she demanded, although her husband's wages at the hotel were so meagre that taxes were the least of his worries.

In the evenings and at weekends, there were always people out cleaning the cars and motor-cycles and messing with the engines. Dick Plesser's combination was the smartest on the block. Lots of chrome, and the sidecar was shaped like a bomb, all red and silver.

Frankie joined the small group of boys who were watching Dick clean the carburettor filter. When one of them offered an admiring remark about the machine, Dick said casually: 'Oh, I'm going to ditch this heap of junk soon.' He was tall, with a lot of lank greasy hair which he made a great show of tossing

78

back all the time. 'After the baby's born, we'll have to get a car.'

'Sports model?'

'Of course. What else?' He could not resist showing off, even to a crowd of children. 'Austin Healey if I can find the model I want.'

Someone whistled, and Dick grinned and tossed back the long hair which looked as if he gave it the same grease as the motorcycle, and did not hear the dirty crack which someone else made about the baby.

When Frankie's mother came round the corner towards the side entrance of Collingwood House, he ran towards her, calling out: 'Hullo, Mum! Hey, Kenny! Mum, Mum – I want to tell you –'

But she was walking with Mrs Bacon, and would not listen to him. Mrs Bacon did not like Mrs Bott. However, like many of the women at the Flats, she maintained a sycophantic show of friendship with her.

It was good policy. Mrs Bott, although she was on the committee of the Nelson Court Community Association, which was supposed to benefit all residents, was, as far as her tongue was concerned, the scourge of the Flats. Gossip, slander and denigration were her familiar spirits. She knew almost everything about everybody, and what she did not know she told anyway, and it was worse than if she had known the facts.

'Mum, Mum!' Frankie pulled at her sleeve, as she pushed Kenny along, her bulk wider than the wheelchair. 'Listen Mum, they –'

'Shut up,' she said without looking at him. 'We're talking. Where's your manners?' and Mrs Bacon made a tutting mouth at him to show that she agreed with Mrs Bott's discipline.

At the entrance to the flats, they talked for a while longer about the Middletons' daughter, while Kenny screwed up his old man's face because he was cold and wanted to be taken indoors. At last they were in the smelly lift, with Frankie penned into the corner of the slowly rising box which was filled with the wheelchair and his mother in her best maroon coat.

'What were you doing out in the street?' she grumbled at him. She knew very little about Frankie's life out of school. She did not care where he went, but she made a show of not wanting him to be a street child.

'You weren't home. I couldn't get in.'

'You dirty little liar. Your Dad's been home all this time, and you know it.'

'I forgot it was his half day. Mum, listen Mum,' he said, as the lift reached the top floor, 'they're going to pull down our school. Pull down the whole lot round there. Cut a new road through.'

'Who says so?'

'Miss Peel.'

'Oh *her*.' Frankie held open the lift door, which would slide back if you were not nippy getting out, and Mrs Bott pushed past him with the chair and walked heavy-footed along the open balcony to her front door.

'It's true, Mum!' Frankie followed her. 'I wish it wasn't.'

'True? Of course it's true. Why shouldn't it be? Come in, son, and tell us all about it.' With one of her swift changes of mood from vile to motherly, Mrs Bott pushed Kenny into the middle of the living-room and bent her bulk to Frankie, unbuttoning his coat, calling his father to come from the kitchen. Her son had a piece of news which no one else knew yet. Her busy black eyes were greedy to know it all, to be the first to know, the one with the fattest piece of gossip to pass on.

'You know what it means, of course,' she said when Frankie had told all he knew.

'It means they'll get the traffic through much faster,' said Mr Bott, who, although flattened out by life, was quite bright in his way.

'Oh that.' That was neither here nor there. 'It means rehousing, that's what it means. All the people living in the places that are coming down – what's to be done with them?' She did not want an answer. She was going to give it herself. 'In 'ere, that's what they'll do with them. Thousands of poor souls on the waiting list for these flats, and they'll slip these others in ahead of them. You'll see.'

'Oh, I don't think so, Nettie.' Mr Bott sat on the edge of his chair where he had perched in obedience to his wife's command to sit down and shut up and listen to what Frankie had to say. His hands lay patiently on his knees: hands nicked and stained from peeling and chopping vegetables, and shrivelled by soda and hot water. 'The Council wouldn't do that.' As if to make up for his wife's mistrust of all governing bodies, he had a great faith in councils. He even trusted the government, which disgusted his wife, whose politics were neither pro-Labour nor pro-Tory, but anti-everything. 'They take it fair.'

'Ho do they?' Mrs Bott laughed through her broad nose. 'What about the Neales then, turned out into the street lock, stock and baggage to let them flashy Plessers in?'

'They hadn't never paid their rent,' Frankie said. 'They were two months overdue, and it's supposed to be pay up or get out if you go more than three weeks.'

'Who asked you? You shut your face before I shut it for you.'

Mrs Bott did not want to discuss the reason for the Neales' eviction. Mrs Neale used to go out to work, and she had been in the habit of leaving the money with Mrs Bott when it was the rent collector's day. This was a neighbourly service which many of the women at home performed for those who 'went to business'. Mrs Bott had not done it because she was neighbourly, but because by going down to fetch the money once a week, she had the opportunity to get into the Neales' flat and look round, which privilege was normally not extended to her.

Mrs Neale had stumbled into heavy debts over a washing machine and a twenty-one inch television set. For the two months during which she had failed to produce the two pounds two shillings and ninepence, Mrs Bott had enjoyed informing the young lady who collected the rents that 'she's let it go again'. On the last visit before the eviction, the young lady had let out the unfortunate question: 'Did she really not give it to you?' That was merely rhetorical, the young lady being puzzled about the defection of two people who were both in work; but Mrs Bott had chosen to take it as a direct accusation that she had been keeping the money for herself.

Who else might be saying that? It was the sort of thing that Mrs Bott might have said herself about someone else. That was why she did not want to hear any talk about the Neales.

'But in any case, Mum,' put in Kenny, speaking for his brother, since he was often allowed to speak when his brother had been silenced, 'the Plessers had been waiting three years for their own home. She told us, Frankie and me, when she came up with the cakes that day. They'd been living with 'is people all that time and 'is old lady wouldn't speak to Sheila at all at the end. That was why they wouldn't make a baby till they got away.' It was surprising how much Kenny knew at eight years old. He sat listening quietly in his chair, and people told him things because, although he was tiny, his face looked older than he was.

'Don't believe it, love.' His mother had a feud on with the Plessers and would hear no good of them. If Kenny and Frankie had not already eaten most of Sheila's cakes before their mother returned from the grocery, they would have lost them, for she had thrown the rest away, plate and all.

'There'll be some upsets here, you can be sure of it.' She continued to grumble while she laid the table for tea and went into the kitchen to put the kettle on, reviling Mr Bott through the open door for not already having done it. 'There'll be coloured people put in here, and them Poles that come over to get their mothers buried on the National Health – taking the bread from honest people's mouths' (this was an automatic addendum to any mention of the Poles). 'And all the scum from those streets round the school.'

Mr Bott, who enjoyed the conversations of his sons when he got the chance, wanted to discuss the new road with them, but his wife grumbled on between them, passing back and forth through the room. She was not remotely interested in the new road, except as far as it might affect her personally. She had been like that during the war. The tide of battle was of no interest compared to the chances of a cut in the jam ration.

'Come, Kenny.' She lifted him easily out of his wheelchair to carry him to the table. 'My poor little boy, what are they trying to do to you, then? They'll rob you of a home, that's what they'll do, the devils.'

Kenny began to whimper as she fitted him into his high chair and knotted one of Mr Bott's old ties round his waist to keep him from slipping.

'Don't frighten him, Nettie,' said Mr Bott. 'You know that's not true.'

'Who says so? You know what they're like. Didn't that old lady get that ground-floor flat over the heads of hundreds of other poor old souls because her nephew works for the Council? Don't tell me there's no favouritism. If they're going to pull down people's houses, they'll put them into the new flats to stop their mouths. You watch. They'll be turning us out.'

'Nettie. Nettie.' Mr Bott shook his head mildly and put his fork unhopefully into a wizened sausage roll. There was not much for tea today, because although Mrs Bott could have cooked something before she went out, the family might as well suffer for her martyrdom of having to push Kenny to the clinic.

'Tell us what the doctor said,' Frankie suggested, to switch his mother on to another track.

'Fat lot you care.' She cut bread savagely and slapped on margarine. 'Or them doctors either. If they think they're going to twist my Kenny's arm round and torture him, they'd better think again.' She sniffed and sat down.

Frankie looked across the small table at Kenny. Kenny smiled bleakly and made messages with his eyes, until his mother put a square of bread into his mouth and stopped the smile. He chewed obediently, still looking at his brother.

He desperately wanted to have the operation. He knew that it would hurt. The doctors had told him that. They had told him that it might mean weeks in hospital, months in an uncomfortable plaster cast. But they had told him that if it worked – which they could not promise – he might be able at least to pick things up.

When his wife had calmed down and was eating her tea, Mr Bott, who with the best intentions, often put his foot in it, said kindly to Frankie: 'That's bad news, son, about your school. I know you'll hate to change.'

Frankie did not want to discuss the misery and dread that had been burdening his mind ever since he had talked to Miss Peel, nagging at him all the time his mother was carrying on. He would talk to Kenny. Kenny would know. His crazy hope that his mother would understand and comfort him had died as soon as he met her in the street. Now he did not want her to say anything about it, did not want her to know what he was feeling.

But she jumped at the topic. 'Hate to change,' she said. 'That's right he will. What about Miss Grace Peel now, eh, Frankie? No more darling Miss Peel. That won't suit you too well, will it?'

Frankie stood up. In his silly fancies, he had visualized himself crying his unhappiness to his mother and her taking him on to her lap and stroking his hair. Now he would rather die than cry here in the sitting-room in front of her with that scornful face she used for talking about Miss Peel, his father with his nervous, blundering sympathy, Kenny who would cry like a little echo if Frankie cried.

He went to get his coat. 'I've finished,' he said. 'I have to go out.'

'Where to?' She did not care, but she wanted to show that she could stop him if she chose.

He thought quickly. 'Over Bill Ritchie's. Me and him's making a radio.'

'You going on the streets? You going with that nigger?'

'No Mum. Honest.' Lying to his mother was a necessity of life.

'If you're going with that dirty nigger,' she said comfortably, holding the cup to Kenny's lips, 'I'll whip you till there's not an inch of skin left on your back.'

Frankie had only told half a lie, because his friend Edgar Biggs from Trinidad was not out in the street, but upstairs in the two small rooms that were the nearest approach to a flat in Glidden Road.

Several other people were out in Glidden Road as Frankie went by, although it was a sad evening, with a gritty mist that might turn to rain. With all but the night workers home from work, and the many unemployed and the unemployable elderly relatives who were always at home anyway, there was no room for everyone indoors.

Some small babies without pants played in the gutter while their mothers talked, leaning on area railings, or sitting on front steps with their chins in their hands and their slack eyes looking through the drab lamplit houses opposite to warmer memories. Most of the women, except the young girls who were going out brightly dressed and pacing like ponies on their stilted heels, wore headscarves and bedroom slippers and a variety of garments against the cold. Many of them wore gloves, or things that were either mittens or gloves with the finger ends worn away; or else they kept their hands inside their clothes, for the hands of the West Indians were always chapped and chilblained in the winter.

Frankie was not the only white person abroad on Glidden Road, for a few of the younger women were white, and some of the children had skins that might have come from anywhere. Frankie would scarcely have noticed the colour of people, but his mother had been raving against black skins for as long as he could remember. The West Indian invasion was one of her phobias. Although she had not succeeded in making Frankie hate the Spades, for he enjoyed their casual laughter and their music and their do-it-tomorrow laziness, she had tainted his natural liking for them with a nervousness that made him hurry along Glidden Road head down, returning only a sketchy wave to the greetings of children or grownups who recognized him.

Outside the Conga Club on the corner by Edgar's house, a few young men in slick trousers were waiting for Joe Knuckles to open up for the evening's sociability. Some of them milled about with a restless kind of rhythm, as if their feet were in command of their heads. Others leaned against the wall and smoked and watched the girls who passed by in the middle of the street or on the other pavement, showing off their bodies, pretending and not pretending at the same time that they were not hoping for someone to take them into the club. The girls who had steady dates would come later after the door was open, for the steady-going boys did not allow their girls to stand about on the corners of streets like Glidden Road.

One of the girls on the other side of the street, giggling and whispering and moving their bodies about because they felt the men's eyes on them like hands, was the sister of a boy in Frankie's class at Abbot's Road.

She was fourteen. She whistled at Frankie and called out something rude.

'I'll tell your Mum where you are, Jenny Spicer,' he called back.

'So what?' She put a hand behind her small head and flipped her pony tail. 'If you do, I'll tell what you tried to do with me up the Buildings.'

'Dirty liar!' Frankie was afraid of girls like Jenny Spicer, but he could hold his own in a yelling match with the width of the street between them.

'What did you do, white boy?' On the steps of Edgar's house, two men were standing. They were dressed alike in yellow gloves to match their ties and magenta shirts to match their socks. They wore wide-brimmed hats at an angle which Frankie recognized as sinister. He knew that from television. Even in the confusion of a fight or a police raid, you could always tell the heroes from the villains by the angle of their hats.

One of the men was chewing on a matchstick. The other, who was short and wide, was laughing at Frankie. With Jenny and her friends laughing at him from across the road, he started for the steps, but the man moved casually across to block his way. 'Where you going, son?' he asked, still laughing. He had more gold teeth in his mouth than white ones.

'See Edgar Biggs.'

'Who he?'

85

'My friend.' As Frankie stepped aside to pass, the man moved to block him again. He was teasing, but all his mother's bugaboos of knives and voodoo magic went whistling through Frankie's brain and his heart hammered up into his throat. It would be difficult to speak if the man kept him here talking.

'I don't know no Edgar Biggs,' the man said. 'This here is my property. I just done bought it. I don't want no trespassers here. You looking for a room?'

'No sir.' Frankie was small for his age, and accustomed to looking up at everybody, but with the man standing on the step above him, he felt smaller than ever. So small that when the man moved a fraction sideways to flip his cigarette into the area, Frankie sucked in his breath and darted past him like a swerving fly. The man laughed, deep and rich. He had only been teasing. The knives and voodoo vanished, and Frankie turned when he was safely inside the house to stick out his tongue and yell a wordless insult before he fled up the dark and smelly stairs to the top floor.

Mr and Mrs Biggs lived in great luxury. They had two rooms, one front, one back, and their son did not sleep in the same bed with them, nor even in the same room.

Edgar slept on a low camp bed in the front room. In the day-time, the bed was covered with a grey blanket and used as a couch. If his parents wanted to stay up late, or entertain friends, Edgar could not go to bed. He could lie down on his parents' bed in the back room; but it was hateful to be woken roughly and pushed out in the middle of the night when the party was over and his father was in a hurry to get his mother into bed.

Not that there was very much partying. There were only a few of their compatriots in Cottingham Park with whom Mr and Mrs Biggs cared to associate. They were too respectable to enjoy the colourful revelry that enlivened the Conga Club or the rooms of other tenants: going on sometimes all night, so that Mr Biggs had to thump the wall or floor with the stick which he kept by his bed for that purpose. But when their decorous friends came, and there was some wine, it did not take much to make Mr Biggs amorous. Unlike some of the other fathers, when he felt that way he did not want any children around. 'I am a man of morals.'

To look at Mrs Biggs, you could see that it would take a drink or two to make anyone desire her. She was thin and bony, with spare black hair drawn tightly back from a face the colour of cold tea. Although she had no bosom to boast of, she favoured low-cut dresses and sweaters, displaying nothing more fascinating than her collar bones and the bars of her upper ribs.

She was a ward maid in a hospital. When she had first sailed hopefully from Trinidad, inspired by the glowing letters of friends already in England, she had visions of a plushy sitting-down job, her hands unsoiled. It was not long before she realized that the friends, unwilling to admit failure to the envious ones back home, had embroidered the depressing truth.

The hospital job, cleaning the ward and its kitchen and sluice and lavatories, was the best she could get. She despised it. Clad in a long pink overall with the belt tied slackly over her hat-rack hips, she took it out of the patients by banging their beds with her broom when she swept, and took it out of the nurses by throwing dishcloths in with the dirty laundry after they had counted it, or throwing away the last of the milk when it was time for the gastric feeds.

When Frankie came into the front room, sure of his welcome, for Edgar's parents liked him to have a white boy for a friend, she was sitting at the table by the window, playing patience. She played avidly, greedy to win against her nonexistent opponent. The cards were her opponent. She handled them sharply and with interest, her face spiked with odium when the wrong one had the effrontery to come to her hand.

Mr Biggs was sitting opposite her, reading the paper. He was a bus conductor, a muscular, business-like man with a square moustache and much white to his eyes. The bus and its schedule were his religion, and to get it from South Mimms to Victoria in the prescribed time a matter of sacred duty. He dealt briskly with old ladies who were too slow getting on or off, was scrupulous about the number of standing passengers, and his trenchant cry of 'Ay-maw-fa-pee!' produced coppers even from people who had intended to try and jump a short ride without paying.

'See the news?' he asked Frankie.

So it was out already. Frankie said Yes and sat down on the camp bed next to Edgar, who had a large history book from the library on his knees. He had wanted to be the first to tell them. The only thing that had been keeping Frankie going since his talk with Miss Peel was that he was almost the only one to know.

'You don't sound very excited about it,' Mrs Biggs said, picking over the cards without looking at him. 'It isn't every day that bloody murder happens round the corner, even in these parts.'

'Oh that.' Frankie had heard his mother and father discussing the knifing of a gang leader last night. They didn't know then, or they wouldn't call that news. 'I got a much bigger bit of news than that.'

'Somebody shoot Sir Oswald Mosley?' That was Mr Biggs, hopeful.

Frankie told them about the road, and how a great chunk of this area of Glidden Road and the crisscross of crowded streets up the hill to the railway would probably be swept away.

'Like Pompeii under the lava,' Edgar said excitedly. 'In a thousand years time, somebody will dig under that road and find my scout knife and put it in a museum and say: That belonged to a boy in the twentieth century. Gee!'

Mrs Biggs had continued to slap down her cards as Frankie talked, and not until the patience came triumphantly out did she raise her head and look at him.

'You lying to us, Francis?' she asked. There were no nicknames in this family. Even in the interludes that occurred after the wine, she called her husband Cornelius, and he wooed her as Dorothy.

'No, ma'am.' Edgar answered for him. 'He not lying.'

'He *aint* lying.' Cornelius Biggs was particular about his son's speech since they came to London. He wanted him to talk like an Englishman.

'Listen, I tell you one thing,' Mrs Biggs said. 'That Jamaican landlord knew about this when he sold this place out yesterday. Poor Gilroy. So he been taken for a ride. I heard them talking down at the store what he paid for it. He won't never get that back in compensation. It a cheat, this British government. I read where they paid that old lady thirty pound for her cottage, take it or leave it. That dirty Kingston nigger. They're all from the same pot.'

Between the Jamaicans and the people from Guiana, Trinidad, Barbados and the smaller islands, there existed an unseen antagonism called 'the shade bar'. White people classed them as all alike, but between the two groups there was rivalry and deceit, and broken hearts sometimes when a girl fell in love with a boy from the wrong island.

'That's Gilroy's trouble,' Mr Biggs said. 'We have ours. Where are we going to live now?'

'Everyone will be rehoused,' Frankie said, eager to brighten their long faces. 'My Mum says some of 'em will be put in our flats. That be something, wount it, Ed? You and me living next door?'

'With respect to your mother, I don't believe that,' said Mr Biggs in a sonorous, biblical voice. 'It was hard enough to find a room before. Now it will be ten thousand times ten thousand times worse. We'll be back where we was, Dorothy, living at the hostel with all the crying babies. A fine thing for a man in my position.'

Mrs Biggs got up and picked invisible fluff from her green tube dress. 'This may be a sign,' she said, 'to tell us that it time to go home.'

'No, Ma!' Edgar's brilliant black eyes were aghast. London was his home. He had planned to live here all his life.

'You know we said we would, Cornelius,' his mother paid no attention to her son's distress, 'when we got a hundred pound saved. You been putting it off and putting it off because you love that big red bus, but another winter here will kill me, sure.' She manufactured a cough, to prove how much she suffered.

'A hundred pound? You got a hundred pound?' They nodded solemnly at Frankie, and he was amazed. His mother had twenty-eight pounds saved, and that was treasure. But a hundred! How did they do it? The Spades grumbled about how poor they were and how there were no decent jobs for them and food and rent were too high, and yet many of them managed to save because they could get along without spending much on things like meat and cigarettes and beer. This was one of the things that irked people like Mrs Bott. The Spades saved up money and bought houses and fur coats and sometimes cars. To white people without the hoarding gift, it seemed they had no right to them.

Many of them saved because they planned to go back home and cut a figure; but usually they stayed. They all talked about how cold it was, how hard to get a job and find a room. They all talked about going home, but hardly any of them did it. It was always new Spades coming in all the time, and none going out.

'What's it like in Trinidad?' Frankie asked.

'Like Paradise.' Mrs Biggs looked out of the window at the street below, which was beginning to grow noisier as the Conga

Club warmed up, wrinkled her sharp brown nose and drew the thin curtains savagely across.

'That not so, Ma,' Edgar said. 'You know it not. You always complaining about this house, but you was glad enough to see the water tap out there on the landing when we came. Gee, we didn't even have a floor or windows back there where we lived with Tanty in tin-can shanty town.' The grown-ups always talked about the West Indies as Back Home. To children like Edgar, it was Back There. 'You always telling me,' he reminded her, 'how Dad was out of work for years and had to take that job at the slaughterhouse and it made he sick.'

'Him sick,' Mr Biggs said automatically, and his wife said: 'Hush up, boy, that's all past and gone. Things will be different now if we go back. Everything will be better.'

'That's what you said when you wanted to come here.'

Frankie envied Edgar his licence to talk back to his parents. Mrs Bott would have clouted him if he had talked smart to her like that; but Mrs Biggs was better-tempered than she looked.

'Hush, hush,' was all she said. 'You know you was happy back home. You had more fun there, running in the sunshine. You was a laughing child.'

'I laugh now.' Edgar grinned artificially. 'But that's all I'd ever done if we'd stayed back there. I'd never got my learning.'

'You don't get much at Green Lane,' Mr Biggs said.

'I will. I will, Dad.' Edgar sat forward on the edge of his hard bed, his knuckly brown fingers twisting together. 'Mr Ellis don't like me, but they's some good teachers there. They'll help me.'

'No one helped you when you failed the examination.'

Edgar had done well at his elementary school, and had been considered almost a certainty for a grammar school place. When he took the eleven-plus examination, he had barely recovered from severe influenza. His head was splitting. His limbs were weak. His bright little brain could not fight its way through the sick confusion. He had failed. He could have had a second chance, but Mr and Mrs Biggs in a stupor of hurt pride, had refused. No use telling them that Edgar had failed because he was sick. They knew better. He had been failed because he was a coloured boy.

And so Edgar had been dropped into the morass of Green Lane Secondary. Still optimistic, still eager to learn, he had kept his head above the mud. If any boy was learning anything in the hell's kitchen of the middle forms at Green Lane, where most of the teachers were at violent odds with the children and with each other and with the incompetent headmaster, it was Edgar Biggs.

His parents began to talk together again about going back home. Their voices were loud. Frankie and Edgar, side by side on the bed, put their heads close to hear each other talk.

'It's rotten bad luck about Abbot's Road, old man.' Edgar put his arm on the smaller boy's shoulders, manly and British. 'Where will you go? Maybe they send you to Green Lane.'

'That's what I'm afraid of.'

'It aint so bad.' To Edgar any school was all right, because it was a school. 'With me, and all. I'd look out for you. Fight for you. They gang up on new kids sometimes.'

'But you may not be there. We won't be pals any more, if your Dad and Mum take you back over there.'

'Gee.' They looked at each other. Then they looked at Mr and Mrs Biggs, talking animatedly with pushed-out lips and moving hands. Then they looked back at each other, and matched eyes. Out of the eyes, the shining chocolate ones and the blue, looked the knowledge of what they were up against. They were caught in the prison of childhood, penniless, without choice, their lives in the thrall to the decrees of the grown-up world.

Presently Mrs Biggs said that Frankie must go home if he did not want trouble with his mother. She knew about Mrs Bott. She knew that Frankie had to lie when he was meeting Edgar, but that did not make him less welcome in Glidden Road. On the contrary, Dorothy Biggs was glad to assist at the deception of such an ardent segregationist.

'Can I walk part way with Frankie?' Edgar asked.

His mother said that it was too late for him to be out in the streets.

'What about Frankie then?'

'That's different,' Mrs Biggs pursed her rubbery lips, then stretched them back against her long teeth. 'Francis a white boy.'

Frankie wanted to say that there were just as many coloured making trouble against white as there were white making trouble against coloured; but the Biggs were his friends, and so he said good night and suffered Mrs Biggs to embrace him bonily, and ran down the stairs past the babel of babies and radio jazz and voices arguing and a woman's screaming laughter, with Edgar leaning over the precarious banister to shout down after him into the well of noise.

It was late. Would his mother believe his alibi? A confused musical roar came from the Conga Club. Outside the closed door, two men stood arguing, their voices shrill and excited like children. Under the boarded window stood an empty whisky bottle and a milk bottle half full of urine. Frankie ran all the way home.

*

On his way home from work that Friday, Mr Walter Wilson, in a dark blue felt hat and belted overcoat and a simulated club tie, stopped at the open counter of Mrs Angel's newspaper shop to pick up the evening paper and a copy of the local weekly, the *Cottingham Courier*.

Mr and Mrs Wilson, the owners of the furnished rooming house in Faulkner Road, half way down West Hill, used to have their newspapers delivered, until an Indian tenant on the ground floor had started to get up early and steal the morning paper as Mrs Angel's nephew pushed it through the letter box. The Indian had gone now, but there were other tenants, and you never knew; so Mr Wilson fetched the morning paper on his way to work at the Post Office and the evening paper on his way home.

If Mrs Wilson, scurrying about the house with her high sharp nose questing for dirt and cockroaches like a Geiger counter, had a moment to spare in her busy day, she read yesterday's paper: skimming through it for the kind of stories she loved, about mothers who sacrificed their lives for babies in blazing houses, or crippled girls getting married.

When her daughter May was at home during the afternoon break, or on her day off from her nursing visits, she did not often read the newspaper. She read magazine stories about the mating adventures of girls more glamorous than herself, and articles which told her how to be beautiful and sexually desirable.

They did not use the word sex on the beauty page, but sex was what they meant, and May, who had not been kissed since she was ten years old, wished that she had the courage to follow beauty hints and see where it got her.

Living at home, it would have taken more courage than she possessed to weather the personal remarks of her parents, whose comments and pleasantries were no less brutal for being masked in illusory good intentions.

When she had tried lipstick two years ago, her father had rested his knife and fork at breakfast and observed amiably: 'I thought it was last week we had the raspberry jam.'

Experiments with face powder had produced jaunty remarks like: 'Been in the flour bin, old girl?'

Any new garment which her mother did not help her to choose was prowled round with tightened lips and murmurs of: 'A bit tight behind dear, isn't it?' Or sharply: 'That hem will have to come down!'

When May's friend Veronica, who was a hairdresser in a large department store, fixed her hair one day in curls and swoops that flattered her pudgy face, the screams at supper of: 'What has that girl done to her hair?' had sent May upstairs to the washbasin to damp it back into its unenlightened bob.

May did not need to live at home, for she earned about six hundred pounds a year as a district midwife; but on the theory that she was devoted to her parents, she stayed. When she talked about other nurses who had flats of their own, she was told how lucky she was not to live a lonely life like that. It was assumed that she agreed, and in a way she did, to the extent of not allowing herself to recognize that she did not.

Her rebellion had come some years before, when after a year as staff nurse in her training hospital, she had accepted the post of maternity sister at a small hospital in Scotland. Steeling herself against the dismay of her parents, to whom Scotland was almost another planet, she had worked happily there for three months. Then her mother had managed to get herself struck by an electric milk van humming quietly round a corner, and May had to come home and nurse her and look after her father and the rooming house.

The Scottish hospital had not kept the job open for her. There could have been others, but she did not try to escape again. It was not worth it. She took her District training, and stayed in the basement flat with her parents and gave them part of her salary and put the rest by for her old age. Mr and Mrs Wilson thought that it was for her old age. Actually it was to be for her second and last rebellion. If she was not married at thirty-five, May was going to advertise in a matrimonial newspaper and use her savings as the lure which her looks had failed to be.

At the draughty newspaper counter, Mrs Angel, in a mud-coloured coat and mittens, was talking over her shoulder to

93

someone at the back of the shop. Mr Wilson, who liked his little joke, tapped a coin on the PDSA collecting box and said: 'I'll have the local Threepenny Dreadful, if you please.'

'And dreadful is the word, if you want to know.' Mrs Angel turned round, picked up the paper, handed it to him and took his money, all in one movement.

'How so?'

'Don't pull my leg.' Above the eternal cigarette, the tip of Mrs Angel's nose was a pink cherry in the dead white plate of her face. 'There's no call for that. It was in the morning paper, just as I said it would be. One of these days, I said, we shall see it in black and white. Those were my very words. I don't care what you say.'

'I don't doubt –'

'I sold you a paper this morning, Mr Thingummy. You can't deny it. How can you stand there and tell me you don't know what I'm talking about?'

'I haven't read it right through.' It took Mr Wilson hours to plod through the *Daily Herald*, exclaiming and chuckling and reading bits out at work or at home to anyone who would listen.

'Well, you've got a shock coming, Mr Thingummy,' Mrs Angel said nastily. She had not liked Mr Wilson since he had stopped delivery of the papers. He had tried to explain, but she held to the fixed idea that he was accusing her nephew, not the Indian.

'My house afire?' Walter Wilson gave his loose-lipped grin.

'Worse than that.' Mrs Angel's cigarette went up and down in the middle of her bloodless mouth. 'They're going to pull it down.'

Triumphantly, she turned away and began again to call behind her to her niece who came once a week after school to dust and tidy the stationery and toys. 'So never presume to tell me I'm wrong again, Edith,' she shouted. 'Just never try to tell me that.' Edith shouted something back, and Mrs Angel continued to talk to her and hand out papers and cigarettes and take money and give change all at the same time.

Weak at the knees, Mr Wilson trotted down West Hill reading the front page of the *Cottingham Courier*. He turned off automatically at Faulkner Road, still reading, bumped into a large dog and said: 'Excuse me, my dear,' thinking it was a child, tottered down the basement steps and in at the back door, calling: 'Norma, Norma! It's the end of the world!'

It was not as bad as they thought at first. After reading the story three times and puzzling for an hour over the chart in the newspaper, they saw that the new road, which would cut diagonally across the top of West Hill, with a flyover at the junction of Park Road, might just miss the houses in Faulkner Road.

'Look – yes, yes!' Miss Beade, who had come down from the top floor to beg a little milk for her cat, had stayed to exclaim and speculate. 'It's because of the railway, don't you see? Here, in the dotted lines.' They bent again to the paper, argued, protested, stabbed fingers at the chart. Then they stood back and stared round the table at each other with a new hope. It looked as if the hated Underground, which could rattle a plate off the dresser on a dry night, might save them in the end.

'I shall have the laugh on Mrs Angel yet,' Mr Wilson said gleefully. 'When they come to pull down her shop, I shall stand by and ask her if she'd like to rent a room at my place.'

'We might be glad of her at that,' said Mrs Wilson, who had a sharp habit of removing the humour from her husband's jokes by turning them into sense. 'How is it going to be, living on top of a highway full of racing cars? A death trap to get across.'

'They don't let you cross them, not the new roads,' May put in, and her mother flagged her down, but accepted the thought without seeming to.

'How are we going to get to the shops?' she asked no one in particular. 'Or up to Park Road? We'll lose tenants over this.'

'You needn't worry about that.' Miss Beade's grey cat, which was draped now round her neck like a choking stole, was only in the house on sufferance, and so she often found herself being sycophantic with the Wilsons. 'You'll never have any trouble letting rooms in your nice house.'

'Did I give you the milk?' asked Mrs Wilson tartly. She did not add: Then why don't you go? But the words were there in the air. She did not like Miss Beade nor her cat, and she preferred to keep her distance rather than have the woman smarm all over her as if she wanted to get her rent reduced.

'Well then, I think I'll be running along,' Miss Beade said, as if it were her own idea. She was a tall nervous woman with restless hands and a crooked face. Her piebald hair, coarse as a horse's tail, was worn in a long, too youthful bob, tied round with a piece of red dressing-gown cord, the ends trailing on to the cat.

For a moment her eyes rested on the fat fruit cake which stood on the dresser with a sharp knife beside it – too tempting for words. But there were no cosy evenings with the landlady's family in this house – not like there had been up North when Miss Beade was younger and all those jolly travellers came and went – not even for that dreadful little man who was her neighbour on the top floor, whom the Wilsons were trying to get for May.

So Miss Beade said: 'A thousand thanks for the milk, says Christopher.' The cat, who never said a word that anyone except Miss Beade could hear, was frequently quoted. 'Good night, May. I hope you won't be called out again tonight. Any little ones expected?'

'At least half a dozen.' May laughed. 'There always are. But they'll have to wait if they want me to do the honours. I'm not on call tonight. I'm going to the cinema.'

'With Veronica?' Mrs Wilson asked as soon as Miss Beade had left. 'I thought it was your night for washing your hair.'

'No, because this is the only night Ronnie can manage. Fred has to take his mother somewhere.' Veronica's fiancé, an arrogant man known as Mr Frederick to the rich and titled heads of hair he dressed in a West End salon, subjected her to his beck and call. She could only take a night off from him with his permission. 'So my old hair will have to wait,' May said.

'Well, it looks awful,' said Mrs Wilson complacently. 'It's a good thing you wear a cap at work. You'd scare the patients half to death.'

'Leave me alone, Mum,' May said unexpectedly, and bit her lip.

'Hoity toity!' cried Mr Wilson. 'Since when do you talk to your mother like that?'

'Oh, she's just excited.' Mrs Wilson would not even concede to her daughter the normal spirit to answer back. 'She's all in a stew over this new road, and no wonder. Such an upset coming to God-fearing people who've never done anything worse than mind their own business. And I wouldn't put it past that map to be wrong, and we'll find ourselves right in the middle of things when it comes to the demolition.'

'Nothing like looking on the bright side,' said Mr Wilson. He had started again on the *Daily Herald*, and had found quite a long story about the Expressway on the middle page. It was gratifying to think that their little corner of the world was news in a paper that was read all over the country.

'Don't give me your sauce.' Mrs Wilson took a friendly swipe at his head with the oven cloth as she passed behind him on her way to the stove. 'I'll bide my time before I give an opinion on this so-called Expressway.' She had already given at least thirty opinions. 'I'm not inclined to believe everything Miss Eunice Beade says. She doesn't know what she's talking about half the time. Gets it from those books she reads. The library must be sick of seeing that face coming in. Whatever she thinks about the Underground, I wouldn't be surprised to see our house go along with the rest.'

'Where shall we live? Let's make plans for where we shall live. Perhaps we could go out of town. I've always wanted to nurse on a country district. They give you a car, you know.'

May's neck was flushing as she became animated. Her mother cooled her down with: 'Don't take me up so, old dunderhead. I'm not saying it will happen. But whatever does come of it, it's going to be no picnic living here in Cottingham Park with all the noise and upset and dust they'll raise. My sills will be coated. It will be damp rags for me all day long. You wait.'

'I think it will be exciting,' May said slowly. She stood by the table with her stomach stuck out, tearing little triangles unseeingly off the corners of the *Cottingham Courier*. 'I think it will be very exciting. Something happening at last.'

Her parents were just opening their mouths to suggest that she should go and have her head examined, when the telephone rang. It was May's telephone, paid for out of her allowance from the District Nursing Association, but her mother always answered it if she could get there first.

'I'm afraid it will be Mrs Nixon,' May said, as her mother went out to the passage where the telephone hung uncomfortably on the wall among the coats, so that you were half suffocated by the smell of Mrs Wilson's plastic mackintosh as you talked.

'I promised her she shouldn't have the relief nurse. There goes my evening out.'

It was May's friend, Veronica Duke. 'She wants to know whether you're going round there or shall she come here?' Mrs Wilson shrilled.

'Let me talk to her.' May went into the passage.

'I suppose I'm capable of giving a message to your grand

friends.' Mrs Wilson held her hand over the earphone, under the impression that she was blocking the mouthpiece. 'What shall I tell her?'

'It depends what time supper is. What had you –'

'Oh dear. So now the whole household is to be organized round your comings and goings. You'd better come round here, Veronica,' Mrs Wilson told the telephone. 'May doesn't seem able to make up her mind. Have you seen the news? No, not that. That's all you young girls think of – murder and rape. About the road, I mean.'

May heard Veronica's voice clacketing excitedly. Her mother said: 'Oh.' Then she said: 'This will kill your poor mother,' and hung up.

'Their flats are coming down,' she said, her small, highly polished brown shoes clicking briskly on the linoleum as she hurried back into the kitchen. 'Where will the Dukes be now with their central heating and their porter and their stereo what-is-it and their grand ideas?' The Dukes had once lived three doors away from the Wilsons in Faulkner Road. Mrs Wilson had never forgiven them for moving, when Mr Duke got a better job, to a block of flats with a porter. 'All this is going to be a great leveller, that's what I say.'

'It is death which is the great leveller.' Mr Wilson made his cultured crossword face.

'Well, it will be death then. The death of a district.' Mrs Wilson liked that. She said it again. 'The death of a district.' While the potatoes were cooking, she went upstairs with a plate of staling shortbread, so that she could say it once more to Jim and Annette Carey, who were under notice to leave the two rooms on the ground floor because they were going to have a baby.

Miss Beade's cat was Mrs Wilson's last concession. New-born babies, no. The Careys were having difficulty finding another place, with Annette sticking out a mile, but no one was going to say that Mrs Wilson was hardhearted. Hence the plate of shortbread.

Veronica Duke was four years younger than May, and it was odd that they had remained friends after the Dukes had moved, because Veronica had grown so far away from May that they now had very little in common.

Veronica was a neat little curly blonde with a high pointed bosom and a tiny waist, and only her legs, which were her despair, to betray her peasant ancestry.

Her unpretentious mother had remained a country-woman, with a village drag to her speech and a habit of making her own bread and setting it to rise in front of the polite tiled fireplace in the sitting-room of the flat. However, she was very proud that Veronica, through mixing with the smart girls at the hairdresssing school and the lovely class of clients at the beauty shop, had made something of herself and could now go anywhere.

May was also proud and flattered that one so attractive and sophisticated as Veronica should still find time to bother with her bumbling self. But Veronica was flattered too, although May did not know it. She was not as confident as she appeared, and May's uncritical admiration of what she was and did and said was comforting.

Although May, after thirteen years of nursing, had actually seen more of life than her friend, it was always assumed that Veronica was much more experienced. She could tell May what to do, which suited her. She was by nature a rather bossy girl, but she could not boss her fiancé, Mr Frederick. She took orders from Fred and then turned round and gave them to May. It was like the hierarchy of the ward staff, which May knew so well from her hospital days. The second-year nurse, blasted by the staff nurse, could recover her self-respect by blasting the senior probationer, who could in turn go out among the bedpan racks and take it out of the junior pro. In the same way, Veronica used May to bolster her ego, which was always being deflated by the bumptious Mr Frederick.

When she arrived at the Wilson's house this evening, the queer jerky man with the fluffy hair, the one who was a gardener and lived on the top floor, was going up the steps. He heard Veronica's heels on the pavement and turned when he reached the porch. You could not call it a stare. It was just the flick of a glance before he whipped round again and went to the front door.

Veronica had only seen him once or twice before in the hall or on the stairs, and he had sidled away without looking at her. Because he always seemed so nervous, she called out in a friendly way and started up the steps saying: 'I've come to see May. Will you let me in?'

She preferred to go in by the front door and up to May's bedroom on the first floor rather than down into the basement flat, where Mrs Wilson would want to talk about the new road. Veronica had heard nothing else but that ever since she came home from work, and she was sick of it.

With his back turned to her, Arthur Sears fumbled in all the pockets of his thick green jacket and his loose overcoat with the big poacher's pockets. Veronica waited behind him in the porch. There were broken black and white tiles underfoot, and plaster flaking in lumps from the canopy and the two cold seats on either side.

Presently Arthur turned round and said in a casual voice, as if he had suddenly lost interest in the project of the front door: 'Forgot my key.'

'We'll have to ring,' Veronica said brightly, as if she were talking to a child. And although the man's face was coarse-skinned and weatherbeaten, there was something rather childlike about his eyes, which blinked and opened stiffly wide and blinked again when he had to look at you.

He ran his earthy finger up and down the vertical row of verdigrised bells with the cards tacked up beside them. The coloured medical student, 'Mr Constantine Porter', was the only one who had a clean card, with his name typed on it. Miss Beade's card said in green ink: 'Miss Eunice M. Beade and Christopher.' Arthur's bell at the top was still labelled on a torn card hanging askew: 'Miss O. G. Sandowsky', a relic of the Polish woman who had been in the room before him.

'The house of many bells,' he said to Veronica. 'Shall I ring them all?'

'Don't be silly.' She stretched past him and pressed the bottom bell, which said in May's writing: 'Wilson. Ring this bell for Nurse.'

When Veronica reached forward, Arthur stepped back hurriedly. He was still standing at the other side of the porch when May opened the door.

'Oh!' May said. She looked taken aback. She made that mouth when she did not know what to say, pulling it stiffly down with the cords of her neck stretched.

'We met on the steps when I came, so I asked him to let me in, and then he hadn't got his key, you see, but – oh well. Here we are anyway.' Veronica giggled and stepped into the hall. Surely poor old May wasn't trying to get hold of *this*? But perhaps it was better than nothing. It was a man, at least. Because it was a man, Veronica took off her coat in the hall instead of upstairs, so that he could see her sweater.

Veronica was in no way promiscuous. She was actually very virtuous and rather prim, and could not wholeheartedly enjoy the liberties which her fiancé demanded. She felt at the same time that it was wrong to allow them, and yet her duty. Worrying about that, she could not easily accept the manicured hand which thrust inside her blouse, which crept between her thighs.

Fred told her sometimes that she was frigid. 'You lie there like a bloody telephone pole,' he had said to her once behind the buddleia hedge at Kew. Although he wanted to touch her all the time, he never told her that she was beautiful, and so sometimes, as now in the Wilsons' hall, she had to show her shape provocatively to another man, to prove to herself that she was not frigid and to try to find in his face that she was beautiful.

'Oh, do you want to stay?' May asked when Veronica took off her coat. 'Don't you think we ought to go right away if we're going to see both pictures?' When she made suggestions to Veronica, it was usually in questions rather than statements.

'Well, but you're not ready.'

'I only have to get my coat and hat.'

'Not that green hat,' Veronica said rudely. 'I won't go with you.'

'All right. A scarf then. My hair's a fright. Come up with me.'

As they went up the stairs, Arthur Sears walked behind them. Veronica knew that her bottom, which was rather broad for the rest of her, moved from side to side going upstairs. She felt it doing that now, and the man looking at it. When they reached the first floor landing, which smelled of the hot spicy soup which Constantine Porter heated on his gas ring to sustain life while he studied anatomy far into the night, Arthur suddenly became very polite and darted forward to open the door of May's room.

Veronica wondered if he wanted to see whether she kept it locked. The other doors in the house were naturally locked because they were the front doors to people's tiny private worlds, but May's door was only a bedroom, an extension of her home in the basement. Remind me to ask her if she locks it at night, Veronica told herself. She had a brief and startling vision of old May lying in bed in that tent of a nightgown and the gardening hands of Arthur Sears trying to do the things that Fred did.

'Have a good time, ladies,' Arthur said, standing back stiffly, his hands by his sides, to let them pass into the room.

'Oh dear, I am sorry.' May turned and stood in the doorway so that Veronica could not get in. 'I never introduced you to my friend. This is Ronnie, you've heard me speak about. Miss Veronica Duke.'

'How do, Miss Duke.' He was still pressed flat against the wall with his arms straight and his hands held in a funny way with the heel of the hand down and the fingers raised, as if he were going to play the piano standing up. His eyes began to blink. 'You live round these parts?' He spoke with a kind of strangled formality, as if they had never had their little session with the bells on the porch.

'At the moment I do.' Veronica laughed. 'We just heard today that this new road will go slap through our flats, if they ever get around to making it. My father says there will be so many objections, the plan will be obsolete before they ever start.' Before she moved away from Faulkner Road, he had been Dad. Now he was My Father, and his coordinating job on the time-tables was Executive with British Railways.

'It's dreadful for you, Ronnie,' May said. 'Those lovely flats. Quite new and everything. Wouldn't you think they would take the road round them? It seems such a wicked waste.'

Veronica thought so too. She liked the warm and comfortable flat, which was near buses and trains and shops and much nicer than the crooked, arty 'studio flat' out at Primrose Hill, where Fred lived with a nest of parakeets and to which he proposed to take her after they were married. But she shrugged and said: 'Oh, no loss really. They're pretty dim. My family were probably going to move anyway.'

'What flats are those?' Arthur Sears asked. He was beginning to move up the stairs towards his room, walking sideways, still with his back against the wall.

'Granchester Mansions,' May said. 'That big brick place at the end of Spurr Road, by the Regal Cinema. You must know it.'

But Arthur Sears, who had seemed to have nothing better to do than hang about and talk, had detached himself from the wall and was sprinting up the stairs as if there were not a moment to spare.

'Queer fish,' Veronica said, as she went into May's room. 'How do you stand living among all these peculiar people?'

102

'They don't bother me.' May went to the mirror, raised her hands to her head in a half-hearted way and then opened a drawer and took out a green wool scarf, which she folded on top of the barren dressing table as if she were making a sling. 'It's company. Someone to talk to. Mr Sears is all right when you get to know him. We have quite nice chats sometimes. You'd be surprised some of the things he knows.'

'I daresay I would.' Veronica studied without enthusiasm the small gallery of babies, some naked, some clad, some with grateful inscriptions, which adorned the mantelpiece above the narrow gas fire. 'But he's dreadfully common, May.'

Veronica had discovered Common after she moved into the overheated stuffiness of Granchester Mansions and the perfumed refinement of the beauty shop. It was her criterion now for many things.

'Who cares?' May tied the scarf round her large head and wondered why it did not make her look like Princess Margaret at the hunter trials. 'So's everyone else round here. Including me, I suppose.'

'If you didn't belittle yourself so much' – Veronica took on the earnest voice with which she perennially attacked the insoluble problem of making something of May – 'you'd make a better impression. People take you at your own value. You always should look and talk your best.'

May hooted. 'When a woman is lying on a bed in agony trying to get a baby out, she doesn't care how I look. She only cares whether I know how to turn a breech presentation.'

'Don't be disgusting. You know what I mean. Aren't you ever going to get married, May? Time's getting on. Why here am I, younger than you, but I'd be worried by now if I wasn't engaged to Fred.' With smugness she tried to quench the little flame of doubt. 'Everyone ought to marry. It's a woman's destiny.' By believing this, she was usually able to quell the small panics which sometimes assailed her when she thought of her life committed to Frederick Baines.

'Married? Me?' May picked up a bulging handbag and moved heavily to the door. 'Go on, Ronnie. Who would want to marry me?'

'I don't know,' Veronica said honestly. 'But perhaps if you –'

'Come on,' May said, 'or we'll be late.'

She said it with unusual asperity. Jealous, you see, Veronica told herself. Jealous because I've got a man and she's afraid she's going to be an old maid.

With such thoughts, Veronica shut out the strange idea that she was just as happy to spend the evening at home or with dull old May as to go tearing about with Fred on his white Lambretta, both of them wearing white helmets and white silk scarves and Fred wearing the big white gleaming grin he copied from a boy he knew who was a photographer's model.

Granchester Mansions, destined, according to the published plan, to succumb to the ravages of the Transurban Expressway, may have been a palace of elegance compared to the Dukes' old house in Faulkner Road, but that was about the best you could say for it.

Many people, after the staggering news was out, were saying, like May: 'It would be a crime to pull down such fine new flats'; but they were not very fine, and they were not very new.

Built before the war, they were nearly thirty years old, but people who had lived a long time in that neighbourhood could remember the Mansions being built, and how they had marvelled at the size and the modern features; and their impression of the flats had got stuck that way and never changed. They were still 'those new flats by the Regal', although they were now several years older than many of the buildings round about, and a period piece compared with the council estate and the massive new glass and concrete railway terminal where Mr Duke worked in sunlight on the fifth floor.

There was not much sunlight in the Dukes' ground floor flat in Granchester Mansions, or in any of the flats on that side below the fourth floor. They were shadowed by tall old buildings across the road. At the back, the deep dark well round which the flats were built kept the bedrooms in a submarine gloom.

The narrow corridors with their rows of cheap metal front doors had not been redecorated for years, and nor had most of the flats. Once so go-ahead and spruce, many of them had degenerated over the years into shabby little bolt-holes which were sub-let over and over again to short-term tenants who did not bother to polish the splintering wood block floors or to clean farther than a half-hearted arm would reach the hanging filth round the kitchen and bathroom walls.

The lifts sounded so insecure that there was little comfort in the annual inspection certificate posted inside. The porters were badly shaven and surly, disillusioned by being expected to work for fly-by-night tenants who did not know how to tip. It was only by handing out more money than he cared to at regular intervals that Mr Duke was able to ensure that his garbage pail – clean coloured plastic while the others were rusty and stinking – was emptied at least half often enough to suit his wife.

Mrs Duke would not do the tipping because she thought, mistakenly, that it must embarrass the porters as much as it embarrassed her. She could never adjust herself to being one who does the tipping instead of one who is tipped. In the days when she had been a maid in the big house in her Wiltshire village, she had always been shy to take handouts, and been afraid when she performed some willing service for a guest that they would think she was only doing it for the tip.

She had enjoyed being a maid. She liked housework actively, instead of enduring it passively. When they lived in Faulkner Road and let rooms, like the Wilsons, there had been plenty for her to do all day. Now in the flat with her husband and Veronica and her son Godfrey out at work, there was not enough for her to do, and so she cleaned and recleaned and scrubbed and polished and shampooed rugs and curtains within an inch of their lives, and there was not a flat that looked like hers in the whole of Granchester Mansions.

In the evenings she sat quietly sewing for her family and watched the television, unless Godfrey wanted to play the Stereo, in which case not much else could happen in the flat.

Godfrey Duke worked as a sales representative to a firm supplying electronic replacement parts to dealers. He got around. He knew people in the trade, and by a stroke of luck he had acquired his stereophonic radiogram quite cheaply. Cheap was a comparative word, and he would be paying out on it for years; but it was at the moment his passion and his *raison d'être* and he did not care if the payments on the set and the expensive records to play on it left him little money to spend on anything else.

Unfortunately for his family. They would have been glad to see him go out more: revive his old interest in football, get his motor-cycle fixed, get a steady girl. When he was at home, the whole flat throbbed with music and the sitting-room was a sound box of shattering noise.

The set, with its enclosed turntable and its panel of buttons and switches which Mrs Duke was forbidden to dust, stood at one end of the room. At the other end in opposite corners stood the two mammoth speakers half as high as a man, with polished cabinets and gold mesh grills out of which sound more real than reality poured forth to penetrate the eardrums and the brain into the very core of the soul itself.

'Why do you let him, Mother?' Veronica asked. (It was not Mum any longer at Granchester Mansions.) 'Why do you let him play that thing all the time when you don't like it?'

'But I do like it,' her mother answered loudly. They were in her bedroom, where Veronica was setting her mother's hair stylishly in end papers and wire rollers. It was possible to have a conversation in there if you raised your voice. 'I have to like it, your brother says. It's culture, Ronnie, all that classical jazz and those steel guitars with their sad melodies. If Goff wants me to like it, I will.'

That was how good a mother she was. Veronica wanted her to like Frederick Baines, and so she liked him, although he was not her type and not at all what she had thought of for Ronnie.

On this night, about a week after the stone of the Transurban Expressway had started the ripples agitating in Cottingham Park, Mr Frederick was half an hour late fetching his fiancée to take her to a dance.

He came on his scooter. How Veronica hated going to dances on the Lambretta! But it was Fred's baby, just as the Stereo was Goff's baby, and she had learned from her mother that whatever you thought of a man's likes or hobbies, you took a back seat and rode along with them.

Fred rang the bell three times before anyone heard it through the noise of Harry Belafonte giving his concert at Carnegie Hall. When Veronica finally heard the genteel chimes and ran to open the door, Fred was cross.

'You can hear that bloody noise right down the street,' he said. 'I don't see how the neighbours stand it, much less all of you. Good evening, all! How's tricks?'

'Shut up, Fred,' Goff said. 'Sit down and listen. This is the best bit coming.'

Fred raised the smooth black eyebrows which a girl at the beauty salon kept neatly plucked for him. He was a tall, taper-waisted man with a fine glossy head of hair and a taste for bright socks and hand-painted satin ties. But discreetly painted. Not mermaids or half-clad hula dancers. Fred was a classy dresser. Never vulgar.

Mr Duke looked up from his book and nodded a greeting. Mrs Duke came in from the kitchen with a smile of welcome on her broad shining face and her head all done up in the rollers like a Martian.

When the music quietened for a moment, her husband asked, as he always asked: 'You going to bed like that?'

'I have to. Ronnie won't let me have pin curls any more.' She bridled a little, pleased with her vanity and the fond tyranny of a clever daughter.

'How you women can sleep in those things baffles me.'

'Il faut souffrir pour ate-ra belle,' Fred said, but the music came up to drown him in a clash and shudder of sound and Goff shouted in vexation: 'Stop yapping and listen, I told you. This disc is history.'

Fred made a face and shrugged his grey flannel shoulders. He sat down impermanently on the arm of an easy chair, and pulled Veronica beside him, putting his hand round her and on to her breast, which she wished he would not do in front of the family.

Ma-tilda! Ma-tilda! sang Harry Belafonte joyfully, and Goff sat entranced by the controls, his light hair flopping on his forehead, his chin on his hand, his tweed jacket all rumpled with emotion. The song paused, the music was soft in the background. An intake of breath, and the singer spoke. Veronica jumped, and Fred's fingers tightened on her jumping breast, for the voice was as startlingly clear as if the man were in the room, disembodied, persuasive, speaking for them alone.

He was coaxing the audience to sing with him. They laughed. Their laughter and excitement leaped at him. He sang the chorus again and wheedled, and the volume of voices grew: *Ma-tilda! Ma-tilda! Take me money and run Venezue-la!*

It ended in a torrent of applause. A roar of voices and hands and delight that was like Niagara pouring out of the loudspeaker.

'Isn't it terrific?' Goff pounded his fist into his hand. 'Terr-r-r-*if*ic. Terr-r-r-*if*ic.' His eyes saw nothing. He was like a reverse Pinocchio: man transmogrified into puppet.

'I didn't quite like the bit about the money under the pillow,' his mother ventured, 'if it meant what I thought it did.'

Goff did not hear her. 'Isn't it colossal? Isn't it absolutely unbearably the most?' He stood up and began to pace back and forth across the floor.

'Calm down,' said his father, 'and get me a beer. Get one for Fred too, if Ronnie hasn't used it all on her mother's hair. They set it in beer now,' he chuckled to Fred. 'What do you make of that?'

'But of course.' No use expecting Fred to be chummily mystified over the foibles of women's coiffure. 'At Alex, however, we use only draught beer on our clients' hair.' He said this solemnly, and no one knew whether he were joking or not.

Godfrey was still pacing the room. Veronica went unasked to get the beer. The women waited on the men in this family.

'Imagine!' Goff raved. 'Imagine Belafonte listening to that disc himself and hearing that applause and those shouts. All for him. How must he feel?'

'Like any conceited damn nigger earning more than he's worth.' Fred puffed out his lips and cheeks complacently. 'I can't see why you bother listening to that stuff. If you want calypso, go into any coffee bar round here. The place is stiff with blacks. I nearly skated into a mob of them just now when I took the corner too fast, hurrying to get to my girl.' He winked.

'Why were you late, Fred? Oh – not that it matters,' Veronica added hastily, for he had often rebuked her for inquisitioning. 'There's plenty of time. I just wondered.'

'Oh now. Oh come now.' Fred looked round at them all with a slow smile. 'I suppose you're going to tell me you didn't watch the Rose Kelly show?'

'Yes, we did.' Mrs Duke was glad to please, because most of the time she hardly knew what to say to him. 'We were having supper. Goff wanted to watch, so we let him keep the set on this once.' As if Godfrey were ever denied his desires.

'How was she?' Fred studied his gleaming nails. His voice was casual.

'Damn good-looking woman.' Mr Duke tapped out his pipe in an ashtray built round a miniature Eiffel Tower, memento of an Easter trip to Paris.

'How about her hair?' Fred's voice was still more casual. He threw the question away.

'It was lovely. I liked that forward lift at the sides, didn't you? Something new for her – that extra heighth.' Veronica had on her professional voice. 'I wonder where she goes.'

'She goes to me. I dressed it for her tonight.' Mr Frederick paused for effect and Veronica gasped dutifully. 'She came into Alex for the first time yesterday. They recommended myself.' He looked down, fluttering his long lashes. 'She liked my styling so well that nothing would do but that I should go to her home this evening and dress her hair before she went to the studio.'

'What was she like?' Goff had recovered enough from Harry Belafonte to be interested.

Fred clasped his hands and looked into space. His dark eyes moist, he gave a low, slow, musical version of a wolf whistle.

Auras of the beautiful television star's glory hung round him. The family listened while he told them some more about her, making up some of it, Veronica thought, because after all, it had only been that once in the salon and then just to comb out at home. Her admiration was piqued with jealousy, as she realized, when Fred shot her a sly feline glance, he meant it to be.

Wasn't she good enough for him then? Suppose he compared her with people like Rose Kelly? She was only Ronnie Duke, who had got somewhere in her profession, but was still a novice in Fred's eyes. The beauty shop of a West End department store was her pinnacle, but it was small beer to him, who swaggered like a spoiled child through the fabulous Alex salon, and talked impertinently to duchesses and film stars.

And this was her family. Goff put on an act sometimes, and talked big, but he did not know anyone who was anybody, any more than any of them did. But Fred had been in the home of Rose Kelly this evening. And now here he was in the narrow cluttered room, with the gate-legged dining table round the corner in the L, and Mother's dried flower arrangements, and Goff looking through his jazz records in a threatening way.

'Does Rose Kelly have stereo?' Goff asked.

'Can't say. I was only in the bedroom. Stereo-sized bed though, I'll tell you. I'll bet that could play back some lulus if it was wired for tapes.' He leered at his future father-in-law. Mr Duke smiled uneasily, and Veronica wished that Fred wouldn't. Sex was a subject that was seldom mentioned at home, even by Goff. Mrs Duke had told Veronica at an early age all the things she needed to know, briskly, in terms of farm animals. After that, the subject was closed. Not closed in a sneaky, dirty way. It was just something they did not trouble to speak about.

Veronica's family would be amazed if she told them some of the things she heard from her clients. Fred said that it was years out of date to have booths in the beauty salon. The Alex salon, like all the newer ones, was just one big room with shampooing and cutting and setting performed in public, and a semicircle of women under dryers in one corner, drinking coffee and speculating on each other's shoes.

But the department store customers, many of them middle-aged or up from the country, liked their accustomed privacy. When Veronica told Fred some of the things they told her about their private lives – she had not the nerve to tell all of them – he said that he could see why they had to have booths.

'Who wants to hear a new Morton Gould?' Goff shattered the sitting-room with a trumpet wail that dragged after it in agonising crescendo a thunder clap of brass.

'Spare us.' Fred got up. 'We're off. Get your coat, Ron.'

The telephone rang and Veronica went into her parents' bedroom to answer it. If she shut the door, she could just hear in there.

'Is that you, dear?' It was a rough voice, slightly cockney, a little breathless.

'I'm afraid you have the wrong number.'

'No, no. Listen, dear. It's you I want. I want you. Listen a minute.'

Sitting on the bed, Veronica listened. For some terrible reason, she could not put down the telephone. She just had to sit there and listen to the filth, the things people never said, the words she only half knew. She was stiff with horror, cold, sick, burning hot. And the awful thing, the thing she would never tell anybody ever in the whole of her life, was that in spite of her disgust, her body grew excited. Fearfully, she put a hand on her breast. The nipple was rigid.

With a gasp, she banged down the receiver, got up and staggered half choking into the other room and flung herself on to her mother in a passion of tears.

'Ronnie! What's happened?'

'What on earth?'

'Who was on the phone?'

'What's wrong, baby?'

They clustered round her and she raised her head from her mother's cushiony bosom and looked round at them in horror with tears running into her distorted mouth. She was contaminated, dirty. They should not ever look at her or speak to her again.

'Tell us, Veronica.' Her mother's protective arm squeezed her gently.

'Oh Mum. Oh Mum.' She looked into the kind fat face, searching the charitable eyes to see if she could tell her. 'It was a man,' she whispered. 'A stranger. He said awful things to me. Things I've never heard.'

'What things?' That was her father.

'I can't tell you.'

'You must, dear,' her father said grimly. 'I shall have to tell the police.'

'Tell us, Ron,' Goff said. 'We'll fix this bastard.'

Uncertain, she looked to Fred for help. He had not said anything. He was standing with his mouth open, his jaw dropped away to nothing. He looked – she let herself see it – stupid, at a loss. She looked back at the concerned face of her father, and her brother with his hair tousled, looking like himself as a little boy half her size, offering to fight a lout at school who had hurt her.

'Well then.' She drew away from her mother and stood alone, clasping her hands. 'He said about – here.' She put her clasped hands over her breast. 'Then he said – oh, filthy things, and he said – he said what he wanted to do to me.' She looked down and bit her lip. 'I can't tell you any more.'

'Come on.' Fred's tongue moved nervously round his lips. 'Tell the lot.'

'She doesn't have to,' Mr Duke said coldly. 'It's enough. I'm going round to the police station now to see what we should do in case the swine calls again.'

'I'll go, Dad, if you like,' Goff said. 'Might be easier for me. Come with me, Fred?'

'I don't see that I need.' Fred's mouth could look like a spoiled baby, not handsome at all. 'They won't want the whole ruddy circus round there. Besides, Ronnie and I have to go. We're late as it is.'

'You're not going to drag this poor child out to a dance?' Mrs Duke put her arms round her daughter again.

'Why not? Do her good. Take her mind off it. We're meeting some people anyway.'

'Fred, I – I really don't feel like going.' She was not crying now.

She just felt hideously wrong. Unclean. Messy, as if she had been a long journey in a train, sitting up all night. She wanted to take a bath, wash her hair, scrub her teeth violently, go to bed in starched sheets.

'Of course she can't go.' Feet planted, head bristling with the grotesque rollers, face red with indignation, her mother stood boldly up to Fred. 'She's had a dreadful shock. She's all upset. Can't you see that?'

'I can't see what there is to be so upset about.' Fred took a comb from his breast pocket and combed his thick hair carefully in front of the gilt-framed mirror over the mantelpiece. 'Some girls I know would be quite thrilled to find themselves so madly desirable.'

'I think you'd better go,' Veronica's father said quietly. 'Go to the dance if you want to. Take another girl. You're not taking Veronica.'

'Fine way to talk to your daughter's fiancé,' Fred swaggered. 'What are you trying to do – break us up?'

Mr Duke did not answer. He went to the door. 'I'll go, Goff,' he said. 'You stay here and look after the girls.'

After he had gone, Fred looked at Ronnie, shrugged, and went with a swinging, self-conscious walk towards the little front lobby that led off the sitting-room. Veronica left her mother and went to him. 'I'll go with you if you like, darling. I'm all right really. Mum's fussy. She –'

Her head sang like a thousand crickets. Her stomach was suddenly full of cold lead. She was going to be sick. No, she was . . . . With a short pleading moan that sounded as if it came from someone else, she fainted on to Fred's feet in the little tiled lobby by the front door.

*

In the fifth floor restaurant at County Hall, known as the Aquarium because of the large glass panels which separated it from the corridor, Mr Robert P. V. Peregrine, from the Press Bureau was lunching with his friend Jack Clew from the Housing department.

'If they're ever going to lay the keel of this Expressway, I wish they'd get on with it,' Mr Peregrine grumbled, making a face at a gull which swooped across the river into a banking turn outside the window. 'I'm finding it hard to dredge up enough news stories. When do you think they'll start?'

'The Minister hasn't set his public hearing yet.' Jack Clew was round and florid and had been frightened by his doctor about blood pressure, which was the reason he was eating egg salad and melba toast, while Robert P. V. tantalized him with steak and kidney pie. 'And after that there will have to be another inquiry to deal with the people who fight the compulsory purchase authority. It'll drag on, the way things do. Of course we'll start on our referencing of the initial section after the first hearing.'

'I don't envy you that job. Counting the residents of half Cottingham Park.'

'Almost impossible, some of it. In those rabbit warrens where the coloured people are, you can count and recount and never get the right answer because the night workers sleep in the day workers' beds and vice versa, and you can't tell 'em apart anyway.' He picked up a piece of thin curling toast and looked at it with distaste. 'Is it cheating if I put butter on it?'

'Not if you can get her to bring some more. I've eaten all there was.'

'Well, that's a sign, I suppose.' He nibbled at the dry toast. 'Referencing.' He groaned. 'When that starts, I'm going to need more nourishment than this. And don't come pestering me for stories, because there'll be none. It's only a tally. Just routine stuff.'

'Oh, I see.' Mr Peregrine twitched his black moustache into an unsmiling smile. 'Just people.'

'Well dammit, Bob, what do you expect us to do? Weep for everyone of them? Personally find a good home for their old pet dog half bald with mange? Give Grandma cyanide because she can't be moved? You could go out of your mind that way. I had a woman in my office the other day. Came sobbing over Westminster Bridge with half a dozen children and forced her way in on me wailing that she'd heard the road was going to push her out of some hovel where she makes stuffed toys out of old hats, and that if I didn't give her a council flat, she'd throw all the kids in the river right outside my window. Refugee. Her husband was shot in Budapest. Excitable. You know the type. Betty had to bring her tea. I told her: "Calm down," I said. "Your house isn't going to be pulled down tomorrow. Plenty of time to fix you up. We'll give you every assistance. This isn't Russia, you know," I told her.'

'That's why she came here presumably. Poor fool. Could be a

story there though. When I was on a paper, I'd have made something good of that. Let me have the details and I'll give it out as a sob story. Keep the boys interested.'

'We don't want them interested that way, Bob. We don't want that kind of publicity. Listen, there'll be thousands of hard luck cases to tackle far worse than hers. You can't build a road through the middle of London without someone suffering. People will cry and wail and object, but the rest of the world needn't hear them.'

'And the Expressway must go through.'

'Well, you know it must. It's the most tremendous thing. It will put us on the map. Show the Yanks they're not the only ones who can handle traffic problems.' He questioned the waitress about the calories in ice cream. She promised a water ice, and cheese for Mr Peregrine.

'What's the matter with you today, Bob?' Jack Clew screwed up his face into fat creases. 'You're talking like a social worker. You'll snarl at me if I try to tell you your job, but it's the road you've got to publicize, you know, not the people it's going to hurt.'

'I know, I know. But that's so damn dull. Trouble is, I've been cruising around Cottingham Park a bit lately. It's a shambles, I agree. Dirt and poverty and flashes of chic and stuffy shabbiness. But it's – oh, you know – liveable. I'm getting to like it. My wife and I saw a house – a little pale yellow house in a street filled with blossom. Cul-de-sac, you know. No traffic. Babies in prams in front gardens. Someone playing a piano, tinkly, tinkly through an open ground floor window. It was for sale. We wanted to buy it. We could too, and live in it for six months or a year before the Council forced us to sell so that they could pull it down. Poor Georgette. It was all on one floor. Perfect for her chair. She hates the flat, you know.'

'They'll not move me,' Mrs Saithe said to her lodger Eileen Kelly. She put in her teeth and closed her jaws with a snap, grinding the teeth back and forth to get them settled.

Eileen's mouth fell slightly open, as it did when she stared. 'But you'll have to go when they pull the mews down, won't you?'

'Ah, but will they pull it down?' Mrs Saithe closed one small eye and laid a finger on the side of her nose. 'I've got my rights, same as anyone else. So has all of them in the mews – even that Commie and her. There's ways and means to object, you know, and don't think we shan't use 'em. We can even make them alter their plans, Lewis Basset says – take a loop 'ere round Armstrong Mews. A detour, Lewis says.' She nodded knowingly. Her scant grey hair was pulled so tightly back that the places where it came out of her temples stood out like little goose pimples. 'A detour.'

There was comfort in knowing the official word. Ever since Lewis Bassett, who had once been chauffeur to an M.P. and was something of a village leader in the mews, had suggested that they all go in a body to the public hearing and demand their rights, the agitated women had been telling each other 'a detour' and taking heart.

'You mean they'd change the whole road and make it not straight just to please a handful of people in a crummy little dead end that's been marked down for a slum anyway?' They might do that in Ireland, but that sort of whimsical tolerance had not been Eileen's impression of England so far.

'It's been good enough for you for near on a year,' Mrs Saithe said sharply. 'You'd better watch your mouth, young lady, and not talk so crude about crummy. Where else would you have found a good clean room in such a respectable house for the money – you and that shedding little bugger? Bless his heart though,' Mrs Saithe added, for she admired the little dog for his gaiety, and would not want to hurt his feelings. 'Apart' – she cleared her throat and looked at Eileen sideways with her best eye – 'apart from other things.'

Eileen's professional life was never directly mentioned between them, although Mrs Saithe had always known about it, and Eileen knew that she knew. But as long as the girl paid her rent and kept the men away from under Mrs Saithe's slate roof, she would do no more than hint about it when she wanted to score a point.

'If this lot does come down, I'll have to chance my luck,' Eileen said. She did not really believe that the puny residents of the mews could pit themselves against the might of Government. 'Perhaps I'll go back to Wicklow.' She did not say anything like: 'I'll be sorry to leave,' or: 'It's been nice being here.' She and Mrs Saithe enjoyed an amicable enough relationship, but they did not say things like that. When they gave each other something at Christmas, or a small chocolate egg at Easter, they did not say Merry Christmas or Happy Easter. They just handed over the gift with an air that they suspected the other would not think much of it.

'Where will you go, Mrs Saithe?' she asked, although she did not really care.

'Me? Nowhere. I've told you.' Mrs Saithe turned her back and rummaged in a drawer full of brown paper and string, giving Eileen the back view of her apron strings to show that she was beginning to be irritated. 'This 'as been my home for forty years. I never did like cars – saving Mr Saithe's taxicab, which was more like a household pet, you might say, living right here below us – and I'm not going to move out of my home so that them as can afford to go on wheels can juggernaut over all my memories.'

She did not mind Guy Banning and his car coming in and out of the garage below her where the domesticated Beardmore had once lived. Mr Banning was all right. Gave you the time of day and a bit of sauce along with it. It was the motorists on the road who were her enemies, and she took it out of them by marching suddenly out on to a zebra crossing with her umbrella raised and taking a thump at the back end of cars which sneaked by her without stopping.

'From what I hear,' said Eileen, who got around at night and heard most of the current gossip, 'if they start to smash up Cottingham Park, they'll have to rehouse everybody. A council flat perhaps. Wouldn't I like that?'

The thought of herself and Toodie in a council flat with a window box full of ferns was delightful. She might, if she was cunning, be able to run it as an office as well and not bother with Carbine Road. That would be a laugh on the government though, wouldn't it, with their talk of stern measures against the deplorable vice blatantly paraded by these women in the public streets. They were always making it softer for the queers and harder for the honest girls.

Seeing herself as a high-class call girl in a négligée in a subsidized flat, Eileen had to laugh. Life was a joke really, she told the little ginger dog as she prepared his supper at the washstand in her room. Just one thing after another, and though some of the things seemed bloody miserable, in the end they often turned out quite comical.

Half a mile away, in the Scotneys on the other side of Park Road, Miss Sutcliffe and Mrs Vulliamy were also preparing for siege.

Not, like Mrs Saithe and the other mews dwellers, with indignantly gossiping groups and loose mouthings about what they could do and what their rights were. The old ladies who lived in what remained of the oldest house in Cottingham Park were attacking the enemy in a more practical way.

They were helping to start a society, the Scotney Society, for the preservation of the world they knew. The new road was not scheduled to hit their house – 'Though I'm surprised,' said Miss Sutcliffe, 'after all the years they've been after us for owning too much land, that they've missed this opportunity to put us out.' If the published plan were correct – 'and since the Press have got hold of it there may be some doubt about *that*' – marginal development of the road would run somewhat below Park Lodge along the side of the gentle slope that had once been the lush parklands of the big house.

Scotney Lane, Stable Way, and Scotney's Passage would disappear; streets which contained some of the oldest houses, one of them with a notable Georgian curved staircase. The view which the old ladies now enjoyed, of uneven roofs and mellowed chimneys and the rounded green tops of tenacious old trees bursting out of tiny walled gardens, would be swept away. In its place, after the road was finished, would be a development of one-storey houses. Miss Sutcliffe could just see them: flat-roofed boxes, cheaply built like everything nowadays, with laundry lines among the brussels sprouts and broken tricycles askew outside the back door.

'But we shall be dead by then,' Mrs Vulliamy said.

'You might. I shan't.' The challenge of the Transurban Expressway had given Jessie Sutcliffe a new lease of life.

The Scotney Society was going to fight. There were enough people in this corner of London who cared enough to stand up against the vandals. It was true that only a few of the old houses would be lost, but that was too much. The other pleasant streets that remained would be marooned in the corner between the costive traffic of Park Road and the speeding nightmare of the Expressway, crossing over Park Road in a big flyover that would loop an arm round the Scotneys and crush them spiritually to death.

'They will never do this in my lifetime,' Miss Sutcliffe said to Mr Davenport, Our Local Antiquarian, who was secretary-treasurer of the Society, and he was polite enough not to say: 'No, because you could be dead before it's finished,' but realistic enough to think it.

His house in one of the higher terraces would not be directly

117

affected, and he did not really believe that the fragile little dyke of local protest could stem the tide of the Masters' ambition, but he had made the neighbourhood his pigeon and he could not see its wings clipped without at least some show of struggle. He had written thousands of words about the Scotneys, given talks to hatted ladies' groups, unearthed old prints for his unique collection. He was also fond of the old ladies at Park Lodge, and so he readily agreed to work for the Scotney Society. Even if it could do no more than make a well-bred noise, it was one way of calling attention to the treasures of his beloved neighbourhood, and it would at least needle the Powers, and might even hold up the work. That was a good thought to both Mr Davenport and Miss Sutcliffe. Whatever the outcome, there was a gremlin pleasure in putting spokes in wheels.

Old Pringle, the decrepit maid at Park Lodge, had been roped in to be the first member of the Society. Miss Sutcliffe had paid her subscription and shown her where to sign.

'What's it all in aid of?' she asked, making the chicken scratches which were her name.

'To stop this new road.'

'With my five bob? Oh well, nothing venture, nothing win, and I suppose you know what you're doing Miss Jessie, for I'm sure I don't.'

By the end of three months there were nearly two hundred members. Mr Davenport, a widower with one uncongenial daughter, who had known time hanging heavy, had found an absorbing interest in soliciting recruits and collecting subscriptions and sending too-diffuse press releases to the *Cottingham Courier* and composing reports and taking them to Miss Junip above the furniture shop in Park Road to be roneoed.

'It's going ahead,' said Miss Sutcliffe; and Mrs Vulliamy wrote to her niece Anne in America, to whom Miss Sutcliffe would not write because she was living with a married man, that she knew how Lord Francis Scotney had felt three hundred and fifty years ago when he rode forth at the head of his pikemen to trounce the robber barons.

With a month to go of the summer term – the last term of all the terms, winter, spring and summer, that had ever been within those grimy brick walls – Abbot's Road Secondary Modern was performing the Summer Play.

118

It was *Macbeth*. A mistake really, John Ferris said, because a lot of the parents would stay away if they heard it was Shakespeare. 'Give 'em *Charley's Aunt*,' he said, 'and they'll pack the hall.'

'The boys want *Macbeth*,' said the headmaster, who had taught them to want it. 'You can do *Charley's Aunt* at Haileybury.'

Mr Ferris, who had been expected to retire and nurse his peptic ulcer when Abbot's Road closed down, had surprisingly been the first to fix a new job. He was going to teach history in Hertfordshire to boys who had at least three of every piece of underwear instead of one at the most, and that doubling as pyjamas.

'Reverting to type,' Geoffrey Savage told him, and Mr Ferris, surprisingly meek, had said: 'Don't jeer. My wife likes the little house they've offered.'

The play was a success. It was a boiled-down version, with much of the text taken out and all the action left in. The girl who played Lady Macbeth, a coloured girl who looked grown up at fourteen, was startlingly good, and there were moments when she surprised some of the audience into finding the words exciting, worth listening to after all.

There were enough murders and woundings and violent horseplay to satisfy both children and parents. It seemed to Grace Peel, who was not very strong on Shakespeare, that towards the end there were far more bodies twitching about the stage than there should have been. Barney Gilligan, a wild hilarious boy with a shock of raven hair who was doing most of the killing with a purple wooden sword made in the art room, finally finished everyone off and then stabbed himself, and the screens were pulled across by at least ten more of Grace's Class 1B than was necessary, to shrieks of laughter and an uproarious stamping of feet on the gritty floor.

Frankie Bott helped to push the screens back. The cast got up grinning to take a bow. With scuffling and giggles, the screens were pulled across again, so energetically that one fell flat to reveal James Knight in torn brown paper armour taking a swing at Barney Gilligan for kicking him in the stomach after he had killed him.

Frankie looked down from the platform to where Mr Rawlings sat at the side with his long legs crossed and his glasses off so that he could enjoy his laugh better. The headmaster was not going to make a speech – this was the children's entertainment, not his, and he wanted it informal – so Frankie left the screen where it lay, pushed through a tangled bunch of boys and girls fighting over the oranges on the banquet table, and went to find his mother. She was liable to barge off home without waiting for the refreshments, because she did not trust publicly offered food for Kenny.

Frankie had never thought that she would come. He had not risked telling her about the play, since anything good about Abbot's Road was likely to touch her off; but he had told his younger brother, and Kenny had begged to go.

Mrs Bott said No, bluntly. Kenny pleaded, and she said No with embellishments. Kenny, who was sharp enough to know how far he could go, had dropped the whining in favour of the silent tears which he could summon at will into his shadowed eyes. When they slid unchecked down his thin white cheeks, Mr Bott, with surprising pluck, had declared that he would take a day off work and push Kenny's chair to the school himself. His wife was so nettled at the thought of Mr Bott both taking a day off and going somewhere where she was not, that she had said that she would go, announcing it belligerently, as if it were her own unique idea and not a concession.

She had sat stolidly through the performance in the back row, looking like a bulldog with a hat on, with Kenny beside her, his chair piled with cushions from the staff room so that he could see, convulsed with laughter and excitement.

When Frankie got to them, his mother was on her feet in her black edge-to-edge coat whose edges did not meet by twelve inches; but there was a crowd in front of her and she could not get the chair going.

'Wait, Mum. You said you'd say hullo to Miss Peel. You said you would.'

'Where is she? I don't want to stay 'ere forever. It takes it out of Kenny.'

'It don't,' Kenny said, but she told him; 'It does,' so he said to his brother, his thin little voice scarcely audible in the hubbub of the hall: 'Smashin' play, Frank. What price all them murders?'

'Just the thing, eh?'

'Too much for 'im,' Mrs Bott pronounced. ''E was 'alf off 'is 'ead.'

'You all right, boy?' Frankie bent to tuck the grey rug more tightly round Kenny's useless legs. Their faces an inch apart, they

120

smiled close, like lovers, in a way they had of talking without talking.

'May I meet your mother, Frankie?' He jumped up, and there was Miss Peel just behind him, her gorgeous hair all piled up on her head like tarts on posters. Darling woman. How had she known that Frankie wanted her, but was afraid to barge in where she was talking with Mrs Bowden and old Pegleg?

'Mum,' he said, faint with pride, 'this is Miss Peel.'

Grace held out her hand, and the big pugnacious woman took it in the hand that nearly all the mothers had, rough and swollen, the pitiful future of the graceful grubby little hands of the school-girls.

'I'm glad to meet you,' Grace said, and the woman muttered something that was reasonably polite, although her eye was suspicious. 'And this is Kenny, of course.' She bent to take Kenny's hand, which lay stiffly on top of the rug palm upwards, the fingers curved like a little harmless claw.

'Pleased to meet you, Miss,' Kenny said, and grinned like an old gnome.

'How old are you?'

'Eight. More than. Coming on nine.'

'Heavens, quite big.' Grace tried hard to avoid the special saccharine voice which sneaks unwanted into the throat with a child like this. 'Where does he go to school?' she asked Mrs Bott pleasantly.

Frankie, who had been standing smugly by like a successful impresario, felt his heart lurch down into his stomach. Oh cripes. He should have warned her not to ask that, but you can't think of everything, and if he had, she would have wanted to know why, and he would have had to tell about Mum and the education lady and – oh cripes.

The meeting between his mother and his goddess was going to ruin. Mrs Bott's mouth had snapped into a bitter slit. ''E don't go to school. They want to send 'im away. 'Aywards 'Eath, if you please.' She pronounced the name as if it were Moscow. ''E'd die if 'e was took from me.'

Grace looked at Frankie's anxious face, then at Kenny, gazing blankly ahead. Should she say something to try and help? She looked at the mother, coloured up like a great tough beetroot. How was anything, short of legal force, going to help?

Mrs Bott had her hands on the back of the wheelchair. There

121

was room now to move, and Grace saw that she was going to nod roughly and go. She must say something pleasant to retrieve the meeting for Frankie, say something nice about him that would make his mother smile and go home mellow.

'I want to tell you,' she said quickly, a little breathlessly, to Mrs Bott's half-turned shoulder, 'how much I've enjoyed having your Frankie in my class this year.' Better not be too effusive. This woman was the kind who mistrusted all teachers and would wonder what she was after. 'He's worked hard and he's been a good boy.'

Frankie scuffled his feet and ducked his head, turning up his eyes sideways to see how his mother was taking it.

'Well, I'm glad to 'ear that,' Mrs Bott said, as if it were the first passable thing she had heard all afternoon. ''E's breaking 'is 'eart over the school coming down, you know,' she said in a matter-of-fact voice, with no pity. 'Though I'm sure I don't know why. One school's much the same as another, I suppose.'

'Yes, of course,' Grace said, for Frankie's sake. He was looking up now, his round eyes with the starry lashes trained on her in torment. The younger children had not yet been told where they would be going next year. Grace had not told her class where she thought she might be going. The time of parting from them next month was going to be unhappy enough by itself. They asked her sometimes: 'What you going to do, Miss? You goin' after another job? You goin' to get married? I say, Miss, if we get sent down Green Lane, will you come with us?'

She had not told them yet about the girls' school in Berkshire whose advertisement she had answered. Swimming pool, tennis courts, model flat for domestic science. How could she tell them that she was traitor enough to think of running from their squalid world to that?

'Where will *you* go?' Mrs Bott asked, although she did not care. She looked Grace up and down boldly, the thoughts written on the front of her forehead: Dress too tight. Silly pointed toes. Them beads. Who does she think she is?

'I don't know yet.' Grace put her hand on Frankie's shoulder and felt him tense and quivering for her answer. 'I – we all like it so much here at Abbot's Road that we haven't wanted to spoil the last bit by thinking too much about the end of it.'

Mrs Bott blew at the sentiment like a horse whose hay is dusty. 'Well, Frankie's thought about it. Leaving you. Miss Peel

122

this and Miss Peel that. Taken quite a fancy to you, the bastard 'as.' With a jerk of her strong arms, she wrenched the chair round and made off for the door before Grace could say good-bye to her or to Kenny, who could not turn to look back as he was wheeled away.

'Aren't you going home with them?' Grace could not bring herself to say: How nice to meet your mother, and Frankie did not look as though he would believe it.

He shook his head. 'Not before the grub. My mate's 'ere. I'm going with 'im.' He watched his mother's broad black back humping through the door. 'Edgar Biggs. 'E wants to meet you. Too,' he added insincerely, as the swing doors thumped and settled behind Mrs Bott.

Edgar had played truant from school to be here this afternoon. He had been in hiding in case there were spies from Green Lane, and also because he could not speak to Frankie until his mother had gone.

Frankie fetched him from the niche where he was lodged darkly between a cupboard and the end of a torn leather vaulting horse, and they went into Mr Goslett's classroom where the desks had been pushed back to make room for trestle tables with sandwiches and cakes. Refreshments could not be served in the dining-hall, for that was where the play had been, the square church-windowed room that was assembly hall, dining-hall, theatre, gymnasium, and playground on a wet day.

Mrs Purdie, in flowered chiffon, was serving lemonade. Mrs Bowden, who never wore summer dresses, was in a sagging green knitted suit, pouring tea from a big tin teapot with two spouts, on loan from a fourth-year boy whose mother worked at a station buffet. Grace Peel was handing a plate of sandwiches to a plump old lady who was wedged so tightly on the small seat behind a desk that it was possible that she would have to be taken home desk and all in a taxi.

'Miss, this is Edgar,' Frankie said when Miss Peel straightened up and turned round. When she had been talking to his mother, it had been agony, sort of. Frankie never should have started it. He saw that now. He was always hoping that it would be all right with his mother, that she would miraculously be different, and then she never was. But this now with Edgar. This was good. Edgar said 'Cheerio!' in his best British manner, and Miss Peel said Cheerio back and made them take three of the best sandwiches each before the salmon gave out. They all stood there talking and laughing just like a party, and Edgar told Miss Peel what form he was in at Green Lane and how he planned to push ahead and get a scholarship for college.

Miss Peel thought that was very fine. 'So many boys don't try for college because they want to start earning money at some job that gets them nowhere, and then they're sorry afterwards.'

'Not me,' said Edgar proudly. 'I'm going to be a teacher.'

'That's wonderful. I'm sure you'll make an excellent one.'

Edgar giggled and wagged his head about and rolled his eyes and dug Frankie gleefully in the ribs, and it made up for everything going wrong with Frankie's mother.

Edgar loved Miss Peel too. Everyone loved Miss Peel. Even that sod Mr Raymond butting in on them with his: 'I say, Grace, I want to show you something. Very urgent,' even he could be forgiven, because he loved Miss Peel too.

Only she would never take up with a twerp like that. They laughed at his back view, because he was wearing tight khaki trousers and trying to walk like a Yank. As she went away with him, Miss Peel looked back with a special smile for the two boys, their mouths stuffed with jam roll, staring after her.

For some time after the unspeakable evening when she had fainted, Veronica Duke would not answer the telephone.

When her father or her brother was at home, one of them would pick it up with a squared, manly expression, ready to deal with the man if he had the nerve to call again.

If the telephone rang when Veronica and her mother were alone in the flat, they would stop whatever they were doing and look at each other.

'Don't answer it,' Veronica said. What had been said to her would be almost a foreign language to her mother, but she did not want her to hear.

'I must dear. It's our duty, that detective said. Our duty as citizens.'

The plain-clothes policeman, who had interviewed Veronica with throat clearings and tactful turnings of the head, had said that if the man called again, someone was to try to keep him talking while someone else rang the engineers on another line so that the call could be traced.

Straightening her dress, Mrs Duke would advance resolutely

on the shrilling telephone, square her elbows and lift the receiver, holding her face back stiffly from it as if it were a pan full of spitting sausages. 'Hullo?' cautiously.

And then when it was her sister, or a friend, or the laundry calling about the missing sheet, she would gasp a laugh and collapse on to the settee, blowing out her stored-up breath, while the voice at the other end cackled: 'Are you there? Who am I speaking to? *Hul*-lo!'

'Just getting my breath.' Elaborate smiles at Veronica and mouthings: *It's all right.* 'I ran in from the back door.' Mrs Duke was not going to tell anyone, even her sister, about the terrible ordeal of Ronnie. This was an inner family secret, with only the police trusted, like priests or doctors.

Once when Veronica was alone in the flat while her mother was shopping on a Saturday, the telephone began to ring. She looked at it. It squatted on the fragile end table by the sofa and looked at her. Veronica let it ring. When it stopped, she got up and went to get a glass of water. The palms of her hands were sweating where she had held them clenched and her mouth was dry.

As she was coming back from the kitchen, the telephone rang again. Be a man, Ronnie, she told herself in the words with which her father used to encourage her when she was afraid of the surf at Marazion. It's probably Fred. He knows you're home. That's why he's ringing again.

She stood over the telephone with her hand stretched down towards it. She remembered the voice very clearly, and word for word, tone for tone, some of the things it had said. When those things came into her mind – unbidden, for she tried to keep them out – her body remembered how it had begun to feel. The disgust and then the treacherous stir of excitement. Like a little extra heart beating. . . .

She stood stiffly with her eyes on the clock, while the bell rang on into the silence. It rang for a minute and a half. Fred would never have the patience to wait that long. Rot *her*, he would say, and either get on to the Lambretta and swing down through Regent's Park to see what she was up to, or go and do whatever he wanted to do by himself. Her hand went down, touched the receiver, its cold smoothness fitted into her fingers.

She lifted it quickly and whispered: 'Yes?' on a held-in breath, and as she said it, there was a click and the dialling tone began.

Arthur Sears sneaked with his clever sideways twist into a telephone box at Shepherd's Bush. Always a different one. That was the way. But they all smelled the same. From long habit, he pressed Button B in case any pennies would come out, then took the black notebook out of the inside pocket of his green jacket.

He glanced over his shoulder to make sure there was no one outside, and just in case, he flipped through the pages non-chalantly, like a businessman checking his contacts. Breathing more heavily, he ran his eye down the list of telephone numbers he had copied from the cards in the glass case outside Mrs Angel's shop. Sheila. Done her. Dead loss. Polish or something balmy. Try the Bust 40. Good lead in there. And she'd talk for a while. The brasses always did, if they could speak the Queen's English, trying to get you to come round.

Come up and see me some time. Arthur laughed that inside laugh that didn't show, dialling. No answer. What was the use of advertising your number all over Cottingham Park and then not answering. Filthy tramp. Out somewhere with some poor bloke who – Arthur dialled again viciously, with a chewed pencil. His thick fingers were clumsy in the holes. Oh well. No loss. It didn't scare that kind like it did ...

Veronica. That was her stupid name. Her telephone number was not in his book. Take no chances, Arthur. All the angles, boy. And her old man was in the phone book. Right here in the little cave under the shiny shelf, waiting for him. A to D. Not yet though. Not too soon again. Keep it for later. If you did it too often to one girl, you were asking for the bogies, and Arthur Sears, he, Arthur Sears, was The Man They Never Caught. Come and get me. The Beast of Cottingham Park. The Scourge. Once, he had shown himself to a girl in the Underground late at night. Had to travel miles out into the suburbs before they were alone in the carriage. She was sitting opposite him in one of those sets of four seats, reading. Arthur had an evening paper on his lap. He coughed, she looked up, and he moved the newspaper. She jumped up with her face all ghosty and went to stand by the door until the next station, and bet your life got off before it was her stop, and half an hour between trains that time of night. *Terrified*, she'd been.

He poised his pencil over the dial again. The redhead? Paris model? Parlie voo, mamzel? Voolie voo – what was it the troops

126

said? Arthur had never been with a girl, and did not intend to if he could stay clear. There were other ways of making love.

May Wilson had sent the man and the children and the dog and the two curious clucking neighbours in curlers out of the stuffy little bedroom, and now she was alone with the woman who was struggling and gasping on the bed and crying on the names of all her gods.

They were not alone for long. May was still turned away, setting up the Cyprane inhaler by the woman's damp restless head, when they were joined by a baby boy, arriving unexpectedly with a yell when he discovered where his journey had led him.

'Surprised me, that did.' May laughed contentedly, working with mechanical ease on the mother and her slippery child. This was the part she always liked best, after it was over, busy and joking if the mother was all right, the two of them rewarded by the presence of the third. Mission accomplished, everything safe.

Not that she was afraid of deliveries. She had lost count long ago of how many successful ones she had done, and you could always get a doctor to come in a pinch. But still, she would rather have the baby out than in any day, and so would the mothers.

'He's a whopper,' she said proudly, holding up the screaming bundle after it was wrapped. 'Nice of him to let you off so lightly, wasn't it?'

'If you can't get off lightly with your seventh,' the woman said, in that drained, exhausted voice they all had until they picked up a bit and started telling their families what to do again, 'you might as well be dead.'

May looked at her. Poor soul. She did not look half as pleased as May did over this nine-pound squashed tomato who had come like a gentleman, giving no trouble. It was automatic to give the babies to the mothers to hold as soon as the necessary things had been done, but for some reason she found herself asking: 'Want to hold him, dear?'

'Oh . . .' the woman turned her head away for a moment as if she were going to cry, then turned it back again on the flaccid pillow and looked with deep eyes at May standing by the bed with the professionally swaddled infant. 'Poor little devil,' she said. 'Perhaps it's best I don't.'

'Why not?' May frowned. 'You're not infectious. That cold you had is quite cleared up.'

'It's not that, Nurse. I wasn't going to tell you, because I thought I wasn't going to mind, but I do mind now, a bit. 'Aving 'im suddenly gone out of me like that – well it makes – it makes you feel empty.'

'But now you can really hold him properly.' May bent down to the bed that was too low to work with, as most of them were. You could always tell a District Nurse by her shins black and blue from iron bed frames. She put the baby under the woman's shoulder, where her arm lay limply outside the blanket. 'There!' she said, as she always did. 'There's a pretty picture!'

But the woman did not bend her arm to hold the child. She did not even look down at him. 'I'm giving 'im away,' she said flatly. 'It was all decided long ago when I first found I was carrying again. I can't . . .' her tired eyes filled with tears. She was only thirty, May knew, but she looked middle-aged. 'First the strike, and then Jack getting turned off only three weeks after they went back. It's too much. I can't do with any more. The kid will get a better deal from someone else.'

'But you could manage. Don't you get Relief? Your husband will find work. You *can't* give him away. How can you, now you've seen him?' It seemed bad enough to have decided in cold blood to give away your child, but to go through with it after he was born, a real someone. 'Oh, you can't!'

'Don't make it worse, dear. I've had it all said to me. My mam played war with me. Don't you start now. It's all fixed up.'

'I'm sorry,' May said. She did not know what to say. Washing her hands in the enamel basin, collecting her things, looking round the room to see if there was anything else she had to do, her heart was crying out in distress. To give away a baby when it was legitimate! If only she could take the child herself. Shut up, you fool, she told herself in her mother's voice. Spinsters aren't allowed to adopt. But May could have loved him as he was meant to be loved, worked for him, made it up to him for the dreadful injustice of being rejected as soon as he was born.

Why do you start these things, she wanted to ask, if you can't carry them through? But that was not her business. She was not supposed to know about things like that; could only guess, from things some of the women said, at the demands and desires. We was having a bit of fun, see . . . 'E come at me . . . It's always like that on a Friday . . .

The door opened without a knock, and the woman's husband,

128

sheepish, unshaven, stepped in, ducking his head under the low lintel. 'I heard the little beggar yell. Another girl? Boy is it, eh? The kids want to come up and take a look. All right?'

The woman shook her head. 'Best not. You know how they carry on.'

'Let's see the little devil.' He came up to the bed awkwardly on tiptoe as if this were a strange room and not his bedroom where he had proved his manhood so many times that a child had to be given away like a superfluous kitten. 'Poor little tyke,' he said sentimentally, touching the baby's head. 'Seems a shame, don't it? You think we –'

His weakening strengthened her weakness. 'No, Jack. Don't ask me. I told you. I can't do it.'

He shrugged his shoulders and straightened up. 'All right, all right. I only thought. . . .' E's a big one though, aren't you, cock? What shall we call him?'

'I don't want to name him,' the woman said stonily, her lips stiff and bloodless. 'I don't want nothing to do with him.'

Nonplussed, the man asked May, as an afterthought: 'Everything all right, Nurse? My wife all right?'

'She's done very well.' There was nothing that May could say to help, so she said: 'I'll be running along then. I'll be back tomorrow, dear, to see to you both.'

'There'll only be one of us tomorrow,' the woman said. 'Jack, I want you to go round to the Society first thing and 'ave 'im taken.'

'No rush,' he said uncomfortably. 'I'd keep him a while if I was you.'

'No.'

He screwed up his stubbled face. 'I don't understand you,' he said, and the woman said: 'I daresay not,' and turned her head away and closed her eyes.

At the door, May sought through her resources for some friendly quip that would cheer things up. None came, so she went out of the room and down the dark stairs to the ground floor, where three or four dirty, half-clothed children clamoured at her and pulled at her dress and ran shouting after her bicycle as she rode away down the deserted street.

Another of her babies was due that night. Overdue. If it did not come tonight, she was going to have to hurry it along, but from the looks of the mother when May had stopped in that afternoon, she should be getting the agitated telephone call or the panting, self-important messenger before morning. She might go along anyway and have a look, but it would be a shame to wake the woman if she was asleep, and the husband was a big black excitable African who frightened May. She did not want to have to talk to him without the small shrill presence of the wife to control him.

Best to go home and get a cup of tea and lie down in her underclothes, and just as she got to sleep, her mother would come upstairs in her cotton dressing-gown and wake May roughly in a fright to get her own back for having been woken herself by the basement telephone.

The moon was high above the chimneys, sailing in and out of thin clouds at a great speed. Edges of white buildings, a puddle by a blocked drain, a strip of stainless steel on a shop front gave back the stunning light for a moment and then were flat again and nothing in the yellow lamplight. Pedalling down a long street of closed shops with padlocked cigarette machines and drifts of paper round their doors, May saw a man stop and hold up a newspaper when the moon rode into a clear patch. When he got home, he would say: 'The moon was so bright, you could read by it.'

Must see about getting that extension. The Association would not pay for more than one instrument. If you chose to live in a tall terrace house where your bedroom was miles away from your living quarters, that was your lookout. But it would be worth paying the extra herself so that she could switch the phone through to her bedroom at night and be able to go out in peace when she was on call without her mother making a grievance about every baby that wanted to be born.

Was it worth it though, if the house was to come down like a pile of bricks, which it was? Better wait and see what was to happen before she made the outlay. Old penny wise, pound foolish, her mother called her, which might have been true if she had been foolish with the pounds.

It was late when May got home, and the house in Faulkner Road was dark, except for the window of the first-floor front where Constantine Porter was studying. Mrs Wilson complained sometimes to her family about the amount of electricity burned, but she did not say anything to Mr Porter. Not because she was sympathetic to his studies, but because she was not going to

130

give a handle to anyone who wanted to say that she discriminated against the coloured. In discussions with her neighbours or at the club where she and Mr Wilson played cards every Wednesday, she would counter the stand-by question: 'Ah, but would you let your daughter marry one of them?' with: 'Why not? They're 'uman beings, same as we are.' But Constantine Porter fortunately had not put her idealism to the test by proposing to May.

Sometimes when May was late home, she would take him a cup of tea and they would talk softly for a moment in the doorway of his room, for May would never step inside, and he never asked her. She would take him up a cup tonight and perhaps tell him about the baby who was to be given away. She was still so upset about this that she had to tell someone, and he might understand. She would tell him: 'When you're a doctor, don't you ever let any of your mothers do that, Mr Porter?' Doctors had that power over their patients, especially the women. Nurses did not.

But after she had carried her bicycle down the area steps and was in the kitchen talking impatiently to the kettle, her mother appeared in the pink cotton wrapper with her hair in a net. Mr Porter would have to go without his tea, because she would want to know where May was going with the extra cup.

'You woke me up, clattering on the steps,' Mrs Wilson said, although she did not look swollen-eyed, with the sleep grease coming out on her long nose, but alert as if she had been waiting up. 'Baby get born?'

'Yes. I almost wish it hadn't.'

'Why? Was it deformed? Oh, don't tell me.' Mrs Wilson was squeamish, although if ever there was something dreadful and May told her, she would listen all ears, even while she was saying: How can you? and Don't talk about it.

'It was a lovely baby. Popped out all in a flash, like the big ones do sometimes.'

Mrs Wilson made a face. Sometimes May wondered how she ever stomached giving birth to her. 'But, Mum, it was' – no use telling her because she was only half listening, but here goes anyway, better than talking to yourself, like Miss Beade with that cat – 'it was so dreadfully sad.' The woman's stony face, not letting herself love the baby, the misery and guilt in the little room, with the sleeping child, the cause of it all, the only one who could not feel it.

May tried to show it to her mother, and Mrs Wilson did listen, but she licked her lips quickly and said: 'Bit of a scandal though. I read something like that in the paper. Some woman wanted to give away her baby and they had scores of offers for it. Why don't you call the *Express* and tell them about it? They might put your name in.'

'Mum, how can you? The poor woman is unhappy enough without being made a public spectacle.'

'Don't be daft.' To Mrs Wilson, it was enviable to get your name in the paper, whatever the cause. 'The neighbours will know all about it anyway in a street like Maynard Place.'

'Oh dear. I hope not. It seems so sad. Do you know, I wished I could have taken the baby. Almost I could have picked him up and brought him home with me tonight.'

May spoke dreamily, trying to share her vision, but her mother said briskly: 'Kidnapping now, is it? If you want a baby as much as all that, why don't you marry some man and have one? You'll soon find out how much of a pleasure a baby is.'

'Yes, Mum, perhaps I will,' May said patiently.

'Though I'm sure I don't know how, since you never go anywhere or meet anyone, and if you did you'd scare him off with your funny ways.' Mrs Wilson laughed to show that she was not being unkind. 'You don't seem to have got far with that Arthur Sears, though you've been trying hard enough.'

'Mum, I haven't!' The blush came up May's neck to spread like fire over her jawbone, pricking up under her eyes. Her hand shook as she poured out her tea.

'Ah, ha-ah!' Mrs Wilson sing-songed lightly. 'Someone's blush-shing! Your mother knows what goes on in that funny old head. What's the matter? Too nervous to offer your poor little mother a cup of tea?'

May swallowed hard and thought quickly about ice . . . glaciers, eskimos, riding a bicycle in winter without gloves. She could sometimes push down the blush that way and control her breathing, which was apt to let her down, like an asthmatic. 'At this time of night? You always say it keeps you awake.'

'Don't tell me what to do. I'm not one of your patients. I'll take a cup, to celebrate.'

'Celebrate?' May said stupidly. What was her mother trying to get at now? 'About that poor little baby?'

'Heavens, are we to hear nothing else but that all night? If you'd been home this evening instead of pedalling about like a mad thing when I don't believe it was even your night on duty you'd have heard what I heard. I got it from Mrs Crocker. Her son told her. He hears everything, naturally.' As the driver of a large rumbling vehicle which sprayed water on the road and swept it with a revolving brush, Mrs Crocker's son was the eyes of the Town Hall. 'It's all to go, he says, from the Antelope corner *up to here*.'

'This house? Oh, Mum, I know you and Dad won't like to move, but this street's not what it was anyway, and I must say, in a way I –'

'Who's talking about moving? There will be a cleaving,' Mrs Wilson said dramatically. 'Right through.' She swept the side of her hand down like a knife blade. 'We'll be the end house, that's what they're saying. Us and Crocker's across the street. They'll make good the wall, of course, between us and next door.' She made a pinched face to go with talking about her rights. 'They'll have to do that. But we'll be here standing, while all else falls!'

She drank her tea thirstily, holding the cup with both hands and raising both little fingers, her eyes gleaming over the rim at May.

'Well, not really all else – only about half of Faulkner Road.'

'How much do you want, old dunderhead? Do you want to be thrown out in the street without so much as a how d'ye do?'

'Oh, I'd take my how d'ye do with me.' May joked to hide her silly feeling of disappointment that it was true. Reg Crocker was usually right, for all his swank.

So they were not going to have to move. Oh well. She had never believed they would, not really, and it would have been hard to give up her district, especially after that successful argument with the superintendent who had wanted to switch her to another section. When you were a midwife, it was difficult to transfer, because there was always someone counting on you being there months ahead.

Well, but this would at least make a change. The outlook would be different from the end of a row instead of in the middle. The road would be a cul-de-sac with their house blanked off and just a drop into space where the Mortons used to be. May would be able to look sideways out of her bedroom window at the wonderful new road and see the cars going home from the West End and the lorries roaring out into the night. It would not be like living in dull old Faulkner Road any more.

'Like on a cliff,' she said aloud. 'Like living on a cliff.'

'Nonsense. It will be like living in a house and nothing more. But I'm glad of one thing. When they start demolishing, I'll be able to see into the Mortons' at last.'

Everywhere you went now in Cottingham Park it was the same. People talking, speculating, grumbling, pontificating, passing on crackpot rumours.

I hear they're going to start next month.

They've already pulled down some of them houses behind the old brewery. Found a live bomb under the pavement. It isn't right, you know.

It will take five years, they say, before anything happens.

The district will be ruined. Why do they pick on us?

Bloody good thing to get rid of some of these slums. Should have been done years ago.

What will you do? Will it get you?

It'll cut my journey north by half an hour. But are we going to be able to get to the thing?

It's a crime, I told him. That's what I said. I said: I say it's a crime I said.

Some people, like the old flower woman who sat by her three-tiered stand of summer colour and smiled at nothing, said that it was nice to have a little excitement once in a while.

'Move me? They may do, dear. I shan't complain. Someone will see that I'm looked after.'

Some people, like Zlotnik and son who sat on fake Louis Seize chairs outside their secondhand shop with hats tilted in the August sun, said that the whole thing was only a dream. They would never actually get around to building the road, so why get excited?

'The only thing that would excite you,' Martha Banning's husband said, 'would be if someone managed to dig their way into your shop and discovered that you had something worth selling under all that junk.'

'Hark at the man talk.' Zlotnik junior laughed merrily. 'He thinks we've lost that chair we had for re-caning.'

'I know damn well you have. I gave it you six months ago.'

'Six months . . . six weeks . . . six days.' The old man Zlotnik spread his hands. 'So what is the difference? We'll get to it.'

Some people, like Mrs Angel at the newspaper shop, were

already so excited about the Expressway that if they kept the pressure up like this they would have a stroke long before the first brick was knocked off the first doomed building.

'I'm getting out,' Mrs Angel told everybody. 'Don't think I'm going to sit here and see my home, my very living, knocked away from underneath my feet, because I'm not. We've given the best years of our lives to serving Cottingham Park, and this is how they reward us. Come up to this corner one day soon, Mrs Banting, and you'll find that we've pulled up our tents like the Arabs.'

'That right?' Martha Banning asked Mr Angel, as he gave her her cigarettes and change. 'Are you really going so soon?'

'She says so.' His eyes flickered sideways and he smiled the secret reptilian smile that showed no teeth.

'Take my tip,' his wife said, 'and get out while the getting's good. Whether they pull down your house or not, this neighbourhood isn't going to be worth the price of a packet of Weights once they get started.'

'I was born here,' Martha said. 'They aren't going to get me out so easily.'

'I was born here too,' Bernadette said, the top of her dark head on a level with the counter; but Mrs Angel was sounding off to someone else, and Bernie's elder sister rounded on her with contradictory venom: 'You weren't. You were born at St Mary's. No one gets born at home these days.'

'They do.' Bernie stuck out her tongue. 'Billy Few's baby sister did. All the kids went up to have a look.'

'Perhaps,' Guy said, as they walked down West Hill, with the children running ahead like dogs, 'it is time for us to leave here and go to some charming suburb where the girls could make some new friends.'

Martha took his arm. In heels, she was the same height as he was. 'We'll go if you want,' she said guilelessly.

'I know that docile bit. It's when you mean to get your own way. You'd hate to move, wouldn't you, love? If they wanted to drive their road through 66 Armstrong Avenue, they'd have to drive it through your heart.'

And that was true. It was true. This was her world. Her own place. Her fitted envelope of atmosphere.

Martha could not imagine herself anywhere else, could not see what kind of a person she would be away from this town within a town that had become her own; this queer conglomerate corner of London that had grown from the simplicity of a feudal village into a teeming cosmopolis where all imaginable kinds of people pursued all manner of lives in every possible way.

Was Cottingham Park to die then, with the knife blade of the callous highway thrust through its heart? Or would it stubbornly survive, closing round the edges of the wound, absorbing the bold new infection imperceptibly into its own character, so that in the end it would be still the same inimitable Cottingham Park where anything might happen, anyone might live?

Part Two

IN a sizeable but sunless flat in St John's Wood, Mrs Robert
P. V. Peregrine was preparing supper. It took her a long time to
do this, since she could not walk; but the kitchen was arranged so
that she could reach everything from her chair, and she wheeled
herself back and forth from vegetable bins to chopping board, to
refrigerator, to stove, to sink, to garbage pail, her slim rubber
wheels making for her the myriad picayune journeys of other
women's feet.

When the food was in the oven, she wheeled herself down to
her bedroom at the other end of the flat. She combed her short
boyish hair and touched up her face, which she hated because it
was a cripple's face – pinched and colourless, with frown lines
on the narrow forehead and pain lines from nose to chin. It was
unfair that the lines had come, because she always made a point
of trying to smile and look serene, but every time she went into
hospital for one of the various disorders which assailed her
useless body, the lines were etched a little more sharply when she
came out.

She trundled back to the drawing-room, made a skilful half
turn between an armchair and the cocktail cabinet, and was
measuring gin into a martini jug when she heard her husband's
whistle in the hall.

Robert Peregrine came in quickly, with the slightly anxious
expression that he always wore when he came hurrying to find
her, as if he expected her one day to be not there.

'But where would I go?' she asked him. 'I couldn't get
very far in the chariot, and I can't even get into a taxi without
you.'

'I worry about you.' He bent to kiss her. She had been injured
in the Blitz as a schoolgirl, and he had known when he married
her what their life together would be. He was sometimes cynical
about his job at County Hall, but there had never been any
bitterness or regret about being tied to a woman whom he either
had to push or carry. A nurse came in every day during the week,
but when Robert was at home he performed tenderly for

Georgette all those duties which the average person who has never cared for a paraplegic prefers not to think about.

'There was a woman at the hearing today,' he said, 'with a small boy in a wheelchair – brought the poor little kid all the way from Cottingham Park to County Hall because she couldn't resist the opportunity to protest publicly about something. You know the kind. It turned out after she'd sounded off her horrible mouth for ten minutes that she hadn't got a grievance at all, because the road won't go anywhere near her flats. Someone told her politely to sit down and shut up, and she took it out on the kid. I saw her. She shoved him around. She bumped him down the steps outside the hall hard enough to bring his teeth out of the top of his head. I watched him being wheeled away absolutely at her mercy, and it made me start to worry about you. Am I nice enough to you? I never know. Is it good enough for you to live with a desiccated old civil servant?'

'Silly,' she said. 'I spend half my time worrying about what kind of a life it is for you with me.'

'We're both silly.' One side of his face twitched as it always did just before he smiled. 'I love you.'

'I love you too,' she said, and they looked into each other's faces for a moment with complete understanding.

'I forgot the ice,' Georgette said. He did not go to fetch it, nor even ask whether she would like him to. Georgette's mother, who had tried to make a helpless baby of her before she married, thought that Robert was inconsiderate. She did not know that to help cripples to do those things which they can still do for themselves is worse than no help at all.

'How was the hearing any way?' Georgette asked when she came back with the bowl of ice in her lap. 'Was anything said that could alter the plans?'

'What a hope,' he said. 'It's much too late anyway. With a major scheme like this, it's only a formality, the hearing, so that nobody can say they didn't have a chance to stand up and say: "You can't do this to me."'

'Did many people stand up?'

'A few. That ugly woman I told you about. There's always one of her at all these things. There were one or two rather pathetic people with genuine objections but not enough nerve or vocabulary to make it clear what the trouble was. Oh, the usual collection of cranks. Some sort of beatnik character with a beard

138

and a lot of spit. And a rather sweet bunch of old dears who've started a society for the preservation of something or other.'

'Those nice old houses where we walked that day. The Scotneys, they call it. They've been writing letters to the *Sunday Times*. Will it get them anywhere?'

'It might, if this country were really as whimsically concerned with individual rights as foreigners think it is. I liked their pluck though. For two pins I'd have stood up and cheered them on myself. I talked to some of the Press boys afterwards. They'll try and squeeze in some neat little stories that will get the old ducks a bit of sympathy. Jack Clew will love that. He always says I'm a spy from the enemy camp.'

'Well, we got a good Press anyway,' Mrs Vulliamy said, putting the bunch of clippings back untidily into Mr Davenport's neatly labelled folder. Since the Scotney Society had briskened her life to some purpose, she had taken to using quite go-ahead expressions. 'I would feel sorry for us if I wasn't me.'

'Oh, the dailies.' Her sister gave the dredging sniff with which she saluted even an implied reference to Lord Beaverbrook. 'Who believes what they say?'

'A lot of people do, Jessie.'

'Only fools like you who are gullible.'

'Now ladies. Now ladies. You'll have to come to order.' Mr Davenport tapped his pipe gently on the edge of his desk. 'Don't let the meeting get out of hand.'

The Scotney Society was meeting in Mr Davenport's study, the inner sanctum, all thick carpet and leather-topped furniture and prize editions of books which looked as though they had been read. Mr Davenport sat by the desk with his domed head shining yellow and his Siamese cat crouched motionless by his elbow like an ornament.

Martha was sitting by the window where she could look down at the pretty street when she got bored. She had gone there because she had promised the old ladies that she would. They were so enthusiastic about the Society, and it was never going to get them anywhere. The polite disinterest at the public hearing had made that quite clear.

Martha had joined because they had asked her, and because she was on their side. It had seemed better to join in with even this feeble attempt to stop the rape of Cottingham Park than merely to wring her hands and watch it happen. But she was becoming rapidly discouraged with the Scotney Society, with its primly outraged letters and its blurred bulletins. None of the other members had turned up this afternoon – there was nowhere for them to sit if they had – and most of them had never done any more than pay their subscriptions and give permission for the Society to speak in their name. True, Mrs Estredge had stood up at the hearing, after Mr Davenport had put nearly everyone to sleep with his dusty historiology, but all she had done was rave about her Georgian staircase.

The Society's objections were all too narrow and eclectically personal, of no use at all except for those quaint little half-patronizing stories in the papers which had so pleased Mrs Vulliamy and Mr Davenport. They did not care about Cottingham Park. All they cared about was trying to preserve their own tiny corner of picturesque gentility. Martha cared about the threat to the whole neighbourhood. Her life was here, her youth, her marriage, integrated with the grey crowded streets and all the shabby landmarks. She wanted to preserve this part of her own self, and with it the worst of Cottingham Park as well as the best. Whether the Scotney Society soldiered gallantly on or fiddled itself into oblivion, Martha did not think she would take part in its affairs much longer.

And then there was Zona. If belonging to the society meant rubbing shoulders with her, it was better to fade out while you still had your health and reason.

Zona was Mr Davenport's thirty-year-old daughter, his despair and his scourge. The project of the Transurban Expressway had given them the first grounds on which they had met in agreement for years. Zona did not care two straws about the Scotneys. As far as she was concerned she would be content to see the whole archaic lot knocked down, and make her pad in a concrete hut with a tin roof. Her father had not even mentioned the Scotney Society to her because he knew that she would jeer, but to his great surprise, he had seen her sitting with that appalling fellow with the wet beard and the duffel coat two rows behind him at the public inquiry: on his side for the first time in her life because the flyover which was to carry the Expressway over Park Road would eliminate the Abracadabra coffee bar, the nerve centre of Zona's set.

When Zona slouched into the study to see what her father was up to, Martha changed her seat on the pretext of wanting to talk to Miss Sutcliffe. The only other vacant chair was next to the one where Martha had been sitting, and whatever you thought of Zona's brain or beliefs or morals, there was one excellent reason for not sitting next to her in a small room. She smelt.

Her hair and her skin smelt and her clothes smelt, all for the same reason. They were not washed often enough. Her hair hung to her shoulders, unkempt; not casually windblown, but limp and straggling into her eyes, like the floor mop of a British Railways cleaner dumped at random on her scalp. She wore a pair of greasy black jeans, ending tightly in the middle of her hairy calf and creased into hard folds behind the knee, a torn brown sweater like a feed sack and a man's jacket with the sleeves hanging loose. Sometimes she wore sandals. Today her long flat feet were bare, the toenails bruised and broken. Her face was sullen and heavy; sallow, with thick lips and pale unfriendly eyes.

Zona's appearance was nothing new. She had been like this for a long time. She was the original weirdie, the prototype of all the lank-haired, tight slacks and sloppy sweater brigade who had materialized in these last few years to form a cult, if not a culture. Colourless in face and clothes, with grimy nails and an attitude towards free love at once furtive and defiant, they worshipped strange music glumly in floodlit cellars; lay on the floor in Earl's Court rooms listening to sick, off-beat songs on expensive gramophones until the dawn crept smokily up behind the minarets of the Imperial Institute; exchanged lovers and thought impulses and beatnik California slang, slightly mis-applied, in uncomfortably furnished espressos like the Abra-cadabra, which meant so much to Zona that she was even willing to talk about it for five minutes to her father and his ghastly friends.

'If the Abracadabra goes,' she said, falling into a chair with her stomach and her legs and her lower lip stuck out, 'I might as well be dead.'

'Don't talk nonsense,' said Miss Sutcliffe, who had known her from childhood and was not impressed.

'But it *means* to us,' Zona said, not looking at her, to no one in particular. 'Like it's one of the only places where we can be ourselves. So this means nothing?'

'They will build you another café, dear,' Mrs Vulliamy said, too intimidated by the faroucheness of Zona to remember the

141

motto of the Scotney Society, Queen Victoria's *We are not interested in the possibilities of defeat.* ...

'It's not a café,' Zona jeered. 'You don't dig me, anyway. Like it's the principle. You heard what Roger said at the hearing. We demand the right to live our lives in our own way.'

'No one is trying to stop you that I can see,' her father said, averting his eyes as she began to pick at her nails. 'I gave up long ago, for one. I don't ask where you go or what you do. I let you use my house as a hotel. What more do you want?'

'We want no persecution,' Zona said darkly, looking out with gall from under her matted fringe. 'Are you going to back us or not?'

'We'll back anyone who's against the road, of course,' her father began equitably, but Miss Sutcliffe, sitting very straight, interrupted: 'This society is not formed for the preservation of immoral nightspots, Zona, and you know it. I suggest you go away and brush your hair and let us get on with our meeting.'

'Egad, Miss Jessie.' Zona got up and looked slackly round, hunching the sagging jacket about her shoulders as if she were cold. 'Why formed then?'

'To preserve the irreplaceable beauties of the area,' Miss Sutcliffe enunciated. 'Do you realize that if this – this thing goes through, you and your father will have to look out of these windows every day and see, beyond the gables and greenery of my house, an eighteen-storey office building and possibly two twelve-storey blocks of hideous modern flats?'

'Why look?' said Zona rudely. She went to the door, swearing as she knocked her naked toe against the claw of a small table. 'Roger's waiting. We're going down to Battersea Bridge to swim.'

'Who's Roger?' Martha asked when she had gone out, leaving the door open so that they could hear her feet going flop, flop, flop down the paintwork at the side of the stair carpet.

'Her latest.' Mr Davenport glanced at the old ladies. 'A platonic friendship. Oh quite. They say that they are brother and sister, a reincarnation of a family in ancient Egypt, I understand. He has a share in an antique shop in Fulham, and Zona helps to take care of their stall in the Portobello Road market on Saturdays. A job of a kind, at least. Well, it won't last. Shall we proceed?'

He was going to read them a long letter which he had drafted

142

to the National Trust, his latest hope. There looked like three pages of typescript, perhaps more. Martha looked at her watch and feigned amazement at the time. She made her excuses, and Aunt Jessie said: 'You're such a busy woman, Martha. It's kind of you to spare us even this much of your time.'

Mrs Vulliamy came quickly out of the room behind Martha, and took her arm in the white panelled passage that ran like a gallery above the entrance hall. 'I told them I'd forgotten to give you your monthly bulletin.' She whispered, although no one was about and the closed door behind them was thick. 'I wanted to tell you. I heard from Anne.'

She was smiling and wagging her head delightedly, as she reached through the clutter of a pot-bellied handbag. 'I must have forgotten to bring it, and I wanted you to see it. It was a birthday card. All quilted satin, with embossed violets, scented even. The most beautiful card I have ever had. I didn't dare show it to Jessie, because she's still – you know. . . . But I did want to tell you.'

'I am glad. How is Anne? I've written twice to that address you gave me, but she hasn't answered. Did she say anything on the card?'

'Well, not exactly. She didn't even put her name, as a matter of fact, but she knows I don't know anyone else in New York.' Mrs Vulliamy seemed to be having some difficulty in closing her bag. She was giving it all her attention, keeping her face down away from Martha. 'No . . . she didn't say anything. But' – she raised her head, and the wagging smile was back – 'the card was more than enough. So much loving thought in the choosing!'

Downstairs in the hall, Martha glanced through an open door into the dining-room and saw Zona and a youthless young man with a beard and heavy duffel coat (if it was warm enough to swim in the river at Battersea, why was it cold enough for the duffel?) standing by the sideboard drinking Mr Davenport's whisky out of port glasses.

*

Neither Mrs Saithe nor any of her fellow-villagers from Armstrong Mews had gone to the public hearing, although they had all talked about going, right up to the last minute when it was too late to go anyway.

Their defiance sounded stoutly convincing when it was batted

143

back and forth from door to door across the cobbles of the mews. Better to keep it that way than to risk it in public.

Even Lewis Bassett, who was as much of a leader as anyone could be in this tight little community where all thought themselves as good as the next, had missed the opportunity to air his voice about detours and the rights of individual citizens.

When he was told afterwards: 'We made sure you'd be there, Lewis,' he had replied, quoting his former employer the M.P.: 'Stand fast and keep your head. That's what I always say. No sense going up there and let those smart talkers make a monkey out of you.'

The Commie's woman, who had begun to be on speaking terms with most of the mews now that the existence of all of them was threatened, had given her opinion that Lewis Bassett was all gas and no guts; but the others accepted his excuse and believed him when he said that if they only sat tight nothing would happen, because that was what they wanted to believe.

Hadn't they been officially condemned as a slum now for over a year? And hadn't they been left alone because none of them would play the Council's game and pack up meekly and go? Passive resistance had worked all right with the Cottingham Borough Council, who had too many far worse slums to worry about, so why should it not work just as well with the L.C.C., who had a thousand buildings to knock down before they need bother about Armstrong Mews?

When the Inquiry Officer had arrived in the mews last August, they had not been rude to him, but they had not been polite either. He had come at supper time, because he was a conscientious man who would rather finish referencing the section assigned to him than go home on time. His reception, by slowly chewing men in shirtsleeves or flushed fat women blocking the doorway as if he were trying to sell them something, had been so discouraging that he had had to stop at the Lion afterwards for a bracer before he could face the Underground.

When the letters came offering purchase by agreement, some of the property owners had put them by without answering, because they hoped thereby to make the letters not exist. Those who replied had, on the advice of Lewis Standfast Bassett, said No in various ways. Mr and Mrs Gilbert Hubert – she white and he black as night and given to wearing a striped blanket on chilly evenings, were the only people who said Yes, but they did not count.

144

They had moved into the mews after the first count of residents because they had heard that it was going to take so long to complete that there would have to be a second one to keep it up to date. To be included in a recount of those likely to be displaced was a chance to get rehoused in a Council flat.

They had tried this once already in a tenement block which was going to be demolished under a slum clearance scheme, only to find themselves rehoused in a new tenement almost as bad, but both their horoscopes had been auspicious when they moved into the mews, so they hoped for better things.

The people of Armstrong Mews, though clannish, did not object to squatters like the Huberts, and though narrowly respectable, they did not actively object to the mixed marriage. Gilbert's actions, both marrying lighter and squatting, had been partly directed at paying off a few old scores against the law makers of Britain, and the mews was not going to condemn anyone who found a way to get his own back on the Government.

In the middle of that winter, when Gilbert Hubert took to his blanket for good and sent his pregnant wife out to work because he could not face the cold, the intimidating registered envelopes containing the Notice to Treat arrived for the householders who had refused to negotiate amicably for a sale.

'They got no right to do it,' protested Lewis Bassett, who had promised everyone all along that it would never come to this. 'They got no right to force us out of our homes.' But he protested with less conviction, for he and everyone else had known about the compulsory purchase order for some time, and now that the claim form had intruded into their homes with the offer of free advice from a Council surveyor or solicitor ('what's the use of asking help from anyone who's paid to be on their side?'), there was nothing to do but ask the highest price they dared and hope to make a good thing out of the violation of Armstrong Mews.

'If they don't like it, they know where they can put it,' Mrs Saithe told Eileen Kelly. 'A slum, that long-nosed man dared to say my house was. Officially condemned as a slum and as such only entitled to site value. "The rest of the mews may be a slum," I told him, "but I keep a decent place here."'

'That's what everyone told him, I daresay,' Eileen said, surprised at her own perception. 'Slum or not, don't ask me, because I've seen lots worse than this, but –'

'You've seen none better,' rapped Mrs Saithe, going back and

145

forth briskly in a narrow rocking chair that went click, click at each end of its arc.

'But it's cosy here, that's what I was going to say. Snugger than many.'

Eileen was in Mrs Saithe's kitchen, which was also her living-room. A good little fire burned behind the bars of the range. The dog slept before it in a basket, and Eileen was knitting, an occupation in which she had not indulged since she left the convent school.

Now that the evacuation of the mews had become a probability instead of an unlikely dream, she was not so sure that she wanted that council flat, even suppose she was lucky enough to be offered it. She knew what people were like. Not many were as tolerant as Mrs Saithe. How would it be to live in a great barracks of a place with a thousand other women all whispering against her behind their walls?

But then, looking at it soberly, where could a girl like her be placed? The old red brick maisonettes in Chapel Gate were swarming with Eileen's colleagues. She would not mind going there, because no one minded what went on, but Chapel Gate did not belong to the L.C.C., naturally, or it would not be swarming with girls.

'Maybe I'll go back to Ireland,' she mused, while her needles went a fast click, click – all her old skill was coming back – to the slower click, click of Mrs Saithe's chair.

'Pigs might fly,' said Mrs Saithe, who had heard this too often before.

'Well, I might. My people have a nice place there. I wish you could see the garden.'

'Fine. I'll go with you. Do me good to get a bit of luxury for a change.'

'Well, now, I don't know that you . . .' Eileen was disconcerted, as she was meant to be, for Mrs Saithe knew that her parents and sister lived in three rooms behind a run-down grocery at the end of a forlorn village.

Mrs Saithe laughed. 'Don't worry. I wouldn't go across that bit of sea if they paid me double. When you're in Ballygally whatever it is, I wouldn't be surprised to find myself still sitting on my bum in Armstrong Mews. Just let them spend a lot of money and get a lot of clowns into fancy jobs, and I wouldn't put it past them to drop this whole idea and start on something else.'

'Pigs might fly.' For an Irish girl, Eileen's vocabulary was limited, and she often copied what someone else had just said.

'You should know. In your country they keep them in the kitchen.'

They both laughed. There was no offence. They knew each other too well, and knew how far they could go. Toodie snored in his basket by the fire, and Mrs Saithe poked at him gently with her small slipper as she got up to move the kettle to the front of the range.

Outside, a storm threw dirty rain at the low steamed windows. Eileen was not going out for a night or two. She had been lucky last week. Fine nights and good business and double payment on Friday from a terrified young man who got it into his head that Eileen was going to tell his mother.

The stitches slipped along the needles with hypnotic ease, click, click. Mrs Saithe's chair clicked as she rocked gently back and forth waiting for the kettle to boil, and Eileen wished that time would stop and life not have to be faced, and that she could stay in Mrs Saithe's warm little mews house for ever.

*

On the last day of the last summer term at Abbot's Road Secondary Modern School, the last of all the terms that had muddled and shouted and wandered their way through those drably castellated grey walls for eighty years, Grace wore a bright red dress and big blue earrings the colour of a tropic sea.

'These draughty old buildings,' Mr Ferris murmured behind her when some of the bigger boys whistled as Grace came on to the platform to take her place with the rest of the staff at Assembly for the last time.

Mrs Bowden, square in brown with brown canvas brogues, frowned and flapped a hand towards the back rows in the hall, but Grace was glad about the whistles. At least it was something normal. Everyone had been so nervous and gloomy for the last few days that it seemed almost a relief to get the school finally closed up for good and the strain and the good-byes over.

That was why she had worn her most startling dress and the ear-rings whose colour exulted with her bright hair. Mr Rawlings had never told her to wear sober clothes to school, but normally she did, because the girls in her class were given to shrieking greens and electric blues, and since they always discussed Grace's outfit with her at some time during the day, she had tried to guide them into more restrained tastes.

Today, however, she had felt so miserable when she rolled out of bed on to the floor, trying to stab at the shrilling alarm in her little top-floor flat, that she had almost climbed back into bed and let the school close without her. The terrible good-byes. It was possible that she would never see anyone from the school ever again, even poor Denzil Raymond, for he was practical enough to find himself another girl to answer his searching questions about feminine customs, rather than track Grace down far out in the country.

Even Frankie Bott. Unless she asked him to stay with her some time. But you couldn't have a twelve-year-old ruffian to stay in a girls' school full of clear-voiced girls in grey pleated skirts and clean white blouses. And if she took him home to Cumberland this August, her mother would be frightened of him and lock up the silver at night.

She picked herself up from the floor, admired her nightdress briefly in the mirror inside the wardrobe door, which was hanging open, like all her drawers and cupboard doors, and went into the tiny bathroom not much larger than a cupboard itself in one corner of the kitchen, with plyboard walls that did not quite reach the ceiling. Only another foot or two of plyboard, that was all it would have taken; but the Meikles, who were so generous to Grace personally, had skimped and cut corners when their daughters left home to marry and they had converted their top floor.

'But then we didn't know you'd be our tenant, dear,' Mrs Meikle said. 'If I had known you were going to live here, I'd never have chosen that colour for the walls.'

'Who did you choose that mustard for?'

'Someone I hated. When the girls left, I thought I would hate having a stranger up there. Of course, I didn't know it would be you, and the yellow was being sold off cheap.'

Saying good-bye to the Meikles was going to be as bad as saying good-bye to everyone at the school. Do keep in touch. Be sure to write. Come and see us. Let's meet when you're in London. Both at the school and at the Meikles' these things would be said, trying to evade the finality of farewell with promises that it was not farewell. But when you left one world for another, you never did write more than once or twice. You so seldom went back. The meetings somehow never were arranged.

148

No time for a bath if she was not going to be late and let her class triumph as she panted in after them and slid behind her high teacher's desk only just before they banged and kicked their way behind theirs.

Oh, so you are going to the school? Well, what do you think I am – a coward?

Why that grey skirt then? Because it's raining. It won't be raining inside the school. Wear the red. Everyone else will behave like a funeral. You, Grace, you are the one who shall bring some brave colour to the day of sorrow.

Mr Rawlings was trying his best not to let it be a day of sorrow. He did not conduct Assembly any differently from the way he had been doing it for ten years. He strode quietly on to the platform, took his place in the middle of the row of staff, removed his glasses to quell the giggles and whispers and foot scrapings in the hall with a long look from under his thick eyebrows, re-placed the glasses and led the two short prayers, using his own sincere voice instead of the gabble or intoning wail with which most lay people pray in public.

The staff and the school sat down, and Mr Rawlings read out some quite ordinary announcements about being sure not to leave any personal possessions behind in desk or cloakroom, and the result of last week's collection for UNICEF. Then he paused and took a breath. Grace looked down at her feet. This was the moment she had been dreading. This was going to be it. Denzil Raymond, sitting beside her, sneaked her a glance and then looked down at his own suède feet to show her that he felt terrible too.

'I wish I could think of something to say to all of you,' the Headmaster said. 'But it seems that there is nothing left to say.'

With her red-gold head still lowered, Grace looked out and down at the boys and girls on the rows of folding chairs in the square hall, battered from so many years of all-purpose use by so many children. The school had never sat so quietly. Even the larger boys at the back, some of whom already looked like men of a kind, and many of whom knew something about a police court and almost all there was to know about girls, were not lounging there with detached grins, making signs with their fingers or moving their great unwieldy feet about.

They were lounging, because that was the only way they could sit, but they were listening to Mr Rawlings and most of them were looking at him, not sliding their eyes around to see on what diversion their restlessness could fasten.

'I have talked with each one of you alone.' The Head had taken every single boy and girl into his study by themselves for at least five minutes during the last month. 'And I think that we said the important things to each other then. They were important to me.' He paused and looked at them, his dark bony head slightly forward and his long arms hanging in a simian stance. 'The only thing I want to say now,' he went on, sending his words very carefully out into the hall, 'is that those things you said to me when we had our last talk together are perhaps the most important things that have ever been said to me during the ten years I have been at your school.'

The children looked surprised. Some of them glanced at each other, making a face, wondering what they could possibly have said that would be important to Mr Rawlings.

'Having said good-bye to all of you, I'll only say now just – thank you.'

A girl let off a giggle. A boy behind her said audibly: 'Can it, Doreen.' The Headmaster smiled and shook his head, and the tension was broken.

It was going to be all right. Grace could look up now. She wasn't going to cry out there on the platform in front of everybody. Mrs Purdie at the bronchial harmonium tried out a few pensive chords and everyone stood up, the smaller ones jostling each other, some of the big boys stretching and yawning as if they had been sitting still for an hour.

It was just like any other day. It was going to be all right. And it would have been all right if Mrs Purdie had not upset everything with her choice of the hymn.

Abide with me, sung by a large number of people, is likely to unman anybody, whether in Trafalgar Square on Armistice Day or in a football stadium in the rain before a cup final. Sung by a hundred and fifty vigorous young cockney voices filling all the space between the cracked and peeling walls, the impudent faces strangely solemn with the pleasure of noisy song, it was too much for Grace.

'I say, Miss,' Darlene Archer called out in her piercing Cries of Old London voice, 'you didn't half bawl.'

'I didn't really. It was just that –'

150

'So did poor old Uncle Oswald,' Darlene said with satisfaction. 'I fort 'e was going to 'ave a fit.'

'Miss wasn't crying.' Frankie Bott took a loose backhand swing at her. His goddess was too proud to weep.

'She was too.' Ted Jelks, the coloured boy with the white mother joined in, eager for dispute.

There was no work being done on this last day. The class were collecting their few possessions from their desks and the shelves at the back of the room and cramming them into paper bags and derelict fibre satchels. Grace was in the middle of the room helping them. There was plenty of noise and some fooling. The sad attentive moment with Mr Rawlings was over. It was possible that in years to come some of them might look back and say: 'That was a fine school, that Abbot's Road. It broke my heart to leave.' But now, in the youthful exuberance of the moment, with six weeks holiday before them, they were not aware that this was the end forever of something they had loved. When they stopped to think about it, as the Head had made them think, none of them wanted to leave Abbot's Road, but they were constitutionally incapable of being sad about it for more than a few minutes at a time.

Even Frankie, who had dragged his toes about the school for the last few days, more miserable than anyone, could recapture his sparkle immediately when a fight was brewing.

'She wasn't crying.'

'Was.'

'Wasn't.'

'Was, you clot.'

'Wasn't you – you –' Because of his friendship with Edgar, Frankie could not shout Nigger or any of the deceptively innocent insults like Hovis, Chocolate, Darkie, so he fell back on: 'You lousy Spade.'

They were scuffling on the floor. Grace picked them up. How many small boys had she yanked off the floor in her two years at Abbot's Road? To stop the argument, she admitted: 'It was the hymn. You all sang it so beautifully –'

'Like ruddy choirboys, eh?'

'– that I'm afraid I did cry a bit.'

'For this place?' A boy kicked at a scarred, lopsided desk, and the inkwell toppled to the floor amid shrieks.

'Look what you've done, Terry Raines!'

151

'It don't matter now.'

'No more school. Burn the bugger down!'

Grace had answered: 'Not so much for the school, as for all of you,' but the children were too excited to hear. Someone had found a dead mouse at the back of the cupboard and they were all crowding round with shouted suggestions of what could be done with it now.

Only Frankie Bott stood rooted to the floor with one foot in the pool of ink and his hair on end from the fight. 'You cried for me, Miss?'

Grace smiled, and would have drawn him to her and kissed him, but in Cottingham Park you could not do that with a twelve-year-old, even an innocent one like Frankie, unless you were sure that his less innocent contemporaries were not looking.

She said: 'Yes, Frankie. It's sad when you make good friends with someone and then have to go away from them.'

Frankie stared. 'But I thought you was coming with us to Green Lane.'

It was hard to find places for all the Abbot's Road pupils among the neighbouring schools, and many of them were being pushed into the rough ill-famed school at the edge of the district, because Green Lane was so overcrowded already that a few dozen more could not make it any worse.

'But, Frankie, I never told you that.'

'When I come back from Mr Rawlings' room that day and told you I was going down the Lane with Ted and May and them, and we asked you if you wasn't coming too, you just give us a funny look, but you never said you wasn't.'

'I didn't say I was.'

'You didn't say you wasn't,' the boy repeated stubbornly, as if he could force the truth into the shape he wanted. 'Mr Savage is going. 'E told Stefi's big brother. If you lot can stand it, I can, 'e said.'

'Well, but Frankie, I –' Grace did not want to look at those bright bird's eyes, daring her to admit her disloyalty. She did not want to tell him about the girls' school in Berkshire to which she was not yet definitely committed. She had not wanted to tell any of them. She had hoped that no one would ask her today what she was going to do, because she did not properly know herself. Let her say good-bye to all this first, rid herself of the claims of the tumbledown school and the dirty affectionate children, and then she would decide.

But she had reckoned without the insistent claims of Frankie. 'Aren't you even going to stay in the Park?' he asked, as someone threw the stiff and luckless mouse out of the window and the whole pack rushed shrieking to hang over the sill and see where it landed.

'There are other places. It's not as if my family lived in Cottingham Park, like yours.'

He shrugged. 'That's right.' He stood for a moment irresolute, scowling, and Grace did not know whether he was going to cry, or say something rude to pretend that he did not care if she deserted him.

He did neither. He smoothed out the scowl and said quite naturally: 'I never did love my Mum though, like I love you, Miss.'

He had never before said that he loved her. Grace had not thought that it was in his vocabulary. Now that it was out, he was not abashed, but stood grinning at her triumphantly as if he had won some kind of conflict.

'I love you too,' Grace said quietly, 'but I can't stay with you, and you will always have your mother.'

'Sod *her*,' he said with amiable simplicity, and as the other children came surging round them again, absorbing Frankie into the raucous mass, Grace thought of the clarion upper-class voice which had passed down the corridor outside the head-mistress's study at the girls' school. 'I say, Caroline, my mother's got a new horse!'

'Are you really going to Green Lane?' Grace asked Geoffrey Savage in the staff room where Mrs Dormer had brought the tray of pale tea and dirty cups just as if it were any day, just as if they were not all going to say goodbye to each other, probably for ever, in an hour's time.

'Why not? Right up my street.'

'But I thought you were going with Mr Rawlings to that place in Croydon.'

'Nah.' The Wild Beast flapped a huge powerful hand. 'I thought I might, and it's a good job and all, I don't doubt. But I changed my mind. Had a few last weekend.' He lifted his elbow in one of the extravagant, unnecessary gestures with which he often chose to illustrate some remark that was already perfectly clear. 'I always see straighter when I'm stewed. Look –

153

these kids here in the Cottie are my kind. Call it soppy if you like, but I think they need me. I'm going to stick with em.'

'But everyone says that you can't *do* anything at Green Lane, that it's a waste of energy trying to teach there because half the time you can't even make yourself heard.'

'Who says I can't do anything? They'll hear my voice all right.' Geoffrey pulled out an empty pipe and sucked on it noisily. The pipe was fat and rugged and countrified, like the leather-patched tweeds and sporting ties and scarves which he wore half mockingly, like fancy dress.

'I think you're insane,' Mrs Bowden said. 'This place has often been more than the human spirit could stand. Why deliberately go somewhere worse?'

'Bit of a challenge, Maggie. Something worthwile, eh? Grace knows.' He jerked his bearded chin at Grace and she flicked her head round in surprise. 'Funny, a girl like you brought up so soft, how you've taken to the Cottie. I'll lay you odds right here and now, you'll never fit in with that lot at the girls' school. Hockey and madrigals, and Lord help you if you don't get the titles straight on Parents' Day.'

'Well, I don't know definitely that I am going there,' Grace said weakly. Suddenly she wondered why she had ever gone to the school for the interview. To escape from herself? To try to be someone different? She had a strangled, breathless feeling as if some vitally important decision was rising, fighting its way up through her beating chest from somewhere deep inside her.

She remembered having that same choked feeling one night when she was about fifteen and she had thought that she was being called to be a nun. In the morning, the stifling excitement had gone, but the vague need of dedication had stayed with her at the back of everything, unsatisfied, troubling her. Troubling her all the time she was at the secretarial college learning things that would do no one any good, until finally she had to go away and train as a teacher and then accept a place in one of the most raffish districts of London.

Nervous, uncertain, her mother had tried to understand. She embarrassed Grace by calling it 'this missionary feeling of yours', but it was nothing like that. It was not noble or self-sacrificing. It was merely obeying the compulsion of what her genuine deep-down self, stripped of the cautious refinements of background and upbringing, wanted to do.

Looking at it that way, missionaries were not really self-sacrificing either, because when they went off to sweat or freeze or die over the souls of the natives in some savage spot, it was the only kind of life their real self wanted. A sacrifice had to be something you did not want to give.

'Do you think . . .' she asked Geoffrey through the breathless pulse that was filling her throat – 'I've only got one year's qualification. Do you think they would take me at Green Lane?'

'My dear Grace,' Mrs Bowden began, but Geoffrey cut her off with: 'Would they take you? Listen, if they keep a teacher there two terms they think he's a veteran. They're so short of staff, they'd even take old Ma Purdie. God –' He looked over his shoulder as Denzil opened the door. 'I thought that was her coming in.'

'What's up?' Denzil lifted his head like a dog, smelling excitement in the air.

'Grace wants to go to Green Lane.'

'Oh no!' Denzil took three quick steps to Grace's chair and stood over her, his hand hovering an inch away as if he wanted to touch her but did not quite dare.

'Calm down, lover,' Geoffrey said. 'She can't do it. No, sweetheart. Not you at Green Lane. I wouldn't do it if I was you.'

'Why not? I'm just as anxious to help these children as you are. Shut up, Denzil.' She slapped at his hovering hand. 'It's not your business. And I can shout as loud as you can,' she told Geoffrey. 'If that's all it needs to teach there.'

'I know, dear, I know. But – oh hell.' Geoffrey got up and began to walk about the floor, polishing his pipe on his beard. 'I can't see you there. It's a shocking district. Much worse than this. The kids are . . . well, I've heard tales about some of the things that go on round the back of the bicycle sheds that I wouldn't even tell you.'

'What things?' Denzil's passion for the details of normal or abnormal sex took his mind off Grace.

'Or you either.'

'Well, I haven't got a bicycle,' Grace said cheerfully. 'Why panic, Geoff? I can look after myself.'

'I'll bet you could,' said John Ferris surprisingly. He had been reading a newspaper and Grace had not thought that he was listening, even though Geoffrey had stumbled over his feet a couple of times as he paced. 'Why don't you have a stab at

155

the job? If I was half my age, I'd come with you and watch you do it.'

'Oh no.' Denzil pursed up his mouth. 'Oh no, she can't possibly. Not Grace. I couldn't let her.'

'*You* couldn't let me!' Just because she had mistily allowed him to try out a few amatory techniques last week after a flask and a half of Chianti . . .

That decided it. 'Just try and stop me,' she said. 'I'm going to apply tomorrow. What fun, Geoff.' She laughed up at him as he stopped before her chair. 'We'll be in the thick of it together. I'm not afraid of the kids, but I shall be of the staff; but at least I'll have you.'

Geoffrey grunted, and Denzil, with jealousy now added to his outrage, clenched his fist and cried out in his high boyish voice: 'Then I'll come too! If you insist on going to that – that insane asylum, I shall have to chuck the college thing and go to Green Lane to look after you!'

Grace smiled and patted his hand. 'It looks as though they're going to be quite well staffed at the Lane next term,' she said. She felt suddenly very calm. It seemed that there was no getting away from Denzil, but that did not matter. What mattered, what had emerged from all this, was that for good or ill, it seemed that there was no getting away from Cottingham Park.

*

'Well, well, well.' Barney Gilligan stopped dead from a run in one of the long windowless corridors of Green Lane Secondary, which were like the lower decks of a liner, but without the white paint and clean smells. 'Look who's here.'

'How nice to see you, Barney,' Grace said, and meant it. She had hardly seen anyone from Abbot's Road yet, and she was afraid of the strange faces in the staff cloakroom (she had missed her tea after lunch because she could not face the staffroom), and of the mob of young barbarians who had just hurtled past her with so little regard for her presence that she had to flatten herself against the wall to avoid being crushed to death.

'Fancy you coming to this penitentiary,' Barney said. 'Do they order the teachers where to go then, like they do the kids?'

'I chose it.'

'You want your 'ead seen to, Miss.' A bell clanged sourly from somewhere in the depth of the school and Barney said: 'See yer!' and sped away in frayed gym shoes.

The Green Lane school had been built long ago as a corrective institution for bad boys in the days before they were elevated to the title of delinquents, and it had not changed much since then, either in appearance or in the quality of some of its inmates.

It was a brown glowering pile of square buildings with small windows. There were turret effects on the roof parapets, and the two front corners of the main block, higher than the rest, looked like watch towers for the shooting down of anyone who tried to escape. The playground at the back was larger than the one at Abbot's Road, but even more depressing. It was bounded by an enormous brick wall beyond which was the labyrinth of lines and sidings and roundhouses outside the railway terminus, where all day long trains starting out or coming in belched gobs of filthy smoke over the iron spikes on top of the wall.

Grace's classroom was on the upper floor, in one of the towers. To reach it, you climbed four flights of steep stone stairs, littered with toffee papers and carpeted with wads of gum, standing aside for your life whenever one of the small hordes of boys and girls who seemed constantly on the run from place to place, came hurtling down on you.

Grace had not yet seen the Headmaster. The Assistant Head, a rangy woman called Miss Arbuthnot with a strong nose like a Red Indian, had told her that she would be given a class similar to the one she had taken at Abbot's Road, the younger children who had just moved dazedly up from their primary school.

Grace had hoped that she might get a second-year class, with Frankie Bott and some of the others she had begun to love at Abbot's Road, but Miss Arbuthnot, who perhaps was not as tough as she looked, had said that she was very young and inexperienced for this post and that they would try to make it easy for her, so Grace had accepted gratefully.

Not that you could do anything but accept, gratefully or ungratefully, at Green Lane. It was immediately apparent after only one morning in the school that there was little cooperation or tolerance. Teacher or pupil, you took what came and made the best or worst of it, according to your temperament and the degree of your disillusionment.

When Grace had arrived at the school with Denzil, who had insisted on going far out of his way to fetch her, she had to accept the news that Miss Arbuthnot's desire to make things easy for her had either evaporated or been overruled by the Head. Grace was to take temporary charge of a third-year class whose master had not resigned, but had merely lacked the nerve to turn up at the beginning of the new term.

This was Form 3B. If the C stream of this age group were even less willing or able to learn, it must be bedlam there in the other tower where Form 3C was housed. In this tower, it was semi-, or even three-quarter-bedlam. The morning had been bad enough, while the pupils were still wary and getting Grace's measure; but when she climbed back to 3B after her indigestible lunch, she might, for one moment after she opened the door, almost have slammed it shut again at once and run away from Green Lane for ever.

But only for a moment. Wasn't this what she had come for? Wasn't this the challenge at which Geoffrey Savage had vigorously grasped and which she had been eager to follow? To teach the unteachable. To try out her will on the lawless. To bring some order and manners and hope and – yes, love into lives that had known too little of these things.

There were two fights going on, one in each corner at the back of the room where ancient cupboards leaned forward away from the wall, swinging open their sagging doors on the jumble of ruined textbooks and jam jars and tangled bunches of raffia thrust in among the rusted equipment of some unrecognizable craft.

Several books had been pulled from the shelves and lay straddled on the floor, one of the tables which served as double desks was on its side with one leg broken, and a rude picture had been drawn skilfully on the blackboard.

One of the few reasonable boys in the class, the coloured boy Edgar Biggs who was Frankie's friend, was sitting at a front desk with his fingers in his ears, reading. He gave Grace a gleaming smile as she walked nervously to her desk, and got up to ask her a question about something in his book.

She saw his thick lips moving, talking rapidly through his grin as only a West Indian can, but: 'I'm sorry, Edgar,' she said. 'I can't hear you with all this noise.'

'Want me to shut 'em up for you?' Edgar said. 'I'm a monitor this term.'

'But I haven't chosen them yet.'

'You don't have to. Whoever ask you first, he it.'

'Well, we'll see.' Grace wanted to make the most of Edgar, who so far seemed to be the only one who was on her side, but she dared not risk being a target for the charge of favouritism right away.

'No, you keep quiet,' she said as the boy opened the surprisingly pink cavern of his mouth and clenched his fists to shout. 'This is my job.'

This was the first part of the challenge. She had been told that if you could make yourself heard in the worst forms at Green Lane, you had done half a day's work. She had to achieve it. She had to stop the noise now at once, or suffer it for all her days with Form 3B.

'Quiet!'

She had told Geoffrey that she could shout as loud as he, and perhaps it was true. Her voice came out stentorian, startling her with its strength, for the rest of her was trembling. The two fights stopped in surprise, and those who were cheering them on or talking and giggling in the middle of the room, turned round suddenly and stared in attitudes of arrested motion.

'She can't half yell,' one of the boys who had been fighting in and out of the cupboards remarked coolly, smoothing back his long greasy hair. This boy, whose name was Sidney Goole, had already impressed himself unpleasantly on Grace's notice. He had a lot to say, but he never addressed himself to her directly; always through the class, like an estranged husband conversing with his wife through a third party.

'I can yell louder than that if I have to,' Grace said. 'Now please will you all sit down and keep quiet.'

'She don't know the teachers ain't supposed to yell at us,' Sidney Goole said.

'Sit down,' said Grace. 'Yes, you too, Edgar Biggs. I'll answer your question in a minute.'

'She's going to make pets of the Spay-yades!' sang out Sidney as he bumped his gangling body ungracefully into a seat at the back of the room. He leaned his elbows on the table from which, like all the others, most of the yellow varnish had been worn or picked away, and leered up at Grace from under a seaweed forelock.

There were some groans, and Grace thought she heard someone mutter: nigger lover, as the class banged and shuffled and argued its way into place. This was worse than she had expected. At Abbot's Road, the coloured children, Caribbean or African, had been accepted unquestionably by the white. Whatever the prejudices of their parents, the children seemed not even to notice the colour of skins, or if they did, it was to treat the smaller negroes almost as mascots, to be petted and made the centre of comic situations.

In Form 3B at Green Lane, when Grace had instructed them to choose their places this morning, there had been the usual two rushes: the small rush of the studious and the docile to be at the front under the teacher's deck, and the larger struggling rush to be as near the back as possible. When they had finally sorted themselves out, and Grace had pulled the extra third bodies off benches designed for two and pushed most of the girls into the middle desks, as separate from the boys as possible, she had seen that nearly all the coloured children were together on one side of the room, away from the windows and the hot pipes.

The table which had been overturned by the fight still lay on the floor, two girls sitting casually behind it with their feet on its side.

'Pick up that desk,' Grace said.

'Can't,' said the red-haired girl in the violet sweater. ''Sbroke.'

'What do we do then?'

They sat quiet now and staring.

'Is there someone in the school who mends things?' At Abbot's Road there had been Hermann the cross-eyed Austrian carpenter who hung round the school all day grumbling, to see what odd jobs he could pick up.

The class continued to stare, mouths hanging.

'Well, pick up the desk anyway. Put it at the back of the room.' Grace was aware of her voice's strained patience and wished that she were able to talk to them naturally. 'We're going to have dictation. You two girls will have to write on your knees.'

'Alice can't write anyway.'

'Who says so?' Alice whipped round, her thick red pigtail flailing, and began an exchange of insults in which half the class joined.

'Pick up the *desk*!'

'I warned her about yelling,' Sidney Goole said sadly.

'One of you boys. You, Sidney Goole.' He was one of the few whose names she knew.

'The girls broke it. Let them pick it up.' The bony adolescent boy with the sharply mature face folded his arms and closed his eyes.

'Anyone.' She was not going to take issue with Sidney today. That could come later when she knew his weaknesses and knew how far the laws of the school allowed her to go. 'One of you boys at the back.' That was a mistake. That gave each one an excuse to assume that she meant someone else. Everyone was suddenly very busy doing nothing at all.

She had never imagined it like this. She had imagined the noise and the fights and the rudeness and herself being sometimes afraid. She had not imagined blank negation and herself not knowing what punishment she was supposed to give for disobedience, nor how to make any of them accept it.

In sticky moments at Abbot's Road there had nearly always been someone reasonable enough to say, 'Can it, you lot,' and give Grace some support. Here in this room with thirty-five strangers in varying stages of puberty, Grace looked round and saw only hostility and indifference. Even Edgar Biggs had abandoned her. She realized that however much he liked her and worked for her, she could not count on him, could not count on any of them not to turn their backs on her when she most needed them and retreat into the jungle.

Was it possible that they would ever come to love each other, she and these uncouth pimpled strangers, these half ripe girls with their sliding eyes and precocious bosoms? Love and grow necessary to each other in the way of the foolish conceited dreams which had buoyed her up all through the holidays while her mother nagged gently on about not returning to Cottingham Park?

'I'm asking you for the last time.' Thank God her desk was high and she could lean against it for protection. 'Will someone please – pick – up – that desk.' Her voice was less steady, but not because of tears trying to seep through. This was not time for crying. This was a time for cold, emotionless despair. There was no solution to this deadlock, and she would be here for ever, she and the class staring blankly at each other like people in different worlds.

Suddenly Edgar looked up at her, glanced round the room behind him, glanced over the other shoulder to where the handful of coloured children sat goggling the whites of their eyes, looked at Grace again, then slid gracefully out of his seat and started towards Alice and her companion, who were now in such a catalepsy of silent giggles that they could not have picked up the table if they wanted to.

Immediately, a large boy with a red face and a thatch of yellow hair was on his feet at the back and shambling towards the overturned desk. He pushed Edgar away, set the desk upright and calmly fitted the leg back into position.

'Don't shove me around,' Edgar said. 'I'm a monitor.'

'So am I,' said the boy, who, if you had put him into a smock and a straw hat would have looked like a picturebook yokel. 'I'm a monitor, aren't I, Miss?'

'Does any else want to be?'

There was a clamour of comment, but no recognizable claim.

'All right then.' Grace had no idea what a monitor did. They had not been part of the system of Mr Rawlings, who did not believe in giving any child authority over another.

'O.K., dear,' said the farmer's boy, who was as tall as Grace. 'I'm in charge of general main*tain*ance then. I have to go to the cloakroom now to see 'oo 'asn't 'ung their coats up tidy.'

'Not now,' said Grace. 'Sit down and –'

But the boy, who was not as bucolic as he looked, had already slipped neatly out of the door.

'Gone for a smoke,' someone told Grace, and with deep sighs and succulent licking of pencils and testing of pen nibs on thumb nails, the class suddenly settled down in unaccountable peace to take dictation.

At the end of the day, Grace found Geoffrey Savage in the staff cloakroom, which was not much more than a bulge at the end of a passage, with some rusted lockers that mostly did not lock and an umbrella stand with the bottom kicked out. The lavatories (repulsive) were miles away at the other end of the school.

'How did it go, girl?' Geoffrey asked. 'You're still in one piece, I see.'

'Only just.' Grace made a face. 'It's terribly different, isn't it? I mean –' There was only one other person in the cloakroom, a master sitting on a bench, tying a knot in a broken shoelace, but Grace was not going to give anyone the chance to say that she and Geoffrey and Denzil had marched into Green Lane and started criticizing everything because it was not Abbot's Road. 'I'll do better tomorrow,' she said. 'How did it go with you?'

'O.K.' Geoffrey shrugged his great lumpy shoulders into the camel-hair overcoat which made him look more like a lion than ever. 'I'm going to like it, I think.' He had got what he wanted, one of the top classes, who had only one more year to go before they tried themselves out on the world. 'I've got one bastard. He and I will slug it out before Christmas, I can see that.'

The man sitting on the bench looked up from his shoe and laughed. 'That's Tiger Pyle, I suppose. I had him last year.'

'How did you keep your hands off him?'

'Oh, you have to. If you hit them, the parents come in wrath, or try to take you to court. If you use the cane, they move their hand so that you bruise a thumb or a wrist tendon, and then you get not only the parents, but the health authorities too.'

'How long have you been here?' Geoffrey asked.

'Two years.' He laughed again, as if this were funny.

'Grace, this is Colin Mackenzie,' Geoffrey said. 'Grace Peel – young white missionary from Abbot's Road.'

The man finished tying his shoe and stood up, and he and Grace shook hands. He was tall and muscular, but the general effect was not tough, and his handshake was not painfully athletic. His large inquisitive eyes rested on Grace with a speculative pleasure. His clothes hung on him all right, but they were shabby and needed pressing. He was either poor or careless. Or had a careless wife. He was probably married. They always were when they looked at all interesting.

'I heard about you from the boys,' he said. 'I looked for you after lunch to see if it was true.'

'I couldn't find Geoffrey, and I was scared to go into the staff-room alone.'

'I don't blame you,' Colin Mackenzie said. 'Common room, we have to call it. One of Mr Neilson's foibles. Anything they do in other schools, he does it different.'

'What's he like?' Grace asked.

'Haven't you seen him? God, wouldn't you think he'd at least have the civility to welcome the new . . . well, you'll find out. He won't like you though.'

'Why not?'

'You'll find out.' He laughed, and his eyes still meditated

smilingly on her surprised face. He did not look as though he meant to be as rude as he sounded.

Denzil Raymond was waiting for Grace by the door which led from the basement corridors to freedom up a spiral flight of stairs. She could not walk to and from the Meikles' house now, as she had done when she was at Abbot's Road. She had to walk to the railway station and take a bus from there. The bus did not go anywhere near the house where Denzil lived with his parents and his twin brother on the other side of Park Road, but he insisted on accompanying her.

Grace was too tired to protest. When Denzil asked her how the day had been, she told him: 'Wonderful. Everything is fine.' She was not going to admit to him that it had been perilous and baffling; more perilous than she had imagined in the last days of the holidays, when in the smothering sanctuary of the prim border town, she had begun to get cold feet.

'How about you?' she asked.

'Terrible.' He hung his head and began to drag his toes on the dirty grey pavement. 'Guess what class they've given me.'

'Oh, Denzil – not the Remove again?'

He nodded gloomily. 'You've said it. At Abbot's Road, half the Remove were half wits and the rest were morons. Here, they are all qualified for a criminal lunatic asylum.'

'They'll get better when you get to know them. You'll do wonders. Cheer up, Denzil dear.' Grace took his arm. After all, he had come to Green Lane on her account. Even if she did not need his protection, she had some small duty to protect him.

'Do you think so? I need some cheering up. Come home with me to supper, Grace. My mother loves you.'

'I can't. Mrs Meikle asked me to go down to them tonight. She's making something special,' Grace invented quickly. The only time she had been to Denzil's home, his family had tried to put a stranglehold on her by calling her Denzil's Girl and lavishing on her a flattery too gross to be sincere.

Denzil was squeezing her arm against his side and trying to scratch her hand with his fingers in a way he imagined was suggestive, so she took her arm away.

'You don't like me either,' he said, and walked with his arms hanging straight down by his sides, like a dummy. 'I might as well be dead.'

As they waited at the traffic lights outside the station, Grace looked across the busy road and saw Frankie Bott waiting at the bus stop. His bus, which was also Grace's bus, came and he did not get on it. He was waiting for her. But when he saw her start across the road with Denzil, he looked away at once and ran after the bus and swung on to it as it rounded the corner, his legs flying out behind him, and his old brown coat flapping like a wounded bird.

He had counted on that. At least he had counted on that. He had saved up his shocks and discoveries all day to tell her on the way home, and then she had come along with that creep. Was it going to be like that then, now that he was no longer in her class – was she quite through with him?

She'd take up with Edgar probably. That snake. Sit him in the front row. Make a monitor of him. Let him pass out the milk and take ten minutes mike off somewhere when he took the empties back. That Spade. Battered by his first day in the maelstrom of Green Lane, savagely disappointed because he could not ride home on the bus with Miss Peel – and it had been the discovery of the age when he realized that they would take the same bus home – Frankie was ready to reject even his best friend.

It was Scouts tonight. Well, he wouldn't go. That would show him. Show him what? Frankie shook his head, which was buzzing distantly as it did when he was angry or upset. No, he would go to Scouts and treat Edgar cold. Show him that he wasn't God Almighty just because he had wormed his black skin into Miss Peel's class.

In the lift which took Frankie to the top floor of the flats, two boys from one of the other blocks who were riding up and down for fun stood at the back of the lift and spat gobs on to the thick glass window in the door. Frankie barely noticed them, until as the lift slowed for his stop, he stepped forward and a spitball hit him in the back of the neck.

'Filthy swine.' He got out, wiping his neck with the dirty rag which was his handkerchief. The door slid shut and the boys were carried away down, jeering.

Frankie ambled along the balcony towards his front door, going slowly, slapping his hand at each step on the cold stone parapet.

'That you, Frank?' His front door was open and his mother's voice came piercingly from inside. 'Well, come in, come in.

165

What are you hanging about out there for? Come in and tell us all about it.'

Frankie turned in at his front door like a ship docking, leaning his shoulder on the door jamb and rolling his body round. 'About what?' He looked dully at his mother, what he could see of her. She was standing in the doorway of the sitting-room, a faceless silhouette, blocking the light with her bulk.

'About what? About what?' Her voice rose like a parakeet. 'I suppose you never went to no new school today.'

'Oh that.' When she had stepped back into the room, Frankie went through the doorway and bent to embrace Kenny, who was waiting for him with his head on one side like a bird. 'It was all right.'

'Ho,' said Mrs Bott. When she said Ho, she folded her arms under her massive bosom, heaved it up and let it drop again: 'That's all we're to be told then. Thank you very much I'm sure. Not that we want to know.'

She really did not care about the school, but she was bursting to know one thing. She went into the kitchen to ask it from yelling distance, so that Frankie should think she did not care about that either.

'And how is *dear* Miss Peel?' she asked, clattering pans in the sink. 'The poor old girl got you in 'er class again?'

Kenny's eyes were fixed on Frankie, and Frankie shook his head. Kenny's eager face crumpled, and the back of the stiff little claw which was his hand began to rub aimlessly back and forth across the rug which covered his legs. They did not say anything to each other. Frankie would tell him everything in bed, when they were alone and safe.

'I said, 'as she got you in 'er class? What's the matter with you, you sulky little bugger? I'll take the strap to you, teach you some manners. I'll tan your 'ide. When I'm finished with you, you'll be as sorry you was born as I am.' Mrs Bott was back in the sitting-room, holding a black iron frying pan like a weapon. 'Oh ho.' She saw Frankie's face. 'So that's the way it is. Well, thank Christ for that. We'll get a breather from darling Miss Peel at last. What you got – a bloke this time or some other old cow?'

'Mrs Finch,' Frankie said. 'She's a devil.' He put his fingers up by his head like horns and waggled them. Kenny laughed.

'Well, I hope she gets 'er pitchfork into your backside soon,' said Mrs Bott comfortably, 'then perhaps we'll 'ave some

166

decency round 'ere,' and they all laughed. Sometimes they did all laugh together like this, at jokes that were not really jokes, but too outrageous to be taken seriously.

On Scout nights, Frankie usually met Edgar at the corner of Glidden Road, and they walked to the Community Centre together. Today, however, Frankie went by another route, slipping along through badly lit streets where cats were shadows and old women wandered nowhere and silent-footed boys in leather jackets walked, not in groups of three or four, forcing you off the pavement, but singly, like Indians on the prowl.

Edgar arrived at the Centre late, when the troop was already started on knot practice. He looked handsome in his uniform, and his skin shone like dancing shoes.

After apologizing to the Scoutmaster, who had his hands full of blind cord, he sat down on a folding chair beside Frankie. 'I waited for you,' he said accusingly. 'Where was you at?'

'I can come by myself if I want to.'

'Gee,' said Edgar. 'You sore because I didn't talk to you at school? This was just the first day, man. We get the chance most days. They's places to meet. Dinner, and the playground, and the can and that.'

'I aint sore. I just fetched up in the wrong class. It's all right for *you*,' Frankie muttered, tying granny knots over and over each other.

'Because of Miss Peel. You right, man. She is some doll.'

'Uh-huh.' Frankie looked sideways from under his lowered brows. 'You a monitor?'

'Sure am.'

'Uh-huh.'

'Quit that uh-huh and listen. You know what she said? She said this morning, when we tell our names: "Oh yes, I know you. You Frankie's friend. That's good. He's my friend too."'

'She did?' Frankie felt his face, which had been glum almost all day at school and all the time at home except when his mother had tickled his ribs with her pitchfork joke, stretching into a comfortable grin.

'You mad at me?' Edgar peered at him.

'Nah.'

'O.K.' Edgar was a good enough friend not to ask what the glumness had been for. Now that his anger was over, Frankie hardly knew himself.

167

'Look here, shut up, you two,' said the Scoutmaster. 'This is knot practice, not a gossip session.'

'Very sorry, sir,' said Edgar smartly. 'How is this?' he held up a tailor-made clove hitch.

'Good enough,' said the young Scoutmaster, wrestling with a Laocoon web of cord made by another boy who could not get it undone. He was not interested in Edgar, because he had taken up his work to champion the under-privileged and incapable, and Edgar always did everything the best.

'Can I splice, sir?'

'If you must.'

Edgar took his scout knife out of the sheath in his belt, and shaved a hair's breadth sliver carefully from the top of his thumbnail.

'Here,' the Scoutmaster came across the room, 'how did that knife get so sharp?'

'For my woodcarving, sir.'

Edgar's beautiful ingenuous eyes looked up at him and he nodded and went back to the tangle of cord. He only came down to the Community Centre twice a week from more rarefied parts. He did not know that in Glidden Road it was no use having a knife if it was not sharp.

The following morning when Grace was checking the register of Form 3B, she was brought to her feet in alarm by the shrilling of a bell in the corridor outside. It was not the dismal bell that tolled the unwilling to classes or playground or dinner. It was the strident voice of emergency, galvanizing your head like shock treatment.

'Fire drill?'

The class sat unperturbed, picking at its teeth and at frayed bits of leather on the soles of its shoes. 'Sit down, Miss,' they told her. 'That's only the Indian love call.'

'What do you –' A harsh crackling came suddenly from overhead. Grace looked up and noticed for the first time that a small loudspeaker box was fastened to the wall above the door.

'Attention all classes,' the loudspeaker said. 'Attention all staff and pupils.' It was a contentious nasal voice, metallic and occasionally scrambled, like a wireless tuned a fraction off station.

'Today is Tuesday September the sixth. All those who did not take home the dental examination form yesterday will please do so today and return it without fail tomorrow, signed by one parent.' There was the same sound of amplified breathing that comes through the telephone when someone is listening on an extension, and the crackle of a page being turned. 'Or guardian.

'Since the ground in the park is very muddy, there will be no football until next week at the earliest, and not then unless the sports captains of the various forms will make some effort to count and pair off the football boots. Miss Fraser's mackintosh is missing. Anyone who knows anything about this will please report to their form master. Or mistress. This is not sneaking. I repeat, this is not sneaking. Am I my brother's keeper? the Bible asks. Yes, you are your brother's keeper, and responsible for his conscience and his morals if he cannot control them. I want all you people out there to remember this. Things happened here last term which I prefer not to mention. They could happen again this term if you so choose. It is up to you. If you know of something wrong, a plot brewing, a boy heading for trouble, it is your duty to tell someone in authority.'

Grace sat rigid with surprise, but the class in front of her were scarcely listening. They were lolling and yawning and giggling, and when the voice jangled on: 'If you know of anything wrong, and you keep your mouth shut, you will be liable for punishment along with the offender,' one of the boys made a raucous disgusted noise and spat on the floor.

There were some more items of school information, and quite a bit more moral hectoring, with the morality slightly askew, and then the voice, sounding as if it were being forced through a narrow tin can, began to intone a long prayer, during which some of the boys at the back brought to an argumentative conclusion a game of darts played on the floor with pen nibs.

'The Lord bless and keep you. The Lord lift up the light of His countenance upon you and give you peace, now and for ever more. Amen.' The querulous voice – did God listen to it? – was still. The loudspeaker crackled small thunder and clicked into silence.

'We should have told you, Miss,' one of the girls said indulgently. ''E does that every day. You'll get used to it.'

'Was that the headmaster?'

'Broderick Neilson in person. Radio announcer of the age.'

'Why doesn't he say all this at Assembly?'

169

The class laughed at her, not rudely, but pitying her innocence. ''E give up holding Assembly long ago,' the farmer's boy monitor, whose name was Norman something or something Norman, told her. ''E daren't let us be all together in one place, so 'e 'ad the speaker system put in. Jim Sugden's Dad done it, as a matter of fact. Owns the big radio and TV shop by the station. Did it cheap to oblige. 'E's like that, Jim Sugden's Dad is. Let you listen to records any time, long as you want and never buy. You should drop in, dear, if you like music. You'll always find a bunch of kids in there after school. We –'

'You mean that Mr Neilson paid for the loudspeaker system himself?'

'Well listen, Miss.' Norman spread his hand patiently. 'It stands to reason the school board aren't going to cough up money for a daft thing like that. They'll put up with a lot from Mr Neilson because no one else wants to run this lousy place, but they wouldn't go that far.'

'Yes. Well – I see. Thank you for telling me.' Grace knew that she should not allow Norman to talk to her about the Headmaster as familiarly as if she were a pupil and not a teacher, but she was not going to discourage him. Not yet. He and some of the others had been friendly at least, which was better than yesterday's solid antagonism. If she could get them to talk to her freely, tell her what they liked and what they hated and what their lives were like at home and why they did the things they did at school, there was a chance that she might be able to begin to do something for them.

Only a chance. As day succeeded day, she found that invariably after a moment of quite friendly communication when they had met each other as human beings across the peeling yellow desks, someone would suddenly remember that this was school, to be despised, and that she was a teacher, to be baited, not listened to, and an ugly remark would scatter the wits of the class in pandemonium.

It was often Sidney Goole who made the rude or vicious or obstinate comment which would rekindle the normal state of rebellion. It was also Sidney who was at the bottom of the Spades v. Jumbles war in Form 3B – Jumbles was a colonial contraction of John Bull. Grace learned from Edgar that Sidney was a member of the White Hunters gang whose oaths signed in blood in a coal cellar showed a racial obsession which, even if it

170

was faked for drama, was a frighteningly good imitation of adult hatreds.

'How do you know about the blood and the oaths and all this?' Grace asked.

'Everybody knows what that lot do,' Edgar said. 'It's no secret.'

'If everybody knows it was this gang who beat up that old man behind the convent, why hasn't someone told the police? Why haven't you?' Grace insisted, as Edgar looked down at his shiny orange shoes without answering. 'Is it because you're a member of a rival gang yourself? Is that it?'

'Oh no, Miss.' Edgar looked up quickly. 'I don't run with no gang. I work. I want to get somewhere. The gangs is for the crazy men who aren't going anywhere but round in circles with the one they think is leader biting after they tails.'

When Grace had been at Green Lane a month, she had taken the measure of the rest of the staff, and had her measure taken by them with a small amount of friendship and a fair degree of suspicion, but she still had not been properly acknowledged by the Headmaster. She met him sometimes in a corridor, scurrying somewhere in a sideways hustle like a sand crab; but when she greeted him, he answered: 'Yes, ah yes. You're Miss Peel. That's right. 3B. How are you getting along?' and was gone before she could reply.

The children in her class hardly ever saw him, and as far as Grace knew he did not know their names, except on paper. He never came into the classroom during lessons. He did not eat lunch in the canteen, nor appear unexpectedly in the playground to stop a major battle that could be heard a quarter of a mile away. His prayers and school notices and captious lectures assaulted the ears every day through the loudspeaker, but there seemed to be no personal interviews: never a line of hopeful or guilty boys and girls propped up outside the closed door of his office, counting on him to play saviour or god of wrath, as the Abbot's Road children had counted on Mr Rawlings.

Once, when a Polish boy with a proud unhealthy face had goaded her all morning, refusing to tackle decimals and needling everyone within range who was attempting, however feebly, to work, Grace had said: 'If you don't behave yourself, Joseph, I shall send you to Mr Neilson.'

The Polish boy laughed, tilting up his bony eagle's nose, and

171

Norman, that ready purveyor of information, said: 'No use, dear. Mr Neilson don't see anybody. Mr Ellis sent me once. Two hours I waited till 'e opened the door. "Please sir," I says, "I've been sent for punishment." "Well go back to your room," 'e says, "and tell your teacher to give it you."'

Applause for Norman's story. Laughter. Fabulous reminiscences of how Mr Ellis received the message.

'Quiet!' Grace banged on her desk with the little wooden mallet which Denzil had bought her from a toy shop for this purpose, since he had found that it sometimes surprised the Remove into attention.

'Of course there's always the cane,' Norman said helpfully. 'We don't care for that much though.'

'There's nothing really she can do,' said Sidney Goole. 'That's why it's all so hopeless.'

'You can give us black marks, so our form won't win the honour shield at the end of the year,' said Edgar, who was one of the few who cared about awards and competitions.

'The shield! Oo wants the bleeding shield? Black marks for black boys!' Sidney Goole shouted, and threw a wad of paper soaked in ink at the back of Edgar's head.

Edgar got up and went for him with a jungle roar, and Norman lumbered wearily to his feet and separated them, which was one of the services he performed now for Grace, except when he was part of the fight himself.

'Sidney Goole,' Grace said, in the new harsh voice she had acquired, of which she was afraid lest it grow on her for life, 'if you do that again, I might have to use the cane. Where is it?'

'Mr Ellis had one, but we took it away when we found he wasn't coming back.'

'So what's a ink bomb?' Sidney Goole jeered. 'Black ink. Black head. Won't show. Black magic. I'll bet she don't know about the voodoo. 'Uman sacrifices. I'll bet she don't know that's how the Spades get rid of all the babies that shouldn't never ought to be born.'

Grace tackled Miss Arbuthnot in the common room, where that massive woman of granite was sitting in an overcoat and a long striped college scarf, because although October had come in like February, Mr Neilson would not have the heating started. 'Why can't I send anyone to the Head when they are bad enough?' she asked. 'Can't he handle them either, is that it?'

Miss Arbuthnot, who never spoke without due thought, which made conversation with her significant but not sparkling, contemplated Grace with her eyes that were set close together above the high bridge of her impressive nose. 'There is no doubt that he could handle them,' she said, 'if occasion arose. But it is not his principle to be the one to administer discipline. That's our job.'

'But I – I can't always. Words just roll off them. If I send them out of the room, they go away and smoke or go home for the rest of the day. They don't care about the black marks, and I can't cane them. Most of them are too big, and I think hitting people is degrading anyway.'

'You can't degrade some of these young brutes any more than they are already.' Mr Partridge, a short mealy man with round spectacles on a round head and a round stomach like an ovarian tumour was always listening to conversations and butting in.

'I don't mean degrading to them. I mean to myself.' In the staffroom at Abbot's Road, you would not have had to explain that. Here in the ugly common room with its unshaded lights and walls of institutional green, people often talked at cross purposes, either deliberately, or because they did not understand each other, seldom seeking or acknowledging a common purpose.

'Great egotists, the young today,' said Mr Partridge, who liked to use Grace's youth as an insult.

'What can I do?' Grace asked Miss Arbuthnot, turning her chair slightly and leaning forward to shut Mr Partridge out.

'You can send the girls to me, if they can find me,' Miss Arbuthnot said. 'I'm not often in my office. But I can scare them sometimes. They don't understand me, because I don't look or talk or move like a woman. That shakes off some of their brass.'

'I should have thought it would be the other way round,' Grace said. 'Not that you don't look like a woman, I mean. I think you are very attractive.' She smiled, wanting to make friends with this female rock, who seemed to be the strongest in the group, but Miss Arbuthnot could not be won this way.

She thought for a moment, her chin resting squarely in the folds of her mannish scarf. 'And the boys,' she continued, 'you can send to Mr Petters, if you positively feel you must.'

Mr Petters was the senior master. He was sixty-five and lazy, with a big puffy head of snow-white hair like a dandelion clock. 'Don't send them to me,' he said. 'I don't want the young devils.

Don't delegate. Always delegating,' he said fussily. 'Everyone always tries to pass things on to someone else these days. It's so spineless.'

'But you must have a higher authority to fall back on,' Grace said. 'It's the whole structure of a school's discipline.'

'That's right,' Denzil backed her up from the piano stool, where he was correcting exercise books on the closed keyboard. 'She's right, you know. The chain of command can't function properly unless each one can trust the one below and rely on the one above.'

Mr Partridge said: 'Listen to the kindergarten. Hark at the experts preaching to us the whole principle of group organization.'

'Look here –' began Denzil, swivelling agitatedly on the piano stool, but Grace made a face across the room at him. This was exactly what they must not do. They must not try to break in here and tell this inharmonious collection of bungling defeatists what was wrong with their school. If Grace and Geoffrey and Denzil were going to do any good at Green Lane, they must share out their ideals persuasively from within, not make enemies by trying to thrust them at the unreceptive. There were too many rifts already. Many of the staff were hopelessly at odds with each other and with the children, and apparently with the Head-master too, although they seldom saw him.

'I would like to see Mr Neilson,' she told Miss Arbuthnot. 'Why can't I see Mr Neilson?'

'Who said you couldn't?' Miss Arbuthnot sat like an Epstein figure with her legs planted solidly apart and her lap at right angles to them. 'I thought you had.'

'I mean really have a talk. Not just in passing. I've been told that I just can't walk in to his office.' Grace had never imagined a school where the Headmaster had not been readily available. 'What do I do? Write to his secretary and ask for an appointment some time before Christmas?'

'There is no need for sarcasm, Grace,' Miss Arbuthnot said. 'Mr Neilson will send for you.'

It was another three days before an undersized boy with a dirty face and a torn green sweater stuck his head round the door of 3B, screeched: 'Miss Peel wanted in Mr Neilson's office!' and vanished.

'Oh – oh,' said Sidney Goole. 'She's going to get 'er cards. Must be the sack if 'is lordship sends for you.'

174

Grace was having an art lesson. There was no art teacher at Green Lane this term and no art room either. The school was so overcrowded that the speciality rooms like the art room and the ill-equipped laboratory had been usurped for classrooms.

It was the worst time for Grace to have to leave the room. Jars of water, paints, sopping paint rags, glue pots, scissors – it needed close supervision to prevent the inevitable relaxed disorder of an art class from becoming anarchy.

'The monitors are in charge,' she said without much hope, for Edgar was absorbed in a neat architectural drawing of a railway crane which he could see from the window – and the white children paid no attention to him anyway; and Norman was playing soldiers with a red-painted rag tied round his yellow head – and the coloured children paid no attention to him.

'Please,' Grace said, brushing chalk off her skirt, 'don't let me find paint and water over everything when I come back.'

'Why give us the idea?' Alice asked. 'We hadn't thought of that.' She yelled with laughter and flipped a loaded paint brush at the soot-streaked window, and Grace went quickly out.

She had not been in Mr Neilson's room for long before she began to understand what was wrong with him, and what was wrong with the school because of him.

He was afraid. Afraid of his pupils. Afraid of his staff. Afraid of losing his job.

He sat Grace down opposite him at the other side of a desk covered with the paperwork silt of months, behind which he sat on a low chair looking like a disgruntled gnome coming up for air.

'I am very busy,' he told her. 'I can spare you' – he squinted at the clock on the wall – 'exactly ten minutes.'

It was quite a large office, but every piece of furniture was loaded, and so was most of the floor. Before she could sit down, Grace had lifted two boxes off the chair, since Mr Neilson did not come round the desk to do it for her. The walls were covered with notices and directives from the education authority and other bodies, some of them issued years ago, as far as Grace could see. The floor was stacked with cartons of stationery and tottering piles of papers and textbooks, and in one corner was a jumble of football boots, their strings entangled. There had been a lot of strictures over the loudspeaker about sports captains being irresponsible in the tally of football boots. But how could they count them when some of them were locked away in here?

'Exactly ten minutes,' Mr Neilson repeated, bringing her nervily to the point, and Grace tried to relax him – and herself, for he made her jumpy – by leaning back and crossing her legs and saying with a smile: 'It was nothing special. I just wanted to talk to you. It feels funny to work for someone you don't know at all.'

'I'm always glad to see you, of course.' The Headmaster's nasal voice sounded almost as tinny as it did over the air. 'I'm often too busy to chat with all the new teachers. There are always so many new teachers. They come and go. It's disgraceful. Nobody stays anywhere these days. They won't put up with anything. They want a soft life and a soft job.'

'I don't,' Grace said. 'I know this neighbourhood. I knew it wouldn't be easy here and that the children might be tough to handle, but that seems to make the job more worth while. Don't you think?'

He ducked his eyes. He did not like to have words put into his mouth in the form of questions which presumed the answer Yes. 'Well, I don't suppose you'll stay long,' he said. 'The women never do. Especially the pretty ones,' he added uneasily, turning his bald head half away and looking at her sidelong as if being pretty were immoral.

'Miss Arbuthnot has been here a long time.'

'Oh, Miss Arbuthnot. That's different. She has a lot of power here. That's why she stays. She likes to order people about.'

Hating him for his disloyalty – immediate and despicable disloyalty at a comparative stranger's mention of the most loyal member of his staff – and for his off-hand assumption that Grace might be gone tomorrow and that he would not care if she were, Grace controlled her dislike and said: 'I mean to stay. I think that perhaps I can help some of these children. Someone has to help them, and I want it to be me. I want to be the one who teaches them that there are more things in life than the cage of dirt and poverty in which they were unlucky enough to be born. I want to show them that someone is really interested in them and in what becomes of them later. That someone – well, loves them, if you like. That's what they need most of all.'

She knew that he would reject that, and he did. All the things that Mr Rawlings had taught her and that she had learned for herself at Abbot's Road, all the truths about their desperate

176

needs which the children had taught her without knowing it . . .
here in this littered funk hole of a man who should never have
been given this job, she knew now with absolute certainty that
these things were true and right, because a man like Mr Neilson
rejected them.

And was afraid of them. 'Love!' he exclaimed. 'You stay in
this game as long as I have and you will bite out your tongue
before you'll use that word in a neighbourhood like this. Some of
the children here are barely human beings. They are devils, some
of the boys, and a lot of the girls are no better than animal filth.
You talk about love – they don't know what the word means.
They couldn't recognize it if you handed it to them on a silver
plate. They are no more capable of loving, or being loved, than' –
he kicked at something under the desk – 'that waste basket.'

'I don't agree,' Grace said, wondering if Sidney Goole would
be proved right, and she would be fired.

'Oh, go ahead. Go ahead. Break your heart. Dozens of others
have. It doesn't matter to me. Keep your registers up to date,
complete all the official forms, don't make a mess of the dinner
money and don't come late or leave early, and in between, you
can get on with the job in your own way. You're supposed to be a
trained teacher. I shouldn't have to tell you what to do. Just don't
come bothering me, that's all. I'm a very busy man. Very busy.'
He looked at the clock and stood up. 'You teachers think that it
is all on you, but you have no conception of how much work is
involved in the organization of a place like this.'

'But there is one thing I must bother you about,' Grace said,
sticking to her chair and leaning forward across the desk.
'Discipline. There seem to be no punishments that the boys mind.
Why can't I send them to you when they deserve it?' She could
not see that it would be any use sending boys like Sidney Goole
to Mr Neilson, but she wanted to see what he would say.

'You could, of course,' said Mr Neilson, wrinkling the front
of his flat-topped head, 'but I don't like it. I'm too busy to
lecture them, and I'm against caning. I would never cane a boy
unless he agreed to it, and do you think any of these cowardly
young gangsters would agree? They've no sense of right and
wrong. No conscience, Miss Peel. No conscience at all. But my
own is clear. I have never laid a finger on a boy in the whole of
my time at Green Lane.' He drew himself up to his full incon-
siderable height, his skull waggling slightly on the inadequate

177

neck. Perhaps he was wise not to open the office door to offenders. A boy like Norman could make mincemeat of him.

'And then, you know.' He suddenly bent and became more confidential, across the desk. 'There are the parents. If a boy was caned, the parents would come and make all kinds of trouble. Very unpleasant. We don't want that. This is an explosive place, this Cottingham Park you know, Miss – er – er – Peel. Why deliberately set a match to it?'

He was afraid of his job and of his staff and of his pupils, and of the parents too, and of the teeming district of which he could have been, if he only knew how, the moral and intellectual leader.

With no one to back them up – and how staunchly Mr Rawlings had always upheld a teacher's decision, even if he told you afterwards that he thought you were wrong – it was not surprising that the staff at Green Lane came and went like birds of passage. The ones who stayed to roost were the duds, the clock-watchers, the untalented men like Mr Petters, who were too lazy or too disinterested to look for another job where education meant more than merely filling in the hours marked on the time-table and throwing dull facts at the children without regard for whether they were dropped or held.

The morale of the school slopped round in a vicious circle. The uncertainty of seldom having the same teacher for long was what helped to create problem children; and the number of problem children on hand to disrupt any class – and it only took a few outlaws to demoralize a class of forty-odd – was what made so many teachers abandon them in despair.

Geoffrey would stay. He was actually teaching something by sheer brute force and strength of will. He liked Green Lane – not the school itself, or the headmaster, but the boys who went there. It was said by the unperceptive that he would get a knife in his ribs some night, but the boys bore him no grudge. He was tough with them, but he was fair, and he went unscathed. Not content with spending his days at Green Lane, often staying late to coach the ambitious or thrash out a boy's problem, he took over the leadership of one of the youth clubs at the Community Centre. He now lived almost permanently in the half world of Teddy boys and hipsters and junior thugs for whose destiny he was battling: freedom and work and a future, or the corruption of petty crime, the tyranny of drugs or alcohol or vicious women, the end disease or gaol.

'He's lost to us, old Geoffrey,' Denzil said. 'We'll never see him again in our world. He's like people who go out and live with the lepers. They never come back.'

Denzil would not stay at Green Lane. That was obvious. His class had a certain contemptuous affection for him, because they enjoyed his boyish lack of guile, but he could do almost nothing with them. He struggled to teach, at least to equip them for some low pressure job, even if they never learned to write their name – and there were plenty of people employed in the country who could not have endorsed a cheque if they were not paid in cash. The Remove, however, would not assimilate what Denzil felt they should know, but only what they wanted to know. It often seemed as if instead of Denzil being in charge of the class, they were in charge of him, carrying him jubilantly along on the current of their illiterate vitality.

The only reason he had stayed more than two months was because of Grace. He had abandoned the idea of protecting her, since she was so obviously better equipped to look after herself than he was, but he was still trying to interest her in his courtship. He had even hazarded a moody 'I'm in love with you' over stew and mashed potato in the canteen, but Grace had answered briskly: 'Of course you're not. You just imagine you are because I'm the only girl you know. Get another girl. Try Miss Jasper. She's gasping for a man.' Miss Jasper was a pudding girl, temporarily on supply at Green Lane and pushed from class to class and subject to subject with a face of anaesthetized resignation.

'Too fat.'

'Well, I'm too thin,' Grace said, eating the unpalatable food with the youthful appetite that Denzil found unnerving when he took her out for a meal. 'Miss Jasper will make a nice change for you, something different to practise on.'

'You used to be so nice to me,' Denzil said, as they plodded together up the stairs to the common room, 'but you're cooling off. I see the signs. You don't like me to touch you, even on the arm, and if I was to put my hand here –'

'Stop it!' Grace pulled her arm across her breast.

'Don't be afraid. I just wanted to see your reaction. I know what's wrong. You've got a thing about Colin Mackenzie.'

'I haven't. How ridiculous.'

'Oh yes. I see how your colour comes up when you speak to him. And that breathless little laugh. "Oh Colin, listen to this. It was a scream!"' Denzil pitched into a female voice and jiggled his sapling hips along the corridor. 'But I'm not going to bow gracefully out and leave a clear field for him. That's why I'm staying here, although if it wasn't for you I'd leave tomorrow and take up tutoring.'

'You're jealous?'

'Yes. Isn't that interesting? I've never felt like it before. It makes me hate the man, although I really rather like him.'

Grace wondered why Colin Mackenzie, who had the class above her, the A stream of the third year group, had stayed so long at Green Lane. He had been there two years, which was a fair record for anyone who was both honest and clever. When she asked him, he said shortly: 'You don't just chuck a job because it's hopeless,' leaving her with the idea that she had not made as much headway with him as she thought she had before she asked the question.

He was rather mysterious. Grace knew that he was not married. She knew where he lived, in a flat quite far from the school with a friend who was a writer. He had asked her out once, to a tiny theatre miles away from anywhere, because the play was written by his friend and he had to see it. A perfunctory invitation which Grace had accepted because you never knew where an evening might lead. This one had led nowhere.

Colin was five years older than Grace. He was too casual with her, too clever for her, and he either had a girl already or was not interested in cultivating one with long unruly arms and legs and a blaze of red-gold hair that was prettier than her face.

One Friday evening after the children had gone stampeding home, she went to his classroom, which was the only place where she could talk to him alone. If she started a private conversation in the common room, Mr Partridge would move up his chair and join in, or Miss Jasper would stare like a china owl, or Mrs Fitch would find something to fiddle with at the end of the room so that she could hear what they were saying. Mrs Fitch did not like Grace being young and attractive. She had said so quite openly – 'with some of these great brutes there are in the school'. She saw sex everywhere and always saw it dirty, and forbade the girls in her class to wear tight sweaters.

When Grace opened the door, Colin turned round impatiently. 'Oh, it's you.' He smiled briefly. 'Want something? I've got to rush off. I'm going to the country.'

'Lucky. Shall I keep it, if you're in a hurry?'

'No, tell it. I'll clear up.'

He dealt with the papers and exercise books on his desk swiftly, without looking at her, while Grace stood in front of him as if she were a pupil standing out to recite, and told him about Edgar Biggs.

She was very worried about Edgar. At first, finding him so alert, so willing to work and to hear everything her voice could impart above the background clamour of 3B, her worry had been how to give him his chance. He and a few others could have learned fast, but they were constantly held back by the turgid mass of near-illiterates who made up the body of the class. Many of them at fourteen had a reading age of six or seven years. Any calculation that could not be done on the fingers was out. Grammar and spelling were mysteries so unfathomable that they could not make the effort to penetrate even the crust. The only subject to which almost everybody listened was Current Affairs, and then only if they could seduce Grace away from her simple explanations of world and national events into a discussion of murders or the love lives of recording stars.

There were thirty-eight in the class when no one was ill, or playing truant, or kept home to mind the nippers or because My Dad's gone to hospital, which could mean prison. It was impossible to give individual attention, but Grace helped Edgar as much as she could. At the risk of favouritism and of the half audible accusation of sucking up to the Spades, she had set him special problems, given him homework which it would have been a waste of time even to suggest to the others, advised him about library books and let him stay after school to ask questions or expound his developing ideas.

His enthusiasm was delightful. His mind, although still cluttered with some half-baked ideas from his parents and a great deal of crudity from Glidden Road, was energetic and hopeful. A lot could have been done for him at Grammar School. But he was not at Grammar School. He was here at Green Lane in the wilderness of Form 3B and he and Grace must do the best they could together.

Then suddenly, Edgar stopped doing his best. From one day

to another, he suddenly would not work at all, but sat loosely at his desk like a dropped marionette with his large dark eyes staring moistly through the blackboard at nothing. The watermelon smile was gone. He answered Grace in monosyllables or not at all. He would join in nothing. He was a rock in the stream of argument, laughter, and horseplay which flowed on without him.

'And only today I've found out why,' Grace told Colin, 'half an hour ago in that little cave off the boiler room where the boys go for dice or a smoke. It's taken him more than a week to tell me, because he minds so much. I hate to see the coloured children cry. They do it like babies, bawling with the whole of their bodies. Poor Edgar. His parents are going home. They're taking him back to Trinidad and he's desperate. He loves England. He wants to be a teacher. He's going to lose everything he's worked for and dreamed about.'

'What can I do?' Colin shut his desk lid with a bang. 'Have them seized at Liverpool and put back on shore?'

'It's this. I'll tell you quickly because you want to go. The parents might leave him behind with someone if I could offer them a concrete hope for his future. I want you to ask the Head to put Edgar into your A class where he'll have more chance to get ahead. And I want you to help him, and if he does well, to get him recommended for a transfer so that he could get at least three years of grammar school.'

'You don't want much, do you?' Colin stepped down from the low platform on which his desk stood.

'Not much. It's just one boy. When I came here, I thought I was going to help all of them, revolutionize their lives right away. I haven't done much so far except keep Dilys Sweeney from breaking her probation. But Edgar. Here's one thing I really could do . . . we could do . . .' He was smiling. 'All right then. You could do. Would you, Colin?'

'For you or for Edgar Biggs?'

'I don't care which.' She went with him to the door. 'I just care Yes or No.'

'All right,' He opened the door. 'I'll have a try at it.' He put a hand on her upper arm and gave her something that was not quite a pat, not quite a squeeze, and went loping off with books under his arm down the pit of the stairs before she could thank him.

Mr and Mrs Biggs did not want to come to the school, because Mr Neilson had once been rude to them, so Grace went with Edgar to the flat in Glidden Road.

It was quite a formal visit. No one sat down. Grace explained the possibilities for Edgar, and his parents said that they would think about it, and stood politely with closed faces waiting for her to go.

The following week, Edgar told Grace that they would like to talk to her again. He delivered the message with the air of a royal invitation, more her honour than theirs. Mr and Mrs Biggs were slightly less formal this time, although Mrs Biggs was dressed to the nines in decolleté watered taffeta, with a heavy necklace of multi-coloured beads lying uncomfortably on the bones of her upper chest.

They poured Grace a glass of sweet purple wine and sat with her at the table by the window, drinking only when she drank and talking with stilted courtesy. It was difficult at first to find out what was in their minds. 'It is very agreeable of you,' they said, and: 'We are indeed exceedingly obliged for your trouble,' while Edgar sat with his cheeks blown out on the hard edge of a bed pretending to be a settee, looking as if he would explode at a touch.

Finally after another glass of wine, it began to leak out from the thick lips mouthing so cautiously round the correct words that perhaps something could be arranged. They might consent to leave Edgar behind. Just for a while, just to finish his education. There was a lady, a Mrs Ambrosia Drinkwater, a distant relative of Mrs Biggs living on a lower floor of the same house, who might take Edgar in. When the time came for the Glidden Road residents to be rehoused to make way for the new road, he could go with her – for a price.

'She only distant kin,' Mrs Biggs explained. 'She don't do nothing for nothing.'

'But she's a fit person to have the care of your son?' Glad though she was, and proud, that because of her they were going to let Edgar have his chance, Grace was slightly alarmed by the disparaging rasp which Mrs Biggs' voice accorded to her son's future guardian.

'Yes, ma'am. Oh surely.' Mr Biggs dropped in the weight of his deep voice. 'This is a very fine and respectable woman. Yes indeed.'

'Don't go back, Dad,' Edgar suddenly said, jumping up and standing with his brown blunt hands clasped before him, his eyes a little wild. 'You stay and Ma stay and we'll all go on the same together.'

'Here, here,' said his mother sharply. 'What's this turnabout? You want to come with us, after all your begging and pleading? We only got two passage booked, you know.'

'No, Ma.' Edgar dropped his eyes and dragged a foot out sideways in the beginning of a dance shuffle. 'I don't want to change my mind. I only thought . . .' He flashed a smile at Grace to assure her of his gratitude and confidence. 'I got so much now. Miss Peel and Mr Mackenzie helping me. Why can't life ever be perfect and a man have all he want?'

'If it were, what point in heaven? No, son. We must go. It is decided.' Mr Biggs' voice was sonorous, as if he spoke of the Lord, but he looked at his wife and it was obvious who had decided.

'You going to miss the buses though, Dad. Best conductor on any route, my Dad is,' Edgar told Grace.

'Of course. I've travelled with you, Mr Biggs, and noticed how quick you were,' Grace said, glad of an invention that was impossible to disprove.

Mr Biggs flexed his muscles a little and showed more white in his eye. 'You see, Dorothy. People do remember me.' He bowed to Grace. 'I'm glad that when I'm gone, you will be able to think of me that way, Miss, in the days of my glory.'

His wife clicked her long teeth at him like bones and said: 'How you talk, Cornelius. Your glory will come when you get back home like the prodigal son.'

'Will *you* be glad to go?' Grace asked her.

'My lady,' said Mrs Biggs, looking not quite straight at her, because her eyes were pulled slightly outwards by the drag of her hair, 'you can keep your London. And your tales of colonial brotherhood and our glorious heritage. So my heritage turn out to be cleaning up the muck and vomit of them old sick people who are never too sick to forget they skin is white. Listen here, next time I go to the movies in Port of Spain and they play God Save The Queen and the people all standing up so loyal and thinking they so British, Dorothy Biggs will get up and walk out, and if any one call me, I shall say I do no more than copy the demeanour of our dear brothers and sisters in the mother country.'

'If you feel like that about England,' Grace said, as she got up to go, 'why do you let Edgar stay here without you?'

Two glasses of the purple wine had loosened prudence from Mrs Biggs' lips. 'You offer him a good education for free,' she said. 'I'm not so dumb I can't see the value of that. He a smart boy. He'll use it. He'll snatch a job from under a white man's nose one day, you'll see.'

'I hope so,' Grace said. 'Then I shall feel rewarded.'

She smiled and shook hands. Mr Biggs put a broad arm round his wife's lean waist and squeezed to make her keep quiet while he said: 'Don't mind her, Miss. It's just that she been fed too much of this crap back home about how all the British is ladies and gentlemen. You want to be young, like our boy here, and expect nothing. That's when you find everything.'

Edgar took Grace downstairs. When they came down the broken steps into the noisy night of Glidden Road, she stopped and looked at the small crowd moving restlessly about on the corner.

'What's that?'

Music and excited voices spilled out on to the pavement as two sharply dressed men and a pigeon-breasted woman went in through the narrow doorway.

'The Conga Club. Come on, Miss. You don't want to stand here.' Edgar stood on the bottom step and clicked his fingers nervously for her.

'It sounds gay. I wish I could go in there.'

'Hush, you mustn't say that. Please come away.' A man leaning on the railings between Edgar's house and the club gave Grace a trilling whistle like a bird, and suddenly there were other men, moving closer from the corner. Edgar grabbed her sleeve and pulled her away. 'Come, Miss. You shame me. You shaming yourself, letting these wise guys stare.'

He sounded like a grown man. Grace went meekly with him down Glidden Road past the eyes of the muffled figures on the front steps all along the terrace, and the eyes behind the windows, some in lighted rooms, some in half darkness. Facetious greetings were bawled out to Edgar, and he yapped back, bristling like a terrier at Grace's side with the importance of piloting her through this hazardous street which was his home.

When he said good-bye to his mother and father at Euston, he

185

cried, and his mother kissed him with her nose cold and said: 'Do your best. Get all you can out of the Jumbles.' His father did not say anything. He was crying too.

It was Saturday and it was raining and Edgar had some weekend work to do for Mr Mackenzie, so he went back to Glidden Road to his foster mother, Mrs Ambrosia Drinkwater. She had taken the name of Drinkwater when she was old enough to need a surname, and she had taken the 'Mrs' for convenience some time ago when she was shacked up, and had stuck to it after the man moved on.

Mrs Biggs, who prided herself on being above the scurrilous level of Glidden Road gossip, had not known that Ambrosia Drinkwater was living with Gilroy. Edgar had not troubled to enlighten her, although since the children always knew who was laying who, he had been aware of it ever since Gilroy moved in shortly after he bought the house from the Jamaican.

Gilroy officially lived in one of the basement rooms, but that was only his office. That was where the weed was, hidden up the chimney and inside the door knobs, and the boys could come for it any time they had to have a charge of hemp. Gilroy himself was charged most of the time.

He was fairly high when Edgar went into the ground floor front room which was now home to him. He was sitting on the lopsided couch, his stomach bulging over his legs in a pair of violent striped pyjamas, picking thoughtfully at the strings of a guitar while Ambrosia stirred something peppery on the little electric stove that stood on a board over the washtub.

'Hullo all,' said Edgar. Mrs Drinkwater had been nice to him while his parents were about, but she turned on him with a nasty face and told him to bugger off. She was a small, hectic-looking woman with a square bunch of frizzy hair and a jaw like a naked skull, with long lower teeth rising high and yellow above the gums.

'I won't bother you,' Edgar said. 'I have some work to do. I'll stay in my room.'

Edgar's room led out of the wall without a door and had perhaps been a pantry for glass and china in the days when this was a private house and Ambrosia's room the dining-room. It was a mere slit of a room, just large enough for a narrow iron bed and a chair and some hooks for his clothes.

'You heard what I said. Out.' Mrs Drinkwater jerked her jaw

towards the door, and Gilroy smiled his sinister golden smile. 'We don't want you around today. You got some money if you're hungry, aint you? All right. What are you standing around for like a lump of coal? Sod off.'

Sometimes they turned him out in the evenings after supper, and never asked where he went or what he did. Sometimes they let him stay in his tiny room, and he would struggle to study on his bed under the dim unshaded bulb that hung from the ceiling, and try not to hear the noise of Ambrosia and Gilroy and their friends in the outer room.

They were a sociable couple. Gilroy was quite a notable figure on his side of the shade bar, and there were always people in the room, talking, laughing, drinking, making music, dancing or cuddling with the women they brought, or happily smoking hemp with their minds turned inside out to the inner glory which the weed revealed. Apart from the public service of supplying sticks of charge to those who could not live without it, there was always a welcome at Gilroy's place for those who had no place to go and for newcomers from the Caribbean who were flagging in the miserable extortionist round of ungracious landladies. Singly or in groups they all came to Gilroy. He was always kind, even to those he swindled.

At the cost of being cold, Edgar hung one of the thin blankets from the bed over the doorway for privacy, but people often jerked it aside to toss him a word or a joke or an invitation to come on out and be sociable and give his brains a rest. 'I knew a boy was driven insane with studying' was one of Gilroy's favourite reminiscences. Once when Edgar came back from Scouts with his old clothes on over his uniform, there was a coloured man with a white girl on his bed behind the blanket, and Edgar had to wait in the other room until they came out, hunched on the floor in a corner while the party fluctuated round him.

One day when he came home from school, there was a large man asleep on his bed. The man's lumber jacket and jeans were hanging on the hooks, and Edgar's clothes were in a heap on a chair in Ambrosia's room.

'What's this now?' Edgar asked his foster mother, shaping up to her boldly where she sat contemplating her turned-up toes in a paintless rocker by the paraffin stove. He was wary of Gilroy, but at nearly fourteen he was bigger than Ambrosia and was not afraid of her because he knew too much about her.

'You'll have to give up your room,' she said casually. 'A special friend of Gilroy's just arrived in town. You wouldn't expect us to put him homeless on to the street, would you?'

'My mother pays you for a room for me. I'm going to write to her.'

'What good is that? She can't write back.'

'She can too. She can write almost as good as me.'

'So what? She won't excite herself. Things don't look so serious from three thousand miles away.'

Edgar was afraid that this might be true. Letters from Trinidad took for ever to reach London. He had only heard from his parents once since they returned, and their only comments on the complaints he had written to them were: 'Glad all is well with you. Work hard. Be a good boy.'

'Anyway,' Ambrosia said, 'you have a room. You can sleep in here with me. That chair lets out from underneath to make a fine bed. A bed of your own. I'd say you was luckier than most kids.'

So Edgar lived in the corner of the room, with Gilroy's friends shooting the breeze half the night, and Ambrosia and Gilroy's noisy acrobatics on the complaining bed in the other corner taking up where the friends left off.

Mr Mackenzie was giving Edgar quite a lot of homework to make up for all that he had missed under the lax tuition of Mr Ellis; but it was impossible to study. He visited round among his friends in the neighbourhood, many of whom were sympathetic to his ambitions, but in none of their rooms was any peace, and their sympathy did not extend to creating some for him. He tried the Community Centre, but there was always something going on there in all the rooms, and no escape from the racket of teenagers. Sometimes he trekked up to the public library, and worked there until the reading room was closed. It was beautiful there, with everyone's head down and the mouths shut and even the feet muted, but he did not go often because he could not afford the bus fare, and it was a long way to walk, and when he got home there was little chance of rest or sleep. Often he was so tired that he could hardly keep awake in school.

When Mr Mackenzie asked him: 'What's wrong? You're not working half as well as you did at first,' Edgar shrugged his shoulders and fabricated a grin and said that everything was fine.

He had not been too well, he said, but he was all right now. Everything would be fine. He was not going to admit the comedown of his circumstances and risk losing Mr Mackenzie's interest because he thought it was not worth working with a boy who had so little chance.

Then Mr Mackenzie, who had quite an urge for Miss Grace Peel, as Edgar could detect, although, like many Jumbles, the man lacked the guts to do anything about it, must have talked to her about Edgar. She tackled him one day when he came up the little staircase from the boiler room where he had been shooting crap during recess with Big Morris from 3A and some older boys.

Big Morris, an undersized boy from Dominica with a huge head like a pumpkin, had made up to Edgar as soon as he was moved into his class. He was a member of the Zorro Men, one of the local coloured gangs, and he had been after Edgar to go in with them right from the start. Edgar had shied off at first, but since he was so often out on the street in the cold evenings with nothing to do and nowhere to go, he had become acquainted with some of the rest of the gang. After living for a while with Ambrosia and Gilroy, it was not so easy to feel himself as superior to them as he had when he was influenced by the queasy respectability of his parents.

Big Morris, whose voice had scarcely broken, was one of the youngest, a shrill and comparatively innocent hanger-on. Most of the others were older and more dangerous, and the *élite* among them wore the barbarous fish hooks sewn into their jacket sleeves near the cuff as emblems of top rank.

As Edgar's home life became more and more unappetizing, it was hard for him not to be tempted by the gang's adventurous company. If they would have him, he might join up with them for kicks. A Zorro Man. When they were on a job or looking for trouble, they wore black masks and dark pants and sweaters, moving like shadows of vengeance through the fearful streets.

'What have you been doing down there?' Miss Peel asked him. 'I've been looking for you all over the playground.'

'Oh —' Edgar cocked an ear back at the stairs. He had been sent up first as scout, and the others had stopped and stayed quiet at the bottom when they heard Miss Peel's voice. 'I went down there to be alone. Have a think to myself.'

'I thought that might be it,' Miss Peel said in her clear smiling voice, while Edgar started to edge down the passage, trying to

189

manoeuvre her away with him so that the others could come up before the bell rang. 'Something is wrong, isn't it? You're worried about something, and you're not working so well. No, don't go. Stop a minute and talk to me.'

'There aint much time to get back, and Mr Mackenzie won't have us be late. Can't we talk while we walk, Miss?'

'All right. But tell me what the trouble is.'

'It nothing.' He got her away from the stairs and safely round a corner. 'Nothing is wrong.' He was not going to admit the truth to her either. He wanted her to think well of him. 'I been a little sick in this cold weather, but I'm fine now. Doing just fine.'

'You haven't looked sick,' said Miss Peel, who was more perceptive than Mr Mackenzie. 'I watch you, you know, and I ask Mr Mackenzie about you, because this was all my idea and I want it to turn out well.'

'It will, Miss,' Edgar said, although his heart was heavy, because her enthusiasm made him more shamefully aware of his weakening struggle and of how he was letting her down.

'It must.' She put her hand on his arm and stopped him as they reached the door of his classroom. The bell had rung, and the room inside was fulminating with shouts and the banging of desk lids. 'There is something wrong, Edgar, I know there is, because nothing could stop you from going ahead before, and now I think you are slipping back.'

She looked at him with those eyes. They had brown and green and grey in them like lake water, rounded at the top and straight at the bottom where her lower lids came often up to smile. Edgar looked at her and all of a sudden, without warning of its approach, a lump started up his throat and exploded in his mouth like a sob.

She still had her hand on his arm, and he was ashamed for her to see that his jacket had a hole at the elbow and no edge to the cuff. 'Is it difficult at home?' she asked. 'Is it something about your foster mother? Isn't she good to you?'

'Oh yes, ma'am.' Jeepers, if he were to tell her even one hundredth part about Ambrosia, she'd die! 'She pretty good to me.'

'But it's difficult to work there perhaps?'

At the end of the corridor came the long legs of Mr Mackenzie, his arms full of books. If Edgar denied the truth, they would both think he was dumb, that he was wasting his opportunities, that he must be written off as worthless.

'I can't work at all.' He let it all out to her in a desperate gabble. 'They's nowhere. She stole my room ... friends all the time, and noise. ... I can't do nothing ... nothing ... nowhere to go ...' The long legs approached. He struggled to control himself against the cheating tears, and very coolly Miss Peel stepped in front of him, guarding his distress.

'Edgar and I have been talking,' she said, and Edgar mastered his babyish blubbering behind her calm voice and her straight narrow back. 'He has a small problem about his homework. Not enough peace at home.'

'The usual problem.' Mr Mackenzie smiled as Edgar turned his reinstated face to him.

'But Edgar is not a usual boy,' Miss Peel said. 'I've got an extra little room in my flat. I don't see why I couldn't take Edgar home with me two or three times a week and let him work as long as he wants.'

Mr Mackenzie raised his eyebrows, and Miss Peel said quickly: 'I know Mrs Meikle won't mind. She'll be glad to help. She'll give me her card table. Would you come, Edgar, if your foster mother agrees?'

Why did he hesitate? Why, even for the fraction of a moment, did he hesitate to grab the spar of wood she had floated to him in the dark sea where he was drowning? Didn't he want to make the effort and save himself from the wreck? Wasn't he good enough?

'Gee, thanks, Miss,' he said, with such swift ardour that he did not think that she had noticed the hesitation. 'You bet I'll come!' He plunged headlong through the classroom door, but pulled himself up and held it open for Mr Mackenzie, poised courteously so that everyone could see that here was Edgar Biggs, the model pupil, the boy who was going to beat his wings away and up to glory.

Edgar had thought that everything would be different and wonderful now, and at first it was. He loved going to Miss Peel's flat and having cocoa and sandwiches and sitting at peace in the little square room with his legs stretched out under the card table. Sometimes he worked like a black fury with a lifetime of ignorance to make up in one night. Sometimes he did no work at all, but just sat and dreamed, enjoying the warmth and comfort and the sounds of Miss Peel on the other side of the door, getting her supper, dressing to go out, singing to the wireless, talking tenderly to Mrs Meikle's ugly cat.

When Edgar got home, however, it was always so horrible that he wondered whether it was worth it. Ambrosia and Gilroy had seized on his visits to Miss Peel as an enormous and salacious joke. They jeered at his learning, asking questions to test his knowledge and then shrieking with silly laughter when he gave the answer. They jeered at Miss Peel, and made up a whole disgusting saga for their friends' amusement about the reasons for her interest in Edgar and what went on when he went to her flat.

When Edgar protested, they only jeered louder and stretched their crude imaginations wider. When Edgar continued to stand up for Miss Peel, Gilroy knocked him sprawling a couple of times, and the next time stood him against the wall and belaboured him thoughtfully about the head, still wearing his gold-plated grin. Being hit on the head made Edgar vomit, and he could not do any work for two or three days.

He tried not coming straight home, but drifted round the streets, joining up sometimes with Big Morris and his gang, in the hope that he would get back to Glidden Road late enough to be let alone. But it was never too late for Gilroy and Ambrosia, who did not get up before noon. Never too late for their scurrilous jokes, and if he was late, the jests had more scope. Edgar would slump on to his sagging chair bed in the corner and put his hands over his ears and try to hide out the taunts in silence. It was becoming increasingly hard to bear.

Every night he vowed bitterly that he would not go home with Miss Peel again. The next time she looked out of her classroom window and waved to let him know that she was on her way down, he would not be there waiting by the railing. At first he always was, but as the weeks went by and Christmas came and went and Edgar did not go to Mass, as he had promised his mother he would, and Ambrosia and Gilroy did not slacken their hilarious torture, there began to be many days when Edgar was not waiting, and it became harder to find excuses for Miss Peel. Sometimes his foster parents found reasons themselves for keeping him away. When they wearied of the Miss Peel jest, it still irked them to find Edgar studious and ambitious. 'Wanting to set himself above us. Think he too good for us. I seen Spades get that way. Next thing you know they marrying white and making laws against they own people.' They gave him jobs to do, messages to carry, packages to deliver: little envelopes which burned Edgar's frightened fingers as he clutched them with his hands in his coat pockets, ready to throw them from him at the slightest hint of danger.

'Don't walk that way,' a man called out to him once as he skulked past a café where the patrons were half inside and half out. 'You can always tell what a Spade has on him when he hold his hands that way.'

When Ambrosia and Gilroy were feeling generous towards Edgar and anxious to bring him up in the way he should go, they would give him a drink or two and fuddle him into joining a party. A light-skinned little girl who did not look much older than Edgar had come to the room one evening while her man was negotiating a deal with Gilroy in the basement. The occupant of the closet bedroom was out – there had been two others since the first one had usurped it – and Ambrosia had pushed Edgar and the girl in there with the admonition to have some fun, dears.

Edgar did not think it was much fun, because the girl was domineering; but at least it was experience. At least it was growing up. So was blowing the hay. Gilroy started by making Edgar take a drag on his cigarette from time to time, and then gave him a butt to finish by himself. It took only a few puffs before the weed hit him and he began to know the elation, the inturned, prideful, cock-a-hoop enjoyment of the supremeness of himself. His mind was clear like glass. His legs and arms moved cleverly by themselves, without effort.

He stayed out of school for almost a week in a happy stupor. On Thursday night he woke sweating with terror, and went dully back to school thinking that he had learned his lesson. The next time Gilroy offered him a butt, he refused, but the time after that he took it.

One day while he was at school, Ambrosia sold his Boy Scout uniform to the secondhand clothes dealer in the next street. Now that he did not go to Scouts any more, Edgar hardly ever saw Frankie Bott, for he would not invite him to Glidden Road now, even if Ambrosia allowed it. He did not want Frankie to know what his home life was like. Frankie was friendly with Miss Peel. He often rode home on the bus with her. He would blab to her about Edgar, and Miss Peel, who meant so bloody well, might come nosing down to see what was going on.

Frankie was only a kid anyway. Edgar was outgrowing him fast. They met sometimes at school where Frankie tried to inveigle him back into intimacy, but Edgar could not be too friendly in the playground, not if he wanted to keep in with Big Morris and his lot. The Zorro Men did not make friends with Jumbles. The White Hunters, the gang of some two hundred Cottingham Park youths with attendant Teddy Girls and chicks, to which Sidney Goole and some of the bigger boys in Edgar's class belonged, were chiefly responsible for fomenting the inter-racial prejudice at Green Lane. The Zorro Men, who were their enemies, kept it on the boil.

The gangs were not the direct result of coloured immigration. There would have been juvenile gangs anyway in Cottingham Park, as there were all over the world; but it happened that here one gang was white and another black, and to Teddy Boys looking for trouble, the Spades were a natural target. In London and Birmingham and Manchester and Liverpool, it was not the colour problem which created the gangs, but the gangs who helped to make the colour problem.

'I'm worried about Edgar Biggs,' Frankie said to Miss Peel on the bus.

'I'm worried too,' she said. 'He's not working properly any more. He's always got some excuse not to come and study. If he doesn't get going again, he isn't going to have a chance in the exams. I wouldn't even have the nerve to send him up for them.'

'You'd set your heart on that, 'adn't you, Miss?' If only she had set her heart on Frankie Bott! He would have shown her. He would not let her down.

'I had,' she admitted. 'Perhaps we've been working him too hard. People do get stale.'

'You're telling me they do,' Frankie said. 'I been stale on algebra ever since I took it up. But it's not that with Edgar, Miss.'

How much to tell? Unhappy though he was because his friend was slipping away from him, gone all nigger on me, as he put it to himself, Frankie was not a sneak. But this was not sneaking. This was no secret except to somebody like Miss Peel who would never really know the score at school because she was a teacher, and a lady at that.

'What then?' Miss Peel turned her flattering attention to him.

194

''E goes with that gang. The Zorro Men they call theirselves.'

'Oh I don't think so. Edgar told me he hated gangs.'

Frankie shrugged. 'I seen 'im with them. 'E'll get in bad, Miss. The coppers is always watching them boys.'

Miss Peel still did not seem to believe it. Not of her precious Edgar. But she could not say he had not warned her.

And what if someone were to warn her about Frankie? Would she refuse to believe that too? Frankie did not think that anyone but Gary Steptoe knew, but in a school like Green Lane, you could never be sure.

Gary Steptoe was in his class and Frankie had drifted closer to him as he realized that he was losing Edgar. It was a friendship of necessity. He had to have someone. He disliked Mrs Fitch, who had a face like the business side of a saw and was always suspicious even when you were honestly trying. The class was overwhelmingly big, and those who had been together the year before ganged up against the newcomers from Abbot's Road.

Because Frankie was small for his age, the bolder girls had called him Baby and the larger boys had pounced on him with squeals of joy as someone new to bully. They punched him and tripped him up and took his cap and his moth-eaten gloves and spoiled his work and pulled his spiky hair, just for giggles. Gary Steptoe, who was on probation for robbing his stepmother's gas meter, was the only one who had been friendly. Frankie knew that he was bad. He had done far more than the magistrate's court ever heard about, and would be lucky if he was not hauled back in there before his probation was over; but so what? He was a friend. He was respected in the class because he was handy with his fists, and Frankie began to be left alone after he took up with him.

Gary was attractive, with a dark Mediterranean skin and a slinky way of getting in and out of crowds unnoticed. When the school had started a charity collection shortly before Christmas, and each child who volunteered was given a box to beg among family and neighbours for the destitute of central Europe, Gary was probably not the only one who begged successfully and slipped all but a penny or two from the box for himself.

'All the kids are doing it,' he told Frankie, and showed him how to tease the coins out of his box without a mark. Frankie spent the one-and-ninepence quickly, because it hung on him like leaden gyves.

What would happen about the collection money? No one had said anything, although Mr Neilson had raved over the speakers about the total being so small. If his mother found out, she would kill him. Mrs Bott was a devil with her tongue and would lie as soon as look at you to make a scandal, but she would never take anything that was not hers. She had nearly blown a gasket that time when people thought she had taken Mrs Neale's rent.

Often in the old days, Frankie had thought that life was tough; but now he knew he'd had it easy. These days he hardly knew where he was going any more. It was a mess. Nothing was the same since Abbot's Road closed down.

One afternoon after school, Grace Peel and Frankie Bott, both suffering from a wave of nostalgia for Abbot's Road, decided to go home a different way and walk past the school where they had been happy.

While Grace was combing her hair before the blotchy cloak-room mirror, sagging at the knees because it had been hung for dwarfs, Colin Mackenzie dropped wearily down the steps and asked in an unusually dispirited voice: 'Who are you getting prettied up for?'

'My steady. We're going to walk round by Abbot's Road and have nostalgia.'

'The fog's coming down.'

'Never mind. Abbot's Road is all browns and greys anyway.'

'Can I come with you?' Colin asked very suddenly, as if the words had come out by themselves.

'Of course.' Grace turned round, surprised. 'But it's out of your –' She saw his face. 'What on earth's the matter?'

'I need company. You and Frankie Bott. I'm sick of myself.'

'What's happened?'

Colin stood slumped in his bulky tweed overcoat, looking at her moodily, with his head poked forward and his dark hair rumpled.

'I lost my temper and lashed out. Caught the young brute hard on the side of the head. Too hard. I lost control in a blind way I hoped I never would. If you lose your grip on yourself, you lose your grip on them, you know.'

Grace nodded. 'Was it Darby?' Darby was a fiend in skin-tight pants and a long Italian jacket who had been tormenting Colin with insults and sly mutinies for weeks.

'Yes. He roared at me like a savage. It was disgusting. And the class was worse than ever after it happened. The gang element at the back rumbling and snarling like the Mafia. Darby stuck his head out of the window and pretended to be sick. Maybe he was. I was too angry to look.'

Frankie was waiting outside the school in a drift of thickening fog, jerking with the harsh cough that so many of the children kept all winter. When the three of them turned the corner, they found Edgar Biggs leaning against the railings with crystals of damp on his crisp black hair.

It was so long since he had come home with Grace that she had ceased to expect him. 'Hullo,' she said. 'Are you going to come and study? We thought we'd walk. It's such a lovely night.'

Edgar laughed shortly, jerking his head, and then glanced at Colin and quickly away, with a sidelong roll of his eyes instead of his former direct gaze. 'I might.' He pushed himself away from the railings, and they walked on together. At the end of the street, where a straggle of coloured boys were kicking something in the road, Edgar dropped behind the other three. Frankie stepped back to join him, and Grace, trying to talk cheerfully to Colin, had half an ear on the boys, wondering why they walked in silence.

When they reached Abbot's Road, the fog was coming down like a blanket over the high brown wall, shrouding the stone carvings: BOYS, GIRLS, INFANTS, over the doors scrawled over with love pledges and rude opinions; drifting in acrid folds across Grace's face as she stood with Frankie on the chill familiar pavement, wondering what she had expected to find.

Abbot's Road Secondary looked just the same. Not a brick had been pulled down, not a slate cast off the roof. Why had they been turned out? The school might stand there for another year at the rate the road scheme was progressing.

'We could have stayed in it, you know,' she turned to tell Frankie, and out of the fog came the sound of running feet, and a shout, and suddenly Colin was in a fight with three hulking boys who had him rammed against the wall, flailing and cursing to get free. Edgar was in the fight too, mixed up with his head down among the legs, and Frankie, shrieking with excitement, swung a futile punch at a denim thigh, and someone took a backhanded swipe at him and knocked him to his knees.

Grace jerked him up and screamed to him: 'Run! Get away

from this!' He looked in horror at his raw bleeding knee and ran stumbling and sobbing across the road, and disappeared.

Colin was on the ground against the wall, and one of the boys was kicking him. Grace was shouting for help. She could not see Edgar, and then she saw him struggle to his feet from under a rolling body and spring like a cat. A yell, a roar of unintelligible profanity, and suddenly the white boys were gone again into the fog, and people were materializing from the houses across the road.

'The White Hunters,' Edgar said, breathing fast and jiggling on his toes like a boxer. 'He ought to be more careful who he hit.'

Two or three women and a mob of dirty children were bearing down on them, and a small crawling car had stopped a little way along the street, and a man was running back.

'Get away from here,' Grace whispered to Edgar. 'Get right away. And thanks.' He gave her a quick gleaming grin and was gone soundlessly into the vapours under the wall.

'That nigger done 'im?' The women were jostling and clamouring at Colin, who was sitting against the wall with his feet sprawled, holding his head. Grace knelt between him and the women. 'Go away,' he said thickly, and turned his head to be sick.

'Has there been an accident?' The man who had got out of the car was excited. His face was white and jumping under a prim hat that came down too low over his ears. 'I wasn't going to stop. In the fog and everything. This is such a dreadful neighbourhood. You never know ... And then I thought, it's someone in trouble, I thought, and I couldn't bring myself to go on, so I ...' No one paid any attention to him as he gabbled on, hopping nervously on and off the kerb.

'It's all right.' Grace was wiping the blood from the back of Colin's head to see what had been done. 'Please go away. We'll be all right.'

'Fetch a copper,' the women said. 'He looks rough. Someone ought to do something. Take 'im to 'ospital,' while one of the children wailed incessantly: 'What's 'e doing down they-er?'

Colin muttered: 'No ... God, no ... just get me out of here.'

Still kneeling, Grace looked up at the bystanders, who were keeping their distance as if the huddle on the pavement were explosive, and said: 'It's all right. He's with me. I'll take care of him. I'll take him home.' Can I get a taxi?'

'On a night like this?' One of the women laughed in a cackle, and the children laughed too, wildly, like mad gusts of wind. The man from the car stepped forward with his adam's apple bounding and said jerkily: 'Please let me. I'd like to help. I'll take you.'

Colin got to his feet, pressing heavily on Grace's shoulder, pinching the bone so that she gasped, but turned the gasp into: 'Can you walk?'

'Go ahead.' With one of Colin's arms round her shoulders and the other across the narrow shoulders of the agitated Samaritan who staggered more than Colin under the weight, weaving his feet about in the road, they got to the car.

The man would have been a bad driver on a clear day. In the fog he was terrifying. He was up on the pavement twice, the flimsy little car teetering from wheel to wheel, and once into someone's driveway, and once almost into a bus that loomed suddenly ahead with yellow lights blindly seeking, and the people inside sitting stiffly, as if they were already dead.

At the top of the hill the fog was not so thick, and they bumbled along under the ghastly lights of Park Road with the man muttering and thumping his brakes and screeching his gears and shaking his mittened fist at passing drivers who hooted him out of the middle of the road.

When they were on the pavement outside the blackened stone flats where Colin lived, Grace leaned in at the front window to thank the man. 'No, no,' he said. 'I was glad. I liked to do it,' and let out the clutch with a jerk that nearly decapitated her as the little car jumped forward and went chugging away down the middle of the street with a blue cloud swirling from its exhaust.

Colin's friend Peter was not in the flat. Grace bathed the large shallow wound at the back of Colin's head and felt his bruised ribs, trying to judge by his yells whether they were broken.

He seemed to be all right. He would not let her call a doctor. 'I'm just beat, that's all. I'll sleep. Be better tomorrow.' He swayed through to his bedroom and flopped down on the bed with his clothes on. Grace stood uncertainly in the untidy, bleakly masculine sitting-room, and he rolled his head round and looked at her through the open doorway with one bruised eye open and the other screwed up against the pillow.

'I don't like to leave you here alone.' She went through into the bedroom and stood looking down at him. He took her hand and

199

pulled her down, and she sat on the floor and put her head on to the bed beside his. 'I'll stay till Peter gets home.'

'I would have to be knocked half silly,' Colin said, 'with you here like this.'

'Will you come back?' he asked presently.

'I expect so.' She turned her head and smiled into his bruised face and his kiss tasted of the dried blood on his lips.

Just before he went to sleep, she asked him: 'Did you see about Edgar? He had a knife.'

'Most of them do,' he murmured with his eyes closed.

'Yes but ... this is what I mean. He used it.'

It was different after that at Green Lane.

The school was not any different, and Grace had her full load of worries.

Sidney Goole was picked up in a café brawl, and when Grace went to court to speak for him, his father shrugged him off with: 'I can't do nothing with him. Don't ask me where he goes at night.'

Sidney was now on probation, with the threat of an approved school if he broke it. Having avoided being sent away this time, thanks chiefly to Grace and no thanks to his objectionable father, he was more triumphantly insolent than ever. He still addressed Grace insultingly in the third person. He told dirty jokes to the girls when she turned to write on the blackboard. He continued to bait the coloured boys, and to knock the smaller ones about whenever he got the chance. This was his thanks to Grace for having committed mild perjury in court to save him from detention.

'Next time you get hauled before the magistrate,' she was goaded to tell him, 'I shan't come and speak for you.'

'So who wants her?' he jeered. 'I can look after myself.'

And now Sidney Goole had a rival troublemaker in the class. Patrick's mother had been an Irish tinker. When the boy was too sick to go on the road with her, she had left him with the friend of a friend, who had passed him on to her cousin. The cousin brought him to England. The mother was never heard of again.

No one knew Pat's real name nor his exact age. He thought he was fourteen, but he looked ten and behaved even younger. He was loud and free-fighting and less willing to learn than anyone else in the class. Grace could get nothing into his head, not even the idea that he could not roam at will round the class, insulting people, kicking over desks, putting nails down the backs of the girls' necks, making feeble attempts to burn down the school with little smouldering piles of damp newspapers in the cloakroom, which Norman imperturbably kicked out when he made his monitor's rounds that always brought him back reeking of cigarette smoke. When Grace referred Pat to the educational psychologist for possible transfer to a special school, she was told that it was impossible to judge his intelligence without knowing his age.

Remembering how she had kept Louie Maule content and busy at Abbot's Road, Grace would have done the same with Patrick, but there were no jigsaw puzzles at the school, and when she bought some, the other children jeered and knocked the pieces off the table, and Pat was in more fights than ever.

Rita Patterson, who had been playing truant on and off for weeks, forged a letter from her mother to say that she had been ill. When Grace took her by force to the school doctor, he confirmed what Grace believed the child already knew: that she was pregnant at thirteen. Grace saw the mother, expecting her to be frantic and needing help, but she covered up for the girl and protested that it was only a billiards attackt, and soon after, Rita left for good. No one knew where she had gone, nor what would become of her.

Frankie Bott grew less like a small confiding bird and more like an urchin, was in trouble with Mrs Fitch, kept bad company, and hardly ever waited to go home on the bus with Grace because he thought that she would be with Colin.

Grace worried about her class, and about Frankie, and about Edgar, who would not work any more, and about Mrs Fitch, who had tried to make the Head get rid of her by saying that she favoured the boys over the girls, and about Denzil Raymond, who had pronounced himself through with women and ready for the monastery, and about Mr Neilson's senseless threat to move her after Easter away from Form 3B, just when all of them except Patrick had written at least two lines about the Armada, just when Norman had written a poem.

The unstable days at Green Lane were turbulent with worries, but Grace could weather all of them, could struggle through anything, because she was in love with Colin.

*

The Scotney Society was gaining no ground. Its complaints were heard, its pamphlets dutifully read, one in ten of its Letters to the Editor published when there happened to be a dearth of 'period' material. People with no authority agreed that something should be done, but no one with any authority at all gave any assurances that the plans for the Transurban Expressway would be modified by one inch to suit the cave dwellers.

Not a pickaxe had yet been laid to a mellow red brick, not a bulldozer come ambling like a truffle-hunting pig down the narrow streets where chestnut and sycamore mingled their bright new abundance with the sad citified plane tree. This spring was the same as any other; but who could say what havoc might not have been wrought before another spring came to the treasured village?

'Like it's no use kidding yourselves,' Zona Davenport told her father. 'The only reason they haven't started on the road is because they're not ready. Not because they're paying any attention to your groovy complaints.'

'There is to be a question asked in Parliament.'

'I know. Roger and I and some of the cats are going to the public gallery in our craziest clothes, and –'

'Crazier than those?' She was wearing greenish-black trousers cut off raggedly below the knee, and a boatman's sweater with her name spelled backwards across the chest.

'Yep. And Roger is going to stand up and yell: "Freedom from tyranny!" and I'll hold up a placard saying: "Hands off the Abracadabra."'

'You think that will do any good?'

'Nope.' Zona smiled, which was rare. Her mouth was so often dropped sulkily at the corners that the lines which the thirties were bringing to her face were all heavy downward ones, so that a smile could be little more than a stiff grimace. 'But it will be a ball, and we shall be eighty-sixed. Like it will be good publicity.'

'It won't help the Scotneys much.'

'So who wants to? You think we'd go to all that trouble just to help Miss Jessie to stay in her own private morgue?'

But Miss Jessie was already beyond help. The letter had come – addressed to her sister, which was an insult in itself, since Miss Sutcliffe was the elder – the letter which spelled death of the heart and ruin and the end of everything that mattered.

202

In view of the shortage of school accommodation in this area and of the urgent need for up-to-date educational facilities for the young people of Cottingham Park and a catchment area defined by the Education Committee, plans for a modern Comprehensive school with full technical and recreational equipment had been initiated. . . . Park Lodge and some adjoining property the ideal site for erection of London's finest school north of the Thames . . . conveniently consentaneous with the redevelopment already proposed in connexion with the new Expressway. . . . Negotiations for purchase by agreement. . . . Compulsory purchase authority. . . .

'They've done us!' Miss Sutcliffe slapped the letter on to Mr Davenport's desk with the flat of her hand, and the Siamese cat shifted its crouching paws and made a noise like a child in pain. 'This is the end of everything. We are finished.'

'But you're not.' Mr Davenport put a hand on her shoulder, surprised to feel the bones so frail in one who was always so inflexible and erect. 'This is just the beginning. You'll fight this, of course. You and Celia.'

Mrs Vulliamy had wandered quietly into the room behind her sister, and had taken a seat on the edge of a hard chair, holding a tapestry handbag primly on her lap, as if she were being interviewed for a job she did not hope to get. 'We can't,' she said dully. 'Jessie says it is too much for us.'

'You're always putting words into my mouth!' Miss Sutcliffe spun round instinctively to argue, and then she remembered that it was true, and shut her bony jaw with a little quiver. She was no longer the leader, the elder sister, the energetic champion of her toppling world. She stood there with all the fight gone out of her, only a skinny old lady with her long canoe-shaped shoes sinking into the velvety rug.

'Yes, it is too much,' she said. 'We cannot fight any more.'

'But you *must*!' Mr Davenport beat his fat sedentary fist against the side of his shining scalp. 'This is where the Society can come into its own. You've done so much already, you can't give up now, just when we have a concrete new injustice to work on. There are all kinds of things that can be done. Sit down, I'll make some notes. Let's see . . .' He sat down in his polished revolving chair and began to jab at a long yellow pad. 'Legal advice first, I think, to see where we stand. Then –'

'No, Maurice.' Miss Sutcliffe came behind him, and with a

203

return of the old imperiousness, tore the sheet of paper off the pad. 'Please leave it alone. We didn't come to ask your help, but just so that you could be the first to hear the news. You have always been our good friend, and you believe in all the things which have meant so much to us.'

'Don't talk in the past sense like that, Jessie.' He swung the chair round. 'They still mean everything. You can't let them rob you of your home! You've held their meddling hands off for so long. At least refuse the purchase by agreement until we see where our best strength lies.'

'You see.' Mrs Vulliamy spoke slowly and quietly and looked down at her little woollen paws clutching the bag, as if she were talking to herself. 'You see, we have done as much as we can, and there must come an ending. We are too old. We have fought with you against the road, and been glad to do it, and been some help, I hope. But this, coming on top of everything – we have no more strength for it. We are too old.'

'Neither of you is too old!' Mr Davenport's gallantry went unacknowledged. He stood up. 'You can't let them get away with this. A school here in the Scotneys – every Tom, Dick and Harry from the slums running shrieking through these streets. A playground for savages in your garden, right outside my windows. It's unthinkable.'

'Dear Maurice,' Miss Sutcliffe said. 'Egotist to the end. I wish we could help you.'

'Don't twist me, Jessie.' He shook his fist at her. 'I want to help *you*.'

'Thank you,' she said with dignity, 'but Celie is right for once. We are too old. We do not want to fight any more.'

'Where will you go?'

'We don't know yet. It depends what price they give us for our house and land. There will be a lot to do, packing up, deciding what to sell. We shall perhaps put things in storage and go to an hotel while we catch our breath and decide what comes next.'

'I'm truly sorry, Jessie.' He stepped towards her.

'If you're sorry because we are letting the Society down in the chance of a new tussle,' said Miss Sutcliffe with a snap of the old censorious spirit, 'that's very selfish of you, Maurice.'

He laughed, and for the first time in his life he kissed her on her cheek, soft and rumpled like unironed silk. 'You think you are

204

beaten,' he said, 'but you are unconquerable really, my dear. I apologize for insulting you with pity.'

*

Out of the blue, and not in answer to anything that Martha Banning had written, came a letter from Anne. There was no address, and it did not come from New York, but from some small, unheard-of town in Connecticut.

'Everything has gone wrong,' Anne's loose, hectic writing said. It had never been neat, but had it always been as disorganized as this? 'I'm coming home. Do you think the Aunts will take me in?'

'Who writes to you from America?' Guy asked, picking up the empty envelope.

'A girl who used to do my hair. She went over there to get experience.'

'What kind?'

'Every kind, from what she writes.' She did not often lie to him, but she could not tell him yet, because of what she was going to write to Anne.

She wrote: 'The Aunts are gone to the Camberley Hotel in Victoria Street. Their house is being pulled down to build a school up there. They are terribly upset, naturally, and haven't decided what to do next. I don't think they will be able to do much for you.'

If Martha had written the truth, she would have said: 'I don't think they will do anything for you.' 'We are finished with Anne,' Miss Sutcliffe had said, and she had not spoken of her since.

'This whole place is being torn apart,' Martha wrote, 'and a lot of our old places and the people we knew, like old Zlotnik and the Greek and Mrs Angel (remember the baboon collar? She still has it) are being pushed out for a new road that's coming through. Everything will look different, but we'll stay, and get used to it, I suppose, when the dust settles. So come to me, Anne darling. If you have nowhere to go, please come to us. The children can go in together and you can have the little front room you used to have when you and I were children.'

That was why she had to lie to Guy. It would be time enough to tell him when Anne wrote to say that she was coming. No sense in having the argument yet, because she might not come. She might not even get the letter.

Martha sent it to the old address in New York, and in a few weeks it came back to her stamped *Unknown*.

Anne Rogerson had two pounds and a dollar and a few American pennies in her bag, and that was all. All she had in the world, apparently, unless something happened about Alan's lapsed insurance, which was unlikely, and too complicated to bother with any more.

She could have left her bags at the station and taken the Underground to Cottingham Park, but the taxi was a necessary expense, to show the Aunts that she was not destitute.

Just as the bar bill on the ship had been a necessary expense. After paying all that for the fare, was she then to be one of the sickly figures wrapped in plaid rugs on the deck, who only crawled out for meals or bingo and missed all the fun? There had been plenty of people on the boat willing to buy drinks for her, but one did not drink that way, trading on being a woman alone. One paid one's way and stood one's share of rounds, and stopped at one's own pleasure, not somebody else's discretion.

First in and last out, she remembered saying to the cynical bar steward as she walked carefully past him on her way to the saloon, very late for a dinner she did not want.

Or was it the master-at-arms she had said it to? He was cute, and it was not his fault that he had been summoned to put her to bed like a child; although he had not put her to bed, but had pushed her gently inside the cabin and shut the door. And locked it? Or had she locked it herself? At any rate, the mattress salesman had not been able to get in when he came discreetly knocking. The mattress salesman had not ever got in – or had he? It was hard to remember. Anne had been more or less drunk most of the time between New York and Southampton.

Driving through the London streets, so familiar and yet so strange, like going back to school on the first day of term and being surprised that everything looked the same because you were different after each holiday. Anne sat on the edge of the seat in a thin suit that was too light for the English June and the neck fur made of five poor little dead martens who had looked so glamorous when Alex first gave them to her, and rehearsed again what she was going to say to Aunt Jessie.

Not to Aunt Celie. It would not matter much what she said to Aunt Celie, who would kiss her squashily and ask no questions, just as she had asked none in her letters. But the questions that Aunt Jessie had not asked because she had not written, these would be there, in the air if not on the lips, and the atmosphere would be thick with Sutcliffe disapproval until Anne could melt her down a little.

'I have come home,' she would say. 'Please let me stay with you, only for a while, until I find something. You are all I have.' Why hadn't Martha written? She was completely under Guy's thumb by now probably. That often happened to women when they married late. It could have happened to Anne, only Alan's gentle thumb had been taken away from her. 'I have no one,' she would tell Aunt Jessie. 'No one but you.'

And the mattress salesman. He would wait alone at the Piccadilly Hotel tomorrow, for hours perhaps, and then go away and drink horse's necks and think wistfully about ships that pass in the night. Or perhaps he would not be at the Picca-dilly, but at home with a wife, perspiring guiltily as he thought of poor jolly Mrs Rogerson waiting for him in vain.

Through the narrow leafy streets of the Scotneys the taxi took her, and Anne squeezed her eyes tightly then opened them stiffly wide, trying not to cry. Her hands were trembling. She should have had a drink at Waterloo. Absurd to think that she could fool the Aunts by just staying sober this afternoon and putting on a lot of gay make-up.

Changing gear, the taxi turned the sharp corner into the little rise that led to Park Lodge. The uneven pavement with the trees sprouting from it, nourished by God knew what except dead rats. The doll's cottage wedged like a captive child between two tall brick houses. Someone had painted the door primrose yellow and made Austrian designs on the window boxes. The gate of the Peevys' house, all heavily scrolled iron. Dr P. had brought it three hundred miles, weighing down the back of his car; but now he was gone, apparently – two puttied-over nail holes marked where the brass plate had been – and left his gate behind. Now the long plaster wall with the tiled coping broken like old lower teeth; the birch hanging over, reaching down for the street, grown half into the bulging wall that had been built too close to it, the front porch, sublimely hideous with the dark dusty ivy and the three marble steps, pride of Aunt Jessie's grandfather.

The house stood solemnly, self-consciously enthroned at the top of the little street. The blinds were neatly half-way down in

207

all the windows. There was some litter on the front steps. Old Pringle was long past washing them, and no cleaning women ever stayed long enough to get through the interior and out to the steps with the combination of Pringle and Aunt Jessie to tell them what to do.

The taxi driver rang the bell, which rang too far away to be heard, so that when Pringle took a long time to answer it people would think the bell was broken, and start to thump on the square oak door with its green and yellow glass panels set between thick leading. One of the panels was broken. There was a jagged two-inch hole, surrounded with cracked rays. Aunt Jessie must be slipping to let even that much air from the outside world penetrate into her hall.

When the driver had put all the bags in the porch, Anne paid him – less than thirty shillings left now – and said: 'Don't wait. I can manage.' She did not want him to see whatever scene was enacted when the door was opened, depending on who opened the door. She should have written to them. Why hadn't she? Because she wanted to surprise them, of course, not because she was afraid that if they said No she would have nothing left.

She stood in the porch for quite a long time, pushing the big bell button into its moulded plaster casing, banging on the wooden part of the door, noticing vaguely the cobwebs in the corners of the porch, and filth on the opaque glass of the narrow side windows. Then she put her eye to the hole in the glass. The hall was dim because the thick coloured panels let in almost no light. She waited until her eye grew acclimatized and saw that the grandfather clock was not there. The vast hat-stand, antlered like a bachelor herd, was not there. The umbrella stand of glazed pottery shaped like the trunk of a tree was not there. Nothing was there except black whispering shadows, the spirits of the Aunts and all their family before them, rustling their long dusty skirts. Everyone must be dead.

If I could have a drink. Just sit down somewhere and have a drink and then I'll think what to do. Anne left her luggage in the porch. There was no one in the street except a very young man in a bowler hat and a Guards' tie going downhill fast, and at this point, she did not much care if everything went. Her clothes and possessions were a nuisance. They cost money to transport from place to place. You had to have somewhere to put them when you got wherever you were going. One might be better off with nothing at all, roaming free of the absurd conventional trivia of life. With her head and its heavy black coil of hair which nested in the slipping marten stole poked slightly forward because it was suddenly too heavy to hold upright much longer, Anne walked away round the corner and down the hill towards the sound of traffic in Park Road.

When Martha and Guy went into the saloon bar of the Lion to get a drink on the way to the cinema, they saw that there was a little commotion at one end of the broad semi-circular bar.

A thin woman in a rumpled silk suit, with a long strand of black hair slipped loose down her back was loud in argument, with sloppily despotic gestures.

Nancy, with no annoyance showing on her firm unblemished face, was trying to quiet her down. Jack was polishing glasses with brisk detachment and saying his stock piece for trouble-makers. 'Now be reasonable, madam. We're trying to run a decent house here.'

'Listen to me,' the woman slurred, wiping out their faces with a sideways sweep of her hand. 'Just you listen to me a minute. . . .'

'Oh dear.' Martha made a face. It was tiresome to sit in the bar with a drunk dominating the scene. Especially tonight when the trouble with Bernadette at bedtime had given her a headache.

She had put the child to bed early to make it easier for Mrs Pellew, and before she reached the foot of the stairs, hideous roars began to come from the bedroom.

'Don't go back,' Guy said. 'She's only trying to keep you from going out.'

'I must.'

'If you do, she'll be worse next time.'

'He's right, you know.' Terry put on the businesslike face she wore for doing things with her father, like carpentry. 'You shouldn't give in to that child.'

'All right, you go and see what's wrong then, if you know so much about five-year-olds,' Martha said, and as Theresa took her saffron hair and solid legs up to her sister's room, the roars rose to a scream: 'My mother's gone away! They've taken my mother to the cemetery!'

'Now I'll have to go up.' Martha looked at Guy.

'Too much television,' he said.

When Mrs Pellew arrived, flustered and hot although the

209

evening was cool, with the ribbon of her hat unstitched and two buttons unfastened at the waist of her dress, Martha said brightly: 'Bernadette is in bed, and I don't think she'll give you any trouble tonight.'

She should not have said this, should not have admitted the possibility of trouble; but Mrs Pellew's martyred face as she began to go slowly dot and carry up the stairs made reference to her last skirmish unavoidable.

'I'm sure I hope not.' She sent down the remark without optimism.

Before they reached the gate of their small paved front garden, where some irises and distorted lupins struggled gallantly out of the gravelly earth through a shroud of wet newspaper blown or thrown over the wall, Martha remembered the letters to post.

They went back into the house. From the hall, they heard Bernadette, out of her room, screaming at Mrs Pellew: 'I wish you'd go away! I wish you dinta never been borned!'

Martha started wearily for the stairs, but Guy pulled her back. 'She's paid to cope with it,' he said. 'I'll deal with Bernie tomorrow.'

'That will be too late. That's like going into the stable and beating a horse when it's forgotten what it did.'

'She won't forget.'

'But it wasn't fair of us to listen. She thought we'd gone out.'

'Oh – fair. Too late. These kids are not as subtle as you think.'

'They are more subtle than *you* think.'

They quarrelled mildly all the way up West Hill. It was almost the only thing they ever quarrelled about, the eternal conflict that was perhaps essential for parents if they were not both to be too hard or too soft. It always gave Martha a headache.

As they walked past the bar in the Lion towards a corner table, the noisy woman with the slipping hair dropped her bag on to the floor. It splattered out powder compact, lipstick, pills, pencil ends. Money rolled.

'Whoops!' She half stepped, half fell off the stool. When she crouched down unsteadily to retrieve her things, her limp marten stole swung off her neck and lay dead on the floor.

'Let my help you.' Martha was glad that Guy bent down. The other men at the bar only sat and stared, and one of them was laughing.

On all fours, stretching to grab a coin, the woman tossed back the loose hank of hair to look up at Guy, and then turned her face to Martha.

'Anne!'

Much later that night, when Anne was asleep at last in Bernie's little room with the street lamp shining cruelly on her sad white face, Martha climbed into bed beside Guy and said: 'Thank you, darling.'

'What for?'

'For letting me bring her home.'

He turned his head to look at her, his face deliberately blank. 'What else could we do? If we'd left her there she'd have finished the night in a police cell or the DT ward. I don't mind. Just keep the girls away from her, that's all, until you've sobered her up enough to decant on to the old ladies.'

Martha turned out the light and settled her body into the position of closest contact with his. 'But suppose,' she said after a while, 'Aunt Jessie won't do anything for her. They could hardly have her at that stuffy hotel in this state.'

'She'll look better tomorrow.'

'You know what I mean. Getting drunk – that wasn't just tonight. Not just because she'd been to the house and found everyone gone. I think this must happen quite often now. You can see that by looking at her. That naked need in her eyes when she asked you for a drink downstairs, and the way she pawed for the glass.'

'That's Jessie's worry, not mine. She can send her to her father. He's practically an alcoholic too, so they should be able to set up a charming household.'

'How can you be so savage? Anne was never like this. This is just something that's happened to her, horribly quickly when you think that it's less than three years since Alan died.'

'Lovers and liquor. Such a sweet widow.'

'You never liked Anne. I knew that. She was too big a part of my life before you. Old friendships are one of the things that get knocked about when you marry an aggressive man.'

Guy turned and put a hand on her and she said: 'You're trying to shut me up. Listen, darling, about Anne. I –'

'Forget it. Forget it, I said!' His voice and hands were suddenly brutal. 'God dammit, why do you have to come to bed in a shroud?'

Anne was not sober enough the next day to be presented at the Camberley Hotel. Martha tried to keep her in bed and make her eat, but she had to go out to buy food, and when she returned, Anne was in Guy's study with a bottle of whisky. They did not talk about her drinking, not yet. That could come later. Martha kept up the pretence that she was ill. She got her back to bed, where at least the children could not see her falling about and losing her shoes, and when they came in from school, feverish with curiosity, they were allowed to talk to her from the door of the room where she lay with her hair streaked on the pillow, smiling over-effusively at the nonplussed girls.

'She has the measles?' Bernadette asked when she came downstairs, dragging her feet on the paintwork because she was thinking.

'We don't know yet.' Martha found herself using the bright nursery school clap-hands-and-stand-up-quite-quite-tall voice which was supposed to jolly the girls along, but usually made them suspicious. 'Until we know what it is, you'd better not go too near in case of catching something.'

'I like her,' Bernie said. 'She smells like Uncle James.'

'That's the medicine.'

'That's what Uncle James calls it. The best medicine in the world is a dthrop of Irish whisky,' Bernadette said in a passable imitation of the overdone brogue of Bessie Myers' middle-aged cavalier.

As soon as the children were in bed, Anne came downstairs in a stained dressing gown, and into the kitchen where Martha was finishing dinner.

'Martie,' Anne said, 'can I have a drink?'

'Not now. We're going to have some food in a minute.'

Anne stood propped against the refrigerator, her chicken bone hand clutching the big shiny handle, and Martha stood by the stove with her hands in the deep pockets of her apron. They looked at each other long and steadily, and the truth of all that had not yet been said was between their eyes.

'Do you have to have it?' Martha asked.

'Have to? Have to? Who *has* to do anything?' Anne said irritably, switching her eyes away. 'Of course I don't have to have it. I just could do with it, to steady my nerves. I haven't been well, you know.'

So it was not time to talk yet. 'Of course. You haven't been

212

well,' Martha said numbly, and Anne went to the cupboard under the counter. In less than twenty-four hours she knew every place in the house where there was a bottle.

She drank the whisky straight, with a gasp and a shudder, and Martha watched her. This thing that had happened to Anne made her able to believe in the Gospel stories of possession by devils. This was Anne – narrow white face, the skin still miraculously pearl-smooth; straight black hair; beautiful legs and feet – and yet not Anne. Someone else in possession of her body.

'Have a drink,' Anne said, pouring another for herself. 'Don't stare at me.'

'No, I'm too hungry. Come on, you must eat something too. It will – it will keep you going. The Aunts are expecting to see you tomorrow, you know.'

'How gay,' Anne said. 'How too damn utterly disgustingly gay.'

But after she had fiddled her way disinterestedly through dinner, holding her fork in her right hand like an American, her left hand always touching her glass, she began to grow a little sentimental about the Aunts. Tolerant because he thought she was going tomorrow, Guy was drinking with her, teasing her along quite amiably. Only Martha sat stiff and silent, hating everything.

'The old dears will be so glad to see me,' Anne said, with the kind of artificial optimism which a shot of morphia can bring to the dying. 'Everything will be all right tomorrow. I knew I was right to come home. They've always been so good to me. They'll let me stay with them until I find a job.'

'How are you fixed for money?' Guy asked.

'I'm not,' Anne laughed hysterically. 'Isn't that absurd? But I'll get a job. There are hundreds of things I can do. In New York, I was a receptionist to a Swedish dentist. With a white dress you could see through and white shoes with soles like truck tyres. I was a waitress for a bit before – well, no one you know. I can get a job tomorrow. No difficulty. No one need worry about me.'

I must. I'm worried sick. Martha looked at Anne, sprawled in the armchair, spouting fuddled courage because of the glass that had been in her hand for hours. She looked at Guy and saw that to him Anne was no more than a faintly and temporarily entertaining soak. He did not understand at all. Tackling the

213

Aunts tomorrow was going to be a picnic compared with what she might have to say to Guy after she came home.

Martha watched Anne all morning until it was time to leave. She was sober, but cold and clammy, and her limbs seemed to be empty of power. Martha took her to the mews to get the car out, because she did not dare leave her in the house alone, and Mrs Saithe came and stood at her front door and exclaimed: 'It's Miss Holder! I'd have known you anywhere, though I must say you've changed since the old days. Been to America they tell me. No doubt that's what's done it.'

'Mrs Rogerson now.' Anne kept her chin in the marten stole which she insisted on wearing because it disguised the thinness of her neck, and made an effort to be cordial, although Martha, trying to open the garage padlock, could feel her trembling as she stood by her.

'That's right. And how is hubby keeping?' Mrs Saithe asked, although Martha knew that she had told her when Alan died.

'I'm sorry to hear you have to move,' Anne said. 'That's bad luck.'

'It'll be bad luck for 'oomsoever tries to move me.' Mrs Saithe stood with the toes of her grey gym shoes lined up on the step, and craned a malevolent glance down the mews as if the eviction crew were even then advancing. 'You talk of America! That's nothing. You know where they want to send me? Kensal Rise.' When she laughed, her mouth was a pink cavern, like a yelling baby. 'Special block of flats for old folk. *Old folk*, the lady said to me. Go and live in it yourself then, I told her, for she was no chicken, mind.'

The aunts would not receive Anne and Martha in their bedrooms, so the meeting had to be in the warm soporific lounge of the Camberley Hotel, with the sun struggling to penetrate the heavy net curtains in pale shafts for dust to dance in, and a party of schoolgirls and ingenuous women with florid hairy cheeks having lemonade and biscuits all over most of the furniture.

Aunt Celia kissed Anne warmly and exclaimed at her thinness, then bit her mauve old lip and looked as if she might cry. Aunt Jessie offered a cheek to kiss graciously, and bade them all sit down as if it were a formal party.

Jessie Sutcliffe was stony. There was no other word for it. She had never been spryly convivial, but she had usually been animated in argument, lively in censure. Now she was stony. She seemed to have become calcified with the loss of her house. She was not interested in Anne. She did not bicker with her sister. She hardly spoke at all to Martha.

Mrs Vulliamy moistened her lips once, and asked Anne what her plans were, but she hardly listened to the answer, glancing nervously over her shoulder as the schoolgirls raised a shout of laughter. No one said anything about Anne moving into the hotel. It was so obviously impossible that it would have been indecent even to hint at it.

Aunt Jessie talked quite amiably about the hotel, and the food, and the poor quality of the mattresses and the staff and the other residents. She spoke of old Pringle and of the Home where they were trying to trick her out of her annuity, and of her own contest with the Lands Tribunal to get a better price for Park Lodge. She spoke without sentiment, impersonally, as if the old maid and the old house were already something in a past, forgotten life. She did not speak about Anne, except to say: 'I am glad that you are staying with Martha. You and she were always such friends.'

When it was time to go, Aunt Celia pulled Martha aside and said: 'She looks *ill*.'

'She hasn't been well.'

'Oh please look after her!' Aunt Celia whispered. 'Please look after our girl.'

'Our girl,' Anne said bitterly as they drove away. 'I'm still that to Aunt C. But Jessie seems to have cut me out of her life, which means Aunt C's life too. How much do they know? I can't remember what I wrote to them. Everything was in such a mess then.'

'They know about that man – Alex, was it?'

'Oh. Did I tell her about Alex? Big mistake that.' Anne spoke lightly, but she frowned as if she was trying to keep her face in order. 'I'd go back to the States,' she said presently, 'if I had the money. John – the people I was with in Connecticut before I came over, I could probably go back there. Let's stop somewhere and have a drink.'

'No.'

'Would you lend me the fare?'

'No.'

'Some friend.'

'I want you to stay with us.'

'Guy won't like that.' They did not look at each other. Martha kept her eyes on the traffic. Anne stared ahead without looking at anything.

'No,' said Martha honestly, 'and neither shall I unless you let me help you.'

She was afraid that Anne would say: 'I don't need help.' She waited, and then Anne said quickly: 'Stop drinking, you mean?'

'Yes.' It was said.

Anne did not answer. Later when they were driving through the Park, where people were sitting under the trees on green chairs or on the new summer grass, she sighed and said: 'It isn't any good, you know. You get dried out – oh, all the time you think: Look at me. I can leave it any time I want. But there's always an excuse to start again. Just one little shot to steady my nerves. Ah, that's better. Just one more and I'll be on top of the world. . . .'

As the days went by, Martha kept hearing Anne's defeated voice: 'It isn't any good, you know,' and her own bewilderment replied: No, it isn't any good. I don't know what to do.

If she locked up all the drink, Anne went out for it, or went down to the basement flat to see what Bessie Myers would give her.

Anne had not told the old ladies that she was practically penniless, but Aunt Celia, risking the consequences when her sister examined their bank statement, had sent her a cheque for a hundred pounds. 'Buy yourself pretty things,' she had written, and so Anne bought drinks in bars, and bottles which she brought home and hid in different drawers every day in a pitiful attempt to keep Martha from finding them.

The children knew. It could not be hidden from them.

'Is Anne ready?' Martha asked one Saturday when they were all going out to lunch.

'She won't be able to come,' Terry said casually. 'She's drunk.'

One morning, Bernadette said: 'You'll have to excuse me from doing my teeth. Anne is in the bathroom throwing up.'

The door was not locked, and Martha went in. Anne was crouched over the washbasin, her arms spread out, her hair splattered over the taps, retching as if her soul were trying to leave her body.

When it was over, Martha washed her face and smoothed back her hair. 'Have you had a drink?' she asked, and it was not hard to make her hands callous and her voice severe. Because she had never wanted a drink before breakfast, the thought of it made her sick too with disgust, and with shame for Anne and the memory of all the mornings when they had woken together and Anne had been the one who got up to take the dog out, the one who had a face on for the day long before Martha had wandered to a bath, the one who got them both to work on time through the shattered City streets after a night of cocoa and accordions in an air raid shelter.

'I just put a splash in the cup,' Anne said. 'I can't drink your coffee by itself.'

Once when Martha went down to Bessie Myers' flat to collect Bernadette, Anne was there drinking rum with James Donahue on the lopsided sofa which had sunk so low that they were practically sitting on the floor with their legs straight out. Uncle James' roguish crimson leer was very close to Anne's face. His hand was on her knee. She was not looking at him, and did not seem to notice the hand, but Martha said abruptly – she seemed to do nothing but bark out governessy orders these days – 'Come on up, Anne. It's time for dinner.'

'She's going to have dinner with us,' Bessie said, coming out of her odorous little kitchen in which nothing seemed to be cooked but garlic and tainted grease. She wore a lardy melon-coloured lipstick and an apron over a pair of shorts, which looked all right from the front but ludicrous from the mammoth back view. 'I've got two extra pork chops.'

Bessie was not jealous of Anne, although James Donahue had taken on a new frolicsome lease since she began to wander to the basement. Martha suspected that Bessie deliberately encouraged her to come down here and deliberately plied her with drink as a means of getting her own back on Martha for the imagined injustices of her basement tenancy.

'Anne doesn't like pork,' Martha said shortly.

'Not like pork? Not like pork?' cried Uncle James, reaching

behind him for the bottle. 'Nobody can not like pork. Me staple diet, if you want to know. Ask Bessie. But I'll share me portion with this little lady, and gladly. Reach me the bottle, Bernadette, love. Either me arms have grown shorter or the sofa has walked away from that little table.'

'I might as well stay.' Martha thought that Anne was laughing somewhere inside, although it did not show on her face. 'Dear Guy will be delighted. Don't pretend he won't.'

Martha did not answer. When Bernadette came round the sofa with the bottle, prancing a little in the sickening actressy way she affected down here, she grabbed her before she could kiss James Donahue goodnight.

'Don't be angry,' Bernadette said as they went upstairs. 'You're supposed to be sorry for Anne because she's ill. That's what you told us.'

When Guy realized that the children knew, although with the instinctive diplomacy of innocence they did not talk about Anne to him as they did to Martha, he said: 'You must get her out of here. I don't care where she goes, but get her out.'

'I can't. She has nowhere to go.'

'She can go wherever she would be if you hadn't brought her here.'

'I can't,' Martha said again, hating to oppose him, hating his hardness, not knowing how to make him understand how she felt. 'She's my friend. It's all different, I know, but underneath this – this sickness, this disease, obsession, whatever it is, she's still my friend.'

'Your friend! A hopeless lush. Do you want me to admire you for your saintly efforts to redeem your old drinking companion? Well I don't. I blame you for mixing our children up in this.'

'It doesn't hurt them. We've always said we'd never shelter them too much, or tell lies. They know about people drinking. They saw you drunk once as a matter of fact. I wasn't going to tell you. They take it all as it comes. They're much less critical than we are. And they like Anne. When she's sober, she's sweet with them.'

'When is she ever sober?'

'Most of the time. She's getting better, you know she is. I *am* helping her.'

'You want to think you are because it was your idea. You started this crusading bit, rushing in where even the old girls knew enough to keep clear, and now you're stuck with it. Well, get unstuck. Listen, Martha, either you get her out of here, or I'm clearing out.' He did not mean this. The discussion was still on a reasonable level, but it was a code phrase to show her that he was genuinely angry.

That night, Martha lay awake with her mind in turmoil. She knew that her husband and children must come first; she knew that she had to help Anne, and knew what might become of her if she sent her away. If Anne would not change, would not break down and admit that she was lost and that she needed help to find the way back, life would rapidly become intolerable. Their happy life here in this comfortable old house, so familiar that Martha did not see it in detail any more, would be ruined. The children might grow away from her. She and Guy might wound each other so badly in a quarrel that it could never completely heal. And all because of Martha's stubborn . . . stubborn what? Conceit, was it? An overblown view idea of herself as the saviour of the fallen?

But if friendship was worth anything, surely it was worth this. If she were now to reject Anne, who was more wretchedly unhappy than she revealed, all the affectionate years of experiment and adventure which they had built up behind them into shared memory would be wiped out; worthless.

She owed more to Guy and the children than to Anne; and she loved them more. Yet for that very reason, Anne could not be cast out to gratify Martha's supplanting love. Anne had nothing. Martha had everything.

She got out of bed and stood looking down at the road shining black under the street lamps. A few doors down, three very young people spilled out of a tiny car. They called a dozen goodnights, banged the car doors and shrieked after the unseen driver as he drove his little car up the kerb, between the wall and a lamp post and away down the empty pavement like a maniac perambulator.

Martha looked back at the bed. Guy was sleeping through the noise. She had a vague idea of going round to St Joseph's and ringing the bell for Father Mack and asking him what to do. He was always willing to talk. Even in the middle of the night, he would be ready to pour reason on these fretted loyalties.

Here's a facer for you, Father. Whatever I do, I'll hurt somebody.

219

Not necessarily. You know that there is really only one thing to do. That will be caring for all and neglecting none. Too difficult? But the more you give, the more will come to you. The Franciscan Brother Giles put that the other way round, but it means the same. No, there is more truth in it: It is only the salvation of yourself that can achieve the salvation of those you love.

Martha went into Anne's room and woke her up. Anne slept lightly. She sat up at once, pushing away her tumbled hair, staring with midnight eyes.

'What now?' she asked. 'Is the house on fire?'

'I have to talk to you.' Martha sat down by Anne's feet. 'It is this. Either you let me help you, or I'm going to get a doctor and have you sent away somewhere for a cure.'

Anne made a face. 'Don't talk to me as if I was a hopeless alcoholic. It's enough to make me one.' She laughed and leaned forward to look out of the window over the bed, drumming her fingers lightly on the pane.

'You're doing that for yourself,' Martha said roughly. 'Stop pretending and admit it. I can help you to fight it, I believe, but only if you want that as much as I do.'

'What could you do?' Anne asked the question casually, as if it related to someone else.

'There are ways. Filling you with food. A lot of sweet things. Big doses of vitamins. One small drink every hour, then every two hours, then every three until it gets to none at all. But if you cheat, I'm through. You'd have to go.'

'You're hurting my legs,' Anne said inconsequentially, and Martha jumped up in a fury.

'If you haven't got the guts to face it, then get out! Get out and sicken someone else. I'm not going to let anyone spoil my marriage, and especially not you, you sloppy, drunken bitch!'

Kindness and patience had done nothing for Anne. At the shock of abuse, she crumpled and sobbed and held out her thin bare arms to Martha, crying: 'Help me – oh help me! I need your help!'

They talked all the rest of that night. Anne told Martha many things; all the worst of the things that had happened in America after Alan was killed.

The day I was going through Alan's papers. That was the day

when everything started to go wrong. Not finding out that there wasn't any money. I knew that, though not quite how bad it was. I was feeling fairly all right. I was in control of myself. I had made the decision about not coming back here. I had got a job. I was tough, the girl I worked with said. That was her best adjective. I'd depended on Alan for six years to show me how to behave – you know how you always said I switched personalities according to who I was in love with? Now I was depending on myself. Being myself. Being very adult, I thought.

Then I found Alan's passport. I knew that he meant to renew it, because we had talked about coming home if he didn't get this job. I saw that it had not expired while he was alive. It expired on the day that he died. A passport to death. No further.

That was the night I met Alex. I had to go out. I went to a bar. I met some people I knew, and Alex was with them. We had a lot of drinks. It made me feel better then, but worse afterwards, of course. But I kept seeing Alex – God knows why because he wasn't my kind at all, nor I his. I stopped being tough. The girl I worked with said it was reaction setting in, but it was more likely hangovers.

A passport to death. Less than six months after Alan's death, I was living with a man who never told me the truth about whether he had left his wife or she him. I had lost my job. Not being fired, or fired myself. I just wasn't quite sober enough to go there for three days, and it didn't seem worth ever going back.

Alex had enough for us. The apartment was much nicer than the filthy place where Alan and I had lived. I was quite domestic for a while. Had some vague idea of domesticating Alex, and he liked it for novelty at first; but then it began to go the other way round, and he undomesticated me. It began to be not worth bothering to cook a proper meal, if neither of us was sober enough to eat it when it was done. We'd go to bed, wake up and go out and do the town, get something to eat – nothing ever closes in New York. Bed again about dawn until the maid came banging in to clean.

That was only the beginning. That was when we were still keeping civilized drinking hours. As long as you don't start until lunchtime, or even half way through the morning, you're still fairly safe. But when one day you have to have a drink as soon as you wake because you can't get up or dress or face the day at all without it, that's when everything lets go. That's when Alex and I really got lost. Suddenly we were so damn sick of each other that if we didn't have a drink before we looked at each other in the morning we'd have vomited right there on the carpet in that bedroom which was quite classy before we got it all messed up and the maid wouldn't come any more. We vomited anyway. The first drink to make you sick, and the second to pull you together.

Then Alex went out one day and didn't come home, and I never saw him again. I couldn't pay the rent of the apartment, of course, so I got a room somewhere on the West Side. That was when I was a waitress. I couldn't afford to drink, so I didn't. I thought I was safe because I'd been able to lay off, even though I still couldn't eat properly.

I met John and we went around together for a while, and he had a ramshackle sort of cottage on a lake in Connecticut and we were there most of that summer, and I stayed on last winter and John came at weekends. It wasn't heated. You've no idea how primitive some American houses can be when they try. But I had wood for a fire and a lot of houses to go to. The people round there are very friendly as long as you drink. A glass permanently in one hand is the passport to society.

A passport to death. John was all right as an outdoor person, when we'd fish, or swim, or sail a dinghy; but indoors – I don't know – it wasn't his fault that his hands and nails were never clean. He had his own printing plant and didn't just stay in the office. But the other things were his fault. When I left him, he followed my taxi to the station in his seedy old car and cried on the platform while we waited in the wind for the last train to New York. It didn't move me a bit. Some of his dear old pals came swooping into the station with the mistaken idea that I was merely going on a visit and must have a send off, and they rode in the club car with me to New Haven and got a bit more stewed. God knows how or when they got back. Or John either. He had got swept along with them by mistake, after we had been through the big farewell weeping scene. But he talked to some other woman all the time and fell off the train at New Haven without even saying good-bye to me.

When Martha woke Guy in the morning, he said: 'You look ill, What's the matter?'

222

'I didn't sleep. I've been talking to Anne.'

'Did you tell her to go?'

'Give her one more chance, will you, darling? It's different now. She's facing it. She wants to get back.'

'I've heard that before,' Guy said. 'On the rare occasions when my mother came to see me, she used to say: "Everything will be different now. I'm going to stay out of the pubs. I'm going to save money and take you away from there."'

'Oh God, I'm sorry. I should have thought of this. Is it because of your mother that you hate this thing so much with Anne?'

'Let's not be too psychological. I was better off at the Home than I would have been with poor Mum. I don't resent her. Do I?' He sat on the edge of the bed considering this.

'Can Anne stay?' He looked up and shook the old thoughts from his head as Martha broke in. 'Please let her stay. If I can see her through this, it will be the one really useful thing I've ever done in my life. Brother Giles –'

'Not Brother Giles before breakfast.' He stood up and took her hands. 'You want this so much?'

'Only if you want it.'

Guy looked at her and sighed. 'She stays. God help us, for we knew the worst too young. Let me get into the bathroom before she crawls in there to find the bottle that's floating in the cistern.'

*

'The Street Offences Act, they call it.' Eileen Kelly jabbed a thick finger end at the newspaper. 'Are you listening, Denise?'

They were in a cafeteria, having tea and jelly trifle. After they bought the paper and saw the headlines, they had to turn in somewhere to mull over this new development in the threat to their professional life.

'Lead on, Macbeth,' said Denise. She was the educated type who had fallen, so she said, on hard times. 'If I were to tell you who my family were, your eyes would drop out,' she often said. Eileen, who could spin a tale herself, knew why she resisted the temptation to amaze. As long as the family remained mysterious, they might really be someone.

'Well, it says . . .' Eileen stuck her tongue between her uneven

223

teeth and ran her finger slowly back and forth across the printed column. 'It says ... Oh I see, this is in the House of Lords. All those old geezers in coronets and ermine cloaks. Mother of God!' She threw back her head and neighed. 'What a time of it they had this day! Peers and peeresses, it says. Trust the old girls to be there.'

'What does it say?' Denise spooned delicately round the bottom of her cup for the sugar. She was a tiny dark girl like a glossy bird, almost two feet shorter than the coloured ponce she worked for. You had to laugh to see them together. The long and the short of it. Eileen liked to clothe her thoughts in familiar expressions, to label intelligibly the bafflements of life.

'A public nuisance, it says. Common prostitutes and that. The Prostitution Act, this buzzard says it should be called.'

'That's fair enough.' Denise rested her sharp little chin on her hands and gazed rationally at Eileen. 'Street Offences makes you think of dog shit.'

Eileen clicked her teeth. 'Oh listen here. It says there are one eight nought nought prostitutes in the metropolitan area. One in five four nought adult women in central London is a har-lot.'

'Shows the crying need,' said Denise. 'There's no supply without demand.'

'That's right.' Eileen read on, shaking her dull blonde head over the unfamiliar words as if they were water in her ears. She read about the danger of vice being driven underground. Well, there could be something in that, but you couldn't have it both ways. If they didn't want the girls on the streets, they must put up with having them holed up somewhere on the end of a telephone, and that would be more danger to the girls than anyone else. There'd be all sorts of middlemen springing up like super pimps, Denise said, trying to get everyone's good money in return for the use of addresses and telephone numbers.

'It says about the ponces too,' Eileen said. 'You'll want to hear this. Lord Muck. "I talked to a street walker," he says, "a sensible and if I may use the word, a decent woman."'

'Dig that,' said Denise, getting out her lipstick.

'"You will never drive us off the streets,"' Eileen droned on like a child reading from a primer. '"The threat of prison will not stop the girls. If they wanted to stop, the ponces wouldn't let them."'

224

'Too true, if they're all like Rocky.'

'Why don't you shop him?' Eileen asked. 'You could get him jailed tomorrow.'

'Sure,' said Denise. 'And get myself marked up with a razor as soon as he came out. No thanks.'

Eileen shrugged. Denise was caught, she knew, and so was that black man. Denise was afraid of him, and he was afraid of what she could tell the police, and so scared of the money she gave him that he threw most of it away on drink and gambling.

Eileen plodded on to the end of the newspaper story. It was full of good laughs. A peeress had said that the queers should be thrown off the streets too. Hear, hear. And some joker said that any man who went with a girl had degraded himself and should be brought to court along with her.

'Handcuffed together?' suggested Eileen.

'Dog knotted,' said Denise, and they had a good laugh about it. A good laugh was a tonic, Eileen said, but the cafeteria was filling up, and some old trout in a sea-going hat came and put her tray down at their table, and they thought they might as well go.

Life was going to have more problems now, if the bill went through. Some of the girls were saying that they were going to chuck it and find other work. 'I might go into cabaret,' they dreamed. 'Or try the films. There's always modelling. Nice money there.' But Eileen was not so dumb as to believe that she could land any glamour job if she left this game. Film extra? You could starve that way, if you did not die of boredom first. She'd get by somehow. Most of the girls would. Even the ones who boasted that they were going to get out would probably be going strong two years from now if their health held up.

When it was established that it was still not going to be an offence to get screwed, only to solicit, Eileen found that she was quite glad that circumstances were going to force her off the streets. She had had the streets. They were not what they were, especially up Cottingham Park way, which was getting such a notorious name, because it was a respectable neighbourhood gone a bit off the rails, that all kinds of people were about who had no business there.

Debutantes for instance. The Queen had killed them off, it had appeared, by having no more presentations, but here they were, all dead but they wouldn't lie down, with layers of petticoats and double-barrelled names and chinless boy-friends with the fluting oh-my-dear-it-was-a-howl voices. They had a new game. It made a nice change from throwing champagne glasses off roofs and tipping waiters into fountains. Tart baiting, they called it. Oh, it was a shriek.

After a party, all dressed up like Christmas, they would cruise along in a car, just two men in front it would seem, when you were on the pavement or in a doorway and they stopped by the kerb and called you over. You went. You never knew; and there might be good money here, because this sort was usually too scared of you to haggle over prices.

'What are you doing out so late?' asks this daisy-faced boy, innocent as you like.

'What do you think?'

'What's the price?' asks his dear old college chum, almost swallowing his Adam's apple. And when you name it, they get to asking: 'What do I get for that?' and leading you on, and you're giving back as good as you get, still thinking there may be something in it, when up from the floor at the back jumps these two giggling tarts whose Daddies should have warmed their bottoms long ago, and the whole outfit is making game of you and laughing fit to bust a blue blood vessel.

It made Eileen sick. Once when she was with Denise, and they had both thought that the boys in the car were genuine prospects before the half drunk girls exploded with laughter, Denise had taken a swing with her handbag at the slicked blonde head of the gurgling boy in the front seat and said: 'What's so funny? Those amateur whores you go about with are much funnier. They don't even know enough to get paid for it.'

Denise was sharp like that though. Eileen was always left dumb and furious. Once she had taken off her shoe because it was the only thing she had to throw and it had gone inside the car window and she was left hopping on the pavement, with Toodie barking like a fool while the jolly crowd drove away. Oh, they had loved that, all right.

Denise was sharp, but she had fallen for the line that time when those two boys in the Jaguar picked them up and said they were all going out to their place in the country and spend the night. The price was fixed and the price was good. Eileen sat beside the one who drove, and he had his hand all over her and was getting quite steamed up. He said some fancy things too, and

Eileen, letting the hand rove, began to play with the old idea of taking up with one man who would be good to her. They were out near London Airport when the boys suggested stopping for a drink. Outside this pub, Eileen and Denise got out first, and then the boys quickly slammed the car doors and drove away shrieking with mirth. Shouting after them and futilely running a few steps, Eileen could see the silly head of the one in the back wagging about as he killed himself with the fun of it.

Eileen felt hysterical, but Denise was practical. They went into the pub and had a drink. They sat by the window, and when a car headed towards town stopped and a man came into the bar alone, they got talking with him and asked him for a lift back.

'How did you get out here?' he asked. 'Where do you come from?'

'Oh,' said Denise, very casual, very classy. 'We just flew in from New York.'

That was the way Denise was. Sometimes you could believe what she hinted about her family. But when they were in the car, all sitting in the front seat together, and the man was so agreeable: no passes, but just chatting with them in his easy way as if they were old friends, they told him the truth, just for the laugh.

He did not laugh. He looked almost as angry as Eileen had felt when she found herself out by the side of the road, only now she did not mind so much because it had turned out all right, except for the loss of an evening's work.

'Look at it this way,' the man said after a bit. 'You know why those useless young fools think it's clever to take the mickey out of you girls? It's because they're scared of you. They're pretty green, you know. A lot of these college boys are virgins, though I can't see why, since the girls they run around with are more than willing. A deb dance isn't much more than one huge brothel, with the hostess procuring, although she doesn't know it.

'These boys would be scared to death to go with you. So they play smart with you because they're afraid that just by looking at them you'll guess how inexperienced they are.'

'You've nailed it,' Denise said. 'I've had a few of them. Give you the jitters. I'd rather take on their grandpappy. He might pop a blood vessel, but at least he knows his job.'

When the man put them out of the car at Park Road, they said good-bye like old friends, and he gave them his card. The girls stepped into the Underground station to read it after he had gone. His name was Detective Inspector Buller.

Denise recovered first. 'Ah well,' she said, while Eileen still stood flabbergasted in the dim old brown-tiled booking hall which wouldn't be half itself if they modernized it when they built the new road flyover, 'if they put him on the street cleaning squad, perhaps we shall see him again after all.'

She was like that, Denise. She could turn a joke about everything.

A telephone. That was the thing. It was clear that it was going to be difficult to sustain professional life without it, unless you wanted a ten pound fine or two weeks in the cooler. Even Hyde Park was going to be cleaned up, which was not strictly fair. The streets was one thing. But people did not have to walk through the Park at night. If, like Billy Graham, they did not like what they saw there, they could stay the hell out.

The Brass Monkey and some of the little back street clubs – and there would be new ones springing up like toadstools to meet this new situation – would be more useful than ever, as long as the sharp characters like Si Robbins didn't rocket the commissions. But it would be the girls with a card in the showcases and a telephone number who would be doing the really good business, Eileen knew. More classy too. 'Do you wish to make an appointment?' You might even put a better price on it with that kind of stuff.

Mrs Saithe had no telephone and no intention of installing one; but the Commie's wife had a telephone, God knew why, since they did not seem to have any friends. It was one of the flamboyant extravagances of junk dealers, like Mother Sternkopf's mink coat and the electronic organ in the home of old Zlotnik above the shop at the top of West Hill.

He had told Eileen about it. He talked to all the girls, and took a professorial interest in the composition of their cards in the showcase of Mrs Angel's shop next door. He had told Eileen that no one could play the organ, but that he and his son were going to take lessons one day.

'You mean you bought it first and learn to play it after?'

'Of course, dear.' Zlotnik junior sat on the pavement the wrong way round in a high ladder-backed chair, his round pink

228

chin resting on the top rung. 'We couldn't learn to play it if we didn't have it, could we?'

Zlotnik and son always had an answer to everything. They were like Denise in that.

The Commie's wife, who preferred Eileen to anyone else in the mews, because they were both on the outer edge of the tightly respectable community, agreed, for a price, to let Eileen use her telephone, and to come across the mews herself with messages.

When Mrs Saithe heard this, however, she turned belligerent. 'I will not have that woman coming to my house,' she announced, and Eileen could not talk her round. When she folded her short arms and clamped her empty jaws like that, there was nothing to be done with her.

She had never cared what Eileen did for a living, as long as she took her clients somewhere else, and she did not especially object to her professional life being brought closer to home by the telephone. But receiving visits from the telephone's owner, who was not only in the pay of that godless lot in fur hats, but living with a man who was not her husband – that was something else again.

Worried about what she was going to do, Eileen was provoked into accusing Mrs Saithe of being bloody narrow, and it started a quarrel between them, the first openly abusive one they had ever had.

At the end of it, when Eileen picked up the little rusty dog and went off to her room with her chin in the air, Mrs Saithe called after her, standing on her toes to make the words travel: 'You'd better get out! That's all I can say. You'd better get out of here!'

Eileen did not go out that night. She was too upset. She stayed in her stuffy little room and shared a packet of biscuits with Toodie and only crept downstairs to the little lean-to washhouse at the back when she was sure that Mrs Saithe was in bed.

If she were to see her, she might be provoked into saying something else that was too hasty – my Irish paddy, she thought with some pride, although she was normally as mild as a cow, and bloody narrow was the first direct insult she had ever sent Mrs Saithe's way. She must not make it worse, because she intended in the morning to smooth things over so that she could stay a while longer. She was not angry now. She had prayed to the Holy Mother, and the Holy Mother, practical as always, had told her that to apologize would not only redeem the sin of calumny, but might enable her to stay in the mews at least long enough to be included in the recount for the rehousing list.

Mrs Saithe, however, being a dirty black Protestant, did not see things in this light. She gave no answer to Eileen's mumbled apology, and asked her briskly when she proposed to move her bits of things.

'I thought perhaps I might stay a while longer,' Eileen said diffidently. 'Give myself time to look round.' But Mrs Saithe said that it might as well be sooner as later, 'seeing as you have to move anyway when they start to pull this poor old place apart.'

She spoke pleasantly enough, and gave Eileen a good breakfast. She pretended to be interested only in giving her the chance to find a nice place before the bricks began to fly and everyone and his uncle was looking for a room; but Eileen, brooding over her tea at the linoleum-topped table with her unbrushed hair hanging over her face, thought darkly: She's glad of the excuse to do me down.

She was sure that Mrs Saithe had remembered about the recount. It seemed to be in the air between them, and they walking round it like two dogs round a bone. But if Eileen were to mention it, Mrs Saithe in her present mood would choose to take offence at that being the only reason for Eileen wanting to stay.

It was a reason, but not the only one. Recount or no recount, Eileen craved to stay in the cosy little flat as long as possible. It had become as near like home as anything she had known since Mam put her out of the tumbledown cottage behind the grocery. Where would she go now? What was to become of her?

I hate you, she mouthed silently at the back of Mrs Saithe's black apron with the big squashed roses. But when she went out into the sunshine later with Toodie jumping at the end of his leash, to ask Denise for advice, she had already forgotten hatred because she had thought of a joke against herself.

Life gave you the knocks, but it did hand you the jokes too. How comical it was to think that only a little while back she had been dreaming of herself set up so handsome in a council flat. Subsidized, mind you, subsidized – what a laugh – by the very government who were after her neck on the streets.

When you wanted to put a card in Mrs Angel's showcase, you did not hand it over the counter; you went through the narrow side door into the little closet of a shop and spoke to Mr Angel privately. You handed over your three quid for three months in advance, and Mr Angel read the card and looked at you with his slot eyes, comparing your picture or your advertised measurements with the reality. It was curiously embarrassing, even to girls who thought that life had stripped them of embarrassment long ago, but it had to be swallowed, because Angel's, being so near the bus stops and the Underground, was one of the best placed showcases in the neighbourhood.

Eileen had been in there with Denise when Rocky had moved her into the rooms in Chapel Gate, and she had to change her card. Denise had not been embarrassed, but had managed to embarrass Mr Angel by saying, loud enough for the newspaper-selling back of his wife to hear: 'Special terms for you, love, after last time.'

Eileen wished that Denise was with her when she took her card up, but Denise was off with Rocky to see women wrestle in mud, so she stopped to have a word with Zlotnik and son before she tackled Mr Angel.

They were out as usual on the wide pavement among the furniture lined up in rows for the benefit of the Saturday afternoon crowds. They could not have been inside if they wanted to, for the chairs and chests and rusted wrought iron lamps and brass kettles and broken gramophone records and carriage harness and dressers and piano keyboards were piled from floor to ceiling right to the front of the small shop, so that no one could now open the door. The Zlotniks went in and out by a side door and up a ladder staircase to the living quarters above, where the electronic organ and old Mrs Zlotnik were housed. At night, the furniture that stood on the pavement, not only to attract customers but because there was no room for it inside, was piled into the doorway and lashed there with ropes.

'Want to buy a nice set of nesty tables, my dear?' Old Zlotnik nodded and twinkled at her like a toy leprechaun.

'When I win the pools,' Eileen said. 'Wish me luck. I'm going to put a card up with my new address. The mews is coming down, you know, so I'm moving in with a girl-friend in Chapel Gate.'

'Let's look?' Holding it close to his clouded blue eye, the old man peered at the card, which had a blurred photograph of

Eileen in her cerise and said: 'Beautiful blonde model now available for engagements.'

'Bust thirty-nine?' He squinted up at Eileen under his cotton wool eyebrows. 'Steady, girl. You go too far there. They'll expect Marilyn Monroe.'

He hooted with laughter, tipping back his tapestry chair and running at the eyes, but Eileen said seriously: 'Her bust is only thirty-seven.'

A girl in a cotton dress and a languid young man in a pork pie hat with a feather in the band had stopped to look at the congested windows of the shop and were laughing together. The Zlotniks liked laughter. They were always cracking jokes with passers-by out here on the pavement, and they often laughed at themselves. They did not mind the man giggling with the girl, but they did not pay him any attention either when he called to ask the price of something he saw wedged behind the dirty glass.

He came over to them, threading a relaxed path between the tables and stools and coal scuttles, with the girl following to see the fun.

'Here,' he said to young Zlotnik, who sprang smartly to attention and touched his flat cap in a derisive salute. 'Here, I say. How much do you want for that copper urn sort of thing you've got in there?'

'The embossed one? Ah, that's a rare piece that is. Real collector's item. I've got a pair of 'em in there, if you're interested.'

'I might be. How do you get the stuff out?'

'We don't.' The Zlotniks were sick and tired of being asked that. It was no longer as funny as each new questioner thought.

'Well, I want to buy that copper urn. How are you going to get it out of here?'

'It's not for sale.' Young Zlotnik turned away and winked at Eileen. 'Ask a bloody silly question,' he said without lowering his voice, 'and you'll get a bloody silly answer.'

Denise's flat in Chapel Gate, whose rent was paid by the coloured giant Rocky, was two rooms on the top floor of one of the tall ornamented brick houses which had once been a terrace of quite fashionable dwellings. Chapel Gate. What chapel? Gate to what? No one knew for sure, but it was said that once long ago there might have been a back gate here to the big estate, when all this was the country.

232

The big houses had gradually emptied of their single families and been converted into flats. After the war the flats had begun to be sub-divided into smaller flats and to them had drifted the same kind of tenants, until the terrace was now, like Carbine Road, a free-going rabbit warren of girls, and women who were nothing like girls, of all races and colours operating just within the Law.

Rocky did not live there. He lived in Shepherd's Bush with a middle-aged woman with a skin of yellow satin. As far as Eileen knew, he seldom visited Denise except for his money. He had quite a stable of girls, this big buck negro, and only slept occasionally with all of them to assert his rights. They stayed with him because they were one-third afraid of him, one-third in some form of love with him, and one-third too lazy to set up an establishment on their own.

The girl who had occupied the other room in Denise's flat had gone off suddenly with a troupe of dancers to Tunisia, so Eileen moved in, with the half promise that she would go to work for Rocky if she stayed. She had no intention of doing that. She was not going to get caught in the ugly bondage of ponce and prostitute from which there was no escape; but she needed the room badly and the telephone three floors below, and Rocky was no problem at the moment because he was interested in a pair of Vietnamese twins and not paying much attention to what Denise did.

The room was not as comfortable as her little room at Mrs Saithe's, which had been cosily filled with a married life's accumulation of furniture and ornaments and pictures and slippery crochet mats. The Chapel Gate room had nothing much in it except an iron bed and a yellow wooden washstand and a clothes rail behind a corner curtain, for the other girl had paused briefly in her flight to Tunisia to sell everything that was saleable.

It was a home of a kind, however, and financially good. With no rent to pay, Eileen was putting by a bit, and thinking of a holiday, or of a trip home to Ireland with new clothes and a suitcase with leather corners. It was also an economy not having to hire the Carbine Road rooms, for sometimes a client would not pay the extra for that and you had to take it out of your regular fee. And it was a comfort to be free of the Park, for apart from the bogies on the prowl trying unsuccessfully to look like ordinary people, the nights were drawing in and it was getting to be no weather for the grass.

Denise's room next door was nice, with bright curtains and cushions and long-legged dolls perched everywhere. She had a gas ring where they heated soup and coffee and made raspberry custards, and in bad weather when business was slack, they would sit in there by the hour and talk and knit and do crossword puzzles. There was usually some kind of a bottle going, and some of the other girls would come in and they would all sit about on the floor in a fug with the gas fire blazing and Toodie panting in his sleep, and talk by the hour about all the things they were going to do when they got the chance.

I might go back to Ireland, Eileen always said, and she knew that one day she would, for she could not go much longer without a sight of her dear sister Olive who loved her, and Mam and Dad would surely welcome her after all this time.

Maria was Italian, and she could play a guitar and sing in that voice that was soft and raucous at the same time. They would sit round her and sing all the sad songs while the autumn afternoons grew dark, and it was a shock to turn on the light when Mrs Slattery, who answered the telephone downstairs, rapped on the door with her big gold ring to call someone down. Whoever it was would curse, and Mrs Slattery would curse back through the door, because although she was paid for it, she did not like to climb to the top floor. 'If you had my mucking legs . . .'

One sad afternoon when Denise and Eileen were eating crumpets and swapping tales about their childhood, Eileen told Denise about how she had first come to England. She had never told anybody the details. She didn't know why, because there was lots had much the same tale to tell, but she had never brought it out, even to that boy she had gone with for a while, who might even have married her if he had not had a wife. Perhaps she had not been able to tell it because it was the first thing that had given her life any real sorrow.

I had been a gay girl, you know, always one for fun. Olive was the good one, staying home to mind the shop and do my work in the house so that I could get out nights. There were boys, of course, nice ones too, and it's funny that the one who brought me sorrow I didn't even like too well. A cross-eyed runty boy, he was, with a thick foot. Mam and Dad were strict, like many of them. There was no going to the pictures with a boy, or to a café, or a dance hall, supposing there had been such a thing in our village. There was nowhere to go and nothing to do. They say that's why there's not a girl in Wicklow who's a virgin after fourteen. Except Olive, of course. She's different. She wanted to be a nun, but Mam couldn't spare her.

When I knew that I'd bought it, I didn't tell anyone but Olive for a while, but there was no keeping it from Mam. I had always been small-waisted, you know, like my grandmother, who was a dancer. Dad beat me so rough, I thought I'd lose the poor little bastard right there in the wash house with the copper bubbling away like hell's cauldron. That was the last time I spoke to my Dad, when he told me to get up off the floor, and I said: I can't.

They sent me to the Sisters the next day. Well, you know what that means. They'll help you all right, but they'll keep you two years, it's said, to work for them in atonement of your soul. I got out of that pretty quick, you can be sure. I was no fool even then, although I was only sixteen and young for my age as I know now that I've seen the way they are in the city. Olive got her savings to me – the dear Lord bless her for that – and I ran away.

There was a woman at the dock on this side waiting to put anyone such as me back on board. There'd been too many of us, you see, running for the new life. P.F.I., she labelled us, just like we were some class of diseased cattle. Pregnants From Ireland. I gave her the slip and came to London with what money I had left, and when my time came, which was sooner than Mam had guessed because of me being well developed about the hips like I am, I went to this church society. They couldn't send me back then. It was too late, unless I was to drop it on the gangway.

I'd signed to have my baby taken away as soon as he was born, and so when he did come, no one at the hospital thought to ask me if I still wanted that. Well – I daresay anything else was only a silly dream. I never saw the people who took him, but I understand they were quite well-to-do people. Very high class indeed. I wouldn't have put my name to anything else, you can be sure of that.

One day Rocky came and announced in his thick threatening voice like things roaring in a zoo that Eileen must either go to work for him or get out.

'I'll do neither,' she said, keeping a piece of furniture between herself and the big negro. 'You're not putting me out on the street. I'll pay you rent for the room, if that's what you want, but I'll not give you a penny more, you miserable black ape.'

Denise looked scared, suddenly pinched and white and ugly, with all the sharp talk gone out of her. She shook her head and made a face at Eileen behind the negro's back; but he was laughing.

'Who can't put you out?' he asked genially. He crossed the room in a stride, picked up Eileen from behind the table kicking and scratching like a polecat, ran easily down the stairs with her dress pulled up and one huge scaly hand like a vice on her thigh, opened the front door and deposited her shrieking like a thing possessed on the pavement.

Doors had opened all down the staircase, and windows were going up all along the street now, but no one did anything. The sight was not unusual enough to provoke much excitement in Chapel Gate.

Eileen's dress was torn and her stockings were laddered and one of her shoes had fallen off on the stairs. 'I'll sue you!' she screamed, thumping on the black front door with both fists. 'Let me in!'

The door was eventually opened by Marmalade Mary, an elderly tramp with orange hair who had a ground floor room under the stairs.

'Dirty black bastard,' she said without emotion. 'E'd no right to do you like that.' There was no sympathy in her voice. Old Marmalade had been down to the depths so many times that she had used it all up on herself. She allowed Eileen to stay in her foetid room until the thud and squeak of heavy rubber soles and the terrace-shaking crash of the front door told that Rocky had left, and then she put her swiftly out.

Upstairs, Eileen found that Denise had her old suitcase out from under the bed and was putting her clothes into it, folding them quite carefully, but still undeniably packing.

'You leave my things alone,' Eileen said, 'or I'll sue you too, you nigger-loving bitch.' Nicely raised as she had been, she hardly ever said things like that, and Denise sat back on her narrow glacé heels and looked at her in surprise.

'Don't take it so hard,' she said. 'You knew you couldn't stay unless you played along with Rocky. I think you're daft not to, as a matter of fact. It's protection, you must allow.'

236

'Ta very much,' Eileen said, taking off the odd shoe and grabbing at her other pair which Denise had just put into the case. 'When I need advice from you on how to behave, I'll ask for it. You don't even know enough to stick by a friend. Standing there with no more fight in you than a cushion and letting that black devil throw me out.'

'It was your fault. You provoked him. What could I do?'

'You could have done something else but cringe there like a sick lapdog. Even poor little Toodie has ten times more guts than you.' She picked the dog up. He had run down the stairs nipping at Rocky's heels all the way, and been booted through the front door along with his dishevelled mistress.

'You can pack your own stuff.' Denise got up. 'Rocky is putting another girl in here tomorrow. You'll have to be out by morning.'

'You could make him let me stay. You've got enough on him.'

'So have you. You know enough to get him put inside.'

Thinking of the cohort of mean black and tan characters who went around with Rocky, Eileen looked blank and said nothing.

'All right then.' Denise's face was at its sharpest and boniest when she was thinking only of herself. 'Nor would I. I've helped you all I can, kid. Now you're on your own.'

'Some friend,' Eileen said bitterly, clutching Toodie fiercely to her as if he were all she had left in the world, which perhaps was true. 'The prostitute with a heart of gold. Funny joke.'

'Mine's tarnished,' Denise said equably. 'Not been used too much lately.'

*

The police had instructed Veronica Duke what she was to do if the ugly, filthy telephone calls came again to the flat at Granchester Mansions. She was to keep the man talking while someone else called the engineers on another line.

The engineers themselves called her once and told her the same thing. 'Are you a brave girl?' the unknown fatherly voice had asked.

'I – I hope so,' Veronica said, knowing that she was not.

'You must keep him talking. Don't be afraid. We promise not to listen. No one will hear what is said. But you must keep him talking until we can trace the call and get the police there.'

Twice that summer it had happened. The first time Mrs Duke

237

answered, and Veronica, seeing the look on her mother's face, had snatched the telephone away from her, listened for a moment and then clattered it down.

'One of us should have kept him talking,' her mother said as they looked at each other in distress across the silent telephone, crouching like a black toad on the sofa table. 'You know what they told us.'

'*You* couldn't. I don't ever want you to, Mother.'

Mrs Duke nurtured and cossetted and bolstered her family with a countrywoman's placid strength, but her husband and son and daughter treated her as if she were the weakest one, instead of the strongest.

'Then you should have held on, Ronnie.'

Veronica hung her head with its froth of cream coloured curls which Mr Frederick rolled deftly up for her in different directions every week. 'I couldn't, Mum.'

'You must, Ronnie. They said you must.'

'I will next time.'

But the next time, when she answered the telephone, her arm put down the receiver stiffly as if it moved of its own accord. She glanced at her father who was reading by the window in the day's only patch of sunlight that filtered through the starched white curtains and the green leaves of potted plants. He was looking at her steadily. She nodded and picked up the telephone again slowly, but only the dialling tone came up towards her.

'Brace up, Ron,' her father said. 'We'll be out of here soon. Out in the country in the New Town, if my transfer goes through. Then he won't know your number.'

'He'll find me.'

'No, sweetheart. He won't know where you are. If you're not with us, you'll be with Fred somewhere, after you're married.'

'He'll find me. I'm so afraid he'll always find me. What does he want with me? Me of all people?'

What did it mean? Did it mean that underneath, deep down, she was depraved? That this sick and twisted man had recognized her somehow as a kindred spirit – seen her perhaps for a moment and guessed at something that she did not even know herself?

The confident bounce was being sapped out of Veronica. At the beauty salon those of her regular clients who were not too engrossed in discussing themselves told her that she looked tired. She was less bossy with the apprentices and she did not

238

even order poor old May about so much. When she went out with Fred, he was irritated by her silence, and furious when she was not able to stop herself crying 'Don't!' and pushing his hands away.

'When we're married,' she told him. 'When we're married, it will be better. I do love you, really I do.' But why then did neither of them make any effort to set a date for the wedding? Fred had got his rise. There was not that to wait for any more.

The next time the dreaded call came, she was alone in the flat with Fred. Godfrey was at a jazz concert and her mother and father had gone to the Palladium to celebrate their wedding anniversary.

Veronica had washed her hair. She was in the kitchen with a towel round her wet head making coffee for them to drink while Fred was putting in the pins and rollers.

The telephone rang. Fred answered it in the sitting-room, and Veronica heard him say: 'Hullo?' and then nothing more. She turned and he was in the kitchen doorway, his face agitated and sallow-pale against the dark patch of his evening chin.

'Quick.' He clicked his fingers at her. 'I think it's him. I told him to hold on. You know what we're to do. Take it, and I'll nip next door and call the engineers.'

'Fred . . . I can't.'

'You must. This is it, Ron. This is when we get him. You do your bit and I'll do mine.' He was curt, heroic, like a character in a television play. He wheeled and was gone.

Like a sleepwalker, Veronica went without vision into her mother's bedroom and picked up the telephone from the table by the bed.

It had never been as bad as this. Keep him talking, they had said. But they didn't *know*. Didn't know that things like this could be said. That a man – any man – a maniac – a creature from the pit – could think of the things that the hoarse excited voice breathed into the telephone.

'Are you there?' he said at intervals. 'Are you listening?' and Veronica had to say: 'Yes.' Keep him talking. Keep him talking. Like the flash shots in a film, she saw the boots of policemen pounding along some pavement, heard a patrol car screech round a corner on the side of its tyres, nearer, nearer, while the man kept talking, spilling out lovingly the vile words and savouring them like a serpent feasting on its own poison.

She heard Fred come back into the flat. Thank God he didn't come into the bedroom, for when the man began to say the worst things, and then whispered to her: 'Wouldn't you like to do that? Wouldn't you love it?' she had to say 'Yes' to keep him talking. 'Say: "I want you to do that to me. . . . I want you to make me do that.' *Say* it. . . .' And from somewhere in the depths of her terror and disgust, she had to drag the stammer: 'I want you to make me do that . . .' to keep him talking.

Where were the police? Why was it so long? Hadn't Fred called? Oh God . . . Oh God . . . When at last suddenly the voice broke off and there was a clatter and then nothing but confused background noises, she thought that she was going to faint.

She put the telephone down carefully and stayed sitting on the bed with her head down, unable to move, her thighs squeezed rigidly together, her eyes staring at the floor. The towel had slipped from her head and tendrils of wet hair hung on her cheeks like tears.

Fred came in. He had his jacket off, and his throat was working inside the open collar of his white shirt. He sat on the bed and put his arm round her and his lips against her neck, while she still sat stiffly.

'It stopped,' she said numbly. 'I think they got him.' She could not look at him. She could do nothing but sit with her knees tight together and her hands flat on the edge of the bed, staring at the wall where the enlargement of the beach snapshot of her and Goff as children hung. 'It was horrible,' she said; but nothing she could ever say to anyone could make them understand.

'It's over now.' He began to caress her. His hand went casually over her breast and then stopped there, more urgent. Did he know what the call had done to her, why her body was paralysed, unable to move for loathing of itself?

'Don't touch me,' she whispered. 'If you knew . . . I want to die. If anyone knew what he said to me, I'd die. But the engineers didn't listen. They promised.'

'More fools them.' He laughed shakily. 'I did. I heard it all on the other phone.'

'Damn you!' She struggled to get up, but he had her pushed back on the bed, pinned down, fighting, sobbing, while all the time his voice beat at her like blows, inescapable, insistent, like the voice on the telephone. '*You liked it. You know you did. Admit*

*it. Tell me . . . say what you said to him. You can't pretend with
me now because I heard you. You'd like me to say those things to
you, wouldn't you? Wouldn't you? You want it, don't you? You
want it. . . .'*

She had always planned that the first time with Fred it was
going to be so beautiful. In a little bedroom in a country hotel
with flowered curtains waving at the casement window and the
night scent of pinks coming in from the garden below. It ought
to be like a poem, and she would make it so, with all her fears
and inhibitions cast aside for the joy that she would give to her
husband.

Not like this. Not like a degraded, disgusting battle with her
head half buried under her mother's pillow, and the pillow soaked
with her wet hair and sweat and tears of pain and terror.

She saw Fred combing his hair in front of the mirror on the
door, and then he went out without looking at her. She heard the
front door shut, then the racket of the Lambretta starting up,
running smoothly, accelerating, fading, and then cut off round
the corner.

She lay on the rumpled bed, not knowing what time it was,
knowing that she must straighten things up before her mother
returned, unable to do anything. The telephone had rung while
Fred was there, unheeded. Three times it seemed that it rang
again for a full minute, but she was only aware of it from far away.
She could not reach out to it.

She was still crying weakly without sobs when she opened the
door to the two detectives. 'Poor kid,' one of them said. 'Don't
mind us, Miss. That brute. It's enough to make anyone cry.'

May Wilson was going to bed early. She had been up nearly
all last night with slow-moving twins, and she was tired. She said
goodnight to her parents, who were watching television and did
not answer, and went up the basement stairs and along the dimly-
lit hall – there was not a bulb in the house stronger than forty
watts unless the tenants had bought it themselves. As she
paused yawning to look at the few circulars on the coat-stand
shelf which no one had bothered to pick up, she heard a key
scrabbling incoherently at the lock of the front door.

Someone the worse for drink? May reviewed the roomers
quickly. No one like that in the house at the moment, thank
goodness. She opened the front door and the dishevelled figure

241

of Arthur Sears, with his fluffy hair on end and his key held out before him like a dagger, fell into the hall.

He fell on to his knees. He was panting, and his face was red and oddly suffused, with the eyes flatly staring. He jerked his head to look back at the door as May shut it.

'Whatever is the matter? You look as if you'd seen a ghost.' May stretched out her strong arms to help him to his feet. He stood up, swayed a little and then clutched at her again. He did look rough. 'Are you ill then?' she asked.

He gave a wild sort of a laugh that was not a proper laugh, flinging it sideways out of his open mouth, but with only breath coming out, not sound. He was still holding her arm, and he squeezed it so that the muscle ached, and stared into her face with those queer bloodshot eyes that were flattened back like a dog with its face hanging out of a car in the wind.

'What's the –' May started again, but he hissed at her to be quiet, and still stood staring dumbly at her with his head cocked as if he were listening to the sound of his own rasping chest. May could have broken away from him. She was strong enough, but she didn't like to, with him in such a state. It was not that she was frightened. She felt more concern than alarm at the way he looked; but all at once he took hold of her other arm and rammed her back against the wall with his shuddering body pressed against hers.

'Oh – you mustn't!' May gasped in confusion. 'Someone may come in!' and instantly he was gone from her and stumbling up the stairs. She heard his feet pounding on the carpet of the second flight, clattering on the linoleum higher up, and the slam of his door at the top.

Out of the shadows of the first landing where the stairs turned, the tall figure of Miss Beade loomed like a shrouded statue. She was wearing her coat slung round her angular shoulders, and carrying her cat and a large torch like a shining weapon.

'What's the matter with *him*?' she asked, as she came down the stairs. 'Pushing past me like that. Poor Christopher got a fright. See how my fur is up, Auntie May.' She put the cat down in the hall. He was attached to her by a red decorated collar and a thin leash. His fur was not up, but his fat grey tail was puffed out like a dusty flue brush. 'I'm just off for my nightly prowl with Mother.'

Miss Beade continued to produce dialogue for the cat, but her long green eyes were looking at May too intently. Had she seen anything? How long had she been on the landing? May felt the blush starting, but managed to keep her head up and stare right back at Miss Beade until she had taken her scarecrow figure and her supercilious cat out of the front door and down the chipped tile steps, holding the torch before her as if she were in the blackout, although the street was quite brightly lit.

Poor old soul. Let her think what she liked. No one had ever pressed Miss Beade up against a wall with quite such urgency, May would be bound. If it meant anything, if this was to be the start of something between Arthur Sears and May – and May's thoughts, tumbling about like dice in a mug, did not know whether to be afraid that it might, or afraid that it might not – Miss Beade would know about it soon enough anyway. When you let furnished rooms, there were no secrets.

'Quite romantic,' she heard her mother say. 'Yes, we're very pleased.' Only she would not say that. She would be more likely to say, with that laugh that was meant to make it look as if she did not mean to be rude: 'Better late than never.'

Dreams, May Wilson. Might-have-beens. For that silly old tongue of yours had probably lost you your chance. 'Oh you mustn't,' indeed. No wonder he had run away. Now he thought she didn't want to have anything to do with him. She had hurt his feelings.

She went back down to the basement. In the kitchen, her mother and father were sitting like dolls in front of the television set, and May stepped over their legs to light the gas. The ring of flame licked up yellow and blue in the darkened room, misting the shiny sides of the kettle.

'Brewing again?' Her mother looked round as the News became dull: someone sermonizing about the United Nations. 'I thought you'd be in bed and asleep by now.'

'It's for Mr Sears,' May said boldly. 'He's not well. I felt sorry for him, all alone as he is. A cup of tea will pick him up. I think he has the flu.'

'Cups of tea for the tenants?' Mrs Wilson grumbled. 'What do they think this is – the Ritz Hotel?'

'No, Mum, he didn't ask for it. I just feel sorry for him.'

Her father snorted. 'That's a new name for it,' he said. 'I didn't know you had the savvy to think up such a good excuse to get into a man's room.'

'Leave off that sort of talk, Walter Wilson,' his wife said. 'It isn't nice and you know it.'

'Can't a man even talk now?'

'Not like that in front of May. You know how she'll take hold of any idea in her silly old head.'

'She wouldn't take hold of that one if it was shoved at her on a silver plate, would you, old blunderbuss?'

May stood silently by the stove, begging the kettle to hurry. On the screen the announcer continued urbanely to address Mr and Mrs Wilson while they jousted back and forth across his well-bred face. When she heard the sound of water being poured into the pot, Mrs Wilson said: 'Don't bother to ask us if we want any. Be sure not to trouble yourself.' And added as May went to the cupboard for two more cups: 'And you're not going into anyone's room, never mind your father's silly jokes. If you must give away tea by the pound to every Tom, Dick and Harry, you can just leave the cup on the floor outside.'

At the top of the house, May knocked on Arthur Sears' door. No answer, but she heard the bed creak, so he was in there sure enough.

'I've brought you a cup of tea,' she called. 'I thought it would make you feel better. I'm sorry.' He could take that which ever way he liked: she was sorry that he was ill, or sorry that she had said: 'You mustn't.'

No answer. Knowing that Miss Beade was still out, for her nightly prowls with Christopher took her on witch's journeys far afield, May pounded on the door and called louder. 'Are you all right? Is something the matter?'

She put her hand on the door knob, but could not bring herself to try the door to see if it was locked. She thought that she could hear him breathing in there. If he was very ill, her duty as a nurse would be to break in and give him help. But if he was only angry with her for what she had said in the hall, her duty as May Wilson was to set down her peace offering and leave him alone.

She called out: 'The tea's outside!' and went away down to her own room below his, where she listened in vain for his feet dropping on to the floor and his door opening. Presently she heard Miss Beade go up the stairs, purring to the cat. The forlorn pink and white cup with the skinned-over cold tea would still be sitting on the floor. Oh well, Miss Beade and Christopher could think what they liked, May was not going to care.

Now that she was in bed and comfortable with a cardigan over her nightgown and the film magazines and the tin of biscuits, the incident in the hall was receding into improbability. Her opinion of herself, beaten down to rock bottom over the years, could scarcely credit that it had happened. The darkening bruise on her arm – she pushed the nightgown sleeve down again guiltily, as if someone were looking – told her that it had. Well, all right. He had the flu didn't he, or something like it? Fevers ran high this year. When he caught hold of her like that, perhaps he didn't know what he was doing. Delirious even. People did some funny things.

After Denise had put her out of Chapel Gate so cruelly, Eileen slept for two or three nights in a hostel, but they took Toodie away from her and tied him in a box in the storeroom, and she could hear him crying half the night. She found another room, where she had to use up nearly all her savings in key money to the black-souled robber who owned the house. Looking for a room in a hurry, you never had a chance. It was either pay the extortionists or sleep on a park bench until some kindly narker gave you the sort of roof over your head which you would be glad to do without.

Where Eileen lived now was called a Hotel, the 'Cavendis otel', with two porcelain letters missing from the fanlight, but it was only a peeling slice of a house between two bombed plots that had never been built up. And no wonder. The neighbourhood was such a sewer that no one in their right mind would deliberately want to build there.

Life was very difficult now. You could risk it out on the streets, but you dared not stand still for long, and hardly dared speak to anyone, for the heat was on, and any likely client might turn out to be a sodding snooper.

In the good old days, you turned up in court off and on and paid your two quid to keep them sweetened up and no hard feelings. Now it was jail as soon as look at you if you couldn't pay their wicked fine on the spot. But if you'd had that much in ready cash, why would you be out on the bitter streets anyway?

The card in the Angels' showcase was not much use to Eileen now. She could not have used the telephone number of the Cavendis otel even if there had been a telephone. It was a fag end of a place, but not that kind. She had the card taken out, and

245

in the back of the shop with Mr Angel breathing sourly over her shoulder, she crossed out the Chapel Gate telephone number and wrote her new address. 'Ring and ask for Eileen.'

The first time a man answered the invitation, the robber had let him in, thinking it was a friend. When the next man came, asking for the 'the model', he caught on, and threatened to put Eileen out in the street if she tried it again.

'I've half a mind to fetch the police to you,' he told her, but she did not think he would, because from the looks of the two pals he had holed up in the second floor back, he didn't want the police in the house any more than Eileen did.

She took the card out of the showcase – just her luck to have paid for it three months in advance – and began to go the rounds of the little mushroom clubs, where you could usually pick up a bit of business of a sort. Some of them had rooms upstairs, but the extortionists were here too, and there was not much in it when it was always pay, pay, pay commissions.

Almost better to have gone with Rocky after all. At least she would have had a decent room instead of this freezing box hanging out over the railway, where the rain went ping, ping into Toodie's enamel water bowl on stormy nights, and the rusty vent pipe outside her window made spectral music when the wind was in the wrong direction.

But maybe next month, next week, tomorrow, something would happen to swing her fortunes up again. You never knew with life. It was so up and down. Only a short while ago, she had been so well placed, living warmly in Armstrong Mews with business fair and a bit of money put by. And now look at her. Toodie did not go hungry, but the gold anklet was loose on Eileen's leg, and her hair was growing in patchy brown like a tortoiseshell cat, because she could not afford to have the roots matched in all the time.

When she said her prayers, the answer was: *The Lord giveth and the Lord taketh away*. She tried again with her eyes screwed tighter and this time the answer was: *The Lord helps those who help themselves*. She decided to swallow her pride and go crawling back to the mews to see whether the Lord would make Mrs Saithe think better of her hardness and take Eileen back in again.

She knew at once what had happened. As soon as she turned off the street under the archway of the mews, it was like being on the moon. It was a cold day and you would not expect to see

246

people outside, but all the normal signs of life were gone. No overflowing dustbins chained to the old horse rings in the wall. No tricycles, no pushcarts, no armless dolls and tin cans half full of sand lying about outside the house where Mrs Dewey had lived with her feckless grandchildren. No crumpled paper boats in the perpetual puddle where the central gutter dipped in the middle of the cobbles. No washing – not a stitch. Even the lines and pulleys were gone, and the empty windows stared like black eye sockets, with no curtains, no flower pots, no milk bottles setting cream on the sills.

So they had got them out at last. Where were their bold words now? Where was their Hold tight and Stand fast? 'They'll never get me out,' Mrs Saithe had said and although Eileen had not believed her, she had believed it herself and refused to make plans or give ear to the Council's suggestions. 'Over my dead body,' she had said, and Eileen saw an image of Mrs Saithe, very small under a sheet, being carried down the mews on a stretcher in slow march time.

Well, it was her own fault. There were others in the same boat and lots far worse off, and Eileen was not going to waste time being sorry for her. She had too much to do being sorry for herself. Even if they had carried Mrs Saithe out feet first, it was no worse than she deserved. She had thrown Eileen out when she needed help, and added the insult of not being here when Eileen came looking for a reprieve with her pride in her pocket and her hand held out for friendship.

Toodie, smelling the old scents of home, ran with his tail up down the crack of passageway between the side of Mrs Saithe's house and the high blank wall at the end of the mews. Eileen followed him. He was round at the back where the little wash house was. The outer door of the wash house was open, dropped slightly on a loose hinge. Mrs Saithe must have left in a great hurry or a great temper. She was usually so careful about things like that, going down two or three times in an evening to check the bolts front and back and sometimes turning back right from the end of the mews to make sure that she had locked up. Even though she was leaving home for the last time, and there was nothing left to burgle, like a tomb, in case the kids might get some fun playing haunted houses until the wreckers came with pickaxes to exorcise the ghosts of Mr Saithe and the Beardmore.

The kids had been in by the look of it, for the wash house was a shambles and words that had never been there in Mrs Saithe's day were scratched on the plaster wall. Eileen went through into the house and up the narrow stairs into the kitchen. Empty. Cold. Stale-smelling. The memory of all the good fragrant meals that had been cooked there gone as sour as the fusty mouse odour which had Toodie questing with frantic nose and rigid tail at the corners of the wainscot.

The little black range was dead, its bars like the rotting teeth of a skull. Dark patches on the wallpaper showed where the set of Youths and Maidens prints had been. Nothing remained but the shelves over the sink and the old flap table smooth with scrubbing, and a pile of newspapers and rags and the two worn rugs from Eileen's room kicked into one corner.

The abomination of desolation. Eileen had hardly ever cried in her life. Even as a child, she had only stared and dropped her lip when she was upset; but for two pins she could have cried now, in distress at life for never staying the same, and at Mrs Saithe for being a party to it.

She took Toodie back to her room at the Cavendis otel, fed him, and put on some more lipstick and her good beads. Then she put the dog on her bed, kissed his doormat face, locked her door behind her and went out to the Brass Monkey and spent her supper money on a drink to get her nerve back.

A man she had talked to once before came in and sat with her and bought her two more drinks, and things began to look brighter. The man, who was paunchy, with fat white hands and an American string tie – quite flashy – told her some jokes, and Eileen said to herself: Laugh clown, laugh, and was quite merry. 'I'll buy you a drink dear,' she said.

When she went to the bar, Si Robbins gave her one of his sagging gloomy looks and said.: 'You've had it, kid. Out now, with or without the boy-friend.' So Eileen weaved back to the little black glass table where the man was investigating his teeth with a match and said: 'Changed my mind. Let's go out somewhere instead. Have some fun, eh? I know where we can get a nice room. Want to come, love?'

'Find another mug,' the man said. 'I'm meeting a chap here on business.' Eileen looked across the crowded bar at Si. He was making the thumb gesture towards the door, so Eileen picked up her red handbag, said: 'God bless' to the man, with a sweet smile in case she met him again, and went out.

It was very cold. The three drinks hit her when she got into the raw air, which was acrid in the back of your throat as if there were fog on the way. Eileen was not in the habit of drinking too much. She did not particularly like spirits, and usually sipped genteelly while other people were going seriously at the stuff. Best get home to Toodie. Turn in for the night. Turn it in for good, she'd half a mind. Tomorrow she'd go to the Labour Exchange.

Who'd employ me? she thought with a silly smile as she fell over her feet at a high kerb. Either her skirt was extra tight or her heels were extra high. She was no good at house cleaning. Olive had always done most of it at home and covered up for Eileen when she shirked. But she could learn. Get herself one of those pretty coat overalls and clean and scrub and work like a black and stay out of the clubs and save money and go back to Olive who was the only one who loved her, the only one who gave a bent farthing what became of her.

Arthur Sears lay flat on his back on the top of his bed and listened to the pain coming and going in his mouth like waves of sound. That dentist didn't know his job. He had said it wouldn't hurt, and then altered that to: if it did hurt, these tablets would stop it.

Arthur had taken two of the tablets, and when they did not ease the pain in ten minutes, he had thrown the rest away. These good little tablets, the dentist had called them, as if they were something strong and special; but they tasted like nothing more than aspirin, and what use was that to a mouth that had been mauled about for a good half hour while its owner lay helpless in the vicious chair like a victim strapped to the torturer's block?

Arthur had half a mind not to go back to that dentist, even though he was on his panel. Better to pay a full fee somewhere than sit an hour or more in that draughty waiting room that was no more than a glassed-in passage, and then have that dead beat mug hanging over you with a mouth full of gold fillings that he must have put in himself to pass the time when business was slow. But he'd have to go back there because three of the teeth he'd grown up with were in the dentist's waste bucket and the impression of his mouth was made, ready for the plate. Arthur was not going through that again for anyone – a lump of hot wax shoved in your mouth to bite on so that you wanted to heave and spew the whole lot right out into the gold-plated face.

And give the butcher his due, it wasn't until he had met Miss Beade that the pain had really started. Arthur had been headed for his room with the tablets and a bottle of lemon squash under his arm to ease his throat, and there she had been on the top landing. Miss Eunice Beade, all dressed up to go out in a black shroud and that hat like a broken grocery box that came down over her eyes so that she had to tilt back her horse's head to look at you.

She had tilted back her head as he came up the stairs and said, quite jolly: 'Back so early, Mr Sears? I thought you'd be out with you-know-who, seeing that she's off duty tonight.'

'Who knows who?' Arthur grunted as he put his foot heavily over the top step.

'Oh come. Don't think I don't know all about you and a certain young lady of the house.' Miss Beade giggled. It was terrible when she giggled, like water running out of an old bath with the drain clogged up. 'You should find somewhere more private to do your love making, if you want to keep it a secret.'

That was when the pain hit him like a sledgehammer coming in at the side of his mouth. He fumbled for his key, opened his door and got into his room, and heard Miss Beade giggle again as the door banged shut behind him.

Love making. The thought of that made him sweat, but a sweat of horror, not the right kind. When he'd gone after old May in the hall, he had hardly known who she was. It wouldn't have mattered who she was, just at that moment. It might even have been Miss Eunice Beade.

'Nyah-ha!' He laughed out loud, lying on the bed, and closed his mouth quickly, for it stabbed him to stretch his jaws. Did old May think that too then? Had they been talking together? Had everyone been talking, trying to trap him, smother him with the detestable stifling shrouds of femaleness?

But they'd never catch him. Even though they set the police on him, like the other night, they'd never get Arthur Sears. He was too quick for them all. Why couldn't they learn that and give him some peace? They were all about him. Miss Beade and May and her leery old mother and that stammering chick on the phone were all mixed up with the pain in his mouth that was climbing in short jabs up into his head.

He got up and looked out of the window at the choppy black sea of angled roofs and the forest of chimneys and television aerials. What a view. When he was in Wales, it had been a real forest below his window. He would have stayed there, if only for the view, if the man hadn't take against him. That fat girl in the dairy would never have hounded him. He hadn't had to speak to her above good morning. Hadn't even had to ask her to leave her curtains open when she undressed, but she knew he was watching all right.

What now? He had laid off the phone for a while. A real fright, that last time was. How could a man stand that just when everything was going so well? He'd fix that stammering blonde one day. Fix everybody. Fix Miss Eunice Beade. The pain in his jaw was like a swollen finger, tight and throbbing like pruning time when you didn't get all the rose thorns out.

On the narrow roof below his window, a night shape moved, padding purposefully. Miss Beade must have left her window open by mistake. Nyah-ah! She'd regret that. If she remembered it, she would come haring home from the meeting or whatever half-cocked place she was to call darling kitty in.

Arthur would take care of darling kitty. Have no fear, Miss Beade. He rapped on the window and the cat stopped, stared at him with round yellow eyes like traffic lights and showed its needle teeth in a lament.

Slowly Arthur opened the window without noise and called to the cat. It knew him, and came towards him up the slope of the roof, and slowly he put out his arm, grasped it by the back of the neck and held it while his other hand dug into his trouser pocket. Although the cat was heavy, it did not struggle, hanging there by the scruff. It was still looking inquiringly at him as he held it outside the window again and skilfully cut its throat with his sharp budding knife and let the blood run down the slate roof into the gutter.

The neck collapsed in his hand and he shifted his grip, brought the cat inside the room and put it on the evening paper. The eyes were already glazing over and the mouth was lifted in a little sneer at death. No longer conscious of the pain in his mouth, Arthur washed his hands in cold water, wiped the knife on the newspaper, closed it and dropped it back in his pocket. Then he lifted cat and paper carefully like a tray and laid them outside Miss Beade's door.

When he stood up, his head was turning round. He wanted to stay and look at the cat bleeding sluggishly on to the newspaper outside the brown varnished door. He wanted to see that face under the grocery box hat as it came puffing up the top flight of stairs. But he had to get out. The pain had gone. Now he must get some air; walk, walk through the night with his head up and his arms swinging.

He jumped round suddenly on his toes with his arms stiffly by his sides and plunged down the stairs. On the next landing he stumbled and clutched the turn of the banister. The noise brought May looking out of her room. She had on a flannel dressing-gown, loosely tied, and her daft staring eyes were like pale holes punched in dough.

She was moving towards him with her hands out, all loose and coming to pieces with her big sloppy tits. 'Don't touch me!' he screamed, and jumped for the stairs, hearing as he hurtled down the opening of Constantine Porter's door and the deep black voice and the feet running down behind him.

Out in the street, Arthur ran and ran, panicky at first, and then dropping into the training jog with which he kept in trim every day between the suburban station and the greenhouses.

Rounding a corner, he ran smack into a girl who was meandering along on high heels with a big smile painted all over her silly white face.

'What's the hurry, dear?' She caught his sleeve and he stopped and looked at her and the voice inside his head screamed: Don't touch me! but his mouth did not sound it.

Eileen had an idea. The idea to end all ideas. If she had been quite sober, she never would have thought of it. As it was, it came to her in a flash of violet light, and she knew that it was perfect.

The man with the queer flat eyes and the loose brown skin did not seem to relish the Park, and would not agree to pay the extra for a room in Carbine Road. He did not actually say No to either suggestion, but he did not say Yes either; just stumbled along like a doll with her arm through his, muttering something about toothache.

'Oh, we'll cure all that, won't we, dear?' Eileen knew how to be motherly. 'We've got just the cure for toothache.'

'Where are we going?'

'To my home,' she told him. 'Back to my place.' And it was as good as her place, wasn't it, with all the money she'd poured out in rent for nearly two years.

'Back to my place. Not far now.' She hurried him on, her mouth stretching by itself into a mask of triumph. It did not matter that Mrs Saithe would never know, that the blow was to be aimed at an enemy who was no longer there. Eileen was going to have the last word. That was what mattered. Eileen was going to have the last laugh.

Still moving like a sleepwalker, with limbs on strings which someone else was pulling, Arthur groped up the steep stairs and into a small dark room. Automatically his hand brushed up and down the wall at the side of the door, but when he found the switch, no light came.

'What's the game?' There were no street lamps outside, but the London sky is never completely dark, and presently he could see that the room was bare, like an empty box. The tart was sitting on a pile of something in the corner, taking off her shoes. Arthur fell on top of her and knocked her backwards, and then struggled until he got her on top of him.

It had to be that way. That was the horror of it. They had to crush the life out of you, smother you, devour you, force you to sacrifice yourself at the disgusting altar of their flesh. He had known it would be like this.

But not again. Not ever again. When the ritual of immolation was over and she sprawled on the pile of rubbish pouting and rubbing herself where he had bitten her, he had to take out his knife again. There was nothing else to do.

He plunged it awkwardly into her throat, exalted to find how strong he was as she struggled and he held her with one hand. There was a cupboard in the wall at the side of the range and he pushed her body into it, knees to lolling head, and shoved against the door until he could fasten the bolt. Then he went down the way they had come in, and put his hands into the broken basin in the wash house. No water came from the tap, but he made the motions of washing, shook his hands as if they were wet, and went out into the deserted mews and away up the hill towards the railway station.

Part Three

THE sweep of the scythe through the heart of Cottingham Park started slowly and almost unnoticeably at first; then suddenly it began to seem that wherever you looked, familiar landmarks were gone.

The demolition was started in the Valley and spread from there in both directions: up the Rise towards the railway where the big new steel bridge was to be, and up West Hill towards the place where the much-publicized fly-over would take the Expressway over Park Road.

The cold weather had started early that winter and persisted, iron clad through Christmas and into the soul-destroying months which held back the spring. The men with the ringing pickaxes and the men with the yellow bulldozers and the disillusioned men who held flags for one-way traffic and the men who clung to the jumping drills were muffled to the ears in scarves and greatcoats, their faces red and shiny, their breath like smoke. But there was work for hundreds. No one who was not afraid to work in the cold and use his muscles need be out of a job that winter, and many of the West Indians who were able to wake from their dreams of a high-class indoor job found themselves making their first good money since they came so optimistically to the mother country.

With insurance cards given to him by a boy who had gone back to the Caribbean, Edgar Biggs worked for almost a month loading away lorries before the truant officer ran him down and sent him back to school at Green Lane.

His foster mother, Mrs Ambrosia Drinkwater, was angry about that. Edgar was nearly fifteen and looked older, and acted older still, she hinted to friends with a smirk. Being past her prime, she liked to pretend that Edgar was panting to try his undeveloped manhood on her if she gave him the chance. What difference did a few more months at school make? These British could soon knock down income tax if they put the big boys to work instead of driving them like babies to count up money they would never have and listen to stories about fellars who been dead these thousand years.

It had been Ambrosia's idea that Edgar should work on the demolition, for the money which his parents sent from Trinidad was coming in less regularly and she began to wish that she had never fallen for the deal. Edgar as a labourer bringing home a good wage she could stomach. Edgar wasting his time as a schoolboy she could not do with. Useless nigger bum, sloping in every afternoon craving food, and running the streets half the night with the black sweepings of the neighbourhood. But it was her responsibility to keep him within the Law, as the school board man had reminded her on that hectic day when he had taken them by surprise and Gilroy in a panic had dumped a whole heap of weed down the can and pulled the chain.

Although it was such a cold winter, the work of destruction was going ahead quite fast. At first it had seemed that the Expressway would never be started. Then all at once it seemed as if there was no stopping it. People who had begun to believe that nothing would ever happen found themselves being evacuated right and left. Decanting, it was officially called, and many of them objected bitterly to the decanters into which they were tipped out of their old crusted bottles. Some, like Mrs Saithe, turned down six flats or more before they would grudgingly accept.

'You'd think they lived in ruddy palaces,' Jack Clew of the L.C.C. Housing department complained to Robert P. V. Peregrine of the Press Bureau. 'Nearly all of them are going to be better housed, but they won't admit it –'

'Because it was our idea, not theirs,' Mr Peregrine said.

The rehousing went on. Friends, neighbours, time-entrenched shopkeepers, cashiers of poky little cinemas that smelled like sleepers in the eye, bank managers, cripples, boxers, huge half-related families, hermits holed up for years in upper rooms with long curved toenails and newspapers piled to the ceiling were all going out in their turn, one jump ahead of the bulldozer. The shells they left behind came down, or only half down sometimes, as if the bulldozers had gone away to look for something more salubrious, and all at once it seemed again as if the new road would never be started.

It was all pull down and no put up, Mrs Angel told anybody who was not too sick of her to listen; and she for one believed that the Transurban Expressway was no more than a planner's nightmare, and that having knocked down half of Cottingham Park, they were going to go away and leave it to the rats and fireweed.

To the people who lived, unwontedly exposed to light and air, on the edges of demolished sections, it began to seem that way. Like all Londoners, they were desperately loyal about any threat to traditional features, but once they were gone, they accepted the new circumstance with surprising speed. And now it rapidly began to seem as if the patches of level waste and the heaps of bricks and rubble had always been part of the landscape, as if the barricades at the ends of chopped off streets were permanent gymnasia for yelling children.

There was a big black and white barrier in Faulkner Road, just beyond the Wilsons' house. Soon it began to be hard to remember a time when the street had not always been as noisy as this, with children playing and climbing on the barricade and the rubble beyond it, and staging battles and man-hunts and formless shrieking games in the honeycomb of old cellars where the four houses at the end of the road had once been before the big crane with the cast iron ball and chain came swinging at them like a giant's toy.

When the Mortons next door left and their house came down in a week of ear-splitting noise and choking dust, it seemed very odd at first to be living on the edge of nothing. It was strange to go out and look at the naked side of your house and see the peeling wallpaper, the line of old brown dado where the stairs had been, the black mark of a bath on a yellow wall, like the ring that had undoubtedly been round the bath itself (and Mrs Wilson swore that she had remarked it when the bath came down), the pipes hanging out like wild intestines, or chopped off short like cut-through diagrams of the heart and its major vessels.

May had thought that she would enjoy the novelty, but so many other unusual things had been happening recently that it was not necessary to have the house next door knocked down just to make a change. It had worried her at first. Even within her own house, there was a sensation of something missing, an uncanny awareness of nothing but air beyond the wall where the Mortons used to be. When she mentioned this to her mother, Mrs Wilson said: 'If you'd pay some notice to things you *can* see instead of those you can't, we might all be a lot better off,' so May dropped the subject. She had other things to worry about, in any case.

She had Miss Beade to worry about, for one. The death of her beloved cat had become a fixation which dominated all her days. Well, naturally. The poor soul had no one else, and May felt very sorry for her, and had tried to cheer her up in all the ways she knew; but cups of tea and invitations to the cinema and offers of a new kitten with bells on its collar did not help. Miss Beade, with her grey-black hair more unkempt and her long green eyes wilder than ever, was developing what May, from the limited psychological knowledge she had picked up in hospital, recognized as a persecution complex.

'Persecution complex, my Aunt Fanny,' her mother said. 'Who do you hope to impress with your long words, old dunderhead? The woman has got a screw loose, that's plain to see, and if she doesn't soon tighten it up, I'm going to give her her walking papers. She makes me nervous.'

This was not surprising, for Miss Beade's mania of mourning was obsessed with the idea that Mrs Wilson had murdered Christopher.

Although she had never liked Arthur Sears, she would not believe that he had done it. It had to be Mrs Wilson. When Miss Beade came home that dreadful night and found the poor mutilated body and saw that she had left her window open, she knew at once what had happened. Christopher with his clever ways had found his way down to the street and into the area in front of the basement door, looking in his innocence for a kind hand to let him in and give him something to eat. Mrs Wilson had let him in all right. Oh yes. The poor martyred soul had probably called out to her: 'Please open the door!' and the wicked woman had slit his throat with a kitchen knife and carried the body in triumph upstairs.

It was no use denying it. Miss Beade knew. Her landlady had never liked the cat. That was common knowledge. She had begrudged him house room and only given milk with a very bad grace when Miss Beade ran short. She had called him dirty! Christopher dirty! He was a thousand times cleaner than many humans Miss Beade could mention. He had often told his mother that he did not like Mrs Wilson, that he was afraid of her, and now Miss Beade knew that until the end of her days she would never cease to blame herself for leaving him in a house of danger. All this May listened to patiently, for she felt that it might do the wretched wreck that was Miss Beade some good to talk it out; but she could not persuade her that it was not true.

'You are in the plot too,' Miss Beade said, narrowing her eyes. 'Don't lie to me. I know you all. You've been plotting this wickedness for months.'

She went to the R.S.P.C.A. and to the police, and a diffident inspector and an embarrassed policeman came round to Faulkner Road to ask questions. They realized at once that the missing Arthur Sears was the culprit, but neither of them was able to convince Miss Beade. She merely thought that they had joined the league against her too, and began writing letters to the Queen and the Archbishop of Canterbury.

May also had Arthur Sears to worry about. He had killed the cat. No doubt about that, since he had not even troubled to wipe the bloodstains off his window sill or tip the stained water out of the basin. But why? Except for that one incident in the hall, he had always seemed such a mild man. Why had he done such a cruel, unnecessary thing? Why had he run away? Where was he, and why did he not come back? He had not even taken his clothes. May telephoned the nurseries where he worked, but they had heard nothing from him since he took the afternoon off to go to the dentist.

When the policeman came about the cat, May wanted to ask him to have Mr Sears traced as a missing person, but when she opened her mouth in the hall, her mother had somehow sensed what she was going to say and had pushed her back and hustled the officer out herself.

'Whatever has got into you, May Wilson?' she cried when the door was shut. 'I didn't know you were that desperate for a man that you had to set the police after him.'

Icebergs. Deep green glaciers. Chunks of marble left out on a frosty night. The shaming blush would not be cooled. May put her hands up to her cheeks, but her hands were red and hot too, and she turned away when she saw her mother looking at them. 'He might have had an accident,' she said indistinctly.

'If so, we would have heard.' May knew that she was going to say No news is good news, and she did. 'He'll come back, you'll see, if only for his clothes. He's just laying low till all this fuss about the cat blows over.'

Everyone in the house except Miss Beade believed that Arthur Sears had disappeared because of the cat, but May knew better. May thought that it was because she had rejected him. That look he gave her when he came stumbling down the stairs – just after he had finished off poor Christopher, it must have been. May could not recall the look photographically, but memory now began to see it as a face of disappointment, accusation, farewell.

He had run away because he thought that she had spurned him (it might even have been that which incited him to kill the cat), and in her mind, May began to build up the story for the future, for her old age.

'A misunderstanding.' Something that might-have-been, ruined by a foolish word. That would be the secret in her past that would explain everything about her, if only people knew. If she ever did pluck up the courage to meet somebody through a matrimonial agency, she would have that story to tell as the acquaintance ripened. At least it would not look as if she had never had *any* offers in her life.

It was not long before she had something much worse to worry about than the persecution complex of Miss Beade and the disappearance of Arthur Sears.

Veronica had broken with Fred. She was not seeing him, and as far as May knew, she was not going to marry him. She did not talk about him, and May did not risk bringing it up, for she knew what it was like to have Veronica jump down her throat when she said the wrong thing.

Veronica, however, had mysteriously changed. She came more often to see May, and she came in old clothes, not trying to impress with the smart little outfits which May could not have worn even if she knew where to buy them. She was quieter, less domineering. She did not give pert answers to Mr Wilson's feeble humour. She seemed low in spirit and often tired and her hair no longer sprang round her head in lively little curls. But that could be – indeed it all could be – because she had broken with Fred.

One night when she had stayed late watching television, she slept with May in her bed, just as she used to sometimes when she was younger. Mrs Wilson did not mind that. She was glad to see uppish Miss Duke with all her airs and conceits brought down from the pinnacle of Granchester Mansions to Faulkner Road where she belonged.

May was happy to have Veronica with her. It was just like old times, she kept saying, until Veronica, with a flash of the old asperity, said that she would go home if she said it once more. Luckily May was not called out that night, although it would have been just like Mrs Askew to have started labour a day early on purpose to spoil their cosy time.

They lay side by side in the dark and talked, and May tried to keep over by the edge of the bed so that her big body should not crowd poor little Ronnie out. She felt protective towards her, and fonder of her than she had been for a long time. She still did not talk about Fred, but they talked about a lot of things: their views on life and how funny it was, and about Miss Beade and the murdered cat, and about Arthur Sears, and Veronica did not tease May for speculating about him and saying that she wished he would come back.

Gaining confidence, May found herself doing most of the talking. She talked about the maternity home in Scotland and how the floors were polished every day like mirrors, but the maids were always smiling. She told Veronica about her room, which had a blue rug on the floor and a real bed, not the institutional iron cot on which she had courted sleep in other hospitals. She described the country, wishing she knew better how to conjure it up, for Veronica was silent and she did not know whether she was listening. How green it was and always wet, and took the starch right out of your cap, but no one minded because the nurses were not the crisp saucy kind, defying matron with lipstick and two inches off their skirts, but older women who cared more about how the patients felt than how they themselves looked.

She tried to tell Veronica what it had felt like to come home when her mother had the accident, but the words would not come, so she gave it up and fetched a deep sigh, heaving like a walrus under the blankets, and said merely that life was full of funny turns.

Through the fanlight of their door they saw the light behind the fanlight of Constantine Porter's door go out at last, so it must be time to go to sleep. 'If I'm not to go out on rounds tomorrow looking worse than my mothers,' May said. 'We had a nice chat, didn't we?'

Veronica said Yes disinterestedly, and May rolled over to look at her, full of compunction. 'I've done all the talking. You shouldn't have let me run on. We should have talked about you, Ronnie.'

'Nothing to tell.' Veronica turned her head with a blank look.

'I've been worried, you know. I haven't said anything because I know you don't like to be fussed over, but you're not yourself.

261

You're not well, are you? Why don't you see the doctor?'

'Oh no. The doctor we go to – all he ever does is give you a tonic that tastes like rust and tells you to rest. Who can rest? I need my job more than ever now that I – now that I . . .' May waited, and Veronica turned her head away and said in a small voice: 'now that I'm not going to be married.'

She turned over and humped up her shoulders under the thick borrowed nightgown which, although it was ludicrously big, looked better on her than it did on May. She wanted to sleep, or to be left alone, so May said nothing. She would not have known what to say in any case, because all of a sudden she knew something. The worry that had been nagging formless at the back of her mind came to the front and stood clearly in shape.

In the morning, Veronica suddenly jumped out of bed and ran to the bathroom. From May's room, you could hear what went on in the bathroom, which was built on the back of the house at the turn of the stairs. May went down there and rattled the door handle and Veronica called out: 'Go away!'

When she came back to the room, white, and with damp hair and big sick-looking eyes, May plucked up all her courage and said: 'Why didn't you tell me, Ronnie? Perhaps I can help you.'

'Tell you what?' Veronica sat on the bed and lit a cigarette, but put it down in last night's cocoa saucer without smoking it.

'I do know, dear. Don't be angry, because I can't help it. Everything about you shows it.'

Veronica gave a feeble little smile. 'That's what comes of having a friend who's a midwife,' she said, and started to cry.

May made tea and brought it up. What else was there ever to do? People laughed about the English being able to think of nothing in a crisis but making tea, but those involved in the crisis were always glad of it. They could laugh all they wanted. May would continue to make tea.

Sure enough, Veronica was glad of it. She had dressed quickly while May was downstairs, although before when she stayed the night she had dressed and undressed casually in front of May, which rather shocked her.

When they had drunk the tea, May started to suggest a doctor whom Veronica could see if she did not want to go to her own family physician, but Veronica said abruptly: 'Let's not talk about it any more. Perhaps it isn't even true. Let's forget about it.'

'Forgetting about a baby won't stop it growing,' May said

262

practically, 'as many women before you have found to their disappointment. How can you say now that you aren't going to marry Fred? What else can you do?'

'I don't know. I haven't thought about it. I haven't done anything about it. But I'll never marry him. I'll never see him again.'

*

Mrs Humphrey Gordon, tall, with a candid, hopeful face and good feet in expensive shoes, walked right past the wide window of the hairdressing salon, giving it no more than a sideways glance, as if she were on her way somewhere else. The window curved inwards without reflections, and had nothing inside it but a backdrop and floor of billowing black velvet and one huge cabbage leaf on a violin with a broken string.

Two shops beyond, she turned back and walked past the surrealist window again, calling herself a coward in her daughter's voice, which was clear but rather prissy, as if the muscles round her mouth worked by a drawstring. It was her daughter Arabella who had insisted that she give up the little Kensington coiffeur and come to the Alex salon; who had made the appointment; who had even driven her here in her small uncomfortable car to make sure that she arrived.

Ever since Arabella had come out two years ago with a huge and elaborate dance at which Edwina Gordon, smiling fixedly in cloud-blue lamé, had suffered all the time about how much it was costing to feed and intoxicate a crowd of people some of whom she did not like and many of whom she did not even know, her mother's behaviour and appearance had been a source of considerable distress to her.

Edwina was good-tempered enough not to mind most of the time. She had never expected to have children like this, but here they were, and she could love them and try to please them in surface ways without allowing them to corrupt her own ideas. She had married a man who had become rich, and who had spoiled his son and daughter for ordinary life by using his money in tireless pursuit of the Right Thing for them. Edwina had hated the snobbish school and the precocious Geneva pension which had been 'the only place' for Arabella and had turned her out with an upper-class crudeness which was worse than the more natural vulgar variety. She had argued for a time against Eton for Roddy, and she had always known that the enormous allowance at Oxford was wrong for him, as the kind of friends he brought home were now proving; but since it was Humphrey's money, not hers, and since she was amiable and slightly lazy, she accepted her children as her husband had made them and tried not to protest too often.

When she did, they called her a socialist, or a troglodyte, which was what the right kind of people at Oxford called those who came from impossible schools. She did not mind being teased, and she did not particularly resent being ordered about by Arabella. That was why she was now walking dubiously back and forth in the rain outside the famous Alex salon. Everyone was going there, her daughter had declared, and Mama was in a sense someone, if only in relation to her children.

It was strange, this aversion of Edwina's to anything that was expensive or eclectic enough to be referred to as 'everybody goes there' or 'everybody has one'. It had nothing to do with awe, for when she was first grown up, she had had all this, known only this way of living, been perfectly at home at the equivalent of the Alex salon and The Stork Room and Cap Ferrat.

When she married Humphrey, and he was poor and nobody, she had dived down into his lesser world with the same joy with which a girl from his world would have swum up into Edwina's. Blissfully she had lived Humphrey's life of meticulous accounts and rare treats and the coat of the year before last, and they had been in harmony. Then he had begun to make money, rather rapidly, and they became different. Edwina wanted to stay in the world that had been Humphrey's, and Humphrey wanted to get as quickly and completely as possible into the world that had been Edwina's. Hence his upbringing of the children. Hence her suspicion of all places like the Alex salon where she was now to offer up the undistinguished brown hair which she had crammed under a safe hat of her own and not Arabella's choosing.

The plate glass door was in two halves, each with a massive chrome handle; but only one half opened. This was to show you up immediately as a tyro if you pushed the wrong door.

Edwina pushed the wrong side, tried again and went inside, and the door swung behind her on the black carpet with a perfumed sigh. At the low rosewood desk sat two glorious women with unbelievable hair, one clouded like agate, one pale lemon like tired daffodils. The daffodil one was quite young. The agate was about Edwina's age, but beautiful. Her skin was like cream mixed with the juice of tinned peaches. The few imperfections of her age – the thread of lines round her mouth, the bones at the base of her throat – only added to her air of having arrived aesthetically at the ultimate peak.

Edwina had an idea that she knew her. Some ex-debutante's mother? A lot of them were working these days, and Edwina would too, if Humphrey would let her. When she told her name, the agate woman greeted her like a welcome friend. Not a friend with whom she had drunk inferior champagne or played bridge while the elegant young tramps jived and pushed their bodies against each other to the music of the band that 'everyone has'; but like a cordial mouthpiece for the salon, part of the general decor, which was more like the entrance hall of a regency love nest than anything else.

If she knew Edwina by name or by sight, she was not telling. That was natural no doubt; but then it seemed insulting, for as Edwina turned towards the curving white staircase, a well-known actress came bumping through the door in a grubby raincoat and was greeted with shrieks of joy and the exchange of some ribald laughter. So agate and daffodil were permitted to be familiar. When they put on the elegant hostess act, it implied that you were on the outside track.

'With Mr Frederick, on the second floor,' Edwina had been told. She walked up. There was a lift behind the stairs, but it looked as precarious as a wicker commode, and there was no one in charge of it. After the first flight of stairs and a glimpse of the first floor, where two girls in primrose overalls argued bitterly over a tray of cosmetics, the Alex salon deteriorated rapidly. The stairs were steep and narrow and not very clean. At the top they led straight into a large low room with dozens of plastic-gowned women sitting about in various stages of coiffure; basins in one corner, driers in another, bare mirrors and shelves along the two walls like a chorus dressing room.

There was no receptionist. No one took any notice of Edwina, and she stood for a while, interested enough not to be embarrassed, and watched a ferocious little Frenchman and two bored young priestesses in black rubber gloves paint the sparse hairs of an ancient but still living skull strand by strand with woad. Eventually a thin woman in a black dress who was leaning listlessly near the door and might be either a customer or an employee said: 'I'll take your coat,' revealing herself as an employee while looking more like a customer than ever.

Edwina handed over her coat, wondering briefly why one English girl should grow into a gifted actress uncaring in a dirty raincoat, while another grew into an ex-debutante's mother diffident about her best Persian lamb and uncertain whether, since it was too expensive to have pockets, it would be common to put her gloves in the sleeves.

'Mr Frederick!' the customer-employee called vaguely into the dedicated hubbub of the room, and a tall young man with glossy black hair and skin which looked more like a sun-ray lamp than a ski-ing holiday turned briefly from his work at the mirror.

Seeing that he did not know Edwina, he did not smile, but told a passing girl in a yellow overall: 'Get Madam shampooed, Audrey.' Edwina had wanted to sit down first and let him see how her hair was done now and explain what she would like, but there was nothing much that she could do about it. As she went away to the basins with Audrey, who had white eyelids and white lipstick smeared over pink, she realized that she was as helpless as a new admission in a concentration camp, and resigned herself to accept what came.

What came was that after the shampoo, she sat waiting in front of the mirror with wet hair for a quarter of an hour, during which time Mr Frederick paid her one flying visit, not from courtesy, but as if to remind her that he really existed and was not too good to be true. He rested both manicured hands on the sides of her head, looked in the mirror – but at himself, not at Edwina – and said: 'I just have my lady to comb out,' and was gone.

When he finally came back for good with an old cigar box full of rollers and pins – how absurd all the pretence of sterilizing brushes and combs when they coiffed you with devices full of other people's stray hairs – Edwina began to tell him what she wanted done; but he pursed up his mouth and raised his eyebrows and without actually saying that he knew what he was doing, managed to imply that she had implied that he did not.

Her hair had only been cut three weeks ago, but to her horror he whipped out a cut-throat razor and began to slash all over her head with no recognizable design. It was impossible to protest, not only because it was obvious that at Alex you were no more than a gratefully acquiescent bust in a plastic cloak, but because

266

Mr Frederick, working swiftly, with petulant lips, poured forth a flow of words that discouraged customer opinion.

Edwina was surprised. In her experience, it was the customers who talked incessantly about themselves, and she had often wondered how hairdressers could stand it. But here at Alex – and looking sideways, and in the mirror to the other wall, she could see that the dozen or so male artists in the short cream jackets without lapels were all hard at it too – the hairdresser talked incessantly about himself, so that it was surprising how the customers could stand it.

As he wound her hair on to enormous rollers that swelled her head like a balloon – what on earth was Humphrey going to say? – Mr Frederick insisted on telling her, with no more prompting than her casual remark that her children were as yet unmarried, a great deal about his fiancée and the intricacies of his relationship with her.

Having absorbed the shock that this slick, too-handsome young man who looked – let's face it – like the more masculine half of a homosexual *ménage*, was going to marry and live in a flat on Primrose Hill and raise children just like anyone else, she must now also adjust herself to the fact that he was revealing quite intimate details of his love life to a stranger in the open salon, with an elderly lady whose face was familiar to Edwina from *Tatler* pictures in company with the horses she narrowly resembled, listening with throaty chuckles from the next chair.

'She's not a very experienced girl, you see,' Mr Frederick informed them both. 'Unawakened, as the saying is, and what with one thing and another, it's led to this bit of a tiff. These long engagements are a bit much, you know.' He winked in the mirror at Edwina, and when she did not wink back, he transferred it to the horse lady's reflection. 'Says she never wants to see me again. Can you believe that, Madam?' As Edwina opened her mouth to say Yes, he chattered on: 'But I'm not worried. I know the ropes. She'll come back. They always do if you just lay low and do nothing. It's their curiosity, you see, Madam,' he informed her factually, as if this were a subject, like toadstools, about which she could be expected to know nothing. 'They have to come back to see what you're up to.'

He put a large net over Edwina's head, low over her forehead. When she pushed it up to where it did not look so hideous, he firmly pushed it down again and clicked his fingers for a girl like a ballerina who took Edwina away and put her under a drier among the semicircle of pudding-faced women staring into space or reading about each other in glossy magazines. Edwina was the only one who read a book.

Then she was back at the mirror with the rollers and pins taken out by an undersized boy who was studying to be a Mr Frederick. He came at her after a while with a brush in his hand, squaring his elbows, and beat her head with the torturous attack of an Edwardian nursemaid. He was not talking now. He seemed morose, and Edwina realized why when one of the other men stopped by to ask: 'Aren't you ever going to lunch?' and he answered with a grimace: 'As if I'd had the chance!'

She wondered whether she should whittle down his tip to show him that she thought he was rude and conceited; but when he had finished with her and she sat looking at a stranger with a head like a full-blown chrysanthemum, she liked herself so much that she gave him more than she had intended.

'For God's sake don't put a hat on it,' was his farewell to her, as though she were obviously the sort of woman who would not know any better.

As if she could put a hat on it! She would not be able to wear any of her hats, and she would have to go to church on Sunday with that black lace square over her head, and Arabella would say she looked like a Neapolitan Catholic. What about Dee Dee's wedding? Carrying her puffed-out head carefully erect, she went downstairs, bade a gracious good-bye to agate – daffodil had gone to lunch – and worried all the way home in the taxi about what she could wear at Holy Trinity Brompton if the white hat would not go on.

'Damn the wedding,' Humphrey said when he came home. 'You look a new woman, Weenie. I fall in love with you all over again.' (Had he ever stopped then?) 'Wear it like this always.'

'Suffer Mr Frederick for the rest of my life? He was so rude.'

'They all are,' Arabella said. 'The ones who are any good. You have to be rude back. That's what they like.'

Arabella and Roddy were dressed for a party. She wore black tights and an Italian sailing sweater and had her hair twisted into a high pony tail which did not suit her. He wore blue jeans which looked wrong on his chubby British bottom and a striped American T-shirt with a packet of cigarettes sagging the chest pocket.

They were going out to the country in a flock of sports cars to hold an orgy in an empty farm cottage belonging to the father of a character who was called Sack Wallace because he had a paunch at twenty-two.

Edwina knew Sack Wallace. That is to say, she had met him trundling in and out of her home as part of her children's comings and goings, but since he was convinced that he was to die young, he did not waste time talking to people's mothers. She did not like the sound of the party, but it was no use telling Roddy and Arabella so, because they would not care, even if they listened. Humphrey, who was in the mild form of exophthalmic coma with which he often came back from the office, had merely said: 'Good show. Have a ball,' groping vaguely for the right idiom. As long as his children did not get injured or arrested, he did not mind much what they did provided they did it with the right set.

Roddy, who had mixed cocktails with all the ritual expertise of an American making a salad, poured one for his mother, and bent to kiss her as he put the glass into her hand. He was very fond of her, when she did not try to interfere with him. She was very fond of him.

His hair was too long. He did not take enough exercise. He had no ambition, because he assumed that he could sail without effort into a desk in his father's business. He only worked just hard enough to avoid being sent down; not that he considered being sent down a disgrace, but he was having too good a time at Oxford. These things were far away from his mother's dream of a son, but she loved him because he was always charming and gay and because there was about his sophistication an unawakened naïveté that she found rather touching.

When she asked him whether the father of Sack Wallace knew about the invasion of the empty cottage, she was the one who was naïve. 'How much fun would it be if he did?' Arabella asked impatiently, holding on to a chair and circling her long black leg at waist level. Three years ago everyone had been going to ballet class. She had abandoned it because it was too much work, but she had never quite got over it. 'He's in Bermuda anyway. That's why Sack thought of it.'

'And Mrs Sack?'

'She's always drunk by nine o'clock. The cook shovels her into bed when she puts the cat out. She'll never know a thing.'

'Roddy darling . . .' Feeling exotic in her fantastic coiffure, which she was scared to take to bed for fear of its collapse, Edwina twirled the stem of her glass and copied the faint wailing drawl of the mothers of her children's friends. 'Is there no one at Oxford except people like Sack and Peter and Fernando and that shocking little boy who tipped Bella out of the canoe?'

Roddy sighed. 'Here we go again. You should have it tape recorded, Mama. You know perfectly well there are. Thousands of people. At least –' He grinned and giggled across the room at his sister. 'I suppose they call themselves people.'

'One imagines that they do. At least they might risk it in the privacy of their own homes,' Edwina said, and Humphrey asked her not to tease the boy. He did not enjoy this kind of talk. He did not personally like Roddy's friends any better than Edwina did, but he liked their families or respected their fathers' money, and since he had worked for twenty years to bring his son to this point in society, he was not going to admit any speculation now on whether the whole thing might have been a mistake.

'Don't be so acid, Mama,' Roddy said, bringing her another drink. 'Here, just the thing for acidity. You always make me sound like such a damn snob, but I'm not at all, honestly, and nor is Bella. When she had that thing with the lift man before they fired him – you could hardly call that snobbish.'

Arabella did not mind him bringing this up, although the episode had been a squalid one. She was interested in remembering about the lift man.

'It's just that, well –' Roddy screwed up his face of an adolescent cherub in the effort to explain himself. 'It's just – well, dammit Mama, you know as well as I do that nobody mixes, I mean really *mixes* with the trogs. Honestly, people just don't speak to them.'

'That must be awkward when there are so many of them up now.'

'Oh it is. It's frightful.' Roddy was serious, thinking that she was serious. 'The place is going to ruin. It's got so bad at Balliol that there's only a few people in the college you'd dare to be seen around with.'

'Let's go.' Arabella went to the door. She never said good-bye to anyone. It was one of her Things, like not keeping her shoes on after midnight. 'We have to pick up Cheese and Jessie, and we'll miss the race down if we don't get out to Chiswick when the others do.'

'One question?'

Roddy knelt before his mother in his jeans and put his arms in her lap and gazed at her with his beautiful childish eyes. 'Speak,' he said. 'Speak to me, Mother.'

'It was only this. What about the hundreds of people from public schools who do make friends with the grammar school boys? Do you bar them too?'

'Have to, if that's the way they want to play it.'

'Doesn't it worry you, being in the minority?'

'God no. Why should it? The corps of *élite* is always the smallest.'

Edwina sighed. 'Well then, this. Has it ever occurred to you and the rest of the *élite* that these same impossible troglodytes whom no one speaks to are going to be the bosses some day in the future when you and your friends wake up to find you are unemployable except for small fry jobs?'

Roddy stared at her blankly, and then looked over his shoulder at his father.

'Nonsense, Weenie.' Humphrey shifted his large body in his chair, recrossed his thick thighs and made a little complacent munching movement of his shiny blue jaw – it was sometimes almost impossible to remember him gangling and eager and vulnerable as he had been when they married. 'If the boy goes into the firm, as of course he will, he won't be small fry for any longer than it takes to learn all phases of the organization.'

'But if you're to go on making money you can't afford to put him anywhere near the top!' Edwina's eyes pleaded with him for contact across the softly waving top of Roddy's head. 'You'll have to take the troglodytes into the big jobs. You can't afford not to if they have the brains and training to give you what you want.'

Humphrey shrugged, and his protuberant sea-green eyes glassed over like a window closed against the rabble. She was sure that he agreed with her, because she knew the history of the brilliant men he employed; but he would not say it. Why not? Was he too lethargic at home or too indifferent to her ideas to bother with them? Or was he afraid of his children? Was he perhaps afraid of admitting to them that he had sidetracked them away from the real world of the future into a world which did not really exist at all outside the tiny circle of unenlightened egos?

She should not have started this. It was a mistake to have had two Martinis. Better to lie low and keep her own convictions, for they would not take her seriously, and she wanted the security of

271

all their love. Arabella had come back into the room in an Austrian loden jacket with a bottle of gin sticking out of each pocket.

'Oh do be careful,' Edwina said, involuntarily, for she was not allowed to say it. Arabella scowled at her with her face which was striking because of the way she made it up, but too cramped and finicking for beauty.

'The idea, Mama, originally at least, was more for fun than caution.'

Edwina was standing up, and Roddy kissed her. He was slightly smaller than she, which chagrined him, but he made up for it in bounce. He always kissed her before he went out – thank God, because one day he was going to be killed in a drunken car smash and at least she would have said good-bye – but he drew the line at waking her up to tell her what time he came home. Perhaps it was just as well.

'I worry, you know,' she said futilely, knowing that it made no difference to them. When they had gone down and eased the car out from the tightly packed line in front of the flats by bumping the cars before and behind them, Edwina turned from the window and went to reassure herself by a long look in the mirror over the fireplace at her staggering sophisticated hair.

*

In Granchester Mansions, doomed to extinction in less than six months, and steadily emptying as the families and bachelors and career girls and widows in the ugly brick honeycomb flew off to other hives, Mrs Duke was in the bathroom with her arms round her daughter.

They were both sitting on the edge of the bath – it did not seem nice to sit on the toilet lid – and Veronica was crying. She had not deliberately picked the bathroom to tell her mother that she was nearly four months pregnant. After days of irresolution, the courage had come suddenly while she sat deafened by Godfrey's Stereo, and it was now or never, and her mother happened to be hanging washing on the ceiling rack which dripped into the bath.

'Mum, oh Mum.' Telling the truth had made the tears come, but now that it was said, Veronica realized, sitting on the uncomfortable bath rim with the warmth of her mother enfolding her, that she was not going to cry any more.

She kept her eyes screwed shut and let her mother rock her

272

gently from side to side. Mrs Duke was not angry, and if she was shocked, she did not say so. She had not said anything yet. When Veronica told her, she had only held out her arms and pulled her close.

'Mum, oh Mum.' She had not called her primly Mother since that last evening with Fred which had stolen what little self-confidence the voice on the telephone had left her, and cracked the thin refined shell which had grown round her as she moved up from her origins. She opened her eyes and saw her mother's vast legs planted squarely apart on the shining tile floor, and saw her own unconsciously planted like that too. Five minutes ago she would have drawn them quickly together and crossed the thick ankles which had always been her bugbear. Now she left them as they were, because it was more comfortable. The ankles did not seem to matter.

'Are you going to marry Fred?' It was the first thing, apart from gentle babying murmurs, that Mrs Duke had said.

'No.'

'Why not?'

'Because I hate him.'

'Your father will say you have to.'

'Help me, Mum.'

'You have to tell him.'

'You must. I can't. I don't know what to do.'

'No.' Mrs Duke let her daughter go with a pat and stood up, smoothing down her apron over the broad territory of her stomach. 'It's for you to tell him. I think you should do it tonight.'

'Not with Goff there.' Veronica turned her white face quickly towards the sobbing of the steel guitars.

'Yes. We can't run away from this you know, Ronnie. This is something we'll all have to face together.'

'They'll kill me.'

'They'll know soon enough anyway. I can't think how it escaped me.' Mrs Duke appraised her daughter's shape practically. 'It's just somehow the last thing a person would think of with their own daughter.'

'Oh don't, Mum, don't.'

But Mrs Duke was not being tragic. Before they went into the melodious electronic hell that was the sitting-room, she turned back to pull on the cord that raised the laundry rack up to the ceiling. 'Just because we have trouble,' she said, 'there's no sense letting your father's good shirts squelch in the bath all night.'

Outside the sitting-room door, Veronica said again: 'They'll kill me,' but her mother pushed her in and stood behind her.

'Turn off that noise, Goff,' she shouted, and Godfrey looked up in amazement from his Hawaiian dream. She never interfered with the Stereo.

It was rather like a play, Veronica thought. She stood there in front of her mother with her hands stiff by her sides and her head up, trying to be a heroine – though what was heroic about it she could not have said – and her father and brother sat suspended in the sudden silence with their eyes staring and their mouths half open to exclaim: 'What on earth –?'

Before they could speak, she told them what. Godfrey, still like a character in a play, jumped up with his fists clenched and his jaw squared and looked all round him as if he expected to see Fred hanging from the picture rail. 'I'll kill him!' he cried. 'I'll kill that bloody little twerp!'

'That won't help, Goff,' his father said quietly. 'Though if it would, I'd be glad to do it myself.'

Weren't either of them going to be angry with her? They were not even looking at her now. 'What are you going to say to me, Dad?' Veronica asked in a small voice. 'I've brought shame on the family.'

'Don't talk like a book,' he said. 'There's no sense looking at it that way. What we have to do is see what can best be done for you. If we get moving right away, we can get the licence and have everything fixed up in about three days, I should think. Or has Fred seen about the licence already?'

'Don't you understand, Dad? I'm not seeing Fred any more. He doesn't know about this.'

'Then he's going to find out damn soon! What's his perishing number? He's coming down here right away.'

He got out of his chair, and Veronica stepped forward and put her hand over the telephone. 'I don't want to tell him. I don't want to marry him. I wouldn't even take money from him – suppose he thought to offer it.'

'He wouldn't get a chance to think. There's such a thing as a paternity order, you know.'

Flushed and fat and kindly, anxiety gleaming on her face like an apple rubbed up for show, his wife put her hand on his arm. 'She doesn't want to marry him,' she said patiently. 'She doesn't want to have any more to do with him. She broke with him weeks ago, as well you know, and no one was more glad than you when she did.'

'Glad or not glad, what does it matter now? It's what has to be done.'

'Doesn't it matter then, what Ronnie wants?' Mrs Duke spoke gently, stroking his arm, as if she were explaining something to a wayward dog. 'It's her whole life, you know.'

'A whole life lived under the stigma of a bastard child!' Mr Duke cried, with his fists clenched and his face alight with anger. The word rang between them in the little room like a gong. Almost immediately he flinched, as if its sound had hit him, and his face and body slackened. When he held out his hands to his daughter, his brown eyes were filled with tears.

'Oh God, Ron dear.' He squeezed her hands as if he could wring her unhappiness into himself. 'I shouldn't have said that. I didn't mean to. Forgive me.'

'Forgive you?' She looked into his well-loved face which was so ordinary, so very like all the patient, hard-working men she saw every morning on the bus, so harmless, so honest, and she realized for the first time in her life exactly how good he was. 'I came in here to ask you to forgive *me*.'

She had expected anger, horror, at the least embarrassment, had rehearsed how she would stand up to it. Her mother's understanding, her father's apology, his instant realization of the hurt of his words which brought the illuminating certainty that both she and the child would now be safe from that hurt, un-manned her more than wrath could have done. She put her hands over her face and began to cry again, and Godfrey put his young arm round her and thumped her gently on the back as if she were a dyspeptic baby. 'What else did you expect him to say?' he said. 'Don't be an ass, Ron. What else did you expect us to do but all stand by you?'

Hours later, after it had all been thrashed out how her father would apply for his transfer to be put forward so that they could get out of Granchester Court before anyone found out; how they would call Veronica a widow and give her another surname, so that she could make a fresh start in the New Town with nobody knowing, a thought occurred to her in bed.

When she had said: I'm going to have a baby, first to her

mother, then to her father and her brother, they had all assumed without question that it must be Fred. It could, for all they knew, have been someone else after she had broken with Fred, but they all disliked him so thoroughly that they had jumped at this proof that he was even more despicable than they had always thought.

Poor Fred. Now that she was not afraid any more, Veronica began to be a little sad for him. When he had telephoned her that day at work, just as if nothing had happened, and she had told him, whispering and glancing over her shoulder, that she was not going to see him that evening or ever again, he had received a blow to his vanity so staggering that it had knocked the words out of him. She had waited for him to say something, and when nothing came but rapid breathing, she put down the telephone on the desk and went back to the lady she was tinting, walking more lightly. Of course she had not known then about the baby. When she did know, she had never considered the possibility of telling Fred. And that was sad too, to think that he would never see his child.

Her family, who liked to bury unpleasant things, never talked now about the man on the telephone, and Veronica was never going to tell them what had happened on that night when the police had scared him off for good. Let them bury Fred too. They hated him enough without having to know the worst about him.

Magnanimous in what seemed almost like victory as long as you did not look too far ahead, Veronica lay comfortably and was sorry for Fred, and sorry that he could not know that she was sorry.

The next time that Edwina Gordon summoned the energy to take her head – a wilting chrysanthemum by now – to the Alex salon, her greeting from Mr Frederick was more cordial. The first time, when it might be only a one-shot visit, he would not commit himself. Now that she looked like turning into a regular customer, he was more friendly. He was still uppish, and deaf to any suggestion about her hair, but he did not treat her as if she were something that had wandered in out of the rain smelling of wet dog.

He was even gracious enough to ask after her family, so Edwina rewarded him by asking about his fiancée, although he would probably tell her anyway, whether she asked or not.

'Did you make up the quarrel?' she asked. 'Did she come back, as you said she would?'

Mr Frederick shrugged his lithe shoulders and looked at himself in the mirror. 'She wanted to, Madam, but I turned the tables on her. I wouldn't have her back.' It was not unusual that he did not meet Edwina's eyes in the mirror, but she noticed that he did not even meet his own. 'I haven't seen her,' he said, 'but I hear from a mutual acquaintance that she was so upset she had to leave town.'

Edwina thought he was lying, but his armour-plated ego seemed to have been pierced somewhere, so she murmured sympathetically that she was sorry to hear it.

'No need to be sorry, Madam,' he said airily, jabbing a pin into a roller and apparently right through her skull. 'There's as good fish in the sea, they say, for those who know how to bait the hook.'

'He's quite impossible,' she told Arabella when she got home. 'Some girl must be congratulating herself that she was clever or lucky enough to get rid of him before he drove her insane.'

'But he does do wonders for you,' Arabella said. She was not affected by the private lives of hairdressers. 'What the hell does it matter whether he's possible or impossible? He's taken ten years off you. You were beginning to look your age.'

'Thank you, darling.' Edwina chose to take this as the compliment which she hoped her daughter intended, but you never knew with Arabella. Using her finishing school voice and no words that could in themselves offend, she often managed to be more offensive than anyone her mother had ever met.

Roddy and Arabella went out early that evening. Arabella wore a black skirt and a red pullover and long red woollen socks and a beach hat with a ragged brim. Roddy wore an open-necked shirt with a baggy rowing blazer and a pair of cowboy boots. Edwina had no idea where they were going, and they would not tell her. She supposed it was all right, although since they were always late for everything, she wondered idly about the briskness of their departure. Were they anxious to get out of the flat before Humphrey came home and asked them where they were going?

'This isn't going to turn into anything like Sack Wallace's cottage party, is it?' she asked Roddy, when he kissed her good-bye.

The party at the farm cottage had raised the roof in every sense, for one of its outcomes had been a ten foot ladder pushed out through a big hole in the slates from inside the house. Hundreds of pounds of damage had been done that night. The walls were covered with shrieking slogans, and someone had splashed a vast naked woman in red paint on the downstairs ceiling. Furniture had been set on fire. Bottles had been thrown through windows in a fight which raged half the night and woke up all the villagers except Mrs Wallace, who had passed out at nine o'clock, as prophesied.

When Sack Wallace's father flew back from Bermuda to view the holocaust, he threatened to sue everyone, but the revellers had fled before the police arrived, and there was no one to sue.

No one had been there. Arabella and Roddy had not been there, and Roddy's cut lip had been sustained in a contretemps with a revolving door.

'We changed our minds and went to another party,' they said, when their father came at them shaking a newspaper in which Sack Wallace had given a brilliant interview denouncing the unknown vandals of whom he himself had actually been the ringleader.

Edwina felt sure that Roddy and Arabella had been there, but she did not tell Humphrey, because he had already suffered enough thinking that they were. He might become noble and want to make restitution to Mr Wallace; which would be all right, of course, but unless the other fools and their indulgent fathers could be rounded up and forced to pay, Edwina did not see why her family should take all the blame.

Humphrey had remained suspicious, however, and had even speculated to Edwina for the first time on the rightness of the right set. There was a lot of rather sneering newspaper publicity given to the cottage episode, and he disliked that as much as he disliked the episode itself. 'If you ever get yourselves mixed up in anything like this,' he told his children, 'I'll take away your cars and send you both to South Africa.'

They had laughed at him, but the surprising heavy father act had made some impression. It was obvious tonight that they were anxious to be gone before he could ask them where they were bound. So when Roddy kissed her swiftly, and stroked her cheek with his finger nail as if she were a cat, Edwina had to ask: 'This isn't going

278

to turn into anything like Sack Wallace's cottage party, is it?'

'I hope so. I mean of course not. I mean I've no idea what you're talking about, since I wasn't even there.'

'You were though, weren't you?' She caught the sleeve of his disreputable blazer to hold him back.

He gave her his smile at once artful and seraphic. 'Oh well – in a sense. Don't drag things up at me. Is this the thanks I get for trusting you not to tell the old man?'

He was out of the flat before she unravelled what that meant, and realized that it meant nothing more than a good exit line.

It was all over the morning papers. 'The party to end all parties,' they called it. 'The Chelsea set goes to town – and how.' 'Debutantes battle with police in Underground bottle riot.'

The party had been planned three days before, and the news of it had spread by word of mouth to some two hundred of the right people – and also to the police and the newspapers. It was probably the best publicized party of that year, and it certainly inspired less sympathy, both among its unwilling witnesses and those who read about it next day, than any upper class antics since the eighteenth century Mohocks terrorized the London streets.

With bottles and glasses and wearing strange hilarious clothes, the young *élite* had pushed and fought and shouted their way on to a train at a time when tired late workers were going home. Fights broke out, both among the merrymakers and the people among whom they were making merry, for, as the Marquis of Stillwater was quoted by a reporter who picked him up from a platform where he had been kicked out of the train on his back: 'The general public don't seem to be as tolerant as they used to be.'

At every station, police boarded the train and threw off some of the people and bottles. They got in farther down the train, or stormed into the next train, so that the line became one continuous party until the police finally combed everyone out, and the reporters took their stories back to the night desks.

A few of the drunkest and most belligerent were arrested. One girl was taken into custody because almost everything had been torn off her but her dark glasses. A beautiful child with a face like a magnolia and at least three surnames would be charged the next day with using foul language. An elderly lady travelling home from her work as an office cleaner fell out in tears at the wrong station and lost the contents of her shopping bag under the train. A boy in a pink hunting coat went to hospital with a broken ankle, still tooting his horn. A harmless young man going nowhere in particular was knocked down and trodden on and rose to fight back and was punched in the head by a policeman in mistake for someone else and hit the policeman back and ended in more trouble than if he had been on the party himself. A Jamaican porter trying to prevent three half-drunk hooligans from getting back on the train was knocked back by one of them against a weighing machine and taken away chattering with rage to Casualty with suspected fracture of the ribs.

Some of the newspaper pictures were splendid, and the stories wrote themselves. The usual righteous journalistic scorn was not needed. It was enough just to give the facts. The reporters had taken as many names as they could in the mêlée, and the names had been ingenuously given because it was all such a lark, and it seemed a lot of fun at the time to have the publicity of being in the thick of what was undoubtedly the Most party of the year. Laughing still, though jadedly, at its memory, and expecting the world to laugh indulgently with them, the party goers were quite surprised when, at breakfast tables all over the right parts of London, fathers flushed like wattled turkeys and spluttered forth toast, and mothers exclaimed in distress: 'Don't tell me you were there!'

Edwina Gordon pushed aside her breakfast tray and came out of her bedroom to exclaim it. She met Roddy trailing frowsily to the bathroom in a scarlet silk dressing gown, and Humphrey plunging out of the dining-room with a newspaper, his eyes like the glass balls that used to roll in the necks of ginger beer bottles.

'Don't tell me you were not,' he said threateningly to Roddy, 'because your picture is on the middle page of the *Sketch*.'

'Of course we were.' With the lie dead on his lips, Roddy tried a disarming smile and boyish enthusiasm until he could see how the land lay. 'Bloody good party.'

'Bloody damn lunacy.' His father thrust his head forward at him like a dog straining against a tight collar. 'Look at this, Edwina.'

She looked and thought: Oh God; and thought inconsequentially: rather sweet of Roddy.

The boy cleared his throat and flickered his eyelashes. 'May I look?' His father handed him the newspaper. 'It isn't often that I have the distinction of – Oh Christ.' He glanced quickly at his mother and father, then looked again at the photograph and giggled. 'That's me all right. Funny, one never knew one looked like that drinking out of a bottle. Like some kind of rare bird. Bella!' They were outside her door and he went into her room without knocking. 'Cast your sagging eyes on this.'

His sister was half dressed. She stood in a brassiere and a pair of brief pants and looked at the newspaper, while her mother and father stood in the doorway and watched her, waiting to see what she would say before they decided what they would say.

In the photograph, Arabella was sitting on someone's lap with the ragged beach hat on the back of her head and her feet on someone else's lap, sprawled like an abandoned doll. It was hard to say whether she was one of the drunks or one of the casualties.

'Bloody good likeness,' she said.

Humphrey went into the room and took the paper away from her. 'Put some clothes on,' he said, playing for time, although he was used to seeing her wander round the flat in no more than this. He looked at the picture again. 'This will kill your grandmother,' he said.

Arabella raised her leg to pull on a stocking, her small briefly clad behind turned to them indifferently. 'Well, that will be no loss.'

Moving swiftly for a man of his size, Humphrey lunged forward and smacked the silk covered buttock. Arabella screamed and turned to swing a punch at him, but Roddy grabbed her and Edwina sat down suddenly on the bed, feeling sick. In the doorway, the Austrian maid, Loretta, paused with a mop to survey the scene at leisure.

Although he did not care at all for his grandmother, Roddy cared enough about his mother to want to make amends for Arabella. 'Gran won't mind,' he said easily. 'She's used to this kind of thing. Your father burned a hansom cab in the Haymarket at the relief of Mafeking. It was her wedding day. That was why he took the horse and driver out first.' He giggled, and his father said: 'Shut up and listen to me – both of you.' Edwina sat in silence on the bed, while Loretta stood indolently in the doorway and watched the unusual spectacle of Mr Gordon telling his children some of the things he should have told them long ago.

Arabella hardly listened, but Roddy began to look a little hurt. His crushed hurt face was one of his most successful. When his father had finished and gone off to work via the drawing-room fireplace where he was going to burn the newspaper, Roddy said to his mother: 'I don't get it. Anyone would think we'd done something utterly beyond the pale. Why should he suddenly take off like that after years of thinking everything we do is wonderful?'

Edwina sighed. 'So far, you've managed to keep out of the papers. He hasn't seen you before like this, held up to public ridicule.'

Arabella was dressed and painted now, and she put on a coat and went out of the room as if no one else was in it. 'Where is she going?' Edwina asked. It was no use asking Arabella.

'To get the rest of the papers, I expect,' Roddy said. 'They were all there, you know. Crowds of reporters and chaps with cameras. I'll bet they – oh sorry, I forgot. You don't like our party.'

She made a face. 'Don't you see, Roddy –'

'I see nothing. You let me down, Mama. I had such a good time last night,' he whined a little, as he used to when he was an imperious child, 'and I'd looked forward to hashing it over with you and making you laugh. You don't have much fun, God knows, so I thought you'd like to share some of mine.'

Adept at exit lines that left you momentarily without an answer, Roddy went out wearing his sensitive hurt face. In a little while, Edwina heard the front door of the flat slam. He had probably gone out to get all the newspapers too in case Arabella drifted on for coffee with some of last night's people and did not come back.

Neither of them came back until the afternoon. When Roddy came home, Edwina was in the kitchen drinking tea and cutting pieces off a fresh loaf on the table: a luxury she could not often enjoy, for Loretta usually lacked the energy to go out, and spent the afternoons with her shoes off in the kitchen, mooning endlessly over her gramophone. When Humphrey had been poor and they had no maid, Edwina had practically lived in the kitchen of their small suburban house. It was one of the things she missed most about being rich.

282

With both hands on the teacup, she kicked off her shoes and wound her feet round the legs of the chair and stared into space, like Loretta. She felt so tired and dispirited that she had to set the cup down and put her hand up to make sure that her hair was standing out where it should be, so that at least she did not look like the defeated mother she felt. Thank you, Mr Frederick. For this much at least, I thank you.

She had been in the shops all morning, and out to lunch with a group of sensible women from a Children's Home committee, and everywhere she went people were talking about the Underground party. It was the topic of the day for Londoners. The newspapers had seen to that, and the evening papers had taken up where the morning stories left off, with the kind of editorial comment and hastily solicited opinions from key people designed to inflate last night's ridiculous balloon into a symbol of class warfare. Like her children, Edwina had bought every paper, and after reading them would not have been surprised to hear the boots of the revolutionaries on the stairs and the crash of the rifle butt against the polished oak door of the flat.

But since the revolution had already happened long ago, without boots or rifle butts, the whole thing was more pathetic than alarming. It was hard on the children in a way. Thirty years ago, they could have got spectacularly away with something like this. It was all right for people like them to be a nuisance then. It was part of the social scene, and they were either admired by those who had not yet caught up with what was going to happen, or exploited gleefully by those who had, as instruments for digging the grave of the influence of their own class.

Poor Roddy and Arabella. It was not their fault that the scene had been taken over by people who were too healthily interested in their own lives to be either impressed or militantly indignant at the antiquated high jinks of a class they mildly despised.

When she heard Roddy come in, Edwina called to him and he came, a little stiffly, and sat down opposite her at the kitchen table, and she poured him tea.

'Where have you been?'

'Out and about. Catching up on the news. There were fifteen people in court this morning.' His face brightened, then he saw the pile of newspapers on the floor by her chair and wiped the brightness off. 'You've got the evening papers, I see. Now I suppose you're going to be stuffy about it.'

'Don't put on that suffering face. Listen, darling.' Edwina put out her hand to him across the table, but he was fussing with the wick of his cigarette lighter and did not take it. 'Don't think your father and I are picking on you just for the fun of it. You think we're back numbers, I know. Well, that's all right, because we are; but that's why we both hate last night's thing. Because we've seen it all happen before, only on a bigger scale.'

'That's what I meant this morning about your father and the hansom cab. People have been cutting up since the world began. Or since alcohol was invented, at least.'

'But why only one kind of people? If a gang of half drunk hooligans from the East End had tried to take over the Underground, they'd have been called juvenile delinquents and a menace to society. For you young lordly ones to imagine you can get away with it because you think you are the top class – this is what distresses all of us who've seen it happen before. Why do you think we had the bloodless revolution in England? You don't like the Socialists. All right. But it was people like you who forced them into existence – and the trade unions too. People like you who made the French revolution. And the Russian revolution. All through history, your kind of arrogance has been simply begging for Communism. Well, now you've got it.'

'Oh steady, old dear,' he said mildly. 'You can't make me responsible for all the ills of the world.'

'But you see, don't you?' Edwina gripped the edge of the table and tried to fix his insouciant eye. It was essential that she should make him see now. She had left it too late. She should have spoken her mind years before, to Humphrey, to the children. She had failed them all by being too lazy to stop them drifting backwards.

Roddy laughed. 'You are so intense, dear one,' he said lightly. 'I never see you like this. Rather becoming really, when you set the old jaw –'

'*But do you see?*' She beat her fist on the formica table top. 'Do you understand why I can't scream with laughter over last night's party and drool about what fun it is to see the young folks enjoying themselves?'

'Yes, Mama.' He looked up at her candidly, with his unguarded, lovable smile. 'You and Dad are jealous because you're too old to have any fun any more.'

'Oh my God.' Edwina slumped in her chair and ran her hands

through her hair, and Roddy screamed: 'Don't do that! You'll
never get it back again.' Then he said quickly: 'Did I hurt you?
I didn't mean to.'

'No, darling. You just stagger me, that's all.'

'Well, I didn't mean it,' he lied charitably, seeing that he had
said the wrong thing, but mistaken about why it was wrong. 'I
do understand what you're trying to say, honestly. What was it
again.'

She sighed. 'I've been trying to say that all of us – the jealous
old folk – have had to learn the hard way to be democratic. Don't
wince. It isn't a dirty word to everybody, you know. Your father
is really democratic at heart, although for some reason he's
always forgotten to let you know. But he remembered all right
this morning. I think it gave him quite a shock to realize that he
knew what it must have felt like to be an ordinary passenger
going home on that train. It doesn't work any more, Roddy, the
way you want to live. You can't put the clock back and undo all
the sacrifices and struggles and enlightenment that have crept out
of the agony of two wars.'

'You make such an issue of it, when really it's all so innocent.
We were only having a good time. Is that so madly old-fashioned?
The proletariat likes to see us enjoying ourselves.'

'Oh, come.'

'Well, if they didn't like it, they could have bloody well moved
to another carriage. Or another train. We all had tickets too.'

'Innocent!' Edwina bent to pick up one of the newspapers, a
tabloid with a huge front page picture of a young man with long
flopping hair and a girl without a skirt fighting among a mess of
faces and legs and bottles. 'What about this? What about that
shocking picture of Arabella, and those girls lying on the floor
with their skirts up, waving bottles?'

'But they were posed. "Lie down," says this reporter chap.
"Lie down on the floor and take the bottle." My bottle, somebody took. That ghastly tart Judith. "Pull up your skirts, Miss,"
he says. "Come on, let's have a bit more leg."'

'That makes it worse.'

'Why? You shouldn't be influenced by the popular press.
They're only trying to make it look worse than it was.'

'Of course. It's a wonderful story for them. They're delighted
to foster a little class warfare when the news is too quiet. Why
do you help them?'

Roddy got up and went to the window to pick petals off Loretta's geraniums. He was pouting. 'I never thought this was going to turn into a social issue,' he grumbled at her. 'We were only trying to have a bit of fun.'

'At the expense of hundreds of people trying to get home after work.'

'They like it.' Roddy kicked moodily at the radiator grid under the window sill. It was soft thin metal and it gave a little to his foot, so he prodded it again in another place.

'They hate it. Oh dear.' Edwina looked again at the newspaper. 'I hate it too. It's all so vulgar.'

'How can it be?' Roddy put down his foot and turned round with his look of disarming surprise. 'Dozens of them were Lords.'

'Don't.' Edwina waved a hand at him. 'Oh, please don't say any more.'

She got up, and Roddy came and patted her arm and said: 'Don't be angry with me, baby doll. I mean no harm.'

She wondered whether anything she had said was any use. 'I know,' she said, and kissed his long soft hair which it was absolutely Out to keep tidy with grease. 'And it could be worse, after all. You might have been in jail this morning. I wonder what they'll do to the boy who knocked the coloured man down. That was an awful mistake. They can't let that go by.'

'They'll never pin it on anyone.' Roddy took his hand from her arm and stepped away from her. 'There were so many blokes milling around. They haven't a hope of finding out who it was.'

He spoke without looking at her, and so quickly that Edwina asked: 'You know though, don't you?'

He shrugged. 'Do I?'

'Did you see it? Do you know who it was?' Oh God, it wasn't over yet then. If they found out who had injured the irate Jamaican porter, Roddy might have to go to court as a witness, and if he tried to wriggle his way charmingly out of the truth, they would know so easily, just as she always knew. 'Who was it?'

Loretta came into the kitchen with her beret and her black coat buttoned high, looking like something from a pre-war German film. 'Hullo?' she said uncertainly, hoping that everyone would not immediately stop being in the kitchen when she came in, for she was lonely.

'Even suppose I knew,' Roddy said as he went out and left his

286

mother lighting the gas under the kettle to freshen the tea for Loretta, 'I would never tell on a friend. Even to you.'

From the basement window of the house in Glidden Road, Mrs Ambrosia Drinkwater watched the thickset figure of the Jamaican run up the area steps, pause by the top railing to glance right and left, as an animal does before it puts its head down to drink, and glide off into the shadows away from the aimless gathering outside the Conga Club.

'That fellar,' she said to Gilroy, who was creasing a ten shilling note up no bigger than a stamp, the way he always carried folding money, 'he dangerous in his mind. It not like him to come here looking for weed.'

'So who cares?' Gilroy said, his golden smile expansive. 'His loot's as good as anyone's.'

'Maybe,' said Ambrosia, 'but them Jamaicans usually keep it among their own. They must be short of charge up the Harrow Road.'

'And he sure needed it bad,' Edgar said. Ambrosia and Gilroy had got so used to having him about the place like a gangling unwanted dog that they no longer bothered to keep him out of the basement office where trade was done. At fifteen, he smoked hemp now all the time when he could wheedle it out of Gilroy, so he would not squeal on them, for they could shop him right back to the Law quicker than thought. 'He don't care about no shade bar now. He feeling his way about the Jumbles, he got no time to worry about Trinidad.' Edgar no longer strove to speak like a Britisher. All that had gone long ago, along with his ambitions to be something, his chance for the Grammar school place, his loyalty to his parents and to the teachers who had believed in him.

'You shut your mouth,' Ambrosia said, but automatically, for she was ready to agree. 'He dangerous, like I say. When I was to the store for salt fish, the women there telling about after he get hurt on the Underground, he going about everywhere swearing revenge. "I'll kill the bugger who done it," he crying everywhere, even though he all strapped up round the chest like a big cee-gar.'

'When he's all charged up and afraid of no man, I wouldn't like to be a white fellar meets him in a dark alley,' Edgar said, knowing in his mind the soft footsteps, the quick glance of the knife, the weight of the body falling on to the hand, the feet like

287

a swift hare flying away while the stain spread slow and sticky on the pavement.

'Or a white woman.' Ambrosia cackled high and raucous, showing her long peg teeth.

'You would too.' Gilroy grabbed at her and she shrieked. 'You'd like it just fine.'

Edgar left them. Sometimes he stayed around to watch them, because with two such ugly people, it could be curious, like animals. But mostly it was boring. There were more amusing things he could be doing out on the street.

Edwina Gordon switched off the little bedside radio and turned to look at her husband. He was reading in green silk pyjamas, propped uncomfortably against the pillows, like an egg set on end.

'Yes, I heard it,' he said. 'Well, there you are. I told you there would be repercussions.'

He had not said so. It had been Edwina who had been haunted, ever since the preposterous party, by the feeling that this was not the end, that something had been started which would have to go a long way beyond mere tomfoolery.

'Raping a white woman is a damn serious charge for a black man to face,' Humphrey said without lifting his eyes. He did not often read a novel, and when he did he gave it as much ponderously concentrated attention as if he were translating it from a foreign language. 'In the States, he'd be executed, if he was lucky enough to escape being lynched.'

'But being the boy who injured him and provoked him to violence is really just as serious,' Edwina said tentatively. 'I wonder how he feels now?'

'Guilty as hell, I should think.' Humphrey spread the book farther open with a cruel cracking noise. 'Where are you going?'

'I'm hungry. I'm going to get some cake.' Humphrey had suffered enough over the newspaper publicity. Mercifully there were only two people in the office who were near enough to his level to tease him about it. But everyone else – even the little squat girl who ran the stamping machine – had given him that special knowing look they usually reserved for people just back from a honeymoon. Edwina was not going to make it worse for him by telling him that she was sure that Roddy knew who had knocked the Jamaican down.

She went along the corridor and into Roddy's room. He had

stayed at home tonight in a feeble attempt to please. Arabella was still out somewhere in a dress cut as if for sunbathing.

'Asleep?'

'I was. Not now.' He sat up with his hair over his face, and switched on the bed lamp. 'Curiously pleasant, going to sleep early. You should try it some time.'

Edwina sat down on the bed. 'I've just been listening to the News. The coloured man who had his ribs broken during the Underground party broke into a flat and beat up a white girl who was ill in bed, and raped her.'

'How do they know it was him?' Roddy was wearing white shark-skin pyjamas and his face was not much darker.

'They caught him. She screamed and a man got him as he was running out of the flats. He told the police why he'd done it. As an act of revenge.'

'Oh God.' Her son looked at her. She had been going to ask him again: 'Who was it?' but suddenly she did not need to. She said: 'It was you who hit him.'

If he had started to babble excuses, to make a joke, to try to duck out of it with glib lies, she would have smacked him across the face. But he looked helpless and afraid, like a child caught with the forbidden object in his hand, and said: 'Yes, it was.'

What were they going to do? Roddy got up and they had a drink and talked round and round the nightmare until Arabella came home and found them tired and desperate on the sofa. For the first time since Edwina could remember, Roddy's conscience came struggling up from the depths where years of doing as he pleased had buried it. He wanted to make amends. To do something for the girl – but what? To go and speak in defence of the coloured man. But would that help? To make up for what he had done with a large gift of money. But this, as his mother had to remind him, was probably the only time in his life when he could not buy his way out of trouble.

'If you had to hit someone, why couldn't it have been a white man?' Edwina fretted for the tenth time.

'He got in my way. It didn't matter what colour he was. I hardly saw. He had the lousy nerve to shout at me, and – oh, it's so damned unfair! You accused me earlier of fostering class prejudices, and I love the prole – you know I do. Now it seems I've stirred up racial hatred as well. Me of all people! I've never had anything against the coons. There's flocks of people at college blacker than the inside of your hat. They're all right. They don't mix, of course. The do-gooders try to be nice to them, but it's too much bloody work. And they think you're patronizing if you try it.'

'The Jamaican won't think that if you go to the police tomorrow and confirm his story. Evidence of provocation might help him.'

'I'd have to go to court. The papers would go to town on it. How much would that help Dad? Or you? Or me.' He pretended to make that an afterthought.

They did not know what to do. The only thing they could settle was not to tell anyone else until they had decided what to do. But when Arabella came home in the sunbathing dress and found them still talking, she knew already. The boys who had been with Roddy when the Jamaican was hurt had spread the news. It was all over the town, and Roddy's name, as Arabella remarked, not without glee, was on everybody's lips. 'Nice thing,' she smirked. 'You get all the responsibility for the rape without any of its dubious pleasures.'

All next day, Roddy prowled nervously about the flat waiting for the police to come, and trying to summon the courage to go to them before they came to him. Whatever he did now could not be of much practical help to either the Jamaican or the wretched girl, but for his own sake, Edwina desperately wanted him to take some voluntary step towards reparation.

But by night time, it was too late. The whole thing exploded in their faces. A gang of Teddy boys cruising the streets in an old taxi had beaten up an old coloured man in daylight, and left him dying on a street in Cottingham Park. By night, violence between black and white had flared up like beacons all over that part of town, and spread into what the news announcer designated, without a tremor in his voice, as an unmistakable race riot.

In the silence that followed Humphrey's extinction of the wireless, as if his broad hand could switch off the truth, Arabella turned to Roddy. 'Now look what you've done!' she said, and as Edwina sat with her face in her hands, sobbing, her son and daughter spluttered at each other in a convulsion of hysterical giggles.

The knife glinted for a moment in the thick yellow light outside the public house, and the man who had been doing most of the shouting staggered back against the wall with his face laid open from eye to mouth and the blood running over the open bone.

With the knife still tucked inside his hand, Edgar ran, seeking the darkness. He climbed over the barricade of old doors, and waited for a long time in the secret black place under the steps of the derelict house, hearing the sounds of battle and the police whistles and the thrilling ambulance bells.

One by one, the Zorro Men slipped in under the crumbling bricks. 'Five on 'em cut.' Big Phil, the wrestler, came in last, his great chest working like a bellows. 'Get home, fellars, and change them black sweaters. Better for all of we now if we could change these here black skins.'

Months later, the events of that week would be referred to as 'the incidents in Cottingham Park', and played down by the people who ventured cautiously into print to explain them, as isolated outbreaks of lawlessness, with no background of basic racial prejudice. But to the people of Cottingham Park who lived through that week, it was war. Race riots and mob violence, and the hideous spectacle of black against white in a brutal, untimely eruption of age-old cankers.

After the first two incidents, the infection spread rapidly until even those who had barely noticed the colour of the next man's skin were on fire with the disease. The rape, the murder of the old coloured man, and the jostling of a white woman outside the public house, which had flared into an argument, a brawl and a knife fight, were only the beginning.

The Teddy Boys in the lurching ten-pound taxi who had pounced on the old man and kicked him into pulp may or may not have been seeking to avenge the rape of the sick white girl. To the newspapers whose job was to jump to crude conclusions for the benefit of those who had to have slick opinions ready made, it was convenient to suppose that they were. When the banner headlines blared that the Teddy Boys had sworn vengeance, the white gangs in the whole area, who had been more or less keeping the peace, saw themselves as vigilantes, and jumped at the offer of a ready-made target for their restless antagonism.

Almost immediately after the public house battle, the word swept round the dismal streets that the Spades were attacking whites with knives, and people who had lived placidly cheek by jowl with coloured families began to remember all the small grievances they had ever had against the West Indian immigrants. The Teddy Boys found themselves for once not in the distrusted minority, but in the vanguard of a disturbance so wild and unreasoned that in some free-for-alls it was not black against white, but black and white confused together against the police.

On the second night of that week, many frightened coloured people kept indoors, but there were some who were not too frightened to embrace this chance to pay off old scores of unemployment and extortionate rents for bad housing now that the frail barriers of civility were down. There had been minor acts of lawlessness all day on both sides, and by nine o'clock a fair crowd had collected at the corner by the green-tiled public house where the knife fight had been to see what was going to happen now. Some had come to catch any excitement that might show up. Some had come prepared to make trouble. Some of the men and women who moved restlessly about and incited each other with ill-informed talk could not have said why they had come, except they they had followed the crowd drifting up or down West Hill towards Green Man Corner.

A few policemen were there, and a sharp-featured constable who resembled the Alsatian dog which even this mainly British crowd did not attempt to fondle, and for a while nothing happened. The public house emptied, and most of its customers, either afraid to walk home alone if trouble was brewing, or unwilling to miss a possible sensation, stayed on the corner with the crowd. The people were so absorbed in their own conglomerate entity that they did not at first pay much attention to the little band of West Indians who came weaving and crooning round the corner on the other side, three-quarters drunk from a wedding.

Bold in their liquor, the coloured men stopped dead, propping each other up, and began to hurl insults at the gathering across the road. They were too drunk to make much sense, but there were some confused shouts about showing all you —ers whose country this is, and a slice of filthy abuse about the Queen, which sent a beer bottle sailing out of the crowd to crash among the jigging crêpe-soled feet.

When the police grabbed the coloured men, they thought they were being arrested, and yelled like stuck pigs. When they found that they were only being escorted away from the explosive zone, they began to shout over their shoulders again at the white people.

In a temper for action, the crowd started after them, surging down the street, but with one of those dislocations of current that will suddenly sweep a whole mass of people aside from their objective, they turned down a side street and made for Glidden Road.

Gilroy and Ambrosia were in their room on the ground floor with the curtains drawn against the dangerous night. Ambrosia was afraid. Her restless hands, thin and scaly like the feet of an old stewing fowl, could not be still. Her eyes rolled about inside her head like roulette balls. She had not gone out since the trouble started. She had sent Edgar for food, but he had not returned.

Gilroy was afraid because there were too many policemen in the neighbourhood for comfort.

When they heard the noise of the crowd coming into the street, shouting and whistling and still fairly amiable, with dogs and children running in and out among them, like a mob of holiday-makers out on a spree, Ambrosia ran into the little closet bed-room where a Merchant Navy deserter was sonorously asleep, and got into bed with him. Gilroy put one rolling eye to a chink between the curtains, but drew back hurriedly as a milk bottle dropped past his face and crashed into the area.

He had to look out again. Now they were aiming better. All along the street from both sides, milk bottles and beer bottles and empty cans were hurtling down on to the pavements from the windows of the coloured tenants. Black faces and bosoms and arms were leaning out of the windows, shouting and throwing and screeching abuse.

Gilroy left the window and ran up the stairs to his front tenant on the next floor and cried: 'You stop that! You want to get the Law in here, you?'

Young Rogerson turned with his arm raised and said cheer-fully: 'Who's stopping? This more fun than the carnival,' and hurled a fat cider bottle into the milling crowd below.

Almost immediately, a brick sailed in through the open window and knocked down the coloured photograph of Roger-son's mother and father petrified against a crumpled backcloth of palms and Grecian pillars. Their son grabbed the brick and threw it back. 'They tearing down the wall on the corner!' he yelled. 'It's war, man, I tell you!' Rogerson's woman, a little light-skinned girl who might have a baby any minute, sat on the floor in a corner with her arms wrapped over her huge vulnerable stomach and admired Rogerson with large patient eyes.

Gilroy went downstairs. As he entered his own room, there was a crash of glass as a brick came through the window, tore the rotting curtains from the rail and skidded towards him over the floor. With a yell, Gilroy pushed aside the wall blanket and got into bed with Ambrosia and the Merchant Navy man. The man slept untroubled while Ambrosia and Gilroy sat and clutched each other on his feet until they heard the motor-cycles and the black Marias come, and the tumult died down and they were left in temporary peace with the curtains down and the wind biting through a large jagged hole in the window.

Edgar did not come home for three days. His foster parents had no idea where he was, and did not care. They would not care if he stayed away for ever, and if he got himself killed in the riots, like the crazy nigger he was, they would tell his parents he had died of starvation because they were not sending enough money.

Edgar spent most of the week with Big Phil, who took him home to the basement room where he lived with a woman and two children who were not his. They had two major rumbles with their rival gang, the White Hunters, who had been among the first to join the 'nigger hunt', as they brazenly called it in court, where some half-dozen of them were later sentenced to three years for causing grievous bodily harm. The coloured men they had injured were caught from the rear, defenceless in an alley without weapons. The Zorro Men would never be caught like that. They were more slippery than the vapid, clodhopping White Hunters, and swifter and more skilful with their armoury of flick knives, dustbin lids, broken milk bottles, bicycle chains, rubber hose and the deadly fishhooks in the sleeve.

Although he was younger than most of the gang, Edgar was now an inner initiate, since he had drawn blood before witnesses. The cheek he laid open that first night outside the Green Man was not the only blood he drew in that week of lunacy and violence. He was reckless, fearing none of his enemies. He would not get hurt. He would not get nabbed by any of the policemen or the plain clothes men you could spot a mile off, who were swarming like dung flies all over Cottingham Park.

He thought of himself as a hero, but once when he was playing on the floor with Big Phil's woman's babies, and thinking what a hell of a fellar he was and that even the little kids loved him, it suddenly came to him with a chilling shock that he was still only Edgar Biggs who ought to be at school, and that it was the blood that excited him and made him unafraid.

He tried to explain this to Big Phil, with difficulty, because Phil did not absorb thoughts that were too subtle. They rolled off his cropped head like water off a bed knob. When it finally seeped through that Edgar had thought about being afraid, not of the police or the White Hunters, but of himself and what was happening to him, Big Phil expanded his chest to match his grin. 'Why you so stupid, man? We doing nothing wrong. We crusaders, like it have in history. You want to sit back and see you own people crushed under heel by them savage imperialist Jumbles?'

In the middle of that week, a boy in Colin Mackenzie's class at Green Lane came to school with one arm in a sling made out of a torn dish towel and a dirty piece of plaster over one eyebrow, with an expression of foolish triumph below it.

He swaggered into the classroom late, and while Colin was banging on his desk for quiet and shouting at him to sit down, he stood with his head up, looking all about him like an actor indicating that now was the time for applause. He had lately joined the White Hunters as an ineffectual hanger-on, and it was clear that with his honourable wounds he expected to be treated like a hero. Several of the boys left their seats and clustered round him, while he danced on his feet and made neat boxing gestures with the unslung fist, as if he were telling a tale of honest pugilism, instead of the cheating brawl which was more likely to have caused what was under the plaster.

When Colin had succeeded in getting the class back into place, the injured boy still stood smiling foolishly out in front.

'You too, big time,' Colin said. 'You don't look as if you should be at school at all, but since you're here, you might as well sit down and try to benefit from the wisdom of Pythagoras.'

'Aren't you going to ask me what 'appened?' the boy asked.

'No.' Colin did not want to start them talking about the riots. The school was on fire with the subject as it was. Nothing else was discussed. Less work than ever was done, less discipline was possible, and the undercurrent of bad feeling between the coloured children and the white was running right up on the surface for everyone to see.

Many of the pupils did not turn up at all, because their parents said that they were afraid for them to walk home from school through the uneasy streets; so the children stayed away and were able to run the streets looking for excitement all day, instead of only in the evening. The coloured children who had been kept away were probably holed up indoors in their frowsy rooms, for the West Indian mother was often more careful for her children's safety than the average white.

There were still enough coloured pupils at Green Lane, however, to keep the school's personal interest in the riots on the boil. Scuffles and fights had been breaking out everywhere, and the Headmaster would scarcely venture from his office for fear of what beastliness he might see. The staff, for once banded together against a common menace, had asked him for a conference yesterday after school to discuss how the situation could be handled, but Mr Neilson had declared he was too busy, and gone scurrying home sideways even before the four-thirty bell had rung.

Toward the end of Colin Mackenzie's Sisyphean geometry lesson, a galvanic small boy with the whole of his face as red as the pimples which stippled his forehead exploded into the room.

'What's up, young Spanner?' a voice asked. 'You seen that nigger with the knife strapped to 'is jock?'

Through the badinage, the boy panted at Colin: 'It's Miss Peel, sir. She wants you, quick.'

Laughter redoubled. The engagement of Colin and Grace Peel had led to an inexhaustible supply of delightful jokes. Most of the pupils at Green Lane liked them both, but the idea of their coming marriage was too riotous ever to be accepted without irreverent comment.

'What's the matter?' Colin was already at the door.

'A fight, sir. A real bundle. Miss is in the middle of it.'

Without stopping to tell anyone (uselessly) to take charge, or even to care what might break out as soon as he was gone, Colin's long legs hurtled down three flights of stairs, with young Spanner gasping behind him like a tubed horse. They raced along the stone corridor to the Assembly hall where Mr Neilson would not hold assemblies, in which Grace's rag tag and bobtail class 2c, who had never had a proper classroom, were temporarily housed among the draughts at one end.

It was, as the boy Spanner had said, a real bundle. The White Hunter, Sidney Goole, passing through the hall with some cronies, had tripped up a coloured boy who was on an errand with a load of books. The books scattered on the floor. The coloured boy fell among them, picked himself up and waded into a fight. From the other end of the hall, Grace's entire class, including the girls, had joined in with whoops and shrieks, and from an adjoining room, with Mrs Fitch screaming futilely: 'Sit down!', some two dozen maniacs had burst yelling into the battle, which was now raging all over the hall.

Expecting to have to save Grace from injury or terror, Colin saw that she was in the thick of it, her hair flying like a torch in the wind, one shoe off and her blouse flapping out of her skirt. She kept pulling boys and girls apart and thrusting them to the back of the room among the upturned tables and broken chairs that had been her class; but as fast as she pulled them out and went back for more, the first ones were back in again with primitive shrieks of joy.

Every minute, more boys from other rooms came down to see what was going on, and joined willingly in. It was no longer a fight between white and coloured. You punched a black boy if he was near you, or dragged a coloured girl down by the hair, but you hit the white boys too for the sheer fun of hitting, and rolled scratching and shrieking on the floor with any girl of your own skin who got in your way. The school had not had such a real slap-up first class bundle since Coronation Day.

Colin stepped over two struggling bodies, and pulled Grace by the arm over to the wall.

'Are you all right?'

Panting, she nodded, wildness in her shining eyes. 'I tried to stop them. I did try. I couldn't do anything. There's too many . . . Lily! You stop that, you filthy little savage!' Before Colin could hold her back, she was into the turmoil again, slapping the face of a fat harpy who was pulling a pair of tight black pigtails backwards in an apparent attempt to snap off the coloured child's head.

Some of the staff were in the hall now, and the classes they had left were trying to get in after them. Geoffrey Savage, his lion's mane on end, was laying about him effectively and without effort. He had Sidney Goole whimpering against the wall with both hands to his bleeding nose, and Colin saw him for a moment with a small boy in either hand, held up by their collars with furiously bicycling feet before he dumped them both out of a side door like rejected kittens.

'Clear the hall! Clear the hall!' Mrs Fitch squealed uselessly above the din. At the main door, Mr Partridge, with his short fat legs planted and one hand on either side of the doorway was struggling manfully to block the entrance to more combatants, until he was pushed vigorously aside by Miss Arbuthnot, who wanted to get into the hall herself.

Monolithic, Miss Arbuthnot stood with her strong masculine head up and her nostrils flared, surveying the pandemonium. She opened her mouth to shout, then closed it again grimly. Even her powerful voice would be no more than a whisper in the shrieking uproar that raged between the green unfaced brick walls.

'I'm going to Mr Neilson,' she said.

'What good will that be?' Colin, holding two boys apart at arm's length, looked at her over his shoulder. 'He's the last person who'd know what to do. Why don't you call the police?'

'No,' said Miss Arbuthnot calmly. 'This is his pigeon.' As a rigorous second in command, she was usually so determinedly loyal to the Headmaster – the only one who was, who did not eternally tear him to pieces in the common room – but now a queer diabolical smile was making mischief on her craggy features. 'I just want to see what he will do,' she said lightly, pushed a knot of skirmishers out of her way and was gone.

What Mr Neilson did was, surprisingly, the most sensible thing. He sounded the fire alarm. From automatic habit, everyone rushed out of the hall, falling over each other, crushing into the doorway, blocking corridors in a disorderly stampede that could have been fatal if there had really been the fire which they believed had broken out.

'The Spades have set fire to the school! They'll burn us up! Let me out of here! Let me out!' In the near panic, many of the smaller ones were sobbing with terror as they ran with the mob; but the fight was over, and although some ran right on through the side passage of the playground and away into the streets, the staff managed to get the rest of them lined up on the asphalt in some sort of fire drill order.

The loudspeaker system through which Mr Neilson regularly addressed the school from the security of his office had an amplifier over the door at the back of the building, so that no one in the playground should miss his sermons.

As the school stood raggedly, shifting their feet in the cold, restless still, with hair on end and faces streaked with dirt and blood, the speaker crackled and the metallic voice came through, talking rapidly.

'Attention all classes. Attention all staff and pupils.'

Grace and Colin were standing together, with their classes ranged unevenly before them. 'Now,' said Colin. 'Now's his chance. If he doesn't muff it. Let him tell them something that'll hit them. Something they can take home. Oh God, I wish I were up there! Tell them, Neilson, you knuckle-headed old fool. . . . Tell them something real. . . .' His eyes were shut as if he were praying. Grace took his hand and gripped it, tightening the pain in her knuckles where the overturned table had skinned them.

'Go home!' The nasal voice was higher now, and even through the blurred distortion of the amplifier, you could sense the hysteria. 'Go home, the lot of you! School's closed. Go home, I tell you!'

His cracking voice was drowned in a hullabaloo of cheers and cat calls. Without waiting for directions, without even looking at the staff lined up with their backs to the school, the ranks dissolved, swarmed shrieking to the grey side passage and funnelled down it to the street. The staff were left alone in the cold wet playground, with Grace still holding Colin's hand.

They looked at one another without expression. Then Miss Arbuthnot shrugged her broad shoulders and went up the steps to the back door. The others straggled after her. Dropping Grace's hand, Colin raced past them up the steps and turned to face them in the doorway. 'Let's go together,' he said breathlessly. 'Let's all go together and tell that bloody coward what we think of him.'

'I'm with you,' Geoffrey Savage said at once, but the other men and women in their dull teaching clothes caught no fire from the spark. They looked at Colin without interest, thinking only of the unexpected afternoon off, and went on their way up the steps and past him through the door.

'It's no good, you know, Colin,' Miss Arbuthnot said. 'He won't understand.'

'You come,' Colin urged her. 'Stick with us. You said back there in the hall you wanted to see what he would do.'

'Well, and I have seen,' Miss Arbuthnot said. 'It's all I wanted to know.'

Colin and Grace and Geoffrey raced up the stairs and along the corridor to the door of Mr Neilson's office. Grace got there first and lifted her hand to knock, but Geoffrey pulled it down. 'What if it's locked?' she asked.

'Then I'll break the bugger down,' said Geoffrey. He tried the handle with unnecessary force and the three of them charged together into the room.

The headmaster had been standing in gnomish silhouette by the window. He turned at once with his hand up, as if the opening door had been a blow. 'Here, here, here,' he said. 'What's this?' He went forward to grasp the back of his chair, as if they were circus lions. The wide littered desk was between them.

'Don't talk to us as if we were your unfortunate pupils,' Colin said. He was flushed with anger, and his gentle amused mouth was set in unnatural bitterness. His trousers were rucked up at the bottom and the knot of his tie was halfway round the side of his collar.

'You look like a revolutionary,' Mr Neilson said, in a conversational tone.

'I feel like one.' Colin glared at him. 'You let us down. You had the whole school in your hand out there, the whole excited lot of them. You could have done something with them. It was your chance. God knows, you've preached often enough and no one gave a damn, but you could have preached sanity to them and they might have listened.'

Mr Neilson let go of the chair and sat down on it, clasping his small hands neatly on the table. He seemed to feel safer sitting down, as if the very vulnerability made him less vulnerable. 'I have absolutely no idea what you are talking about,' he said.

'Oh yes you have.' Colin stepped forward and banged his fist on the desk. 'You had the chance to say something that could have brought some sense to these lunatic kids. If you'd said it right, it might have reached beyond them, back to their homes, where the race hatred started. Even if you didn't know what to say, you could have given us the chance to talk to them. We –'

'My dear Mackenzie.' Mr Neilson raised his neutral-coloured eyebrows. 'Do you imagine for one moment that they would have listened?'

'They might at that.' Geoffrey Savage's cockney had grown broader since he came to Green Lane. Identifying a little *too* much with the inmates, Denzil Raymond used to call it. 'Colin's right, you know. Dead right. They were in a funny kind of temper just then. I don't know . . . bewildered, like, with the fight over, and some of them wondering where it had gone and what it had been about anyway. They're only kids, after all.'

'Kids! Full grown criminals, a lot of them. Perhaps you are so blind to the activities of your class that you don't know that at least a quarter of them have been out all this week in armed gangs, mixed up in the thick of the riots.'

'Who's to stop them, if we can't? So because of a few thugs, you treat the whole bleeding lot as homicidal maniacs and send them packing as if you were scared to death they'd come up here and do you.' Geoffrey spread his hands helplessly. He turned away and muttered to Grace: 'I wish they bleedin' had.'

'Have you finished?' Mr Neilson drew a sheaf of papers towards him and picked up a pen. 'I'm very busy.'

'We've only just begun. You know what will happen now?' Colin leaned across the desk. 'They've got away with this. They've had their fight, their junior race riot here in the school, and got a half day off as a reward. Most of them will go right out on the streets and start looking for more trouble. God knows there's plenty of it.'

'Let them find their troubles somewhere else,' Mr Neilson said fretfully. 'I can't have it here. You don't seem to understand. What happened today was dangerous. It could have resulted in some terrible disaster if I had not stopped it. I had to clear the school. I had to break them up and get rid of them. It was my duty, both to the school and to the public who rely on us.'

'Duty hell,' said Colin. 'You were afraid. Scared to death of a pack of kids, and they all know it, you rotten coward.'

Grace held her breath, but Mr Neilson did not seem to mind. His waxy indoor face did not change colour. His voice was calm as he asked them to leave; which they did, having no heart to say more. 'And shut the door behind you!' he called out querulously. Of all the people of whom he was afraid: the school board, the parents, public opinion, his pupils, he was least afraid of his staff. He did not care what they thought of him.

'He'll sack us,' Grace said when they were in the corridor.

'Who cares? But he hasn't even the guts to do that. Let's sack ourselves.' Colin took her hands. 'Let's not come back any more. We'll get married tomorrow and go miles away to some place where everyone's the same colour and has the same income, which is nil, and scrape a living out of the earth.'

'Oh lovely.' She swung his hands, catching the quick swoop of his spirits. They had left their anger behind in the Headmaster's office. He could keep it for company among the books and stationery and pen nibs by the gross. 'We'll have babies, and they'll run about naked and never go to school.'

'Old Geoff can come too, and be Caliban. Bring Dora. She's got the hips for the simple life.'

'I'm staying here.' Geoffrey would not join the game. 'You know that. I – I'm committed.' It was odd to see this big shaggy man embarrassed. 'Grace knows, don't you, love?'

She nodded and took strength from him to pull out of the dream before it all seemed too easy. 'I'll go anywhere with you, Colin, you know I will. But let's just stay here until after the wedding, next month as we'd planned it. I did promise my class they could all come. How could I cheat them out of that? The girls are going to make all the cakes in domestic science, you know that, and Mary Oliver's going to hold my bouquet. Her mother sold the gramophone last week so she could have a perm, and –'

'God damn it,' said Colin. 'What's wrong with all of us? I offer you freedom, the joy of living in the way we were meant to live before civilization fouled everything up. But it turns out that our whole life, our stake in the future, our grab at our own kind of happiness has all been quashed a week ago by Mary Oliver's mother's gramophone.'

'But you do understand?' If he did not, she could not marry him.

'Yes, darling. God help me. I understand. I understand about us all.'

'No escape!' shouted Geoffrey cheerfully and bounded away down the stairs, his thick tweed jacket flapping about him like the pelt of a mountain goat.

'What the 'ell you 'ome for at this time?' Mrs Bott welcomed Frankie as he pushed open the flat's front door.

She stuck her head round the kitchen door like a turnip tied up in a black scarf and let out a sharp scream. 'Your face! You been truanting, Frankie Bott. You been out on the streets fighting.'

'No, Mum.' Frankie went to the sink and wiped his face with a rancid dishcloth. 'I was at school. There was a fight there. That's why Mr Neilson sent us home.'

'Them nigger kids started it,' she said quickly.

'They didn't then.' Between thirteen and fourteen, Frankie had suddenly begun to grow. He had not filled out sideways, but although he was weedy, with knobbly joints protruding from his sleeve and trouser ends, he was almost as tall as his mother. It was easier to contradict her when you could talk right into her face. 'It was some white boys started it.'

'Ho,' said Mrs Bott, wagging her great turbaned head at him. 'Don't tell me. I know 'oo starts all the trouble. 'Oo started all the trouble we've got on our 'ands now so that decent folk daren't stick their noses out the door to fetch a crust of bread?'

'The Teddy Boys.' Frankie dried his face on a towel which smelled of carrots. 'That's what they say.'

'You ignorant little bastard. I suppose it was the Teddy Boys who went for that poor innocent girl.' Although she was so crude and vulgar, and her tongue fitted easily round words like bugger and bastard, Mrs Bott would never say a word like rape in front of her family. 'It was the niggers. It's always the niggers, when it's not the Poles – taking the bread from honest people's mouths – the niggers at the bottom of everything, young Frankie, and don't you ever forget it.'

The riots had fed Mrs Bott's racial fervour. Since a few coloured citizens who had been on the housing list had been moved into the Nelson Court estate, her hatred of the West Indians was constantly on the boil. Although she professed to disapprove of the rioting, for she was an individualist, not a mass joiner, it was really just her cup of tea. Anyone from Nelson Court who went nigger baiting might well have been inspired by Mrs Bott's busily venomous tongue.

That night, when the family was sitting in a slack-lipped coma before the television set, a crash and tinkle of glass sounded outside the window far below.

Kenny shrieked like a sea bird and Mrs Bott jumped up. 'It's the Spades!' she hissed dramatically. 'They're on to us now. There'll be a siege 'ere, you mark my words, and all of us innocents slaughtered where we stand.'

'Nettie, Nettie.' Mr Bott switched on the light and went to comfort Kenny, who was crouching terrified in his chair, the tears running unchecked over his bony cheeks. 'Don't talk so daft.'

While she rounded on the little man, Frankie took the opportunity to slip out of the room and out of the flat like a rabbit to see what was going on.

A crowd of white people had come from farther down the Rise and heaved three bricks through the window of an old lady in one of the Old People's Flatlets on the ground floor. They had been aiming for a window behind which a white girl lived with her Jamaican husband; but that did not help the old lady, who had had a heart attack and was now lying stiffly on the floor with her mauve toes turned up, while a bunch of curious heads peered through the door, trying to see her over the haunches of the neighbour who was kneeling to tend her until the doctor came.

The crowd outside had moved away, and nothing else seemed to be happening, except that some small boys were stoning a dog and calling it 'dirty black pig' in imitation of their elders. Frankie threw a brick at the boys, the dog squeezed away through a railing, and he went upstairs to report.

When he told his mother the news, her first reaction was: 'Serve that miserable old woman right. She 'adn't ought to be in that flat in the first place. Never would be if she 'adn't that nephew at County 'All.' But her satisfaction at the old lady's come-uppance was quickly replaced by regret that the nigger-loving tart and her so-called husband had got away with it.

The man had recently got a job on demolition and site clearing for the Expressway, which had been a thorn in the ample flesh of Mrs Bott ever since Mrs Bacon from below had told her about it, less than an hour after the man had left the labour exchange. Mrs Bott's initial disgust about the new road and the threat of its evacuees, whom she saw rehoused *en masse* in Nelson Court at the expense of meritorious tenants like herself, was now temporarily channelled into an indignant supposition that coloured labour was being preferred over white.

That night after Frankie and Kenny were in bed in the tiny room off the sitting-room, Mrs Bacon came up to hash over the brick incident, and she and Mrs Bott carried on at length about cheap coloured labour and other grievances, both real and imaginary. The boys listened idly. They had heard it all so many times before; but when the spiteful voices dropped to whispers, Frankie sat up in bed to hear better, and then padded to the door and laid his bristly head to the keyhole. Kenny could not sit up or get out of bed, so Frankie retailed to him the gossip about the

Spades living off the white girls, which both boys already knew about and understood, and how it was a disgrace to the neighbourhood and hanging was too good for them, and if Mrs Bott had her way she would see every filthy black gagger hung on a lamp post with his guts torn out.

In the middle of the night, Kenny woke screaming from a nightmare of black men and knives and a blood-crazy mob who all looked like his mother.

'Hush now. Hush, my dear. Old Frank's 'ere. There's nothing to cry about.' Frankie lifted him out of his cot and carried him to his own bed, where he lay with him and hushed him tenderly to sleep.

Towards the end of the week, the rioting slackened off, and there were no more major clashes between black and white. More than two hundred people had been arrested, and some of them would have time to contemplate the violence for many weeks from the peaceful security of a prison cell.

The police were beginning to hope that the situation was under control, but they did not relax the extra patrols, and it was bad luck on Zona Davenport and the rest of the cats that they chose to stage the siege of the Abracadabra coffee bar just as a posse of six young constables was unloaded from a van further along Park Road.

The Abracadabra had been compulsorily closed, and was soon to be demolished along with all the shops between it and the West Hill corner to make way for the new road flyover. On this Saturday, two weeks after the Abracadabra was extinguished in an orgy of talk and revolutionary declarations, some of them more or less in verse, Zona's reincarnated brother from ancient Egypt left her in charge of his junky antique stand in the Portobello Road. In a woollen ski-ing cap, his beard looking as though it were slung on hooks round his ears, Roger went from stall to stall where many of Cottingham Park's Abomunist brotherhood were scattered, spreading the word of revolt.

The battle cry was 'The Place', and it was taken up and passed swiftly from bearded mouth to sullen unpainted lips and back under the beards again.

The Runners, mostly out of work ballet dancers who went up and down the market buying odd pieces of silver and china and selling them farther on to other stallholders who tried to guess what the runner had paid before they bid a price, took the pass-word with them. 'The Place.' By nine o'clock that night, just as the healthy policemen dropped unhurriedly from their van, Zona and Roger and some twenty others advanced on the Abracadabra, broke open the famous blue glass door through which had passed so many remarkable minds weighed down by bushes of hair, and began to shove tables against it from inside.

'Like here we stay,' they told a passer-by, who looked in-nocently in through the hole in the blue glass.

'Didn't you get the word, mate?' The passer-by saw Zona peering through her hair in dark glasses in the dark and stepped back. 'All this lot's coming down to make way for the new road. Progress.'

'We are progress,' Zona said. 'This is our place and we're here to stay, like till we die, if necessary.'

'Sooner you than me.' The man scratched his head and walked on. When he came to the policemen, who were preparing to disperse in pairs, he stopped and said diffidently, for he was never at ease with the Law: 'It's none of my business, but there's a crowd of spooks broke into that closed-up caff back there.'

'Here we go again.' The fresh-faced constable sighed. 'Are they after a coloured man?'

'Don't look like it. They wasn't fighting. But they got blacks in there and all.' He watched the police run down the pavement, and turned to go. His part was done. He had been denouncing violence all week at home and in the gasworks canteen, and it was not his place to get mixed up.

In formation outside the Abracadabra, the policemen ordered the rebels to leave. When they refused, the six men kicked in what was left of the blue glass door and went in after them over the furniture.

Roger saw blood from a cut hand and took off mewing like a peewit through the shattered door; but most of the rest stayed to resist, so that they could be thrown out bodily and claim a greater injustice than ever.

The resistance was not strong, since there was not much muscle under the blue jeans and cable sweaters. There were two or three Africans in there, not students, but emblems of the primitive negro culture much admired by the weirdies. They could have fought effectively, but now that it came to an issue with a uniformed enemy whom they knew as all-powerful spoilers of fun and freedom, they found themselves standing against the back wall wondering if it was worth it. They had never liked the Abracadabra coffee, and they could beat bongo drums just as happily anywhere else.

The women held out longer than the men. When all the beards and polo necks were out on the pavement, there were still some girls inside, hanging on to wall fixtures and kicking out with their thin flat shoes, crying hoarse defiance.

The men were a little chagrined that it was mostly women who were taken to the police station, and some of them tagged along with the dishevelled little bunch, hoping to salvage some notoriety. Zona was charged with obstructing the police and wielding an offensive weapon, viz. a stainless steel sugar canister, with intent to cause grievous bodily harm. Her father had to go and bail her out, which made her just as angry as it did him, for she had looked forward to staying martyred in the police cell and writing agonizing poems about it on the toilet paper.

The turbulent week ended with the razor slashing of a coloured prostitute under the railway arch, but since she had recently informed on her ponce, her misfortune did not necessarily bear any relation to the race riots.

A few trivial skirmishes were reported that night, and then suddenly, from one day to the next, peace came to Cottingham Park. The tide of hatred had withdrawn – temporarily, said the realists, who knew the undercurrents; permanently, said the idealists, who did not believe it had ever been at flood. The police continued their vigilance in the following week, but the extra men were gradually removed, wanted elsewhere. The less seriously injured were discharged from the hospitals. Those who had been brutally battered had either regained consciousness or lost it for ever.

The notoriety of Cottingham Park had spread to all corners of the world. All nations, especially the Americans, were shocked that a country so readily critical of segregation and apartheid could not handle its own racial problems any better than anyone else. Sir Oswald Mosley's British Union Movement published a stirring attack on the injustice of the law to the white crusaders. A few coloured agitators raved unheeded among the Marble Arch orators. The Afro-West Indian Union left some slightly Marxist propaganda under the windscreen wipers of parked cars, and the Ku Klux Klan sent inflammatory letters to the relatives of white people who had been arrested or hurt.

As the local excitement died down, and West Indians continued to arrive trustfully in the mother country, the riots quickly became no longer news but controversial history. Editorial postmortems began to dissect the calamity. Articles by the dozen were written to prove that there was no racial hatred: that there would never be racial acceptance. That the violence could explode again at any time: that the rioting was only an unlikely accident. That the Teddy Boys alone were guilty: that the adolescent gangs were no more than the tools of a maturer, more significant force. That the police were to blame (too few and too inept): that the police had been magnificent and deserved recognition by a general rise in pay. Inevitably, letters flooded the correspondence columns from drivers smarting from recent parking or speeding fines, declaring that if the police were not so busy hounding the motorist, they could stop all hooliganism before it began.

You could believe what you liked.

In Cottingham Park, the residents walked a little more warily. Nervous West Indians were for a long time afraid to show lights in their rooms, and both white and coloured preferred not to be out alone in the streets after dark. There was a general feeling that unless you could put all the Spades on one side of the cleaving Expressway and all the Jumbles on the other, with no bridges between, it was impossible to say that it could never happen again.

*

It was towards the end of the week of the riots that Arthur Sears came back to the house in Faulkner Road.

He came back at a queer time, which was like him, because he had always been an unpredictable character. May had just come home long after midnight from delivering a white girl's baby which had come out coal black; not surprisingly, since its father was a stevedore from Lagos.

The delivery was normal and easy, but there had been an unpleasant incident which had made May wonder, with all her experience of birth and death, how much she really knew of life in between. While the girl was in her short labour, two women – a little drunk, they sounded – had come into the cul-de-sac of rotting houses and started to shout abuse. From the uncanny information service that always operated in this area, even in peaceful times, they knew that the baby was coming – had seen

308

May's bicycle perhaps, for the trusty blue and white frame was well known by now in these parts – and had begun to shout with raucous insolence: 'What colour's the kid?'

The girl's mother, who knew about the stevedore, like everybody else, went to the door and threw milk bottles at the women and loyal curses; but then threw away the loyalty with the last milk bottle and came into the room to tell the moaning girl: 'Serve you right if I'd of let them lunatics give you what you deserve.'

Tired and discouraged, for there seemed little future for the black baby or its bewildered mother, May was lifting her bicycle to carry it down the area steps – chaining it to the railing was no good in this neighbourhood where people would saw through a chain as soon as your back was turned – when a creeping sensation at the back of her neck made her turn her head quickly. A man was watching her from the shadow beyond the lamplight.

Instead of hustling away down the steps, May dropped the bicycle back on to the pavement, where it bounced gently on its well-filled tyres, and let it lean against her as she stood trying to get her breath. She had not felt so winded since she used to pound up and down in that hockey field near the hospital with nobody passing the ball to her because she could not get her stick to it if they did.

When she had got enough breath, she began to laugh. She had seen at once, after the first shock, that the man was Arthur Sears in his long overcoat with the poacher's pockets.

'I frightened you,' he said, staring at her with his head poked forward. He seemed thinner and shabbier, and his hair looked as though he had cut it himself, chopped short at the sides and a narrow bush on top, making his head go endlessly upwards.

May nodded. 'It's my mother's fault. Ever since the trouble started round here – you know about the riots?' Where had he been for more than two months? She thought suddenly that he might have been in jail. 'Every time I have a night call, she's made me as nervous as a kitten with her warnings of knifing and murder.' Her mother had also mentioned rape, but Mr Wilson had snorted and told her to put a sock in it, Norma; for who would want to rape old May?

'Well, you're quite a stranger, I must say. Where have you been, Mr Sears?' she asked. She had never called him or thought of him as anything else, even after that rough embrace in the hall, which had started all the funny circumstances of his disappearance. She asked it diffidently, for she still believed that it was her rudeness, and the rejection she had not intended, that had driven him away.

'Oh – round and about,' he said quite airily. 'I been visiting.'

'Do you –' It was hard for her to say it, because it was just as bad to be suspected of chasing him as of spurning him. 'Do you want your old room back?'

'Is it free then?' He looked wistful, as if he spoke of a beloved old home, so May said kindly: 'Of course. We kept it for you, hoping you'd come back,' although the truth was that with all that end of the road torn up and the big machines scooping at the rubble all day and sometimes half the night with floodlights, it had been impossible to let his room.

'And then of course, your clothes. How came you to rush off like that without even a change of socks?'

'Nothing like travelling light.' He laughed and jerked his head in that wry way he had, stretching the tendons of his neck. 'I see you lost something.'

May looked to see if she had dropped a glove, but he was gazing past her to the gap where the Mortons' house used to be. 'Oh that. Yes, isn't it queer to be on the end of the row? They're going to plaster us up, they say, and make it all neat, but they've not done anything yet. Mum's writing to the Ministry.'

Arthur Sears laughed again, more nervously. 'No sense in standing out here all night in the cold,' he said. He picked up the bicycle and carried it down the awkward steps and stabled it for her in the coal shed under the pavement. Wherever he had been, he had learned some manners. May had never known him to do anything like that before.

He was turning to go up the steps and round by the front door, for he still had his key, but May said: 'Come in this way. Mum won't mind.' Mum would die rather than let a tenant come in by her private entrance, but she would be asleep by now, for all her declarations that she could not close her eyes when May was out at night.

Silently, guiltily, she made tea for them both in the kitchen, with only the small lamp on, glancing over her shoulder from time to time, seeing as clearly as if it were actually there her mother's figure in the stiff blue housecoat May had bought her for Christmas appearing in the doorway like Mrs Noah.

They drank the tea standing up – it seemed safer than sitting down – and talked in whispers. Friendly, it was. Arthur Sears seemed different somehow, less edgy. Before, even when he stopped to talk to you, he had always looked as though he were ready to run. May had never thought that he could be so companionable, and liking him, she said when her back was turned to get out the shortbread: 'I was worried about you, you know. I wish you'd have let us know where you were. I thought you might have met with an accident, or been ill, or something.'

'Or in prison?' When she turned round, he was looking at her with his long tufted head on one side, and smiling, showing the gap at one side of his front teeth where he had had the extraction, that very day he disappeared.

'Don't be daft.' She hoped that the light was too dim for him to see the blush that betrayed that she had thought of that.

He put down his cup gently, knowing Mrs Wilson, careful not to let the spoon clink in the saucer. 'The last time you made tea for me,' he said softly, 'I wouldn't drink it, would I?' May could not find anything to say.

'I'm sorry, May,' he said surprisingly. She had never heard him apologize about anything, even when he left a cigarette on his chest of drawers and burned a furrow right through the veneer and into the wood. 'I was a bit rough on you that time.'

May still could not find any words, so seeing that he had eaten three pieces of shortbread very quickly, as if he were hungry, she put some more on to a paper picnic plate that her mother would not miss and told him to take it up to his room. Poor fellow. He did look thinner too. She would have to fatten him up. Sneak cakes and that upstairs when she got the chance. Perhaps give him the money for a proper haircut too, if he was low in funds. Her silly mind began to race ahead, as was its reckless habit, and she jerked it back and scolded it as if it were an impetuous horse.

When they had crept past Mrs Wilson's door and were safely up the back stairs, Arthur Sears stopped in the darkness with one foot on the staircase. 'What about her?' he jerked his head upwards.

'Miss Beade?' Of course. So pleased in the kitchen with the new Arthur Sears, May had forgotten about poor Christopher. 'She's gone. After the cat was – after the cat died, she went very odd, I'm afraid.'

'Always was.'

'Odder than usual. We hardly saw her, and then one day when I was cleaning your room' (she had actually been guiltily looking through his drawers and clothes to see if he had left any clue to where he had gone), 'I smelled a funny smell. I thought she had some meat gone bad – you know, she had that little electric stove to cook on – but the smell kept on being there for days, and then finally we found out what it was. She had told us she'd had Christopher buried in a pet's cemetery, but she hadn't. She had him up there in her room in a shoe box.'

'Go on?'

'Honest. A big shoe box. Well, her feet were outsize. She always had trouble to fit them. She was so upset when Mum said she had to get rid of it – she always thought Mum had killed the animal, you know – that in the end she took herself off. Found another room out Fulham way. Poor soul. I did feel badly for her.' May hoped that she had made him feel badly too, because it was his cruelty, after all, that had caused Miss Beade so much distress; but she did not have the brass to say that she knew he had killed the cat, and he did not admit it.

He said quite airily as they went up the stairs: 'Any other excitement round these parts since I've been gone? Robberies? Murders and such?'

'Not especially – except for the shocking things that happened in the riots, of course.'

He said good night as they reached May's floor and went on up the stairs to his old room, balancing the plate of shortbread.

Although he complained that the racket from the new road site gave him headaches, Arthur Sears settled down again quite peacefully in Faulkner Road. Miss Beade's room was let to an elderly man who cleaned the kennels at the dogs' home, and Arthur was reasonably polite to him, and did not annoy him, as he had always gone out of his way to annoy Miss Beade.

He did not go back to his old job at the nursery. He would not even inquire to see if they would have him, but found work handling vegetables for a Covent Garden wholesaler, which had at least some remote connexion with gardening. His hours were strange. He and May sometimes left the house together in the dark: she on a maternity call, he to greet the lorries coming in with the dawn. He was at home in the afternoons, which was usually May's off-duty, and they fell gradually into the habit of

312

doing things together. They might go for a walk, or he would accompany her if she went to the shops for her mother, or she might even invite him into the kitchen, if the omens of her mother's mood were favourable, for a cup of tea and a chat, or a hand of whist if her father was at home.

Although the teasing about 'Your boy-friend' and 'May's big heart throb' was merciless, May shut her ears and bit her tongue against rejoinder and struggled to endure it. At least her mother had not forbidden her to be friendly with Arthur – it was Arthur now, quite boldly. At least she allowed him occasionally to visit the kitchen, although if he made crumbs on the tablecloth or tapped a cigarette into an ashtray that was only for ornament, Mrs Wilson would stare at him and make an elaborate show of cleaning up.

When he had left, mumbling his thanks, for he was somewhat tongue-tied in the sharp watchful presence of Mrs Wilson, the jokes leaped out of their holes at once, with double energy if Mr Wilson was there.

He would whistle the phrase from Mendelssohn's Spring Song which the cinema pianos used to play when the lovers appeared on the silent screen. His wife would clasp her hands and gaze at the ceiling and declaim: 'In the spring a young man's fancy.' She did not know any more.

May would turn away to hide the traitor blush and try to think herself out without a coat in a snow blizzard, or inside an ice-cream freezer; but one of her parents would pounce. 'Got it bad, haven't you, old girl?'

'To think of our May.' A wonderingly shaken head. 'We'd made up our minds you were on the shelf, you know, dear.' Kindly, with a load of unwanted sympathy.

'It just shows you though, doesn't it? A girl should never give up hope.'

It was torture, but it was worth it. May had never had a friend who was a man, and now it seemed she had one. Nothing would come of this. Her parents would see to that, even if by some absurd chance Arthur did intend something more than a few talks, a few walks, a few games of cards. He probably did not particularly like her. Why should he, when all was said and done? She was nothing to look at, and a lifetime of having her opinions squashed or ridiculed had not helped to make her entertaining. It was just that he was lonely, and for some reason he wanted company, which he had never sought before he went away.

He never touched May, never took her hand when they met, or walked less than a foot away from her when they were out; at the cinema, he leaned his elbow on the far side of the seat. That suited May all right. She would not have known what to do if he had made any of the advances at which her parents leeringly hinted. Hadn't she made a fool of herself the only time he had tried something, and almost frightened him away for good?

If only ... her mind was in a constant runaway gallop these days ... if only you could have a baby just by standing up before the minister to be married, without having to do anything else. But if ... she tugged at the reins of her mind, but it would not stop ... if Arthur Sears ever wanted to marry her, then she would have to let him touch her, and not mind it, and let him – her mind took a swerve away from the word – do what had to be done, and they would have a baby, and May's body and spirit would at last be free.

Once he said to her, in the middle of a conversation about something else, for his mind often jumped about illogically: 'I've sometimes wondered whether I've made a mistake, playing the lone wolf all my life. Other chaps my age are all settled down by now.' May held her breath. She dared not speak for fear of putting her foot in it. 'I could have a smallholding somewhere with a bungalow. Herts perhaps, or Beds. Handy for the markets. Might be better in the country.'

Better? So he was looking for something. Did he mean a place alone, or did he mean a place where a family could find a good and peaceful life? May had always wanted a country district. They gave the nurses a car. . . .

Gaining the courage to show interest in his welfare, May ventured to ask Arthur why he did not go back to the dentist to get the gap in his mouth filled with some new teeth. He kept saying that he would go, but he never did. She thought that he was afraid. He was afraid of many things, like spiders and mice and loud sudden noises. Nervous. Sometimes he was equable with the new steadiness with which he had inexplicably returned from his wanderings. Sometimes he was jumpier than ever, and May's tearaway mind saw that if – if anything should ever come of it, she would have to be the strong one, the protector. Like all sturdy girls who are strong and sensible enough to take care of themselves, she had always dreamed when she was younger of a

314

husband who would treat her like a delicate treasure. But never mind that. You could not have everything in this world.

You could not have anything. That was the truth of it. The very Saturday that she and Arthur were going to the Victoria Palace and tea afterwards, was the day that the police came for him. Not real policemen, taking off their helmets clumsily in the hall, but two men in belted raincoats, who kept their soft felt hats on.

They showed her their authority. She had to let them go upstairs. When they came down with Arthur Sears, he did not even look at her. Just walked through the hall and down the front steps with his legs swinging stiffly as if someone had him on strings from above. His arms were not swinging. He was handcuffed to both the detectives.

'Well –' Mrs Wilson's instinct had brought her up from the basement, of course, and May turned to her with a little laugh. 'There goes my last chance.'

She waited for the pain, but for once her mother was too dumbstruck to plunge in and drive the knife deeper.

*

You could still walk up the street, although it was closed to cars because the mains were being diverted, and the cheap little shops were silent and empty, boarded up and waiting for destruction.

As soon as she turned the corner, Martha remembered that she should not have brought the children this way; but it was too late. They ran ahead and disappeared under the crumbling archway at the entrance to Armstrong Mews.

Martha found them standing in the wet gutter that ran down the middle of the cobbles, looking at the small crowd at the end of the mews, where the demolition had already begun.

'Come on,' she said. 'It's late. There's nothing to see.'

'Look at all those people. There's Hughie Felissa.' Terry put her fingers in her mouth and whistled. A boy in corduroy reach-me-downs tied baggily at the waist looked round, spat, and turned back indifferently into the crowd.

'They're only watching the demolition,' Martha said too brightly, and her younger child looked at her to see whether she could possibly believe that.

'Don't worry,' Bernadette said, seeing Martha's anxious,

315

dissembling expression. 'We know. That's the house where they found the body in the cupboard.'

'Who told you?' Martha and Guy had discussed most things with their daughters, but this they had kept quiet, and destroyed the newspapers. It was too close to home. The children used to see Eileen Kelly occasionally when they were at the garage. They remembered her and Mrs Saithe too well.

'Bessie let us read her paper,' Bernadette said, 'after you hid ours. Everyone at school knew about it anyway. We were the heroines of the hour, knowing so much about the nooberhead.'

Martha took them away from the abandoned mews, littered with the rubbish and broken belongings thrown out by the tenants before they left.

'What excitement,' Theresa said. 'I wonder what else they'll find. They'd already found some skeletons of babies, you know, before they found poor Eileen. In the drains.'

'Who told you that?'

'I read it.' Bessie Myers's Sunday paper never missed a detail. 'You and Daddy read the wrong paper. Did you know that they caught the man because he'd left his teeth marks on old Eileen and they traced them through his dentist?'

'Yes,' Martha said. 'Yes, I knew. Let's talk about something else.'

'Why? This is really interesting. Something happening at last. We're famous. Everybody in the world knows about Armstrong Mews now. When I tell people I live in Armstrong Avenue, they'll say: "Oh, that must be near the place where that terrible murder was."'

'We must pray for poor Eileen though,' Bernadette said piously.

'I'd rather pray for that dog she had. I wonder what happened to him? We could have taken him in perhaps, if we'd only known she'd had it.'

Walking to the house, Martha had thought that she would go down to the basement flat and rail at Bessie Myers for feeding her children on the diet of lurid news she so much relished herself; but by the time they reached home, she had lost the energy of her annoyance. What was the use? Bessie was Bessie. She was something that might as well be stomached, like any objectionable piece of furniture that would cost too much to replace.

If Bessie left, Martha and Guy could not afford not to let the basement flat to someone else, who could easily be worse. At least Bessie did not come upstairs all the time, crying for company. At least she was never late with her rent. At least James Donahue, with his winey breath and clumsily roving hands, had been exorcized for good. One night during the riots, he had left Bessie's flat in the flush of liquor, got into a fight at a bus stop and struck a policeman. Surprisingly, for Martha had never thought of him as needy – what then could be his attraction for bouncing Bess? – he could not pay the fine. He had expected Bessie to pay it, but she announced that she was through with him, and let him go unwept to a week in jail.

Guy had been out during the rioting too. He had always been sympathetic to the dilemmas of the coloured immigrants, as he was to anyone who was made to suffer for having been born in the wrong place, because he knew what it felt like. After the trouble began and the wireless and newspaper stories began to come through and Cottingham Park was afire with rumours, Guy was soon too disturbed and restless to stay at home. The first television news films incited him, as they did the Teddy Boys and the causeless hooligans, to want to be out in it and doing something. Martha could not stop him. He seemed hardly to notice her anxiety.

He came home limping very late one night with the curt explanation that he had gone to the help of an old coloured woman who was being threatened with an axe. He went into the kitchen, and there was a lot of noise of running water. When Martha went in, she found him trying to bandage a two-inch gash under his knee with a wet handkerchief.

'What happened?'

'The chap threw the axe and it glanced off me.'

'Oh God.' She knelt down on the blood-smeared floor. 'Sit down. I'll get bandages. I'll have to call Dr Mayes. Why on earth didn't you tell me? Because you were annoyed to find me waiting up?'

He shrugged. 'I knew you'd fuss. And you are fussing. It's nothing. Don't bother Mayes. I'll fix it. Leave me alone.'

When Martha went to the first aid cupboard, she found that she was crying. Not because of the ugly wound with the glint of white in it that looked like bone, but because a few months ago Guy would have come straight to her with the open dependence of an injured child. He would have wanted her to fuss and make

317

an important thing of dressing the wound. There could never have opened between them these sudden terrifying voids across which he stepped away from her and was alone.

Never before Anne came.

Martha had known that it would not be easy to have Anne and to try to help her to fight back against the poisonous enemy that had invaded her; but she had never thought that it would be so almost impossible. Or go on for so long.

Three times Anne had stopped drinking, with Martha's dogged help. Three times she had started again, always at the worst moments. *Just a quick one to steady my nerves*, when she was going to an interview for a job she might have achieved, if she had gone after it sober. *Just to have something to hold*, when she was invited out by people who did not know what she had been through, and with well-meaning hospitality had laughed: 'On the wagon? You? What nonsense,' and put a Martini into her hand, ice-beautiful as the fatal Snow Queen. When two gins hit Anne as if they were six doubles, then they began to realize. But then there was nothing to do but send her home to Martha, and talk it round in pretended pity.

The third time, when Anne 'cured' herself and wandered haggard and pale about the house like a ghost seeking something it must never find, Martha had been able to push her into a job as an extra Christmas assistant in a Piccadilly store. Anne worked for three weeks, tired but triumphant, and forced Martha to take most of her wages. When the store offered to keep her on into the new year with better money, Martha helped her to find a tiny furnished flat, and Guy became ten years younger and much nicer to everybody at the idea of being rid of her.

The morning when Anne was due to move into the flat, Martha came downstairs at six o'clock to let in the cat which was wailing with rhythmic insistence under her bedroom window. Anne was in the kitchen, sitting at the table with her eyes half closed, a bottle and a smeared glass in front of her. There was about an inch of neat whisky in the bottom of the glass, the way she always poured it when she was drinking steadily. Never a long drink. Never any ice. Just the inch of whisky, topped up before it was finished; the bottle within reach, the glass raised automatically, like breathing, her fingers keeping hold of it when she set it down.

She was in her nightdress, and her long black hair was pinned up sketchily at one side and falling in a slovenly tangle on the other. She looked as if she had been there for some time.

Martha was furious. She spoke her thoughts at once, with none of the understanding and love she had struggled so patiently to maintain these last months. Anne raged back at her drunkenly. 'Go to hell and leave me alone. Stop watching me. I'm not a child. I'll live my life my own way.'

'Not on my whisky, you won't,' Martha said and picked up the bottle. Anne grabbed at her and fell, and lay vomiting on the black and white chequered floor.

That time, the doctor took Anne away from the house, as he would have done before if Martha had not yielded to Anne's pleas to be kept out of hospital. It was the thing she had feared most of all the things that had become ordeals to her since drinking had destroyed her courage.

It was only after she had gone away, trembling and silent, that Martha realized that she must have started to drink again in an attempt to help herself face the ordeal of moving away to live alone.

When she told Guy this, he said: 'God, will you never stop making excuses for her? She doesn't need an excuse to go to the bottle. She just goes to the bottle. Won't you ever face the sordid fact that she'll never be anything but a hopeless lush?'

His small store of sympathy for Anne, his unwilling admiration for Martha's loyalty, were worn out long ago.

When Anne came out of the country clinic a few weeks later, the job was gone, of course, and with it the chance of supporting herself. Her Aunt Jessie Sutcliffe had never weakened in her resolution to have nothing more to do with her. Anne had no money. Nowhere to go. No one to help her. Nowhere but Armstrong Avenue. No one but Martha.

'Just for a week or two,' Martha said humbly to Guy; but he stepped away across the impassable gap that he could so easily make between them now. 'Please yourself,' he said, and his versatile face was coldly without expression. 'It's your house.'

'It's yours too.'

'I didn't buy it. Your mother left it to you.'

'Why throw that at me? It was you who wanted to stay here after she died. If you feel like that about it, why didn't we get out long ago?'

'I would have, if I had known you were going to turn it into a home for incurable alcoholics.'

They were never violent quarrels. They were irritable arguments in which they both said things they had never said before and did not truthfully mean. They had never bickered until now. They had never reached any disagreement that could not be settled with love and yielding. It had usually been Martha who yielded, because her devotion could make her believe that he was right; but now she had to believe him wrong, because she could not let Anne down. She could not yield, and so the little sparks of antagonism flared up with hateful frequency.

Bernadette, who was saturated with television films about divorce and storm-tossed romance, burst screaming in on them one day and beat her fists against her father and cried: 'If you leave us, I'll kill you!'

Guy took the child away to comfort her, but there was no comfort for Martha. When he came back, he said: 'You see. Even the children. Even your children have to suffer because of your pig-headed charity.'

When Anne came back, the hostility between her and Guy was open now and acknowledged. He would barely speak to her, and because he was rude, Anne did not bother to hide how she felt about him.

When Guy's leg did not heal properly after stitching and had to be opened and drained, and he ran a temperature and Martha saw him dead of osteomyelitis, Anne had offered to take care of him so that Martha could go out.

Guy refused. 'Let me die in peace,' he said. 'I don't want her in my room. She thinks I'm trying to be a cardboard hero. When I was going out the night I got this' – he slapped the cradle which kept the bedclothes off his knee – 'she said: "Why the hell don't you keep out of it? No one will thank you for interfering." '

Stronger now and less dependent, Anne was out of the house much of the time, trying old contacts, risking the chagrin of refusals, following up advertisements or abortive recommendations. She could not find a job. She had hardly any money. She had written to her father, who had not answered, and she even went to see her aunts again, prepared to humble herself and beg for help.

It had been a great effort to make herself go back to the Camberley Hotel, for she was as unforgiving as her Aunt Jessie, and when she was told at the desk that the sisters had moved to the country, she went away and walked in the Park in the rain, to keep herself from going into a bar. Cheated of the ordeal, her effort collapsed. She could not summon it again to make the trip out to the country.

Her courage had not come back; perhaps never would. But she was better. It was possible that she was cured. She had not had a drink since she came out of the clinic, and she was calmer, and putting on weight.

'If it had not been for you, I would be dead,' she told Martha. 'Guy would no doubt like it better if I were.'

Martha did not dispute that. She had given up answering any of the acid things that Guy and Anne said about each other. But the first part of the remark could be true. What would have become of Anne if Martha had turned her away when the aunts did? She had done what she set out to do, and what she had promised to do that night when Anne sat up in bed and told her what had happened in America. She had stood by her. She had passed all the most gruelling tests of friendship.

And what was her reward? For not betraying Anne, she was rewarded with the dread that she had betrayed some secret of her alliance with Guy. *The more you give, the more will come to you*; but she was losing something. Could she retrieve it before it slipped away for ever? When Guy was well enough to be left, she would go to the country herself and tackle the old ladies and force them to understand that they must do something for Anne. It's their turn to give, Brother Giles. I wasn't big enough to give to everyone.

*

After the excitement of the arrest of Arthur Sears and the news that he was to be tried for the murder of a prostitute, and the attendant publicity for the Wilsons – 'We're famous at last, Walter. Look! "ARTHUR SEARS WAS SUCH A QUIET MAN *by his landlady*" right here on the front page' – May never properly recovered her spirits.

She tired more easily and was depressed. She found it hard to summon the bright quips with which to help along the labour of her mothers. It was difficult to get to sleep, and then harder still to drag herself out of bed when Mrs Wilson came to rouse her for a night call.

'It was the shock,' they said at the District Nursing Centre. 'It's bound to give you a turn suddenly finding you've lived all those months under the same roof with a murderer.'

'Didn't you used to go out with him too, May?' one of the nurses asked, her ferret eyes bright with curiosity.

'No,' May said flatly. 'No, I never went out with him.'

'Funny,' the nurse said. 'I saw you once in Park Road with a chap who looked like the newspaper pictures. Must have been someone else. I didn't know you had a fellow.'

'I haven't,' May said doggedly, and Ruthie Bowers clapped her hand over her round pink mouth and spluttered: 'Good thing you didn't go with the lodger. What he did to that girl – it might have been you, May!' and dissolved in delirious giggles.

If only people would let it rest. What it would be like when the trial came up, May could not bear to think. It was bad enough now. Every patient, and the relations and neighbours of every patient who had seen her name in the paper, wanted to talk about it and to be told what it had been like to live in the same house with a sex killer and cat-torturer (Mrs Wilson had gladly dug up that bit of history for the reporters). Even her nicest doctor began their consultation on a threatened eclampsia with: 'So you got your name in the papers, I see. It isn't all of us who can claim reflected glory from a murderer.'

It was bad enough out at work, but it was worse at home. Scarcely a mealtime went by without some reference to May's bad colour and lack of appetite. When her mother had delivered the jabs of 'pining way', and 'funny to think that this time last month I was thinking about wedding bells', Mr Wilson would hammer in the nails with: 'Give it a rest, Norma. It's bad enough to lose a man to another woman, but it's a real shocker, when he's the only one who's ever looked at you twice, to lose him to the gallows. How can you expect her to eat bakewell tart?'

When May was wondering how much longer she could stand it without resorting to the breakdown to which some of her more sadly harried mothers occasionally succumbed, Veronica sent an invitation to visit them at the house in the New Town if she could get away. Her brother Godfrey was going up North on a buying tour. May could have his room. The Superintendent at the Centre agreed that it would do May good to have a break, and arranged for her to take her two weeks' holiday earlier than usual.

Veronica was expecting her baby in two months. She carried

322

it awkwardly, as if it were on a tray inside her, and although she seemed to May's automatically professional eye to be reasonably well, her small face under the light hair which was cropped short now, in a kind of indifferent bravado, had a sharper, anxious look, and there were dark shadows under her eyes.

Mrs Duke, who was full of old wives' tales about pregnancy, said that this indicated that the baby was lying high – it's the pressure, they say. May pretended to agree, for the mother's comfort, but her own diagnosis was different. Veronica was jumpy, edgy, quick to irritation, and within two days of May's arrival, back at her old game of picking on her and restlessly finding fault.

May began to wonder why she had been invited. Veronica knew nothing about Arthur Sears, except the sensational surface facts. It was not that she was sorry for May. Was it – with the old dependence on a tame audience – that she needed May to be sorry for her?

No family could have been kinder or more helpful to an unfortunate daughter – May tried to picture how her parents would have behaved if it had been her, and shuddered – but although Veronica's future was secure and her secret safe from the neighbours, May knew that she was nervous and unhappy.

On the third day, they went to the shopping centre for groceries, taking Mrs Duke's favourite toy, a kind of duffel bag on wheels, for it was a half-mile walk each way.

The Dukes' bright new semi-detached house was on the outer edge of the New Town, with a coveted view of rolling meadow and a spread of muddy ploughland on the opposite slope which would soon disappear as the settlement expanded over it like creeping lava towards the resentful Old Town beyond the hill. Already at the end of the Dukes' road a loop of twenty new houses stood almost ready for custom round what would be a little green when the builders had ceased to trample it. All round the perimeter, new houses and low blocks of flats were going up, marching outwards into the countryside.

'They finish five a day,' Veronica said gloomily, as they turned at the end of their road by a little garden neat as a birthday card and walked down the hill past the playing field. 'Five moving vans coming in every day. There seems no end to it.'

'Don't you like it here then?' May was enchanted with the clean and airy town with its sprucely painted houses like the toy villages that were sold in string bags, its gardens and greens and quiet roads where children played in safety. She would love to live here, but you would never catch her father changing his job and moving out. Faulkner Road was good enough for him, even with the Expressway which would stop him walking straight over to the Buffaloes, and it had been good enough for May in its fashion until she saw this modern Arcadia where ordinary people without much money could live in comfort with something nice to look at across the street and sweet new air to breathe. Even Granchester Mansions, step up though it was for Ronnie, had been sunlessly hemmed in and noisy. 'I'd have thought you would have liked this,' May said, as Veronica did not answer.

'It's all right.' Veronica bumped the shopping cart roughly up a kerb. 'All right for now, I suppose.' They walked in silence past a row of yellow stucco houses where pennants of washing exulted in the breeze, and babies slept under cat nets in perambulators in the tidy front gardens. 'I couldn't stick it for long though,' Veronica suddenly burst out. 'I'd go off my rocker.'

'But surely, Ronnie –' May looked at her sideways without turning her face. Veronica was walking with her head down, her lower lip aggrieved, her feet plodding listlessly under her awkward body. 'I thought it was planned that you were to stay on here with the baby and find work locally with your mother to mind the little one.'

'Oh yes, it's all *planned*,' Veronica said. 'Mum's been wonderful. So has Dad. I don't know what I'd have done without them. That's the thing, you see. I haven't any choice. I'll find a job, I suppose, when I'm the proper shape again, working with girls who'll gape when I tell them about the salon in town. There's no style here, you know,' she said in the quick, classy voice the beauty salon had taught her. 'I hate this place. There's nothing to do. One cinema. A social club for the Mums – that'll be me pretty soon – tea and cards and "has your kiddy had his tonsils out, Mrs – er?" A youth club for the savages – they break it up about every other week. Dances at weekends, but the teenagers take them over too, so they're more like free fights. It would be all right here if you had a husband and your own house. You'd be just like the rest of them then, looking to see whose washing was whiter, like the women in the advertisements, and producing a new baby every year. But me – I'll be nothing. I won't fit anywhere, not with the single girls or the married women, and sooner or later, people will find out I'm not really a widow.'

'How can they? Your family would never tell.'

'Oh, they'll know. People always find out the bad things. They're friendly enough here, but they're just as spiteful as anywhere else. More so, I daresay, because some of them have come up in the world, from slums and condemned bits of London, and when they get out here, they kill themselves being respectable. I shan't have a chance. Nor will the poor kid. And Mum and Dad and Goff will pretend not to mind, but they will. Mum likes it here. She's made some friends, which she never did at the Mansions. Goff has a girl. Her father works in the bank and they think they're just the thing. Goff will be lucky if they let him within a mile of darling Jennifer once they find out about me.'

'You mustn't let yourself be depressed, Ronnie,' May ventured. 'It's your condition. I've known a lot of my mothers get like that. Look on the bright side, I tell them. You have someone else to think of now, you know.'

'Oh, tell that to your beastly mothers,' Veronica said irritably. 'I never stop thinking of the someone else, poor little beggar. I can't stay here. I can't go away. Where would I go? It's hard to find a job when you have a kid. And who's going to marry you? Men aren't that charitable. There's no one here anyway. The ones my age are all married. The single ones – well they don't come here with their parents, or if they do they soon get out when they find what it's like.'

When they reached the centre of the town where the buses were, and the supermarket and the Woolworths, and the dress shop with the racks of clothes like uniforms, and the huge glittering chemist, and the antiseptic state-owned pub, and the municipal restaurant which smelled of greens and gravy, Veronica said with a bitterness quite new to her: 'I'll tell you the truth, May. These last two months, since I've had time to think and see what's coming, I'd have got rid of the baby, if I'd known how.'

'Oh no!' May looked round quickly and lowered her voice. 'That's a dreadful thing to say.'

'You're shocked,' Veronica said calmly. 'Poor old May. I thought you would be.'

They went among the crowd, and she talked of something else. When May tried to find words on the way home, groping for a way to give comfort and to tell her that everything would be all right, Veronica shut her up curtly. 'I don't want to talk about it. You're as bad as Mum. She's always wanting to start knitting things. I won't let her.'

'But, Ronnie –'

'Shut up, I told you. Don't keep on and on.'

May felt miserably helpless. Selfish to be enjoying herself with Veronica's friendly parents in the cosy little house. She should not have come. She was no use to Ronnie.

That night May sat up in bed for a long time reading a novel given her by Mr Duke, who was very kind to her and treated her as though she was interesting, which she knew she was not. May had scarcely read anything but magazines, and was surprised to find herself enjoying the story so much that she kept her light on long after midnight.

Mrs Duke insisted on her sleeping late and having breakfast in bed, because it was her holiday and she had had a shock. Luxurious bliss to know that she did not have to get up and be at the Centre for the day's orders at eight-thirty. Paradise to lie in Godfrey's cheerful room with radio parts and technical magazines on every bit of furniture, the garlanded curtains touched gently by the hand of the silent country night, and know that all the babies in the world could be born and she could stay in bed.

All but one. May had turned out her light and was wandering into sleep when she heard a sudden cry and the sound of Veronica sobbing in a panic from her room across the landing.

She was sitting up in bed like a risen corpse. 'I'm bleeding May – I'm bleeding! Do something!' She was terrified.

'Lie down.' May pushed her gently back, and pulled off the bedclothes. The placenta had come first. In a minute or so, the baby would be born. Veronica clutched her arm and screamed, and May said soothingly: 'Don't worry, dear,' just as if she were any scared young mother with her first. 'Your baby's coming, that's all. Why didn't you call me?'

'I didn't know . . . I thought the pain was nothing. It was so quick. Oh God, May. Help me.'

May rolled up her sleeves. It was only afterwards, when she recalled how Mr and Mrs Duke had come to the doorway together, that she realized that Mr Duke had seen her in her long challis nightdress. At the time she did not notice. Afterwards she was glad that she had bought the flowered challis new for the visit.

His wife sent Mr Duke away and came quietly to stroke the cropped head and wipe away the tears. Her hair was tied up in a fancy striped bandeau bequeathed to her by her daughter. Under it, her large benevolent face was troubled, but without fear. Thank goodness she was not one of those mothers who threw fits in an emergency and were far more trouble than the patient.

'Light the oven,' May said brusquely. She never minded whom she ordered about when she was working. 'Warm up a blanket and all the cotton wool you have.'

Without looking up, she heard Mrs Duke's leather slippers creak rapidly away, and May was alone with Veronica in the intimacy of childbirth, the closest relationship possible between two women. Old professional though she was, May never lost that absorption in a warm emotion that was very close to love. As the sobbing, frightened girl on the bed brought forth the baby into her accomplished hands, it was completely love.

The seven-month boy was tiny, about eighteen inches long, and blue. Held up by his feet, as May slapped him gently, he gave one feeble gasping cry and no more. Wrapping him swiftly in the blanket from the bed, May pulled her handkerchief out of her pushed-up nightdress – a part of her mind, far off, laughed triumphantly at the memory of Veronica telling her it was common to carry your handkerchief in the sleeve – put it between her mouth and the baby's and with slow gentle breaths forced her own life into him.

'Finest pie you ever cooked, Mrs Duke,' said the young doctor who came with the ambulance and the incubator and found the baby in the open oven, breathing as steadily as if he weighed nine pounds instead of less than four. 'Bit of a busman's holiday, eh, Nurse?' He turned to May, as the nurse from the hospital went out with the baby. 'Nice work. That one was too small to have got into life on his own. You must be pretty good. We'll be needing a new Maternity sister next month. Want the job?'

Barefooted, wearing Mr Duke's grey overcoat over her night-dress, May felt the blush coming up into her dishevelled hair. Not knowing what to say, she managed a laugh, and the doctor laughed too and said a friendly good-bye and went out.

May went back upstairs to Veronica, smiling at his praise. Between one step and the next she stopped with one foot raised and leaned against the wall as the realization hit her.

If it was not for her, the baby would have died. She could have let him stop breathing and no one any the wiser. But she had done automatically the only things she knew. She had not thought. Old May never thinks what she's doing. Old slow coach. Old muddlehead.

Here she was thinking she was so wonderful over a premature delivery, and she was really not wonderful at all. She was a fool and a traitor. She could have done this for her friend. She could have taken the sin on to herself, a burden to carry for ever, but Veronica would be free.

You must be pretty good, the doctor had said. But not good enough, you see. I never even thought.

With the overcoat buttoned modestly round her bulky figure, May went slowly through the open bedroom door. Veronica was lying on her back with her head turned away. When she heard the slight noise of the bare feet on the linoleum, she turned her head, and May, staring numbly down at her, saw in her shallow little face all the radiance and wonder which she had so often sought in vain on the faces of her mothers.

Veronica put out a hand. 'The doctor told me he couldn't have lived if it hadn't been for you.'

May nodded dumbly.

'If I'd only known it would be like this,' Veronica said. 'I have him. He's going to live. He must live. He's mine. I don't care what happens now, what people say. He's all that matters. Why didn't you tell me I would feel like this?'

'I – I didn't know, Ronnie.' May's heart was bursting, tumbling out of her in torrents of gratitude. She had never felt so happy in her life, but all she could say was: 'I'm glad.'

'I'll never forget what you did. The doctor said: "You pick the best friends." He was right, wasn't he?'

With the grin spreading over her face, May was exalted enough to boast: 'He thought I did so well, he wanted me to apply for the Maternity sister's post at the new hospital.'

'Why not?' Veronica yawned and closed her eyes for a moment. 'Much better for you than sticking on at home. Couldn't be worse anyway. Try for it, love, why don't you?'

May watched her close her eyes again and settle her contented face for sleep. 'I might at that,' she said slowly as she bent to pull up the covers. 'I might at that.'

*

Glidden Road was to come down at last. (And God knows what we'll find *there*, the contractors said glumly. Dead tarts in cupboards will be nothing to it.) It had been condemned for nearly two years, and if abomination gave precedence, it should have been one of the first streets to go when demolition started. Paradoxically, however, the worst streets were going last, because it had taken so long to find accommodation for their teeming inhabitants.

Only those who had been there during the recount could be rehoused, and since scarcely a day went by in Glidden Road without some turnover of tenants or a new arrival from the Caribbean being squeezed in somewhere, there were many who would have to fend for themselves in a district growing ever less hospitable as the path of the Expressway flattened out block after block of the stinking old terraces where coloured immigrants had found refuge.

Some of them had known that Glidden Road was condemned when they moved in. Some had not, and who was a man like Gilroy to tell them, as long as they agreed to his extortionate rents?

In the top floor front, where Edgar's parents had once genteely lived, were Mr and Mrs Macdonald Pratt, an elderly couple from Barbados who had ventured over the sea in search of their son who had found a good job, married, and stopped writing or sending money. The Pratts, who had come, like so many others, confident of finding Paradise, had found their welcoming committee in the mother country composed of sour-faced landladies who took one look at them and closed the door. They had spent a dismal week in a doss house and two nights on a bench near the playground, where at least they could sleep together. Then a compatriot in a café told them about Glidden Road, and two fat women gossiping on a doorstep in Glidden Road told them about Gilroy.

Having heard their miserable story, he pushed the rent up viciously, with the golden smile of a benefactor. The Pratts had no choice. They were so thankful to find shelter that they even believed that Gilroy was kind, with his glistening grin and his guitar and his big laugh.

There was no work for old Macdonald Pratt, even if he had not been too nervous of London to go out and look for it. But they had their savings, and their simple faith that they would find their son just by being in the same town with him, and then he would take care of them. They had been to his old address and found it overflowing with strangers who had never heard of Kylie. They had been, keeping very close to each other to gain courage from the familiar body, to the police station, where an unimpressionable sergeant told them that if he could find every- one who was being looked for in Cottingham Park, he wouldn't have to wait for his promotion. Having done all that they could, they sat back in Gilroy's top floor front and waited for Kylie to come and rescue them.

Because they were shy and cautious, they hardly spoke to anyone in the first few weeks, except Gilroy when he came now and then to jolly them up lest they suspect that he was robbing them – even old fools like this sometimes found their way to the Town Hall – and Ambrosia to whom they were grateful for bringing their small supplies of rice and saltfish, not realizing that she kept the change. It was not until the Pratts began to venture out for shuffling walks in the spring sunshine that they realized that the houses at the other end of the street were empty, their steps piled with refuse, their windows already broken by the children who would make their playground in them until they were torn down.

They turned and went home. They met Edgar coming out of the house in a G.I. khaki shirt three sizes too big for him.

'What this?' Mr Pratt clutched the billowing shirt sleeve to stop him. 'When we come, every damn house in this street running over like flood water. Did everyone dead, boy?'

Edgar pulled his arm away and looked at them. 'Didn't you know?' The old lady with her broad beam and her spread feet and the flower nodding on a little wire out of the band of her hat looked like someone. He frowned. She looked like his Gramma. And just as lost and out of gear as Gramma would have looked if she had been transplanted to London.

'Know what?' The old man poked him with a horny finger. 'Is a plague?' The whites of his eyes rolled fearfully.

'Jeeze.' Edgar dragged his toe. He ought to be laughing at them, as Gilroy must be laughing. 'He'd ought to told you. The whole street's coming down. They finding new accommodations for everybody. Everybody who was here to be counted, that is, five, six months ago.'

'Not we, you mean, boy?'

330

'I guess not.'

The old woman began to cry, blubbing noisily in the street, and the man took her arm. 'Get in, Essie,' he said sharply. 'Where you pride?' and hoisted her up the front steps. At the top, he turned and looked down at Edgar and held out his hand as if he wanted to ask something. His big leathery mouth opened and shut. His pale tongue worked thickly up and down, and finally he said: 'No one don't need to accommodate we. My son Kylie, he take care of that.'

Edgar flapped his hand and turned away. He had a date. They were not his worry.

He did not see them again, except when they were carried out on stretchers with grey blankets over their dead faces. There was an inquest, but Gilroy slid out of it somehow with no blame, and his only comment on the passing of Mr and Mrs Macdonald Pratt was that he would never have credited them with the sense to stuff the cracks in the door and windows before they turned on the gas.

When the rehousing programme had started, there had been some talk of Gilroy and Ambrosia getting married, so that they would have a chance for a council flat. Some of the couples in Glidden Road were going to the Reverend Whiting or to Father Mack at Saint Joseph's, just as Edgar's parents had when they discovered how useful a marriage licence was in England. It usually meant having all the children baptised too, which was accepted with an amiable tolerance for the foibles of the Church – 'To please you, Father.'

Gilroy and Ambrosia, however, although they had been several years out of the West Indies, could not overcome the distrust of marriage which had been bred into their people since the days when marriage was forbidden because a permanent connexion reduced the market value of a slave. A modern council flat was tempting, but Gilroy did not want to be tied for good to Ambrosia, who was increasingly shrewish, and threatening him with the change of life.

They had applied to be placed in another rooming house, and when this was refused, and they were offered the choice of a blackened tenement on the other side of the railway or two piddling rooms in the exile of suburbia, Gilroy told the Council visitor what she could do with her rehousing and disappeared to Liverpool, where he had good connexions in his trade.

Ambrosia, who had not worked for years, surprisingly acquired a job as a resident maid at a women's college in the north of London. God help the college when they find out what she's like, Edgar thought, but: 'That's splendid,' the housing visitor said. 'That's you accounted for. But what about the boy?'

What about the boy indeed. Ambrosia did not care, and said so. She was not legally his guardian. She had only let him stay with her out of the bounty of her heart.

'That not true!' Edgar shouted at her. 'My people paid you. They paid you more all this time than you ever give me for it, you rotten cow.'

Ambrosia dropped her jaw into a grin like a picked skull. 'Don't make me laugh,' she said. 'They aint paid me nothing for months, and you know it. If it wasn't for my charity, you'd been out on the streets long ago, where you belong.'

'I wish I had,' Edgar said. 'It been far better than rotting here with you and that fat weed pedlar.'

Ambrosia winced, but the visitor had too many worries already to bother with suspicion. She said: 'Oh dear' anxiously and took the problem of Edgar back to head office.

Edgar smelled what was coming. A hostel of some kind. An institution. He'd only just got quit of school, and now he would find himself somewhere far worse if he let them get their hands on him. Before Ambrosia left and the last tenacious roomers were smoked out, Edgar took his few possessions and went to Big Phil's place which was farther across the Rise, out of the path of the road.

But Big Phil and his woman had quarrelled. He was moving on, going to Nottingham where the big wrestling bouts were being promoted.

'The kids?'

'They're not mine. She's got a room. She'll easy find another fellar to shack up with her.'

'Want me to stay and take care of you?' Edgar bounced on his toes and flexed his muscles. He had already slept with the girl twice when Phil was out at training. But she said: 'Listen to the child! Phil said a fellar,' and shrieked with laughter, so that Edgar would not have stayed now if she had begged him.

Well, he'd make out. He'd get work on the road again. Move in somewhere. Might even go back to Trinidad. Admit his failure.

Bring sorrow to his parents. He had not written for a year, but when they had written at Christmas on the back of a card all spangly with angels and Holy Ghosts, they said they knew he was doing fine. They would send money soon. His father had been out of work. They should not have come back, but they would never get the money for the fare again. When Edgar had his swell teaching job, he could lend them the money for the fare and they would come back and take care of him. Like hell.

Don Harper, the dauntless young man who ran the Community Centre in the worst section of Cottingham Park, had defied the unrest which had been grumbling round the streets since the riots by inaugurating a club for coloured boys and girls. They had the big room for dances every Wednesday, which Don Harper hoped might keep them away from the regular weekend dances. He was energetic, but there came a limit to breaking up the nasty little fights which erupted when the coloured boys danced with white girls. Don Harper was all for the ideals of integration, but he had trouble enough at the Centre keeping the peace between those of one skin without trying to tackle the racial problems which no one else in Cottingham Park seemed able to solve.

Edgar Biggs normally kept away from the Community Centre. Scouts was a baby's dream of the past, and the Zorro Men had no use for any of the activities, unless they smelled a fight brewing up there and could slide into it while the muscle man on the door was busy chucking people out, or lie in ambush under the tunnelled arch of the tenement yard opposite.

After he was on his own, however, he wandered into one of the dances of Don Harper's Caribbean Social Club, casually, as if he could take it or leave it, to see if he could pick up a piece of news about a job or a room, but mostly because he was hungry.

For a shilling, you could get all you wanted to eat and a bottle of coke, and Edgar had one and sevenpence which he had eased out of a girl's pocket at a crowded bus stop. Don Harper introduced him to some over-decorated girls, some of whom he already knew but did not wish to acknowledge, and tried to make him join the dancing; but Edgar said: 'I broke me foot', and stayed by the refreshment table. He was through with girls for a while. He travels fastest who travels alone was the line, and

Edgar Biggs was going to be a fast traveller, although at the moment he did not know where to.

Travelling alone out of the Centre when the dance was over, he saw Frankie Bott in the hall, reading the notices. This last year at school, he had hardly spoken to old Frank. There was too much between them. Frankie was still in with Miss Peel and them, still in the camp which Edgar had deserted for ever.

He had shot up high since the days when they used to run around on the sly together. He was almost as tall as Edgar, but without any of his bulk, and at fourteen his cheerful face still had some baby traces, while Edgar's was almost the face of a man. Edgar's clothes were usually too big, since they were begged or stolen from grown-ups. Frankie's were too small. His wrists stuck out a mile and his trousers rode high and dry above a pair of clobbering boots.

'Hi Frank!' Edgar moved up to him and put a hand on his shoulder. When Frankie turned, his round face split with genuine pleasure. 'I didn't know you came 'ere,' he said.

'I don't.' Edgar jerked his head towards the door. 'Want to walk?'

'You bet.'

One of the boys who were milling about by the cloakroom door threw at Frankie: 'You ought to lay off them toasted Irishmen. The black comes off.' The others guffawed, and Don Harper called out from his office: 'Cut that stuff out you lot, or I'll knock your ruddy heads together.'

Outside the Centre a young policeman with an Alsatian was waiting by the wall, the man standing relaxed, the dog sitting quietly by him. Since the inaugural meeting of the Caribbean Social, which had been gatecrashed by some of the more violent White Hunters, Don Harper usually tried to get a man up there on Wednesdays.

To show Frankie that he was not afraid of the bogies, Edgar called out as they went past: 'All's quiet, officer. You can take Rin Tin Tin home.' The dog moved a sharp ear, but the man paid no attention.

As Frankie and Edgar walked through the streets down which they used to run home after Scouts, shoving each other into the gutter, boasting and telling impossible plans, they talked spasmodically, in half articulate jerks, as boys do when they are neither exuberant children nor conversational men. Their talk

334

was unrevealing, for they were cautious with each other after the long gap of mistrust, and yet they were at ease and leaning back towards the old relationship. Frankie, younger and weaker, admiring Edgar partly for himself and partly because he was a forbidden companion; Edgar stronger and far more experienced, but seeking from Frankie the mystery that made his life more secure because he was a white boy.

When Frankie stopped at a corner and said: 'I'll have to go this way. Mum only lets me go to the Centre if I come straight home when they pack it up, and don't think she don't know when they pack up,' Edgar was punched in the plexus of his feeling by jealousy and loneliness. Lousy though it must be to go home to Mrs Bott, it was still going home.

'I'll walk with you,' he said, the lone wolf suddenly not wanting to be alone. 'I don't live in Glidden Road no more, you know.'

'Why not?'

'It all empty there now. They going to start pulling it down any day. I'm going to get work on one of the gangs if I can. Fun, huh, to help tear down the crummy old place?' Might even find a screw of weed in some cranny where Gilroy had stashed it in an alarm, and forgotten. Jeeze, he could stand a charge right now to see him through the night.

'Where do you live then?' Frankie asked, already leaning his skinny body towards the side street, as if Mrs Bott had it on a string.

'Here and there. Nowhere special at the moment.'

'Like camping out, you mean?' Frankie's eyes were circles of wonder.

'Camping out!' Edgar laughed. 'Like a bum is what I mean. I'll find something soon, but it warm now, and so what? They's a kind of cellar under one of them –' He stopped. Not even innocent Frankie Bott could be trusted with the knowledge of the Zorro Men's secret place under the steps of the derelict house.

'Tell us then,' Frankie urged. 'I could bring you some food and that. Beer if you like,' he added in acknowledgement of Edgar's graduation from Boy Scout to adult hobo.

'Bring us a stick of hemp too, while you're at it,' Edgar said, and Frankie jumped and said nervously: ''Ere listen, Ed, you never –'

335

'O.K. I never. Get on home, boy, or you'll get your neck wrung like a cockerel.'

'Tell me where you'll be. I want to help you. Honest.'

'Nah. The boys take care of me. They'd kill you if you tried to come in our place.'

Down the street came a line of white boys, peg-topped in tight trousers and loosely draped jackets, weaving and tacking their spider legs all across the road. Edgar was suddenly gone out of the lamplight and Frankie turned and ran in the opposite direction. Even Frankie Bott, who had never run with a gang or seen anything more deadly than his mother with a chopping knife, knew that white and black did not get caught fraternizing. Not if they were alone. Not if it was night, and a mob out looking for giggles.

When school opened after the brief Easter holiday, Grace found that she had been moved again. Form 2c had given her some bad times, but it was typical of Mr Neilson's maladroit methods that just when you were beginning to make something of a class, you were taken away from them.

2c had always been a trouble spot. They were an extra class created to accommodate one of the sudden bulges that appear in school populations, and they had never had their own room. For the first part of the year they were wedged into the end of a corridor, with a blackboard in front of the window cutting off most of the daylight. The move to the back of the draughty assembly hall was not much better, for there was constant traffic passing through and often some noisy activity going on at the other end of the hall.

When Grace acquired this nomad group, it contained two recognized delinquents (it only needed one to demoralize a whole class), one complete layabout whom no one had ever even attempted to teach, one girl whose language split the ceiling, and one who was fetched away by an enigmatic policewoman during Grace's first week and never seen again.

Thanks to Mr Neilson and the constant changes of staff at Green Lane, Form 2c, lost, resentful, disorganized, had been shoved from one unwilling teacher to another, no one's love and everyone's burden. Grace Peel, who had gained toughness at Green Lane, but had gained compassion too, set out to make them love and to teach them how to stop being a burden.

Before the Easter holiday, she was just starting to succeed. They were settling down. They at least listened to her with their ears, even though their minds often rejected the information, or did not receive it at all. Some cautious love was beginning to come back to her. When she returned from a week in Scotland with Colin's family, Grace was determined that there was not a child in that Cinderella class who should not have a better summer, because of her.

When she discovered that Mr Neilson had arbitrarily switched her back to her old form 3B, she stormed in a fury to his office.

He laughed at her. Instead of arguing, or being offended by her anger, he laughed. It was a thin and joyless sound, high up at the back of his nose. 'Why all the fuss?' he asked indifferently. 'You had 3B before. Got along quite nicely with them if I remember right' – as if he didn't *know* that she had wrung out her heart for Sidney Goole and Norman and Dilys Sweeney before they moved up to the dead antipathy of Mr Peters!

'You can't do it!' She was so tense that she felt her toes gripping the floor through her shoes.

'Strangely enough, Miss Peel, I can,' Mr Neilson said smoothly. 'I am the head of this school, it seems. I give orders, and my last order to you at this time is please don't shout. I've had sinus trouble. It's very painful.'

At break, Grace found Mary Oliver and June Ricketts lying in wait for her on the way to the common room. Mary was close to tears, and June had that blank dull-witted look which petrified her face when she was upset.

'Oh Miss!' Mary stepped in front of Grace with her face lifted, offering her distress like a gift. 'Just when some of us was beginning to think there might be some point to school after all.'

Grace put an arm round her. This was probably the warmest compliment that she would ever have. 'You'll be all right with Miss Cramer,' she said. 'But this is her first job in a big school. You'll have to make it easy for her.'

Grace had seen little Miss Cramer and recognized something of herself as she was when she first came to the school: timid, idealistic, pathetically ignorant, but full of good intentions. Eighteen months of experience at Green Lane had taught Grace that she had some rubber in her spirit. Resilience was the last thing to hope for in the new young teacher with her nervous cough and red defenceless eyes, and the disgusted noises which

Mary and June made at the mention of her name seemed to seal the fate of poor little Miss Cramer.

'What about the wedding, Miss? Does it mean we can't come to the wedding?'

'Of course not. Who's going to hold my flowers if you don't come? It will be just the same. I promised, didn't I?' Grace spread reassurance on them like butter, but her heart sank. Would she have to invite form 3B too – all thirty-three of them? It would be a madhouse. Thank goodness Colin's mother was not strong enough to travel south.

Frankie Bott would come of course, whatever happened. He was in her class again. When she went into the room this morning, he had called out: 'I knew it was my lucky day!' impervious to the hoots and sing-song jeers of 'Frankie Bott loves tea-cher!' His transparent joy made Grace feel ashamed that she had let her fury with Mr Neilson sour her opinion of form 3B at first. Getting to know them during the first few days, she realized that there was just as much to be done for them as for the un-fortunate 2C. Just as many trouble makers. Just as many shirkers. Just as many wretched childhoods which cried out for someone to take an interest in them before it was too late.

'In a place like Green Lane,' she told Colin as they walked away from her school in the late afternoon, 'it doesn't really matter where you are. It's like shovelling snow off a mountain. It wouldn't matter where you dug, because you can't do the whole thing anyway.'

'Discouraged?'

'I didn't mean it that way. I meant –' Out of a doorway materialized Frankie Bott in a short tight jacket and threadbare gym shoes. He hissed and clicked his fingers at her as if the police were after him. She stopped.

'Can I speak to you, Miss?'

'Of course. Walk with us to the Underground. Mr Mackenzie and I are going to the cinema.'

'It's private.' Frankie slid a withering look towards Colin. He had never disguised his jealousy. When he was younger and used to be jealous of poor Denzil, it had been comic. Now that he was older and taller and exposed to the self-inflicted wounds of adolescence, it was more pathetic.

'I'll walk behind you,' Colin said agreeably. He used to be irritated by Frankie Bott, but Grace had made him accept the boy, as she would have made him accept a clumsy dog that had to stick with her.

'It's Edgar.' Frankie quickened his step so that Colin could not hear. 'I seen 'im.'

'Edgar Biggs? How is he? He told me he was going to get a job as soon as he left school. I was going to try to get him apprenticed somewhere, but he didn't come near me again. You know how he was after he stopped working for the exam, and –'

'And went to the bad? No kidding, Miss. You never knew what 'e was up to. I could tell you some tales.'

'Don't, Frankie. What are you trying to do? He used to be your friend.'

'That's right. That's what I mean. You got to do something for 'im.'

'Frankie, I can't. I did my best before, you know that. But it went wrong. It's too late now.'

'Listen. 'E's all alone. Parents gone, and that women 'e used to live with, she cleared out too. Got nowhere to live. No money. 'E sleeps out somewhere. Like a bum, 'e said. And another thing, Miss.' He glanced back over his shoulder at Colin. ''E smokes them cigarettes.'

'That's nothing. All the boys do at his age.'

'No, I mean them with drugs in 'em. 'Emp and that.' He looked at her with his eyes wide open. 'You know what that does to a man?'

'No,' Grace said rashly, but luckily Frankie said: 'Nor do I, but it can't be no good.'

After Frankie had left them, Grace told Colin about Edgar. 'Don't you ever let up?' he grumbled. 'I get school all day and school half the night when I'm with you. It seems I'm not marrying a woman. I'm marrying a whole pack of lame dogs howling at her heels.'

'Edgar isn't howling. He's not at school either.'

'Don't feed me technicalities. Just be in love with me, like normal people going out after a day's work. Do they discuss all the time who lost the order slips or why the third girl from the left in the back row of the typing pool got fired?'

'Probably,' Grace said, but she kept quiet about Edgar.

Next day, she went to Geoffrey Savage. Geoffrey, with the crusading light in his brown eye, loaded her with suggestions, since he was in touch with every organization and authority for the care of youth; but the one Grace liked best was that since Edgar was supposed to be a Roman Catholic, she should go and talk to Father Mack about him.

'But then you've got to get hold of the boy. How are you going to find him?'

'Frankie said he might be at the coloured dance at the Community Centre. He goes there for the food.'

'Good enough. Want me to go and rope him for you?'

'No Geoff. He's frightened, I think. On the run from something. I don't know yet whether it's the police or just authority in general. But he'd be less scared of me than of a man.'

'You shouldn't go up there alone.'

'I shall take Frankie Bott,' she said with dignity. 'He may know the passwords.'

'You're a plucky little piece,' Geoffrey said.

'Colin doesn't think so. He thinks I'm silly to get into this.'

'Come off it. Don't you know about men? They pretend they want a woman who can't stand on her own two feet without them to prop her up, but they don't really. When they marry, they choose the one with guts.'

Father Mack was a short energetic man with a square head of brindle hair cut in Germanic bristles all the same length.

Grace liked him at once. She had never believed all the horrors about the Roman church with which her mother had stuffed her, yet as she rang the bell by the peeling arched doorway of the presbytery of St Joseph's, she was nervous.

An old woman opened the door and took Grace into a bleak little room like a cell, with a crucifix, a prie-dieu covered in worn carpet, a bookshelf half full of old black tomes and two hard chairs.

Was the prie-dieu for confessions? It was not surprising that people could strip bare their souls in this uncompromising little chamber which was like a waiting-room between death and eternity. When the priest came in, the chill of guilt which the room imposed was immediately dispelled. Grace sat down again more comfortably and stopped twisting her hands and letting her mind run in a morbid panic round all the sins that she would have to confess if she were suddenly converted. Father Mack was cheerful and friendly, with amused eyes and a brisk voice which cut the corners of speech and enabled Grace to get to the point immediately.

He listened without interrupting. Not many people could do that. Years of patience in the confessional? It was Edgar's trouble she was confessing, not hers; and yet as she talked to the square unhandsome face, Grace found that she was admitting to him her own failure with the boy, releasing the disappointment that she had never quite thrown off since he had slipped away from her.

'But it wasn't your fault.' Colin, Geoffrey, Mrs Meikle, Miss Arbuthnot – several people had said that to her; but when Father Mack said it, she was able to believe him. 'You did your best. If things had been different for him, he might have gone ahead and been able to make use of your help. But then again, even if it had been easy for him – his home I mean – he might still have got away from you.

'There is a sort of – how shall we put it? – an innate lassitude in so many of these people. They're so charmingly lively, but there's an apathy under the surface that turns off the switch suddenly when they're asked for sustained effort. The Caribbean syndrome. One of the doctors round here calls it that. Would you believe that the most common affliction in streets like Glidden Road is a nervous breakdown? Yes, perhaps you would. These people, you see, come over here chock full of innocent optimism about all the good things waiting for a British citizen. When they find they've got to fight for anything they get, and that they are going to be lonely and unwanted – even hated, though I'm not supposed to say that because the government tells us there is no racial hatred – they let go. They're not equipped to face both the disappointment and the struggle. That's often when they start on the hemp, if they weren't on it before. It makes a man feel like a big shot, so why bother working to be one when you can do it with a reefer for half a crown? I'll have to keep your Edgar Biggs off it though. Keep him short of money perhaps. I'll pay him in food and clothes.'

'Then you can help him? I thought you were going to say it was hopeless.'

'Oh no. The presbytery is going to crumble away if we don't redecorate it soon. The boy can do some painting. There's a little room upstairs. He can stay here with me and the two curates and Nellie Moran – she'll keep him working – until I can see what's best to do for him.'

'You're very kind, Father,' Grace said.

'Oh no. You have been kind in giving me the chance to help him. So many of them will tramp round all the welfare offices in London before they'll come to the priest. Welfare will give them something for nothing, you see. We ask that they should give something back, even if it's only sneaking in at the tail end of Mass and gabbling half a Hail Mary.'

That Wednesday, Grace went with Frankie to the Community Centre and stood in the hall pretending to read the notice boards and not to notice the whistles and scuffling bravado of the boys round the pool table. Frankie had gone through a door which had opened on music and a riotous confusion of jive. She did not expect him to come out with Edgar, but he did.

They came out together, Edgar in a grubby sweat shirt and blue jeans which had disintegrated at the bottom. He stood for a moment and looked at her with his head down like a bull; then Frankie, serious with the importance of his mission, prodded him forward across the hall and he stood near Grace, but not close to her.

When she said: 'Hullo, Edgar,' and held out her hand, he still kept his distance, looking at her with his nostrils wide and his neck arched, less like a bull now than a nervous horse.

One of the boys at the pool table said something fairly crude, and Frankie went scarlet into his sticky hair. 'Let's get out of 'ere,' he said, and hounded them both out of the hall.

'Did Frankie tell you what the offer was?' Grace asked when they were outside. 'Are you coming?'

'I told 'im, Miss, but 'e wouldn't say nothing in there.' Frankie's face was drawn with anxiety, but Edgar shrugged a big bony shoulder and said casually: 'I don't care. I'll come if you like.'

That much at least he had picked up and retained from the citizens of Cottingham Park. He might be at the end of his tether and needing help desperately. He might, within himself, be surging with relief, delight and gratitude, but it was: 'I don't care' and: 'if you like', in the true British idiom.

The heavy padlocks on the collection boxes at the rear of St Joseph's were ugly and incongruous in a house of prayer, but essential in a church that nested in a neighbourhood of thieves.

PETER'S PENCE and FOR THE POOR and FLOWERS FOR THE

DECORATION OF THE ALTAR were too tempting. People gave of their penury, but there were others who were not ashamed to take, they had the chance and the right tools.

The church was rarely empty from the first mass until it was locked at night. There was nearly always someone in there, women mostly, praying, or moving slowly round the Stations of the Cross, or just sitting in a pew at the back in peace. There was little opportunity to rob the collection boxes while the church was open, and whoever was doing it this time, was finding some way of getting in after it was closed. Father Mack checked the padlocks each night before he locked the doors; but for three mornings running he had found one of them forced open when he came through the church from the vestry to let in the sour grey air from the reluctantly waking street.

'If anyone wants me,' he told Nellie Moran after supper, 'I'll be in the church. I'm going to ambush myself in the gallery and see if I can catch this pilfering mouse.'

'Want me to watch with you, Father?' Edgar was at the kitchen table, finishing off the pie that Nellie had given to him after the fathers had finished with it. 'I sure be glad to catch that thieving devil – as long as it weren't none of my buddies.'

Nellie frowned and tapped his head with a wooden spoon, but Edgar laughed, and the priest laughed too, enjoying his honesty. There was no mystery about the kind of life he had been leading. He had talked most of it out and sworn that he was through. Soon, he promised, 'when I get my nerve up', he would come to the confessional and receive the only real forgiveness.

'Why not now?' Father Mack always said, but Edgar hedged with: 'I have to get me prepared. I got a lot to remember.'

'Thanks for the offer,' the priest said, 'but I'll watch alone, I think. I may have to stay there until late, and I want you in bed and asleep.'

'That's all he ever does is sleep,' Nellie Moran complained, 'when he's not eating. I never saw such a lazy slug.'

'In that case, why do you take him cake to eat in bed?' Father Mack asked mildly, and she muttered at him with her slack old lips and asked him to do her the favour of going about his business in the church and leaving her alone in her own kitchen.

All that week, Father Mack sat in the dark gallery of St Joseph's and prayed the rosary and meditated and dozed and waited, with the red glow of the sanctuary lamp and all the painted plaster saints for company. He stayed there most of the night and went stiff and weary to robe for early mass, but he heard and saw nothing, and the boxes were untouched.

On Saturday he heard confessions in the early evening. The usual procession. Tongue-tied men giving their sins crude names because they knew none better. Anxious young mothers with their sorry little admissions of nagging at their men and raging at their children, going away in the first peace of the week, although because of the way they had to live, many of them would be back next month with the same story. Girls, both penitent and impenitent, who had committed the commonest sin in Cottingham Park – or anywhere else for that matter. Lonely women seeking introspectively to turn petty faults into transgressions. Mumbling old grandmothers who twisted their confessions of family feuds into grizzling diatribes against everyone in the family but themselves.

Towards the end of the hour, while Father Mack bent his ear to a whispering child, he heard a man or a boy come into the other side of the confessional, stumbling against the step. Newcomer. The old hands knew about the step inside the little dark place. Strangers and novices usually stumbled. When he opened the door on that side, he saw the head of a coloured boy behind the grille.

He knew that it was Edgar, but the boy told him anyway. Then he asked: 'Can you tell anyone what I say?' And the priest answered: 'No. I can't even talk to you about it outside the the confessional unless you give me permission.' And Edgar told him that he had come into the church from the presbytery at night and taken the money from the collection boxes.

'What for?' Father Mack asked. 'If you needed money so badly I would have given it you.'

'Not for weed you wouldn't,' Edgar said breathlessly. 'You don't know what it like to want a charge that bad.'

At the end of the confession, Father Mack asked: 'Will you talk to me about this afterwards? Not the other things. I mean about the money. You have my word that I won't bring the police into it if you do.'

'I don't know.'

'Will you promise God now that you will not steal from His church again?'

'How could I, with you waiting for me up there?'

344

'But I won't be waiting in the gallery, unless you tell me to. Unless you give me permission, I can't refer to what you have told me, either directly or indirectly. That means I can't try to catch you. I can't change my routine and empty the boxes every night instead of once a week. I can't even ask you to leave the presbytery.'

'Jeeze,' Edgar said, as the woman waiting on the other side cleared her throat just audibly as a hint that they were taking too long, 'they sure make it tough for you, Father.'

'It's tougher for you,' the priest said. 'You know now that the church will be empty. But if you won't promise at least to try not to take advantage of that, I can't give you absolution.'

'What you mean?'

'Our Lord's forgiveness. That's what you came in here for, wasn't it?'

'Oh Jesus.' Edgar was breathing heavily. 'I don't know. I came to tell you, that's all. I don't know. I don't know. I'll come back.' He was suddenly gone, and Father Mack shut the door with a sigh and raised his other hand to open the other door, and leaned attentively towards the grille as if the impatient woman's confession were the only thing that mattered.

'Are you not watching any more for the thief then, Father?' Nellie Moran asked.

'No.' Edgar was looking at him, but Father Mack had to turn his head away. Even the implication of knowledge in the eyes was forbidden. 'I shall stay in bed. Whoever it was, I don't believe he'll come again.'

In the morning three of the boxes that had taken money during the week were empty, and Edgar was gone.

*

After they were married, Grace and Colin lived in a miniature house, two up, two down, in one of the streets below the slope of the Scotneys that was growing mysteriously from a slum into an attractive little place to live.

That was the arresting thing about Cottingham Park. The Scotneys had remained the same, tree-stuffed in an undisturbed Georgian dream. The teeming terraces of the Rise remained the same, or got a little dirtier. But in between there were streets and cul-de-sacs and little looping byways that were always going up or down in the world, never quite knowing from one decade to the next what their status would be.

It had nothing to do with the new road, now carving out its relentless path as slowly as a blunt saw through teak. The chameleon activities of these little side streets had been going on for years before the Expressway, or even the internal combustion engine which made it necessary, had first been a brain's unclarified thought.

The houses of Pottery Street, where Grace and Colin lived, had once been the dwellings of craftsmen at the local pottery which made the grey-white Cottingham ware. When the pottery was abandoned, the cottages were taken over by grooms and gardeners and coachmen and cooks who served the big estates. When the large houses fell one by one under the hammer of the changing economy and were pulled down and turned into flats and maisonettes and residential hotels, the neat little terrace cottages began, by some mysterious drift of cliques, to be taken over by poets and painters and essayists who were not quite outrageous enough to be in the front ranks of the artistic revolution. Painted up and prettified with porches and insecure wrought iron balconies, Pottery Street became a sort of sub-Bohemia, still rather countrified, with an odorous livery stable at one end and trees growing out of the uneven pavement. Over the years, as the growing town marched out and engulfed what was left of rural Cottingham Park in a solid lava of new houses and shops and schools, it passed by Pottery Street with one of the strange vagaries of the London current, and left it much the same, except that the livery stable eventually became a garage.

As the horses moved out, so did the writers and the painters; gradually, over a generation or two, until there was only one very dirty old man, who wrote diatribes against God and tried to give them away in Park Road, left to live among the poorer families who were moving into the cheap deteriorating houses. After that, the street went downhill for a long time. The trees developed a cankerous blight and were cut down. The new inhabitants could not afford to repair the neglect which had begun to creep over the quiet street like a mildew. The landlords let the rot continue, since they had written off the property as worthless.

The Germans kept their hands off Pottery Street, and after the war, in the rush of marriages which could find nowhere to

346

live, Pottery Street began to go up in the world again with the gradual reflowering of the spruceness and charm with which it had begun life for the houseproud workers who first gave it its name.

By the time Grace and Colin moved in, about half the street had been painted and renovated and made livable, with bathrooms built into the little yards at the back, and tiny tiled kitchens. Grace and Colin's house down at the wrong, unfashionable end – the ballet people and the actress and the bald young man who designed all-white interiors were at the other end – was still falling to bits. It was the one where the bearded old agnostic had lived, and though it had been empty since he lay dead in it undiscovered for two weeks many years ago, it still smelled of him.

With the luck of optimistic lovers, they got it so cheaply that they were able to pay a local builder to make it safe and comfortable, and they spent the first months of their marriage painting and papering and laying linoleum and setting tiles and making bookcases and coming together in exhausted joy on a secondhand box spring mattress without legs.

As soon as they came home from Green Lane, they were in working clothes, and that was how Frankie Bott found Grace when he knocked timidly on the bright blue door one evening when his mother thought he was at the Youth Club. Grace put her paintbrush across the pot and went to the door, wiping her hand on her encrusted overalls. Her hair was tied back in a pony tail and there was paint on her nose and in her eyebrows.

Frankie stared. 'I'm sorry, Miss,' he said. 'I didn't know you were busy.'

'We're always busy,' she said. 'There's so much to do. I wasn't going to invite you till it was all ready, but since you're here, come in and see what we've done.'

The hammering upstairs stopped. 'Who is it?'

Frankie's face dropped a fraction, as if he had hoped to find Grace alone, but she called up to Colin not to stop work, and took Frankie into the kitchen which was the only room where there was anywhere to sit down.

They sat at the little shiny table and drank ginger beer, and after fumbling awkwardly round several false starts, Frankie finally told her why he had come.

When Grace told Colin afterwards – for she told him everything, even the things she thought he might not like – he advised her not to interfere.

Colin had been at Green Lane nearly three years longer than Grace. When he first went there, from a private school in the Midlands where the masters and parents vied with each other in spurious refinement, he had plunged in with all Grace's zeal and beneficent plans for revolutionizing the shabby lives of the boys and girls who came into his care. But he had had too much of it. He had failed too many times and broken his zeal too often on the shield of Mr Neilson's obstinate inhumanity. Grace was still body and soul absorbed in the school. Colin was beginning to be there in body only. His spirit was drifting away, not from the children of Cottingham Park, but from the ugly, unenlightened school which was their lot. His eyes were turning to the big new comprehensive school which was being built up at the top of the Scotneys to the futile rage of its undemocratic neighbours and an almost defunct protest group called the Scotney Society. If he managed his degree this summer, he would apply for a job there, and if he got it, and he could not make Grace give up teaching by giving her a baby, he was going to drag her in there somehow, even as a knitting teacher, to get her away from Green Lane.

'The kids are one thing,' he said. 'Their parents are another. If this Bott woman is as horrible as you say, I'd stay away. Let the authorities handle it. They've got welfare people for this sort of thing.'

'But they've been trying for more than two years. The doctors too. Everyone has told her that Kenny might benefit from the operation and that she must let him go to the hospital school, but she won't let him out of her clutches.'

'Why would she do it for you?'

'I don't know. She just might. I've got to try. I promised Frankie that I would at least try. His brother means everything to him. They protect each other in some odd sort of lost way. And I've seen that pathetic little boy. He's the nicest child, heaven knows why when you think of the life he's had. I'm scared to death of Mrs Bott, but I must at least go and talk to her. I failed with Edgar, you see. Failed miserably. If I had left him alone in the first place, he'd have gone back to Trinidad with his parents and never known all this trouble. Perhaps I can make up for that by doing something for Frankie.'

348

'I love you,' Colin said seriously. 'You are a meddling missionary, but I shall never try to change you.'

Frightened though she was at the idea of tackling the formidable Mrs Bott in her lair, Grace was glad to have the chance that Frankie had given her. It might exorcize the disquieting ghost of Edgar, who had been on her conscience ever since Father Mack had telephoned her at the Meikles'.

'About the boy,' he had said, and stopped.

'Edgar? How is he? Have you been able to find him a job?'

'Well – no. I'm sorry, Miss Peel, to disappoint you after you've done so much, but the boy has gone.'

'Where?'

'I'm afraid I don't know. He just disappeared. And he won't come back, I know that.'

'But why?'

'I'm afraid I can't tell you.' Father Mack's voice went tight and rather distant. A secret voice, shutting her out from his special world and making her questions sound like unseemly curiosity; but she had to ask them.

'What happened? Please tell me, Father.'

'I'm sorry, my dear,' he said more warmly. 'It's a matter of – well, call it a trade secret if you like.'

What could Edgar have done? What on earth had happened? She would never know. It was obvious that the priest was not going to tell her.

'Don't worry about him,' he said. 'You did what you could, and he'll be all right. He's a bright boy. He got me very neatly trussed up. He'll make out, wherever he is.'

With Mrs Meikle at her elbow, concentrating on her in a bursting mixture of curiosity and concern, Grace did not know what to say. Father Mack sounded so unruffled that her distress and anxiety seemed foolish and out of place. 'I'm so sorry, Father,' she said finally. 'After you took all the trouble to help him. It was my fault for –'

'Gracious,' Father Mack said cheerfully. '*I* don't mind. I got the hall painted and half way up the staircase. An excellent job he made of it too. I'm grateful to you for letting me have him.'

Mrs Bott was furious. She was so angry that she was afraid she would burst a blood bessel in her head and then where would Kenny be, with her in her box and no one to look out for him?

That would show them though, if she died. Then they would realize how great was the burden she had shouldered all these years. In her dreams of revenge, it was not unusual for Mrs Bott to imagine herself dead, in order to spite somebody. It would be almost worth it, if only you could be sure that after you died you could look down and enjoy the discomfiture of those you left behind.

The nerve of that woman – what did she call herself? Mrs Mackenzie, and that was a nerve in itself – coming into her flat and poking her nose into Mrs Bott's affairs. Who had told her about Kenny? Miss Peel – Mrs Bott refused to call her or think of her as anything else – had not said. But it had to be Frankie. Who else?

'You mucking little bastard,' she screamed at him after Miss Peel had finally taken herself off with all that hair which must be dyed or Mrs Bott was a nigger's uncle. 'I'll kill you for this.' She went into the kitchen to look for a weapon, and Frankie nipped on to the little balcony outside the sitting-room and ducked down behind the strings of wet washing.

'Please Mum,' Kenny was crying. He was always crying these days. What the hell was the matter with the kid, a big boy of ten years, with every care lavished on him?

'You're getting to be as ungrateful as your brother,' she snapped at him, and Kenny winced with his face, for he could not move his head far enough to duck. 'I'll 'ave you separated, that's what I'll do.'

Kenny stopped crying, and she wiped his nose savagely with the corner of her apron. 'But you said you wouldn't,' he whimpered. 'When Frank's teacher told you what she'd found out about the school and all – you said you'd never send me away.'

'Who said anything about sending you away?' Mrs Bott stood with her hands on her mammoth hips and glared at the glass door to the balcony. 'I see you out there, Frankie Bott, don't think I don't. It's Frankie that'll go. They've got places for devils like 'im.'

'What's up, Nettie?' Mr Bott came in. He was smaller than Frankie now, and much paler. He walked with a stoop and a slight limp, the rheumatic legacy of an air raid injury, which irritated Mrs Bott.

'What's up? he asks.' She rounded on him. ''E comes in 'ere dot and carry and asks what's up. If you'd come straight 'ome from work instead of calling in all the boozers on the way, you'd have been 'ere to stand by me in the face of insults.'

It was true that Mr Bott had had a beer on the way home. He often did these days to make the homecoming easier. But he was never without his peppermints. She was only guessing, so he kissed Kenny and stroked his thin dry hair and asked: 'Where's Frankie then?'

She jerked her head. ''Iding from me. As well 'e might. Bringing that woman 'ere to make a mockery of me. . . .' With relish, she launched into the tale of Miss Grace Peel. ' "It's Mrs Mackenzie now, Mum," says our Frank, soapy as you please. So I'm to call her Mrs Mackenzie now, am I, on top of everything else?' That stuck in Mrs Bott's maw, the last indigestible insult.

'Well,' said Mr Bott mildly, sinking into his chair and resting his tired head on the torn piece of lace which covered the back. 'But she's right, you know. The doctors have been begging you for months to let Kenny have the operation. Just think if you could use that hand, eh Ken? Wouldn't that be something?'

Kenny grinned, his eyes eagerly on his father, but his mother gave him a push that turned his wheelchair round to face the other way and said: 'You too, is it? Stuffing the poor little devil up with all these notions. Sentencing 'im to torture. Them Russians as got nothing on you. You know what the doctor said because you was there with me at the clinic last time, though what for, don't ask me. It might not even work, 'e said, that young one with the glasses that claims 'e's God Almighty. It would be painful, and 'e'd have to spend weeks in hospital. If you'd condemn your poor little boy to that, I certainly wouldn't.' She bent over Kenny and began to fuss with his clothes and his blanket, clucking at him, smothering him with her monstrous bulk.

'But I wouldn't mind the pain, Mum,' Kenny said out of the muffler of her bosom. 'I've said so. I'd take the chance. I'd 'ave the operation if it meant I could use me 'and.'

'Shut up,' his mother said quite fondly. 'Nobody asked you.'

She was quieting down, and Frankie had put his head into the room, turning a bright eye back and forth like a bird before it picks up a crumb, but he drew his head back quickly as Mr Bott started her off again by saying rashly: 'But the school, Nettie. You'll 'ave to give in over that sooner or later. There's laws, you know.'

'There's no law that says a helpless child can be taken from

351

'is mother,' she informed him. 'What does 'e need with schooling? 'E's never going to be able to work, poor soul. 'E'll get all the schooling 'e needs right 'ere from me. 'E can read, can't 'e? 'Oo taught 'im that?'

'Frankie did,' said Kenny, and Mrs Bott gave one of her bull-fight snorts and went out to the kitchen, because she could not disagree. Frankie could read better than her before he went to Abbot's Road.

But where would it get him after all? She fumed to herself as she bashed about the kitchen getting supper. She'd got no schooling worth the name, she was proud to say. With a smart mother who lied about her age, Nettie Norris was able to be out earning her living at fourteen, without all this nonsense they tried to stuff into the kids' heads nowadays, Miss Grace Peel and her lot. Mrs Bott cut savagely into an unripe tomato with a bone-handled dinner knife honed down to sharpness. And look what she had made of herself. Best mother in the flats, Mrs Bacon said, and everyone admired how she had devoted her whole life to a crippled child who most would have left to wither and die, or shipped off on to someone else.

And everyone knew how much work she did for the Community Association. The day Mrs Bott moved into the flats had been a good day for Nelson Court, that she would say. All she had done for the good of the place – who'd got rid of the postman who used to come and visit that widow all the time? That's what Mrs Bott would like to know. Disgusting. Who'd let the air out of his bicycle tyres night after night until he got discouraged and took his big jock off somewhere else?

Who'd written the letter to Mrs Corrigan and told her that her daughter was going with that nigger? Anominous, of course. When you were as community spirited and well thought of as Mrs Bott, there was no need to flaunt your name.

And who was going to get rid of that great vicious dog and save the flats from becoming a barking, stinking bedlam, which was what would happen if one dog were let in and everyone and his uncle began to clamour to keep one too?

Cutting thick, unappetizing sandwiches, Mrs Bott forgot about Miss Grace Peel – Mrs Mackenzie, hah! – in the pleasure of thinking how she was going to sway the Association committee tomorrow to force the Council to get rid of the collie that girl had sneaked in on the second floor. What if the girl was going blind? She wasn't blind yet, was she? Mrs Bott had seen her walking across the yard just like anyone else. And if she was, she could take herself and her dog off to St Dunstan's. Mrs Bott would have none of them.

The following week, Mrs Bott had something else to occupy her outrage, besides Miss Peel and the girl with the guide dog. The Barrows family moved into one of the larger flats along her balcony, and Mrs Bott was instantly alive to what kind of people they were.

The day that the Barrows family came to Collingwood House with their poor little show of furniture, Mrs Bott kept her front door ajar all day, and went out a dozen times to shake an unused mop or duster over the balcony parapet.

When Frankie came home from school, she pounced on him. 'There's new people moved into 54,' she said, before he had hung up his cap. 'Kids! There's dozen of them. 'Ow will they ever all fit in and keep within the Law, that's what I want to know.'

'I seen one of 'em outside,' Frankie said. 'Teenager.'

Mrs Bott made a face as if he had said homicidal maniac.

'Their old flat in Spurr Road is coming down for the Expressway.'

'And they put 'em in 'ere? With four thousand already on the waiting list for council flats? I told you this would happen.' She turned her eyes sideways to Frankie and put on her quick whispering gossiping voice. 'I told you that very first time you come 'ome and told us about the new road. This is only the start of it. You watch. They'll 'ave us all turned out before they're done.'

'Oh can it, Mum,' said Frankie, who had heard this hundreds of times before. 'Keep your wool on.' When she was scandalizing she was at her most amenable, and he could risk familiarity without getting his ear knocked through his head. 'This boy I met – 'e's got a new scooter and all. Wait till you see it, young Ken – 'e told me they'd been put 'ere because the Council didn't want to move them out of the neighbourhood they knew.'

'Ho,' said Mrs Bott, lifting her bosom with her folded arms and letting it drop again below where her waist should be. 'When there's thousands being turned out would like to stay in the district and can't. Why should these people get it? What's so special about them? It's graft. You'll see.' She lowered her voice. 'Money passed in the right quarter. Don't tell me. I know the way it goes.'

'Well, I don't know, Mum.' Frankie scratched his head. 'Can I take Ken for a walk? It's lovely out.'

'All right. You can take 'im down to the shops and get me a quarter of tea.' She rooted in her great sprung handbag. 'If you don't bring back all the change, I'll flay you inch by inch,' she said easily.

She was glad to get rid of them. As soon as they had gone down the balcony and she heard the lift gate and the whine of the motor, she took off her apron and went along to No. 54, her fat-impeded heart thumping with pleasurable excitement. She knocked on the door. A child's face looked at her through the curtainless kitchen window, and presently the door was opened by a girl of about eleven, with curly dark hair cut short all over her head and a white nervous face which looked at Mrs Bott as though she were a monster.

'Where's your mother, dear?' Mrs Bott asked in a grating moan, which was her kindest voice.

'I don't know.' The girl looked blank. 'In heaven, I suppose. That's what they said.'

'Oh dear, what a shame,' said Mrs Bott inadequately. 'Is your Dad in then? I'd like to 'ave a word with 'im.'

Still staring at her, the child suddenly opened her mouth like a dark cave and screamed: 'You can't – you can't!' and stumbled back inside the flat, sobbing wildly.

In a moment, an older girl came out, with an apron tied tightly round her small waist, her hands dirty and her hair untidy, as if she had been working.

'I'm sorry,' she said, looking calmly at Mrs Bott. 'Dodie's a bit upset. She didn't mean to be rude.'

Using her prepared speech, Mrs Bott said: 'I just came to see whether I could give you any help, getting straight.' She edged her foot forward, and still talking in a neighbourly way, managed to insinuate herself into the hall of the flat.

When Mrs Bott kept coming, anyone but a prizefighter would have to stand back, and the girl was not strong enough or confident enough to stop her. 'It's very kind of you,' she said. 'But we'll manage all right. I'm used to managing, you see, since our mother died.' The child Dodie came out from the back of the flat and stood close behind her, and when the older girl reached out and put her arm round her and drew her close, Mrs Bott saw that she was not grown up, as she had thought, but only about sixteen.

Under the pressure of Mrs Bott's questions, she gave the information that they used to live in a flat over a greengrocer's shop in Spurr Road. 'My brother, Garry, he used to work there, selling and sweeping out. It was handy.' When their home was condemned, along with all that block right past Granchester Mansions, they had been offered the flat in Nelson Court. 'Of course, we're very glad to get it,' she said shyly. She was a quiet, gentle girl, with no lipstick and a cardigan that she had obviously knitted herself, rather badly. Mrs Bott could see all the mistakes.

'I should hope so,' she said. 'There's many people like you been turned out and would give their back teeth to get into these flats. You're lucky, I must say. People have been waiting three and four years to get in 'ere. You're lucky to get in ahead of everybody, aren't you?'

Her voice was beginning to bully, when a man came into the doorway, blocking the light. No, it wasn't a man, it was a boy. Well, it was a young man, with glasses and a long, angular face, but not old enough to be the father of this lot.

'This is Tom,' the girl said. 'He's my brother.' She made a face at Tom, which Mrs Bott intercepted, and vanished into one of the rooms.

'I'm Mrs Bott from down the balcony,' she said, noting the worn suit on the muscular young body, and the machine oil ground into the big square hands. 'I come along to say welcome. Where's your Dad then?'

'He's dead,' Tom said. 'His lorry crashed in the fog on the Staines Road. The day we heard we'd to move out of our place, that was. He never knew about it.'

'Oh dear.' Mrs Bott tried to cover up for the bullying tone which he had heard when he came into the doorway. 'You mean you're on your own, the four of you?'

'Five,' Tom said, 'with young Spud. He's the baby. When Dad was killed, there was talk of putting Spud and Dodie into Council care, but Ruth wouldn't have it. She's looked after the lot of us for nearly five years since Mum died, so what's the difference? We'll stick together. Excuse me. I've got to wash.' He pushed politely past Mrs Bott and went into the kitchen.

She stayed in the hall for a moment, taking in all the details of the coats hanging on the wall and the rug that was frayed at the edges, but very clean. No one came back. The small boy was jabbering incomprehensibly to his brother in the kitchen, but the others were silent, and Mrs Bott thought that they were hiding from her until she gave up and went away.

Something to hide, no doubt. Five on their own, and two of them teenagers. The Council must be mad to allow it. Trouble here. Have to keep her eye on what went on.

She did her best among her neighbours in Collingwood House to spread insidious calumny against the Barrows family, but in spite of all the hints she dropped, people persisted in liking them. Their predicament touched every heart, except Mrs Bott's. Tom rapidly made friends among the men, and there were always women ready to feed biscuits and sweets to Dodie and the inarticulate Spud, and to offer Ruth their help. Genuine offers of help; not manoeuvres like Mrs Bott to go nosing inside flat 54.

Ruth was too kind to reject the help, but she did not need it. She managed the cooking and cleaning and washing and ironing and shopping for the whole family, and still found time to run a small baby-sitting service for working mothers. She had to be at home anyway, because of Spud, she said, so she might as well have a few others tumbling about the flat. And there were mothers who could have told you, if they had not been too proud, that there had been weeks when the rent and the hire purchase instalments all seemed to come tumbling on top of them together, and Ruth would make nothing of letting the sitting money go.

She took Tom's wages from the coachworks and budgeted them precisely, and bullied young Garry about finding another job. 'I'm looking round,' he said. 'I'll get something.' At seventeen and a half, he had grown fast, and he was lazy. He was happy hanging about the flats, where there were a lot of boys of his age, but Ruth's reminder that if he did not find work, she was not going to give him the ten pounds at the end of the month for the instalment on his Vespa, eventually sent him sauntering to the Labour Exchange. He found part-time work as an errand boy. Not much of a job, and there was very little left over to give Ruth after he had paid out on the scooter and some essential articles of up-to-the-minute teenage clothing; but at least it was a job to keep him busy half the day, and Ruth's only worry about him now was his relationship with a pert sixteen-year-old called Lilian, who had migrated towards him smoothly because of the Vespa. If you could go pillion, you had it made. It did not matter too much who was on the front of the bicycle, as long as you could lord it from the back perch over the girls whose boys had nothing but their own two feet.

Soon Garry and Lilian were going steady. They wore each other's clothes, and exchanged toy animals to take to bed, and had some daft sort of private language, and went on runs with the scooter club at weekends, and were together almost every evening.

It was all right for Garry to have a steady. All the boys did, except the real drips, and Ruth's driving ambition was to give her brothers and her sister as much as everybody else. But Lilian unnerved her. She was her own age, which made it funny that Ruth was, in a way, a chaperone, especially since Lilian wore advanced make-up and knew about clothes and talked as if she had ten years more experience of the world. Ruth did not believe three-quarters of the talk, but Lilian still managed to make her feel like a schoolgirl, although if she had one quarter of Ruth's responsibilities, she would have sat down sprawling in her tight black pillion-riding pants and breathed her last.

'Is she the right girl for Garry?' Ruth worried to Tom. 'I'm afraid.'

'What of, Kid?' Tom's duties as a father did not extend to discussing the sex development of an adolescent, and Ruth could not talk about it squarely. 'He's got to have a girl. I'd have one myself, if I had the time.'

Ruth flushed. The time when Tom might want to marry and leave them did not bear thinking about. 'Well, I don't know. Lil is – don't you think she's fast, Tom? They say she's kept company with a lot of the boys.'

'Who says? Lil's a nice girl, under all the play acting. You been listening to Mrs Bott. That's your trouble.'

'Oh, her.' Ruth made a face. 'I wouldn't talk to her at all if it wasn't for going in to see poor Kenny. She only lets me do that because she thinks she might get the chance to pump me about what we're doing.'

Frustrated because Ruth was always close-mouthed with her, Mrs Bott continued to spread ugly rumours, and the obvious target was Garry and the girl Lilian, whom Mrs Bott had classified long ago as no better than a little alley cat. The sycophantic Mrs Bacon listened and sucked her new teeth, but the other women were too fond of Ruth and her family to listen even to the juicier bits of Mrs Bott's scandalizing inventions. But she persevered with her insinuations and her sly efforts to turn the whole top floor if not the whole block of Collingwood House against the plucky Barrows, and it was small wonder that when she unwrapped the crumpled newspaper that was pushed through her letter box one night, she found a little load of faeces, the staple insult of the children of Nelson Court.

*

Martha did not write or telephone to ask Miss Sutcliffe and Mrs Vulliamy if she could come to see them, because they might refuse, or deliberately go out if they guessed that she was coming to ask them to do something for Anne.

However, when she arrived at the little Cambridgeshire town where the aunts had so unaccountably made their home, Martha learned from the postmistress that she had missed them anyway.

'Gone up to London for the day. Took the 9.10.' This was clearly the kind of a place where you could not go to the railway station without everyone knowing where you were going, and probably why.

'Would you tell me where their house is? I think I'd like to see it anyway.'

'They're friends of yours, eh, from the old days when they lived up there?' The postmistress turned her clouded blue eyes aloft as if London were on the other side of the ceiling.

'Yes,' Martha said. 'Very good friends. I've known them nearly all my life.'

This would give the postmistress something to spread round the forgotten little town whose only claim on society seemed to be that it had a yew tree mentioned in the Domesday Book and the tallest church spire in Cambridgeshire. *A very good friend, she said. Known them all my life. Those were her very words. How comes it, then, that she's not been down to visit them before? And that they go away the very day she comes. And that she wants to go nosing round the house when they're not here. Seems funny, doesn't it?*

The village would agree. They probably talked about the old ladies anyway, for in a place like this, with apparently no one of their own kind, they must live like hermits, wrapped close in

358

their proud disappointment, with the village children making signs against the evil eye if they had to pass the house after dark.

It was one of those tender, still days, almost damp enough to be raining, and the yellows and washed-out blues and browns of the plastered cottages set close along the pavement were as quietly pleasing as the dark wet fields of the gentle hill which sheltered them. As Martha drove slowly through the village past the magnificent old church and the thatched institute hall and the butcher's shop painted like a toy and hung with rounds of beef and legs of mutton as neat as doll's house food, she began to see how one might be content to live here and lose touch with a speedier world. If Miss Jessie and Aunt Celia wanted to hibernate, perhaps they had picked the right spot, for surely nothing ever happened here to lure them out of their super-annuated cocoon.

'Last house on the left just before you get to the fork in the road,' the postmistress had said, and Martha had expected to see some kind of quaint old cottage with diagonally leaded windows eyebrowed with reed thatch, and a tangle of neglected rambler roses in the garden. But the last house on the left was a bungalow. A modern, newly painted bungalow with a cinnamon front door and a hideous green roof and a garden newly dug round a tiny symmetrical lawn, with tulips ranged like guardsmen under the windows. Nothing could have looked less like Miss Sutcliffe and Mrs Vulliamy. It was inconceivable that they should live here, and hang their washing on the lines in front of the orderly vegetable plot which ran far back behind the house to a young orchard and what looked like chicken houses.

But they did. No one answered the bell, and when Martha walked round the weedless gravel path to try the back door, she recognized Aunt Celia's indestructible spotted blouse hanging limply in the still air, and no one but Aunt Jessie, even if they had lived seventy years in the backwoods of Cambridgeshire, would wear that endless cotton nightgown with the meticulous pearl buttons all down the pin-tucked front.

After knocking on the back door and making faces at a fluffed-out cat which stared at her from the inside window-sill – 'A cat, Anne!' she would be saying in two hours time. 'A cat, of all things' – Martha went back to the front of the stucco bungalow and looked in at a window. Through the net curtain, she could recognize the old ladies' furniture. Not too much of it.

The sitting-room was positively antiseptic compared to the hot stifling clutter of Father's Den at Park Lodge. They must have got rid of a lot of the old stuff. Even the vases and ornaments were cut down by about half, although there were still plenty of them on every level surface, including the lead soldier who shot pennies into the bear's mouth. Martha was glad to see that. Miss Sutcliffe had always promised to give it to Martha's children for their children one day.

As she turned from the window, she saw a woman standing by the little white front gate which had its bars set like a quarter of the sun's rays. 'I saw you from my window,' the woman said very pleasantly, 'so I thought I'd better come across the road and tell you Miss Sutcliffe and Mrs Vulliamy aren't here today.'

'How kind of you.' Martha smiled. The woman was just how one always thought countrywomen would be, but seldom were: fresh-faced, with clean hair in a thick knot and an aura about her of scones coming out of the oven and towels spread out on gooseberry bushes to bleach in the sun. 'They did tell me at the post office, but I wanted to come and see what their house was like anyway. They're old friends of mine.'

'Oh?' The woman was not curious about that. 'It's a lovely little bungalow, isn't it?' she said. 'Only had the one owner before they came. John Stanton, he built it and worked the garden at the back and set in all the fruit trees. His nephew works it now, and keeps the ladies in fruit and vegetables and eggs in return for the land.'

'They don't charge him rent for it?' Martha said involuntarily. This did not sound like Aunt Jessie.

'Oh no. He's had bad luck, you see. Lost the sight of one eye in an accident, but he's got two kids and they're glad to help him earn a living.'

Martha was too surprised to say anything, and the woman said, with the kind of crooked smile with which people dote over children: 'Ever so kind, they are. Always ready to help. Quiet, you know, without making a show. We think they're dear old ladies.'

Dear old ladies? Aunt Celia perhaps, but Miss Jessie had never been a dear old lady, not by the wildest stretch of imagination.

'They live quietly though, I suppose,' Martha said. 'Keep to themselves pretty much?'

'When they first come, they did,' the woman said. 'Seemed a bit nervous as it were, never having lived in the country before. They thought people might be – you know – stand-offish, like they are in the towns. Miss Sutcliffe, she'd say to me when I'd come over to sweep them through or bring a cake and that: "I always thought the country people treated you like a foreigner till you'd been there five years." Well, I've heard that about places like the West country, where they're backward, but we're very go-ahead here, though you might not think it. We're up to all sorts of enterprises, and the old ladies got pulled into things along with everyone else. Now they're in everything that goes on. Miss Sutcliffe, she's the vice-president of the Women's Institute, and goes to all the county meetings, and Mrs Vulliamy has the children for Sunday school. They're busy all the time. They're both on the committee to raise funds to restore the old wool market, and Miss Sutcliffe has been the one who's had all the say with the authorities about getting a school bus for the kids. She's always in and out of Cambridge. Has her name down for the Rural Council. I hope she gets it.'

When she got back to London, Martha ran up her front steps with her key in her hand, bursting to tell Anne the extraordinary news; but Anne opened the door before she could put the key in the lock, and flooded her with words before she could open her mouth.

'They've been here! The aunts came! They stayed two hours and I gave them lunch. Don't be angry; I used the chicken. But they were so adorable. Absolutely different. You wouldn't believe it.'

'I would,' Martha said. 'I talked to the woman who lives opposite them in the village, and it didn't sound as if she was talking about the same two people we knew.'

'I know. Isn't it fantastic? But they're not the same people. They're quite different.'

'What happened? Take a breath and tell me.'

'Well, it seems that they got claustrophobia living at the Camberley Hotel, because people kept dying, and Aunt Jessie had a fight with the night porter because he wouldn't bring her soda water when she couldn't sleep. They suddenly decided to go to the country – why this particular village, or that bungalow, don't ask me, because I don't believe they knew themselves. I think some estate agent got hold of them, and they went to look

361

at a crumbling old picturesque rectory he couldn't unship on to anyone else, and they suddenly got discouraged with decay and bought the most modern thing they could see.'

'But they're happy there. I could hardly believe it when the woman told me. It doesn't seem like their kind of place at all, but according to her they're the life and soul of the village.'

Anne laughed. 'Aunt Jessie had two sherries and told me: "We've realized we can't hide away from life. The country people have taught us something. Taught us how to take part." And poor Celie cried all over me and said why hadn't I told them years ago that it was possible to live like this, and now it was almost too late. So then they got into one of their arguments – oh yes, they still do that. Sign of good health – and old Jess said that she for one intended to live another fifteen years at least, if only to see some cutting she's managed to root grow into a tree and bear blossom. Imagine.'

They stared at each other. 'If you could *see* the bungalow,' Martha said. 'It just – it just isn't them. It's a good thing they've got old Pringle safely stashed away. She'd die if she had to sleep on the ground floor.'

'But they love it. They told me, in great surprise, that they'd never known that houses were built so conveniently. Well, I mean – after Park Lodge. They eat in the kitchen!' Anne went into peals of laughter, and Martha looked at her sharply.

'You've had a drink.'

'No, I haven't. I don't need it. I'm drunk on happiness. You haven't asked me yet why they came here.' On the white face under the black hair was a closed, curving smile, like a self-satisfied badger.

'To tell you what they've discovered about life?'

'That, but more. They've only just got the payment on Park Lodge, even though it was pulled down long ago and is half-way to being a school by now. They've been fighting it with the Lands Tribunal all this time. Maurice Davenport has been helping them, because he'll do anything to get the better of a government department, and finally – this is the only thing he's achieved since his poor old Society folded – he's got them an excellent price. But now they say – a bit damping for Maurice, but he probably enjoyed the fight for its own sake – that they don't need it, because the bungalow was fairly cheap and it doesn't cost much to live there, and so –'

'And so?' Martha knew it from Anne's face.

'They're giving me half the money.'

'Oh, my darling one,' Martha said. 'My darling.'

'And more. They threw out a diffident suggestion that unless I was set on living in London, I might buy a little house near them. "You ought to try the simple life," they said eagerly, like pioneers. If they could have seen that waterfront shack in Connecticut where I was this time last year! But Aunt Jessie is hand in glove with local government in Cambridge, and she thinks she can get me a job of some kind if I take a refresher course on my typing. "And stay off the bottle," she said to me very sternly. Aunt C plucked at her sleeve and said: "Oh, Jessie, don't," and I just sat there opening and shutting my mouth like a fish. How did she know? I was sober as a morris dancer that dreadful morning we went to the Camberley Hotel, and I know you've never told them. How could she possibly know?'

'Guessing perhaps? Even when we were children, they always had their mysterious ways of knowing things that no one told them.'

'They know more than we think,' Anne said solemnly, and Martha's heart gave a cold lurch as she suddenly recognized the familiar slight slackening of the mouth, and knew that Anne had lied to her about not having a drink. 'Let me tell you this. Those old girls know more than we think.'

*

'It's the last night at the Lion,' Guy said. 'I think we ought to go.'

'To prod at the body with our foot? I think that's morbid.'

'Oh, come on. What's the matter with you, Martha? You're the one who's morbid.'

'But I hate it so. I hate to see all these places go. A whole corner of the Scotneys and those lovely chestnut trees that used to drip blossom on to the pavement. Slade's and Crumper's and the Prescott Hotel where they had the fire and I saw the woman jump out of the window. That shop that never had a name, where the old lady used to give me free sherbert, and the cat sat in the biscuit tins. The Square – I once found a wild strawberry in the rock garden where we weren't allowed to go, and Maimie Fulton's dog was buried there, under the place where all those bulldozers are parked in the mud. It just never stops. Every time I go out, another irreplaceable thing is gone.'

'You can't stop it by staying at home and wailing,' Guy had been surfeited of reminiscence long ago. 'Shall I call Mrs Pellew, or will you?'

'Mrs Pellew has gone,' Martha said hollowly. 'Her road is blocked off at one end, and since she can't get across to the shops she likes, she's gone to live with her daughter and the beast in human shape.'

'Well, ask Bessie to come upstairs. Put some food out for her, and tell her she can play the hi-fi. We needn't be long. But I would just like to say good-bye to the old boozer and have a lot of half-price drinks and get sentimental.'

'I thought I was the one who was sentimental,' Martha said, thinking that perhaps after all he did not mind about that.

'Yes. I want to see what it feels like to cry for things you never thought of loving until someone knocked them down.'

'That's unfair!' Martha cried. 'I have loved all these things, always. They're part of my life.'

'Part of my life . . . part of my life. . . .' Guy put his hands to his head, with the suggestion that if he were less civil, he would have put them over his ears. 'But that wasn't the only reason they existed. They had a life of their own. You never see that. You think the sole purpose of a square half mile of the Cottie was to contribute to the pattern of life of Martha Banning, née Grant. Née egotist,' he said, and went down to the basement flat to wheedle Bessie.

It was still possible for these frightening chasms to yawn suddenly between them. Martha had thought that it would never happen any more after Anne left, that everything would be all right. With the bone of contention withdrawn, the atmosphere of the house was gratefully easier, although the children sometimes said: 'I miss old Anne, isn't that odd? At least she could play the piano.' Now that Anne was in the hotel in Cambridge, looking for a house – and was even that going to be all right? There seemed to be a perilous lot of parties and no sign of a job – Martha and Guy should have got back to where they had been before she came.

But perhaps they never would. Perhaps if you had gone through a time of strain and dissension, you could never quite go back after the strain had been eased and the dissension removed.

Martha felt sad when she left the house, but sadder still when they got to the dying old Lion, which was going down roaring in a riot of drink and back-thumping conviviality.

Jack and Nancy, who were going to a lively pub at Windsor and were not really sorry to leave the shabby old beer palace, were working like whirlwinds behind the bar to serve out an appropriate sentiment along with the half-price drinks. There was a big crowd. Most of the regulars were there, and a lot of strangers had come in to see the old landmark breathe its beery last, and a reporter and a cameraman were holding an unwilling man down at the upright piano, and trying to find an old lady to sing *She was a dear little dickie bird* to satisfy their readers that the great heart of cockney London still beat in traditional style.

Watching Guy at the bar among the crowd who were trying to get drinks, Martha saw the long back of a tall narrow man uncomfortably wedged on a stool with his hands protectively round his glass. It was Robert P. V. Peregrine, the Press Officer, and all her disjointed anxiety and sadness for Anne, for Guy, for herself, for Cottingham Park, fused together in an unbearable memory of the night when he had sat there and turned to her and said: '*Odd, isn't it, how the silliest rumours invariably turn out to be true?*' and she had known that timeless moment of suspended existence and thought: '*That was when it all began.*'

Guy saw Mr Peregrine too, and when he came back with the drinks, he brought him to Martha out of the crowd. There was nowhere to sit and not much room to stand, so they stood close together by the fireplace and looked at each other.

'Strange, that we should meet again in the same place, Mrs Banning,' Mr Peregrine said, the black moustache tilting sideways to the crooked smile that was half shy, half urbane.

'Why have you come here?' Martha said rudely. 'To gloat over the corpse?' and Guy, who had been watching the cameraman, jerked back his head in surprise at the bitterness of her voice.

'It isn't my fault,' Robert P. V. said, standing there with his speckless waistcoat concave and his polished shoes ranged parallel, 'any more than it was my fault the first time we met, and you attacked me.'

'We were rude, I expect,' Guy said. 'I'm sorry. It was a bad shock, you know, suddenly hearing about the new road. My wife hasn't got over it yet. In fact she feels worse about it now than she did then.'

Martha said nothing. Guy was trying to be nice to her, but she could not summon any small talk. Her sadness hung on her like lead, and although she had drunk quickly to lighten it, the whisky had only weighted it more heavily.

'You think it bad taste of me to come tonight?' Mr Peregrine said quickly, as if he were anxious to get at the trouble. 'But I really like this place, you know, and the whole neighbourhood incidentally. My wife and I – we might have come to live here if we'd discovered it before it started to disappear. However,' he said, as Martha remained glum, 'you won't believe that, perhaps, so I'll tell you the other half of the truth, which is that I had to come to see if there would be any kind of story I could feed out to the Press.'

'Headline:' Martha stretched her mouth in a smile. ' "When they called Time at the Lion for the last time. The passing of a beloved old institution." So you'll give out little stories about all these fools swilling in here tonight as hard as they can go because the drinks are cheap, and sobbing into their beer at the death of a tradition they never knew existed. Look at Jack and Nancy. They're delighted to shut up this cumbersome place and run off to their juke box and stainless steel beer handles.'

'Don't you credit any of them with any genuine feelings then?' Mr Peregrine asked, drawing down his lips in concern for her scorn.

'I don't know,' she said, not wanting to talk any more. 'Go and ask them, if that's what you came for.'

'On me,' said Mr Peregrine courteously, and took her empty glass and Guy's.

'You were terribly rude to him,' Guy said as soon as he had turned away. 'That's not like you. I was embarrassed. That's not like me either.'

'I couldn't help it. People like that are so – so remote and callous. Ever since I saw him, I've felt so awful, remembering how we met him here that night and how I felt then.'

'Why take it out on him? He's not callous. He's one of the few human civil servants at large. They lock up most of the reasonable ones in case they should let down the side. What's the matter with you, love? You're impossible tonight.'

'I know. I know I am.' Martha bent her head because tears were coming into her eyes, and the roar of voices and laughter and the jangle of the deliberately untuned piano and the shouts pounded on her ears like a merciless sea. 'I don't know what's the matter with me. I feel miserable.'

A man was standing on a table in the corner pretending to auction off the contents of the bar. No one was taking much notice of him, but he continued to bawl: 'For this beautiful rococco mirror – 'ow much am I bid?' until his voice was drowned in a rise of song from a group who had finally been persuaded to sing round the piano.

The cameraman, walking backwards, knocked against Martha, took her arm and pushed her forward. 'Come on, madam, get in the group. Let's get a nice nostalgic picture.'

She shook off his hand and began to push her way towards the door. Guy struggled after her. 'I want to go,' she said across the shoulders of three animated women in hats, who took no notice.

'You can't. He's getting drinks.'

'You stay.'

'No, you fool.' One of the women did turn her head then, and gave him a long, thoughtful glance. 'All right. Wait for me. I'll explain.'

When Martha reached the door, she looked back once more with a curious timidity into the crowded, sour, boisterous saloon. Guy had reached Robert Peregrine, and he had turned with the three drinks wedged between his hands and was looking at Martha with a face of such puzzled pity that she let out a sob and a man said: 'Watch your step, dear. It's worse when you get out in the air,' and she pushed blindly out of the door as a cackle of laughter exploded behind her.

Coming home on the Underground two days later, the depression was still with Martha, shackling her like a disease. A new station was being built farther down, but the old Park Road station was still open, although all the shops in that block had gone, and the blackened brownstone slabs of the top part of the station along with them. The ticket office was a temporary underground affair, and the grieving lift brought you up into a short passage to the road, walled and roofed with corrugated iron and wet and dirty underfoot.

You could still walk down Park Road from the old station to West Hill corner, but it was not Park Road any more. It was beginning to be like pictures of Berlin after the war, and you could almost expect to smell dead bodies under the rubble that had once been the bakery and the heap of rotting timbers that had been 'Secondhand Clothes. Misfits. Uniforms. Waiters. Weddings. Riding Clothes Bought and Sold.'

Although the secondhand clothes shop was no loss to the community, for no one was ever seen going in or out, it was a great loss to Martha. In a changing Park Road it had always stayed the same, nothing ever sold out of its crowded windows. The uniforms and tropical outfits and beetle-back coats and D. H. Lawrence riding habits and the hunting boots which Martha had once coveted had been there so long that they might have crumbled into dust like an ancient corpse in a cave if they were disturbed. What had become of them when the shop came down? Martha had been in the country when it happened. Were they salvaged reverently, or had they been laid to rest among the dry rot and dead cockroaches which descended on them from the mouldering apartments above the shop?

Round the corner into West Hill, most of the Rising Sun was gone already, and with it the courtyard archway and the old woman who had sat beneath it with her cans of flowers and the bulb sprinkler that Martha had given her one winter when she saw her throwing water over the blossoms with a chilblained hand. The old lady had always been so certain that someone would look after her, but since she had no shop, there would be no compensation and no resettlement for her. Even after she learned this, she had continued to sit and smile at nothing, until one day she disappeared, leaving behind her rusted cans and her three tiered stand which could still be seen lying on its back beside an upturned bathtub on a pile of broken bricks.

Where had she gone? No one knew. Mrs Angel at the newspaper kiosk, which was still standing shakily two doors down like a disappointing mirage in a desert, neither knew nor cared.

'I have my own troubles to think about, Mrs Banting,' she had admonished sharply when Martha asked about the flower woman. 'With havoc all about me, the dust and vibration have all but ruined my hard stock.'

'I thought you were going months ago,' Martha had said. 'You always told me that you were going to go while the going was good.'

'I'll thank you not to put words into my mouth,' Mrs Angel hectored. 'What I said and what you may think I said are two very different things, as I'll challenge anyone to deny. People are still using this pavement, aren't they?'

Mrs Angel's questions were so rhetorical that you could seldom bring yourself to answer them, but when Martha said nothing, Mrs Angel pounded it home. 'Can you stand there, Mrs Banting, in the cold light of day, and try to tell me that people are not still using this pavement? Well then.' She stood back, swanning her stringy neck in the triumph of winning a shattering point. 'Well then, who is going to serve the public if we don't stick to our posts until the bugle sounds retreat? No sir,' she said uncivilly to a diffident man who had been waiting for a chance to ask his question. 'We don't sell the *New York Times*. Why should we?'

Although she needed cigarettes, Martha did not stop at Mrs Angel's shop today. With the hangover of the Lion's obsequies still enfeebling her, she was not equal to it. Ahead of her, an old truck, sagging over one wheel at the back, was standing outside Zlotnik's furniture shop like an overdriven horse. Behind it, like a pack donkey, young Zlotnik's venerable Morris ten, its doors held shut with wire, had a legless Empire sofa and a rolled carpet lashed to its long-suffering roof.

As Martha went by, Zlotnik junior came staggering out of the shop – Martha had never seen its door open before – wearing a small brocaded chair on his head like a turban, with an unidentifiable wrought iron object in his arms, and a brass-bound chest, green and crusted as if it had been under the sea for years.

At the kerb, he set down the chest and took the chair from his head. 'Moving out,' he said with cheerful redundance.

'Are you taking everything?'

'Just the things we like.' He waved a hand at the mound of indescribable junk which teetered on the lorry. 'We'll let the rest go to a dealer. The Council – pardon me.' He spat into the gutter (his father would have done it on the pavement) – 'offered to compensate us for trade fixtures and fittings. We haven't none of them, so we tried to make them buy out our whole stock. Laugh! You should have seen the man's face, shouldn't she, Dad?'

What had seemed out of the corner of Martha's eye to be a piece of junk falling off the lorry was revealed as Zlotnik senior dropping nimbly down from the pile. He dusted his hands. 'The Council' – he spat on the pavement – 'I wanted they should re-establish us in one of them smart little stores under the flats on the new estate.'

'Neat,' said young Zlotnik. 'We'd have done good business. But they told us – ahem!' He whipped a baggy cap out of his pocket and slapped it on his head like a vaudeville impersonator. 'So sorry, Mr Zlotnik sir, I'm afraid your business is not quite – ahem.'

'Where are you going then?'

'Shoreditch.' He removed the cap to speak normally. 'Dad has a cousin in the trade there.'

'I shall miss you very much,' Martha said. They had not been there when she was a child, and yet it was hard to remember a time when they were not sitting out on the pavement on their broken furniture, the father and son, exchanging amiable insults with passers-by.

'Fortunes of war. Don't let's cry about it,' young Zlotnik said briskly and hurled the long piece of wrought iron sportingly to the top of the lorry; but his father came close to Martha, and she saw that his blue eyes were moist and his lip trembling under the ragged white moustache.

'Thank you, my dear,' he said. 'We'll miss you too, me and the boy. I want you to take something, for a *pamiatka*.' He dug in the pocket of his coat and put into Martha's hand an exquisite little china figure of a child with a rose, delicately painted, unchipped, perfect.

'Oh no.' She held it out to him. 'I couldn't. It must be very valuable.'

'That's why it is for you.' He took her hand and closed her fingers gently round the little figure.

In a side street off West Hill, abandoned and half demolished, a giant machine was tearing up the old roadway. Hurrying down the hill with the china child in her hand and an ache at the back of her eyes, Martha saw the teeth of the machine bite off a chunk of macadam and spit it out on one side with a swing of its pre-historic head. As she watched it turn back to bite again, her teeth felt dry and jagged and the nerves jumped to an actual pain at the phantasy of some monstrous warlord who forced her, naked, on hands and knees in chains, to bite up the road with her own teeth.

When she reached home, she met Theresa waiting for her like a one-man dog in the hall, and bent to lay her aching head against the child's ingenuous yellow hair.

'What's the matter?' Guy found her there, for Terry had not moved away from the pleasure of holding her mother close.

'I saw Zlotnik and son moving.' Martha stood up and showed him the beautiful little figure. She was afraid that he was going to say: 'That's nothing to cry about,' but he gave it back to her and said: 'Yes, I see, I see. I'm sorry, darling,' and Terry said practically: 'Where will you put it? Let's go and show Bernie. She'll want it, but you mustn't give it to her.'

Later that evening, Guy asked suddenly: 'Do you want to go away?'

'From this house?'

He nodded, and when she did not answer, he went on: 'I know how you feel about what's happening here, and it isn't going to get any better. When the ruins that distress you now are cleared away and the new road is finished, it will always be there, you know. Down at the end of Armstrong Avenue behind a wire fence like a jail; noisy and ugly, all day and all night.'

'It isn't that,' Martha said. 'It's because you and I have been fighting here, that's what you mean. Perhaps this house is no good for us any more. We've spoiled it.'

'Do you want to move?'

'I don't know. . . . I don't know. Is it time for us to go, darling? Do you think we would be happier somewhere else?'

Part Four

GARRY BARROWS took a decarbonized cylinder head tenderly out of the kitchen sink, wrapped it in a thick wad of newspaper to save his clothes, and was gliding out of the flat when his sister Dodie called out: 'Ru-thie! Garry didn't clean the si-ink!' in the nasty singsong of her age.

'Don't sneak,' Ruth said, as automatically as if she had been Mother for all of the child's eleven years. She came out of her bedroom. 'It's all right, Garry,' she said. 'I'll do it.'

'You'll not!' Tom shouted from the front room. 'Make the boy do it. You get back in there and clean that sink, young Garry. You hear me?'

'Yes, sir.' Garry winked at Ruth. They waited in the hall to see if Tom would come out, and then Ruth whispered: 'I'll do it. You go along. You're late already, and Lilian will pout at you.' She giggled. It made her laugh when Lilian put on a Hollywood tantrum. Once Ruth had heard her say: 'I've never been so insulted in my life,' and poor Garry just stood there and gaped, although if it had been a movie, he would have said: 'Too bad, lady,' and slouched cynically out with his hat on.

Ruth reached up to see if he would kiss her good-bye, but he jerked his head away and passed a hand over the side of his hair, which was swept back in the popular D.A. haircut into a little drake's tail at the back.

Ruth came down off her toes and said to Dodie, low and threatening: 'If you tell Tom I cleaned the sink, I'll eat you. Do you remember, Garry' – she went with him to the door – 'when Dad told me to do something, and Mother would say she'd do it, and threaten you not to tell on us?'

He grunted and went out. He did not relish tales of his childhood. Half man, half boy, there could be no pleasure in reminiscing about boyhood until he was wholly a man. And he could not talk about his mother. It always surprised him that the others could, naturally, as if she had merely gone on a world trip. But Garry had been the worst age when she died. Not quite thirteen, and he had not been able to tell anyone then how it felt, and he could never tell anyone now. Not even Lilian. He could keep up fairly well with her endless prattle, and juggle the current jokes and catchphrases, but if anything serious came up, which it seldom did with Lil, because she was not that kind, his tongue felt like a boiled pudding in his mouth, cloth and string and all.

He did not do much talking tonight, after he had replaced the cylinder head in the Vespa and fetched Lil and run her up to the Community Centre, leaning hard over on the corners like a yacht race. There was a dance on, and he did not dance, although he could click his fingers and jerk his head and hips as if he were the soul of swing. He sat round the wall with the other Sultry Sultans, watching the girls jiving together with dedicated faces. There were not many boys on the floor. They preferred to sit and look broody and sexy, and pretend to be beamed on the girls' legs and the contents of their sweaters. No one would believe it, Garry knew, but Lil had never taken off her sweater with him, or even let him pull it up. She looked like a hot number, but in a dark doorway, or in the cinema, she was just as nervous as Garry, and almost as inexpert.

After a while, Lilian came over to him with her heavily pencilled brows drawn thunderously together across her small blunt nose. 'I've laddered my stocking,' she said crossly. 'That's finished it for me.'

'It doesn't show.' He leered in the approved fashion. 'Your legs look all right to me.'

'You know I can't stand ladders!' She was the petulant young heiress, swearing at her maid. 'It's made me nervous, having that happen. Let's go.'

When Lilian was 'nervous' there was not much to do but fall in with whatever she wanted. The weapon of her nerves was always successful with Garry, although it had no effect at home, where her father would offer the flat of his hand as a cure.

On the way out of the Centre, they passed the open door of one of the rooms that was used for parties and club meetings. If you belonged to one of the clubs, you could have your wedding reception there, as long as you provided the beer and food. There was the fag end of a wedding going on now, and Garry and Lilian paused at the side of the doorway, for they talked sometimes about getting married, although because they were so young and so poor, it seemed almost as far off as getting old.

There were about twenty people in the room, the women with

374

flowers pinned upside down and the men with a single carnation wrapped in foil round the long stem. Two of the women wore silver wreaths. That would be the bride and bridesmaid.

'Look!' Lilian clutched Garry's arm, as the smallest one moved to cross the room with a crazy, hip-tilting walk. Below her bright cotton dress she was wearing built-up boots, her feet turned out at impossible angles like a mutilated doll.

A man standing near the door turned at Lilian's whisper, and saw them staring. 'Gate-crashers eh?' he said amiably. 'Come on in and drink a toast to the happy couple.'

Garry and Lilian looked at each other. She was thinking of her laddered stockings. He was thinking of his promise to Ruth not to take a drink until he was eighteen.

'Come on, kids,' the jolly man said. 'Just a family party. Don't be shy.'

Garry felt his ears and hands growing big, but Lilian said: 'I don't mind' in her best social manner, and the man put an arm round her and drew her into the room.

Lilian accepted a lemon squash, and Garry took a beer because he had not the courage to refuse, and they were taken by the jolly man, who was Uncle Wally, to meet the bride and groom. When they saw that the bride was the girl with the boots and the crazy walk, Garry was afraid that Lilian would giggle or stare or otherwise disgrace them both; but the bride was so sweet and un-ashamedly happy, with confetti on her crooked shoulders and in her dry red hair, that Lilian was able to pull herself together, with Garry standing close behind her for his own protection.

The bridegroom looked ordinary enough – how *could* he? thought Garry, who was afraid of cripples, and didn't even like to go with Ruth when Mrs Bott let her wheel young Kenny out. But when they were introduced to him, he only nodded and smiled, and the bride said quite happily: 'He's deaf and dumb.'

They did not say anything. What could be said? Fancy that ... That's nice ... too bad. Garry gave the words a trial run in his mind, but did not bring them out; so the newlyweds told them, in a three-sided conversation translated to and from sign language, that they had met at the Outlook Club, which was a social group for handicapped people. 'Though it's more like a marriage bureau than a club. This is the third marriage we've had this year.'

Everyone was very nice to Garry and Lil, and although the

party was nearly over and there was not much food left, they were urged to finish what there was, and Garry was made to finish his beer, although he found it as hard to get down as porridge. There was some dancing at the other end of the room, where the bride's family and the bridegroom's mother, a huge glistening woman who had not troubled to wash her hair for her son's wedding, were performing all the hoary old numbers. Uncle Wally whirled Lilian away with his elbows squared like jug handles. *Knees up Mother Brown*, for crying out loud! Garry watched for Lil's face as she came round, thinking it would be dead pan to show Uncle Wally that it stank, but she was laughing and kicking her pretty laddered legs and giving the old buster the time of his life.

Everyone was dancing except Garry and the bride. Standing by her, watching Lil as proudly as the bride was watching her husband, Garry felt ashamed that he had scoffed in his mind about the dancing, and that he had thought at first, when he saw who had got married: Call this a wedding? What a laugh.

Presently Don Harper came in in his crested blazer and slapped the groom on the back and kissed the bride and asked them if they were going to keep the party going all night. There was some suggestive laughter, led by Uncle Wally, but the bridegroom's mother quelled him with a look, and everyone started to say good-bye a dozen times over, and Uncle Wally lifted all the beer bottles to make sure they were empty.

The newlyweds were going to a holiday camp for a week. As he shook hands awkwardly with them, Garry began to think about what they would do in the narrow bed in the little painted cabin. It made him feel queer, and he dropped his eyes and shuffled his feet, wishing Lil would cut short the social gush. She was overdoing it now.

It was too late now to go to a café for a cup of tea to take the beer off his breath in case Ruth was waiting up, so they rode home down the dark dirty hill, Lil's arms clutching his waist, her breath warm on the back of his neck. That was one of the many good things about owning a scooter. When a girl rode with you she had to hold you like this, even when she was angry with you, if she didn't want to fall off or walk home.

Lil was not angry tonight. Her eyes were dreamy in her pale night face as he walked with her across the inner court to the back entrance of Drake House, which was her block. She walked close to him, hip to hip, thigh rubbing thigh, and he pulled her into the covered passage between the courtyard and the street, pushed her against the wall and moved in to kiss her.

'I say, Lil.' He raised his head. There was always the problem of getting enough breath, which he supposed he would solve in time. 'Those two. That girl with the funny legs. Could they – could she – I mean, could they do it like other people?'

She pretended to be shocked, but she wasn't. She was rather glad, because he usually would not talk about sex. 'You never should have had that beer,' she said contentedly, staring at him with her eyes dark and soft and her hair all cloudy against the brick wall.

'No use getting married if you couldn't, I suppose,' he went on expansively, pleased with the idea of himself as a daring inebriate. 'That's why people get married, isn't it, Lil? So they can do it every night and no one to say anything.' He pressed his body against hers and could feel her response, half scared: but instead of scaring him too, as it usually did, it made him feel strong and bold. Must be the beer. Ruth had her nerve to say it would be bad for him!

'Listen, Lil,' he whispered urgently. 'When we get married, we can – we can –' He thought of the cabin at the holiday camp. He did not think of a rough and tumble, but of the two of them just lying there close and peaceful, with the moon making squares on the blanket.

'Oh, God –' He moved his hands, kneading her arms, crushing her. He had not known he was so strong. 'If there was only somewhere we could go. It's not fair. It's not fair! Other people have cars. They have their own place. They can lie down together, like –'

'Oh no, we mustn't. Garry, no. You're hurting me.'

'I wouldn't do anything, honest.' The strength was tenderness now. 'I just want to lie close to you and hold you, like people do when they're married. Just lie together in the dark.'

She sighed and bent her sweet-smelling head to his shoulder. 'Let's go out on the grass there, behind the sheds,' he whispered. 'No one will see us. Let's go and lie down for a little while and be like husband and wife.'

'Just play at it, you mean?' She raised her head to look at him.

'That's right.' She would go along with most things if they were presented to her as play acting.

But this wasn't play. This was real. In the shadow behind the sheds, he took off his jacket and laid it on the grubby London grass. She smiled with pleasure at the gentlemanly gesture and lay down gracefully, and he dropped down beside her and held her. Not kissing her, not moving his hands; just holding her and wanting to lie like that for ever.

Far above them, the craggy roof of the flats reeled through the bright night sky, and they lay in silent wonder below and knew that they were in love.

They did not say anything. They had never spoken of love before. You didn't when you were going steady. You just – went steady, because everyone else did, and it saved the trouble of playing the field. They did not speak of it now. They did not need to, and what few slick words they had to talk of love would have dragged it down from the immensity of the sailing sky.

'This summer,' Garry said dreamily, 'if that old robber gives me my holiday, why couldn't we –'

Lilian was on her feet in a second, flattening herself against the shed. 'She saw us! A woman went by over there. She saw us.'

'So what? We weren't doing anything wrong.' Useless to try to make her lie down again. She was nervous now. 'Take it easy, Lil. There's no harm done. Even if she thought – whatever she thought, she couldn't have seen who it was.'

Mrs Bott had not seen who it was, but she made an optimistic guess, and waited three steps up the stairs at the side of the lift at her end of Collingwood House. Her luck was in. She had not been there five minutes before young Garry Barrows, with his coat over his arm, came wandering through the inner entrance like a moonstruck tomcat, and pressed the button for the lift.

Next day, when Frankie was at school and Kenny settled in his chair on the little balcony in the sun, Mrs Bott did two things.

First she sat down and wrote in pencil one of her anonymous notes to Lilian's mother, and went smiling like a hallowe'en pumpkin down in the lift to post it in the box on the corner.

Secondly, after threatening Kenny with exotic tortures if he got talking to that nigger woman whose balcony was across the corner (she was much less kind to him when they were alone), she went along the balcony and knocked with the heavy hand of doom on the door of No. 54.

The boy Spud opened the door, peering at her impudently

378

through a wing of yellow hair. That child ought to be at school. They claimed he was not yet five, but Mrs Bott thought otherwise, even though he talked so badly. That was some rotten maniac streak in the family coming out.

'Where's your big sister?' She did not bother to smile or call him Dear.

'Wan er ay-er,' he said. 'Spud wattsa, biby, see?' and trotted back to the front room where two babies in crawlers were screaming in each other's faces on the floor. Mad, that's what these mothers were. Mad and feckless to leave their children in a place like this. Mrs Bott advanced through the hall towards the sitting-room, emboldened by the idea of finding some crying scandal she could report to the N.S.P.C.C.

Ruth came out of the bathroom. She had washed her hair, and was brushing it now to dry it. Soft and silky, it hung to her shoulders and irritated Mrs Bott by its beauty.

'Oh, it's you.' Ruth straightened her head and stopped the stroking movement of the brush. 'Did you want to see me?'

'I did,' said Mrs Bott. 'It's not very pleasant, I'm afraid, but I feel it's my duty as a neighbour, for your own good, to tell you what I know.'

'Oh dear. Wait.' Ruth called to Spud to take care of the babies, shut the sitting-room door and asked Mrs Bott to come into the kitchen.

The tiny kitchen – more like glorified cupboards they were, Mrs Bott had often complained to the lady who came for the rent, as if the kitchen in her last residence had been anything more than a grease-spattered corner of the two-roomed lodging – shone like a gay dairy. Red and white check curtains and the stove like new, a military line of hand-painted canisters along the counter, and all the cupboard doors neatly closed, giving rise to the thought: What has she got to hide then?

'Will you sit down?' Ruth put her hands on the back of a chair.

'I'll say what I 'ave to say standing up, thank you.' Mrs Bott folded her arms and told Ruth whom she had seen last night, and in fairly plain language, what she knew they were doing.

Ruth had gone white. 'I don't believe it,' she said, and her knuckles were white from gripping the chair.

Mrs Bott shrugged her fat-embossed shoulders. 'Believe it or not,' she said. 'It's all one to me. I'm only telling you what's

379

true. Disgusting. Them two young codlins out in the open like that for anyone to see. It's a disgrace to the flats, and if you can't undertake to keep that bad boy under control, I'll take it up with the Community Association and blacken your names so thick you couldn't get 'em clean with hearthstone.'

'He's not a bad boy!'

'I say 'e is,' said Mrs Bott, encouraged by the glint of tears in the mild brown eyes. 'And I say as I've said all along, it's wrong to let you kids live 'ere all alone like this. I knew there'd be trouble. It never should have been allowed, and I've half a mind to go to the Council myself and tell them so. With all the decent families on the list for flats, they –'

'You keep your nose out of our business,' Ruth said bravely, although her voice and mouth were trembling. 'It's not true about Garry. I don't want to hear any more. I don't believe it. Please go away and leave me alone!' She was really crying now, pushing the backs of her hands in her eyes like a child; but she was not too much a child to understand the parting shot that Mrs Bott delivered as she went into the hall, past the inquisitive face of Spud peering like a goblin round the crack of the door.

'If you've any sense, you'll get the girl's parents to 'ave 'er examined. Take 'er to a doctor. Then we'll see 'oo's right and 'oo's wrong. Not,' she added as she opened the front door, 'that you could tell much from that at this late date. That girl as been bad ever since she knew what it was for, as I've always told you.'

When Garry came home for lunch, Ruth did not say anything to him. She wanted to talk to Tom first. She was sick with fear all day, but the most terrible thing was that when Tom came home, he did not at once declare that he did not believe it.

'Surely you don't think it's true?' She felt like screaming at him, but they had to talk low, for the walls of the flat were thin and the ears of Spud and Dodie were eager.

'It's possible, that's all I said.' Tom's voice was weary. 'It's possible. Boys of that age – well, you know what they're like round here.'

'But not Garry! He's different. He puts on airs, but he's only a child.'

'He's older than you, Ruthie.'

'I feel ten years older than him. Sixty years older now. Oh, Tom, I feel a hundred.' She sat down on the bed and wept. 'I

380

knew we shouldn't let him go with Lilian. I told you she wasn't the right type, and now look what's happened.'

'Hold on, kid. We don't know yet what has happened. It may not have been them she saw. Don't get so worked up that you believe everything that old bitch tells you. Look, I'll talk to Garry, O.K.? Try and get the truth out of him, and by God, if I think he's been fooling around, I'll take off my belt and thrash him, teenager or no teenager.'

'Don't be hard on him!' She jumped up and held on to his arm.

'You sound like your mother.' Tom laughed without smiling. 'When I was bad, she used to complain to Dad about me, and then when she'd got him all worked up, she'd cry: "Don't hurt the boy." '

When Garry came home late that evening, Tom took him into the little bedroom they shared, and Ruth turned the television up loud, so that she could not accuse herself of eavesdropping.

The next morning, Garry left for work earlier than usual. Ruth tried to ask him something, but he would not talk to her. She too. She was the one who had told Tom. All of them were against him. Just when he had found Lilian – really found her – in that magical closeness under the tilting cliff of brick and stone, everyone was trying to get them apart.

Jealousy, he thought in the lift. Ruth didn't know how to get a boy. Tom always said he hadn't time to find a girl, to cover the truth that none of the skirts would look at him with those thick cheaters and that solemn face.

When he reached the ground, he went quickly across the inner courtyard among the shop and office workers – the factory people had gone long ago – and waited by the wall on the other side of Drake House, where Lilian would pass on her way to the bus. When she came, in a blue pleated skirt and a white sweater and her hair pulled back in a pony tail, he grabbed her arm and walked with her, matching his crêpe-soled step to her tapping heels.

'It was Mrs Bott,' he said. 'It was her saw us by the sheds. She spoke to Ruth, and Tom near went off his nut.'

'So it was her sent that letter. I might have known it.' You didn't have to live in Collingwood House to know about Mrs Bott. Everyone in the whole estate of Nelson Court knew what she was like.

'What letter?'

'To Mum. It was in the post this morning. They started in on me, both of them. I didn't get any breakfast. If I hadn't had to go to the shop, they'd be at it still.'

'I got it last night. Tom asked me right out if we'd been there – where she saw us. Don't ask me why, but I can't lie to him. I – he stares at me with those four eyes, like brain washing. I just can't. But when I told him we did nothing wrong, then he thought I *was* lying.'

'Me too.' Lilian looked at him, and he saw that she had hastily tried to cover the traces of tears. There was powder on her lashes over the mascara. 'Did he tell you we weren't to see each other?'

He nodded. 'And you?'

She nodded. Suddenly he pulled her round a corner into a side street and hurried her away from the crowd headed for the buses and trains.

'Where are we going? I'll be late for work.'

'You'll be worse than that. You won't be there. Nor will I. We'll run away. That'll show them. We'll elope, like the rich tarts do. Go to Gretna. I'll sneak back and get the bike.'

'Oh, Garry, we can't. I –' She stopped and looked round fearfully, as if she expected to see a posse from Nelson Court come roaring after them, headed by her parents and Mrs Bott. 'I haven't got a coat. What if it turns cold?'

He did not love her any less for being practical. He was the romantic one, the dreamer. She could be the one who looked out for details.

'I've got a little cash. And we'll work on the way. Chop wood and that. Help old ladies,' he said vaguely. 'I'll buy you anything you want. Come on, Lil.' He pulled her forward, but she hung back, frowning and biting her lip.

'Joke's over,' she said miserably. 'I've got to get to work.'

'It's not a joke.' He stood in front of her and took both her arms, right there in the street in the broad daylight, with women coming out to shake mats and a child with a broken tricycle staring at them and sucking a filthy finger. 'Listen, Lil. Last night, we – well, you know how we felt. You felt it too, didn't you?' She nodded, and stopped pulling back from him. 'I – look, we love each other, don't we? What else matters?'

'Do they really marry you at Gretna?' The adventure of it was creeping in on her.

'I don't know. We'll find out.'

'Eloping,' she said slowly. 'Eloping to Gretna Green,' and he saw the picture form behind her eyes like a scene from a film, and knew that she would go with him.

They were found two days later by a farmer in the West Riding hills, fast asleep in his barn in each other's arms. They were covered with sacks, but Lilian was shivering when she woke with a scream, and the doctor who was called to the police station said that she had a high fever.

They were sent back to London in a police car, and that was the last time they saw each other. Lilian was in hospital for two weeks with pneumonia, and when she came out, she was sent to an aunt in the country, until her parents could find another place to live.

Ruth and Tom fought a small battle with the authorities, who suddenly became too interested in Garry's welfare. When Tom went to one of the contractors and got the boy a job working full time on the new road, the welfare people were satisfied and the family were left in peace, although it would be a long time before Nelson Court stopped talking about them, or threw away the newspaper cuttings with the picture of Garry and Lilian staring out of it like bewildered children.

Flushed with triumph – for had she not prophesied all along that there would be trouble? – Mrs Bott turned to seek new scandal, and chance provided her with the greatest opportunity of her career.

Even before the excitement over Garry and Lilian had died down, Nelson Court was rocked once more, this time to the foundations, for the word that had been spoken was Murder.

There were many who agreed that it was an accident, but Mrs Bott knew it was murder, or manslaughter at the least, and said so to everyone she met that afternoon. When she had exhausted the pleasure of telling it round the flats, she went to the police station and told it there.

'I knew something like this would 'appen,' she told the detective sergeant. 'That Silverman woman should never have been allowed to have children. They sterilized them in Germany, you know, if you'll excuse my mentioning it. Only good thing that house painter ever did. If the welfare people weren't so busy poking their noses in to see 'oo's on relief that shouldn't be, they'd have taken that child away from her. Knowing what went on, as I did, I should have spoken up long ago, but I've never been one to carry tales. I mind my business and expect everyone else to mind theirs. But it is my common duty to speak, now that it as come to murder.'

'Be careful how you use words like that, Mrs Bott,' the sergeant said. 'And please don't use it before the coroner. You will be called as a witness at the inquest on Kevin Silverman.'

Mrs Bott bought a new dress, and prayed – although she did not believe in God, because she could not conceive of an arbiter more final than herself – that it would stay fine so that she would not have to wear her old coat.

The day of the inquest dawned in a grey-blue haze which lifted before breakfast was off the table to reveal a cloudless July sky with a promise of heat already beginning to shimmer on the roofs and chimneys. Perfect. Everything was going her way. Frankie was kept home from school to watch Kenny, for Mrs Bott trusted no one in the flats now, absolutely no one, with all the funny things that had been going on. Ruth Barrows would have liked to take Kenny, but she and Mrs Bott were not speaking now. That is, Mrs Bott was not speaking to her. Ruth would have relaxed the vendetta, for Kenny and Frankie's sake, and because she hated to fight even with people like Mrs Bott; but Mrs Bott, like an unscrupulous borrower who despises the benefactor he cheats, always hated her victims after the event as much as they hated her.

Mr Bott had to take a day off work to accompany his wife to the coroner's court. He wore a new tie, and she had pressed his blue serge. Although his face was wretched, from his back view they looked as if they were going off on a jaunt as they toddled off to the bus, so big and so little in their Sunday clothes.

Having watched them go from windows and balconies, the women of Collingwood House turned back to their flats, but not to housework. They turned back to cups of tea, in and out of each other's flats all morning long, discussing, speculating, telling over and over again their little bits of information, kind or catty, about Mrs Silverman, whose three-year-old twin had died of a fractured skull.

None of them had known her well. She was not a friendly person, not friendly at all, they said with the pursed mouths of the gregarious who run with the herd for their own safety. She had only been at Nelson Court a few months, and she was always busy, either out at work and pushing the twins to and from the day nursery, or toiling far into the night for the needs of her children and her demanding husband.

However, although she lived at the other end of the block, Mrs Bott claimed to know all about her. Well, she always claimed that, whether she knew or not, and made up what she didn't know. But there was something funny about this case. Too much secrecy. Mrs Silverman would not open the door to anyone after the tragedy, which was a poor way to treat neighbours who came with sympathy and with the gifts of cakes which were invariably baked at the flats whenever anything momentous happened, good or bad. Was it possible that this time Mrs Bott was not exaggerating all the way?

She was home before the lunchtime editions of the evening papers were out. Grim-faced, her feet pounding like pneumatic-dampers, she walked along the balcony with Mr Bott trailing behind like a poor relation, and as soon as the door of her flat had crashed shut, the women heard her yelling at Frankie.

It was all in the evening paper. In the early edition, with not much news yet, it started on the front page and went on inside. In the later editions, it had been put farther back in the paper; but it was all there, and in most of the morning papers too, and there wasn't a soul in Nelson Court, including the children and the groping grannies to whom it was read, who did not know it almost by heart.

There it was, the verdict. Death from misadventure, with a picture of Mrs Silverman with her hair wisping out from under a beret, trying to smile as she came out of the coroner's court. She had told her story. She would tell it many times again to herself, trying to see at exactly what point the cogs of normal life had slipped; but meanwhile, she had done what was required of her. She had stood up and told it in public. She had told how the child had irritated her beyond measure that Saturday dinner-time when she was tired and at the end of her tether already. She was always tired, and she was not well – the doctor had said she had anaemia, but she hadn't found time to go back for the injections – but she could not give up her job because her husband could not find work.

Would not, the women commented. He would not even mind the kids when she was out working for him. She had to push them a mile each way to and from the nursery at the beginning and end of her day's work.

She was devoted to her children. 'I'd do anything for them,' she told the coroner, but when the boy first knocked over the jug of milk and then would not eat his dinner, it was the last straw on the hump of the week. Without thinking – 'I never hit the children in the normal way' – she had swung her arm to smack the boy, he had ducked, fallen off the chair, and hit his head on the corner of the iron grate. When he did not move and she could not rouse him, she had called the doctor.

'When he told me Kevin was dead, I couldn't believe it. I don't know what I said to the police. I was half out of my mind. Yes, of course I loved the little boys. I had never knocked them about. My husband spanked them sometimes, but – No, sir, never. I might lose my temper when I felt so low, but I'd never illtreat a kiddy.'

The husband said much the same. He had been out when the boy died. The first he knew was when he came home and found the door on the chain and his wife carrying on. She was fond of the twins as far as he knew. Beat them? I don't think so, unless she – Of course I didn't. Bruises on the child's body – search me. Must have got them in the fall, or fighting with his brother. They were always fighting. Not identical twins, you see. The doctor had explained that. Yes, he had spanked Kevin earlier that week for bed-wetting, but just a gentle slap.

When Mrs Bott stood up in her new dress, she painted a different picture, a masterpiece of her blackening brush. No wonder there were bruises on the child. They were at them both all the time. Cursing and yelling – it would make you sick to hear the kiddies scream, but she was accustomed to minding her own business. She had seen Mrs Silverman hit the children in the playground. They were always crying and whimpering, and Mrs Bott, who was funny, but she couldn't bear to see innocent children suffer, had said many times that something ought to be done. Oh yes, everyone at the flats knew about it. It was a disgrace to the block the way those children were treated. She did not speak to Mrs Silverman herself – 'she's not my kind' – but a neighbour had passed on that when Kevin was in hospital two months ago, his mother had been heard to say that she would be glad if he never came out.

After warning her against hearsay evidence, the coroner asked her politely whether it was true that her flat was at the far end of the building from Mrs Silverman's, in the other wing. 'Very well.

And I understand that from the location of your flat it would be impossible to hear what went on behind the walls of Mrs Silverman's flat. How could you hear the angry voices and the screaming? Slapping them in the playground is nothing. Any mother might do that. How do you know there was ill treatment at home?'

'I know,' said Mrs Bott contentedly. 'I know everything that goes on at the flats.'

Told to stand down, she sat and surveyed, in caustic disbelief and with plans for future persecution, Mrs Silverman's next door neighbour, who was persuaded to raise her voice above a whisper for just long enough to tell the coroner that she had never heard any questionable sounds coming from the flat.

Within half an hour of the start of the inquest, the coroner said: 'I am perfectly satisfied. I shall record a verdict of death due to misadventure, since there is no case to be preferred for manslaughter. There was no negligence per se, beyond the understandable carelessness of an overworked mother. I do not believe there was any history of ill treatment, nor desire to hurt the child. As to the evidence to that effect – I cannot accept it. The witness who gave it was apparently actuated by malice. We have here, I believe, the local gossip and busybody, who will invent rather than say she does not know. A type of woman not peculiar to our big housing estates. She has always been found wherever people live together. You will find her in the Bible with a stone in her hand – for I have never believed that the accusers of the woman taken in adultery were all men – and I need not remind anyone here present of our Lord's words: *He that is without sin among you . . .*'

The coroner was well known for making quotable comments, and this one was quoted in every newspaper, and used for the headline: LOCAL BUSYBODY WITH A STONE IN HER HAND to the delight of all the tenants of Nelson Court and the bitter chagrin of Mrs Bott.

Her public rebuke marked the beginning of the end of her reign of terror. With their private thoughts corroborated in print, people were not afraid of her any more, and the younger ones sniggered at her openly, and the older ones turned their heads away and would not give her good morning, much less the time of day, so that to venture out of her flat began to be an ordeal from which even her brute egotism shrank.

387

When she was asked to resign from the Community Association, and refused, protesting still that they needed her, a special meeting was called without her and she was arbitrarily deprived of her committee membership. That was the final blow, the retribution that diminished her utterly, not only in the eyes of Nelson Court, but in her own as well.

It was shortly after this that Frankie came back into the classroom after form 3B had stampeded to the cloakroom and said: 'Do something for me, Miss?'

'If I can.' Grace looked up from her desk and pushed back her coppery hair. She was tired. She had just found out that she was going to have a baby, and although she had felt all right before, she had now begun to feel frail. 'What is it?'

'Come and see my Mum again.' He stood up boldly and looked her in the eye. She was quite shocked that he should suggest it after what his mother had said last time.

'I can't, Frankie. I don't believe she'd even let me in. Besides, it wouldn't do any good. She wouldn't listen to me before. Why should she now?'

'But she's changed, see? She's not like she was. You read about that – what the coroner said, and made 'er a laughing stock?' She nodded. He had not talked to her about it at the time, although he had come to school with his fists clenched and started three fights the day after the inquest with boys who taunted him about his mother. 'It got 'er down. She's been low ever since. Don't take no interest in nothing no more. I think she might let Kenny go. All she as to do is go and tell the doctor she's willing, and 'e'll make the arrangements about the operation and maybe getting 'im into the special school after. But we've got to get her to go there. I can't make her. She don't talk to me no more because I go in and sit with Ruth Barrows after school.' He blushed. He was growing up. Although Ruth was more than a year older, it was a practical step down from his make-believe romance with Grace, who was eleven years older. 'But she might do it for you, if you spoke to her right.'

'I daren't,' said Grace honestly. 'I'm afraid of your mother.'

'Nah.' He flapped a hand. 'She's all shut up now. A child could 'andle 'er. Even Dad talks back without getting is ear 'ole smashed in. It's pitiful to see it, in a way. Gives you the creeps. She just don't say much any more.'

Mrs Bott did not say much to Grace. And Frankie was

right: even though she had got less than her deserts, there was something almost pitiful about this elephantine tyrant suddenly shrunk to the spirit of a mouse.

She was bad-tempered still, but she did not shout and wave her gross arms about, and she did give some kind of sullen agreement that she would consider – only consider, mind – talking to that clever-dick doctor again about the operation. 'Only talking to him, mind. I shan't say Yes and I shan't say No, but since everything I do now is wrong, it seems, I suppose it don't matter what I say. They'll crucify me for it anyway.'

Taking advantage of her mood of disillusioned grievance, Grace got Frankie out of the room by pretending that she had dropped a glove on the balcony, and asked Mrs Bott quickly whether she would let the boy spend a week of his summer holiday with her and Colin in the Isle of Wight.

Mrs Bott shrugged and turned away as if she were bored to death with the whole set-up; her children, Grace, the holiday, life itself. 'I don't care,' she grunted. 'As long as you pay 'is fare.'

When Grace bent to say good-bye to Kenny, he said: 'You're a doll, Mrs Mac. I was afraid it was going to be me that had everything, and nothing for old Frank.'

Colin was not enthusiastic, although Grace reminded him that he would be out in a fishing boat most of the time, while she sat on the sands and nursed their child within her; but Frankie entered into his fifteenth year with a new vision and a new hope. He had never been away on a holiday before; he had never seen the sea; and Ruth Barrows was knitting him a white sweater to wear when he walked on the beach in the strong salt wind.

*

Maurice Davenport stood at the bay window of his study and looked through the old rounded glass at cranes and churning concrete mixers and scaffolding and bricks and barrows, and the brown muscled backs of men bare to the surprisingly hot sun swarming all over his view where Park Lodge and the trees of the old ladies' garden used to be.

The school. It was unlike the L.C.C. to do anything at speed, but this monstrosity was going up rapidly, as if they could not wait to pile insults on his disappointment.

The complete failure of the Scotney Society had been a great disappointment to him, although his brain if not his heart had

389

realized from the beginning that he was part of a lost cause. But lost causes in England did not die for lack of victories. Most of the other members, even Miss Sutcliffe and Mrs Vulliamy, the founders, had begun to tire of the Society when its hopelessness became apparent, but Mr Davenport had hung on to it, and continued to write his letters to editors – months since the philistines had published anything – and there was still a fund of subscription money in the bank with which he was going to strike a final blow for freedom if he could think of anything effective.

Even through the closed window, the hideous sounds of construction invaded his house. He had not been able to open a window on that side for months, and when they started work on the fly-over below him on the other side, he would have to live in an airtight box, suffocating slowly in the cause of peace.

What would it be like when the school was finished and the shrieking peasantry came storming up West Hill and across Park Road to occupy the conquered territory? From what he could discover of the position of the entrance, the ones who came from the north and west – and that was where most of the brutes lived – would walk right past Mr Davenport's house on their way to the school. No use trying to grow anything in the front garden. They would pick the flowers and dig up the bulbs and probably wrench all the little knobs off the tops of the stone fence posts. Morning and afternoon, he would have to shut himself away at the back of the house and stop his ears against the tumult.

'Why don't you move?' Zona always said when he grumbled to her. 'God knows, I don't care about this old ruin. I'm not here most of the time anyway.' She was living on and off with Roger at his seedy pad in Fulham. Living like brother and sister, they still claimed. They shared a bed, because there was only one bed. 'Like it's not for sex,' she told her father, who did not believe it and did not want to hear about it.

It was not for Zona that he stayed, although if he ran off to the country like Jessie and Celia, God knew what would happen to her, if the police did not put her safely away somewhere first. He stayed because he loved the house, and because he would not be driven out. If he ever moved, it would not be because the vandals had forced him away, but because he had found a place he liked better, and since that could not happen, he would stay.

He would stay and get used to the school and the Expressway, if he valued his blood pressure. He was supposed to be an intelligent man, after all. There were some who had thought so, and praised his writings highly. Intelligence should be able to adapt. Zona had been an intelligent young girl, though you would never think it now, and she had been able to adapt to all kinds of peculiarities, and to accept grubbiness that would have horrified her when she was a fastidiously coddled child. He, Maurice Davenport, would adapt to the masses. It would be wrong to sit at the back of the house with his hands over his ears. Perhaps he would in time be at this same window, beaming down on the scuffling urchins as they picked the heads off his tulips and played football with his fence knobs. But he would never get close to them. Never go out with bags of toffees, or wish them Merry Christmas as they slid by in the snow. He had never been able to understand people like that. Never tried to, come to think of it. Had he missed something?

He felt vaguely ill. Lonely too. It was Saturday morning and Winnie Leathers was out doing the shopping. He might have started to practise adapting on Mrs Holloway, with whom he rarely exchanged more than a greeting and a request not to put his books back upside down, but cleaning women led their own lives on Saturdays, it seemed.

Zona was in the Portobello market with Roger. She had gone out in a greenish leather jacket that was supposed to be black, with a putty-coloured scarf over her head to match her skin: her standard garb for stall-minding.

Mr Davenport had not been to the Portobello Road market for years. He used to wander down sometimes in the days when it was a genuine market and some of the stall-holders were still so naïve that you could pick up quite valuable oddments for almost nothing. It was quite chic to go then, before the market was discovered and everybody began to go there, and huge American cars stood chrome to chrome all down Chepstow Villas. The stallholders were not naïve any more, and many of them looked like Houndsditch and spoke like Oxford, and they all knew exactly what everything was worth, and would only bargain with you to make you think that you were getting something cheap at double its value.

He wished that Zona would come home. Even she would be better than no one. He did not feel at all well. Nothing he could put his finger on, but he had indigestion, and his breath seemed to be different. Not laboured, but noticeable. He was uncomfortably aware of the process of breathing in and breathing out. Perhaps he should go down there and find Zona and ask her to come home and stay in the house while he went to bed. He did not want to lie in bed alone tallying his respirations.

If he went to the market, he could start adapting a little, look about the shoddy crowded streets at the houses and tenements where lived the same kind of children who were going to be picking off his flowers and fence tops on their way to school. Talk to people at the stalls. Everyone in the market couldn't be like Roger. Some of them must still be the original prole, and perhaps it was not too late to start trying to see their side of things.

On the pavement near the top of the Portobello Road where the market stalls began their crazy downhill chain of copper, old clothes, gramophone records, jewellery, coffee-pots, spoons, swords, pistols, armour and odd pieces of china which might have been worth something without the chips and cracks, a man in a greasy raincoat was squatting to set out his wares. Mr Davenport stopped to watch him as he took them out of a suitcase, unwrapped the newspaper and set them out very carefully against the wall of a shop which had nothing but table legs and bundles of banisters in the window. When the suitcase was empty, the man had on display four unmatching coffee cups, one without a handle and all without saucers, a cork with a wooden Tyrolean figure on top, a broken umbrella handle shaped like a panting dog, a few cards of buttons, some unidentifiable pieces of cloth, six hideous paintings of naked women, too small even to be indecent, and a wheel with a handle on it, which looked like nothing except the remains of a primitive egg beater.

Visibly adapting, Mr Davenport stepped forward and asked the price of the umbrella handle.

'Five bob,' the man said laconically.

Good God, it wasn't worth fivepence, but Mr Davenport was not quite brave enough to say so. 'Would you take an offer for it?' He did not want the umbrella handle except for the pleasure of casting the hideous thing into the nearest rubbish bin, but he had pledged himself to try to talk to the common people, and this filthy man with the shifty eyes and the stained collarless shirt, squatting on the pavement beside his pitiful stock, was probably about as common as you could get.

392

'No,' the man said. 'Five bob. Genuine hand carved.'

Press on, Davenport. 'What's that for?' He pointed to the eggbeater wheel.

'I don't know.' The man did not even look up. 'It doesn't work.'

'Will anyone buy it?'

'How should I know? Some chap with a workshop. I sell everything.'

'Where do you get all your stuff?' Doing well, Davenport. Not only showing an interest, but actually beginning to feel one. Where would a man like this fill his suitcase with such dross, except from a rubbish heap?

'I pick it up in lots,' the man said, and perhaps he did. Impossible to believe that he would take the trouble to steal it. 'Got any more naïve questions?' Pleased with the word, he appealed to a man and a girl who had stopped to look at the naked women. 'What naïve questions he asks, don't he? He's full of naïve questions today. Just full of em.'

Rebuked, Mr Davenport went on his way. How could you talk to them if they would not respond? You could not make contact unless they did too. Perhaps they were no more anxious for it than he was.

He could still feel his breathing as he walked down the hill, but the indigestion was better. It had shifted a little and was now only a slight nagging awareness that he had a stomach. Well, now he knew he had a stomach and a pair of lungs. What other organ of his body was going to intrude itself next on his notice?

He stopped to talk to a slatternly woman in charge of a stall full of medals. She had a sign tacked up over her head: The Medal Queen. Her hands and hair were filthy, and when she saw that he was not going to buy, but only wanted to ask her where she got the medals and was it a hobby or a profitable trade, she said: 'If I had to stand here all day and answer nosey questions, how could it be profitable?' and turned to greet a feminine boy who whispered in her ear and then darted off with a theatrical wave and: 'Bless you, darling!'

Beastly woman. Maurice Davenport was not even sure whether she was a genuine prole or someone like Zona. Horrible, rude woman. He hated it all. The dirty people. The junk. The leisurely crowd who stopped and peered and fingered and jostled him back and front and both sides as he struggled through them looking for Zona. He began to feel terribly ill. He did not know whether he would get much further. He would never find her. He would fall, and these people would trample on over him, or kick him out of the way under a stall. Suddenly through a gap in the crowd he saw her, sitting listlessly behind a stall of china and glass, all hung with silver trays and teapots.

'Zona!' It was not much more than a croak, but she looked up just in time to see him with his mouth open in amazement, for he had never thought that the next obtrusive organ would be his heart, before he toppled forward into a surprisingly small heap among the Portobello feet and legs.

When Miss Sutcliffe and Mrs Vulliamy came up from Cambridgeshire with a basket of new-laid eggs and a huge bunch of flowers for Maurice Davenport, they were shocked, because they had always thought that they would die first, and now here they were in excellent health and spirits, while he . . .

They sat by the bed and made the unconvincing sounds of optimism. 'You must hurry and get well so that you can get out into this lovely weather.' 'When you're out and about again, you must come and visit us. You can sit in the garden and eat raspberries.'

When Miss Sutcliffe went out of the room to fetch water for him, she met Zona plodding up the stairs in bare feet, with cotton trousers wrinkling up her flabby calves.

'Why didn't you tell me how ill he was?' Miss Jessie demanded angrily. 'You told me on the telephone you were not worried.'

'Well, I'm not.' Zona looked calmly up from below with her pale dry mouth open and her hair like wet yarn. 'How would it help him if I were?'

'You are an unnatural daughter, Zona Davenport.'

'I always have been. Didn't you know?' Zona went on past her, hesitated at the door of her father's room, looked back at Miss Sutcliffe and then walked to her room, as if she would have gone in to her father if she had not felt compelled to shock the old ladies.

'About the money,' Miss Sutcliffe said before they left. 'The Scotney Society funds. We don't want to bother you, Maurice, but we were wondering what you planned to do with it.'

'I don't know, Jessie. To be frank, I doubt whether at this

point I even care. I had thought of using it for some kind of final gesture – a condemnation of the bureaucrats, with pictures of your house and the others that are going, to remind people always of what the vandals have destroyed.'

'But that won't bring them back,' Mrs Vulliamy said, leaning forward and looking at him with her big bird's nest head on one side. 'There are all your prints, and the pictures you gave to the Town Hall, and all your writings too, to keep the history of this little corner of London alive.'

'Don't lecture me,' he said weakly. 'I know all that. And I know that hardly anyone will ever look at the pictures or read what I've written.'

The sisters looked at each other across the bed. Celia wet her lips. 'Shall we ask him?' she asked excitedly.

'Calm down. You're red in the face. We might,' Jessie looked at him. 'He might take it better than we think.'

'Stop talking over me. Good God, anyone would think I was dead already. What is the matter with you two chicken farmers?'

'It is this,' Miss Jessie said. 'It's up to you, of course, since you are treasurer, and also the one who stuck by the Society longest, but Celia and I thought that since the battle is lost, it might be a gracious gesture in defeat to give the money to the enemy.'

'Village life has softened your brain,' Mr Davenport said testily. 'What do you mean?'

'We thought of piecing out the money to last – say five or ten years including the interest, and establishing an annual prize for a pupil at the new school who can write the best essay about the Scotneys and their history.'

If Mr Davenport could have sat up, he would have done so. 'Those brutes!' he said. 'Isn't it bad enough to have them taking over so much of what we have loved, without paying them into the bargain? They won't want it, anyway. What do the ignorant wretches care about the Scotneys?'

'But we could make them care, Maurice,' Miss Sutcliffe said eagerly. 'Some of them, at least. They'll do anything for money, even study the history of old Cottingham Park. They'll want to read what you have written. They'll ring your door bell and ask to see your prints.'

'But perhaps he won't like that,' Celia said softly.

'Of course I won't like it. I'll hate it. I dislike these people. I don't want to have anything to do with them. I've tried, but I can't be like you, inexplicably changing your whole outlook on life just because you've changed your house.'

'It wasn't inexplicable. We began to realize what we had missed. It was as simple as that.'

'For you, perhaps, but not for me. I can't. . . .' He was tossing restlessly on the bed, turning his head from side to side, his plump mottled hand banging feebly on the counterpane.

'Hush, Maurice.' Jessie stood up and took his hand to still it. 'Don't get excited. It doesn't matter. Forget about it, and we will too.'

'Forget it?' He stopped moving his head and looked up at her accusingly. 'Don't dare. It's a good idea. I like it.'

'Do you really like it, or are you just trying to humour a pair of silly old ladies so that we'll go away and leave you in peace?' Miss Jessie had known him all her life. She was not going to let him fool her, ill or well. 'I thought you said you hated it.'

'I do, but I hate myself more for hating it. Can you understand that? I envy you what you've discovered. I shall never discover it. And the tragedy is, I don't want to.'

Miss Sutcliffe and Mrs Vulliamy had planned to call the prize the Scotney Society Award, but after Maurice Davenport died, long before the school was finished and the children began to clatter past his house, they found that he had willed his collection of old local prints and all his historical notes to the Scotney Comprehensive School. When Miss Sutcliffe presented the scheme to the new headmaster, she threatened him – unnecessarily, for he did not care either way – that he would not get the prize money unless it was called The Maurice Davenport Award.

*

When it was time to tell her children that Guy was looking for a house outside London, and that they would be leaving Cottingham Park, Martha was afraid.

If they were unhappy about leaving, it would be her own fault. She had brought them up to mirror her own love for these streets and curious little shops and sudden pockets of tree-filled gardens, this patchwork of houses in tones of grey and black and dirty white. It was like a village to them, and they were a part of all its life. They had clean, desirable friends in the new painted houses in the converted streets, and hoarse ragged friends in the streets behind Armstrong Avenue where the Rise began its hopeless climb through shabbiness to squalor. Like Martha, they knew every inch of every pavement, knew everybody's dog and baby, and the fortunes and diseases of the proprietors and their relations in all the smaller shops.

Unlike Martha, they were not much disturbed by the devastation of the new road. The importance of it, and the excitement of something new to watch, the giant machines, and the masked men kneeling with sizzling torches under little round-roofed shelters where watchmen crouched like tortoises at night compensated for the passing of the chocolate shop and the doll hospital, the cheap little cinema, the square with the jungle full of wild cats and zombies.

To Martha, Cottingham Park was being destroyed. To the children, it was merely being slightly changed, and the change was stimulating. One of the cranes on the office building site was over a hundred feet high, and the driver climbed up the open shaft like a monkey on the Eiffel Tower. The crane and the bulldozers and the acetylene torches and the tumbling of bricks in clouds of ancient dust entered into their childhood to be recorded there along with the very childhood sights they were destroying.

'That's why they won't mind moving,' Guy said. 'They live from one new thrill to the next. They're always saying "I can't wait for it" about the most insignificant event, simply because it's something that's going to happen. They'll feel the same way about a new house.'

'I don't know. They love it here.'

'Because you've made them love it. You've taught them to think that Cottingham Park is the only place on earth to live. That was all right when they were little. But hell, Martha. Bernie's seven and a half. Terry's nearly ten. They don't want to live on your nostalgia for ever. I think they'll be delighted with the news.'

'I think they'll be miserable.'

When they were told, the children were neither delighted nor miserable. They knew already, because they overheard many of their parents' conversations, but they put up a thin show of surprise and interest. They said nothing revealing, and when Martha, out of her anxiety, asked them foolishly: 'But do you

397

mind?' Bernadette closed her small secret face, and Terry said in the infuriating voice she had picked up from a girl at school who kept tally in a notebook of her own qualifications for future sainthood: 'It doesn't matter whether we mind or not. We have to go where we are told.'

It was much worse telling Bessie Myers that she must soon leave the basement flat. Bernadette, who had remained thick with Bessie even after the attraction of Uncle James Donahue was eliminated, offered to do it, since Martha baulked; but Guy went down alone and came back upstairs in ten minutes sweating lightly, with his face screwed up on one side as if Bessie had struck him.

'She was very rude,' he said. 'It's extraordinary. You'd think we ran our whole lives for her convenience.'

'Did you tell her she might have to go before the winter if we found a buyer?'

He nodded, and let down the side of his face. 'She said that she wasn't going to pay any more rent money to traitors. She'll get out as soon as she finds a flat, I think. Just as long as she doesn't set fire to the house before she goes.'

'I hope she does,' said Bernadette surprisingly from the floor. 'You shouldn't turn her out. She's my friend.'

'But there will be new friends, new people to love . . .' Martha began soothingly, but Guy cut bluntly in with: 'We can't take Bessie Myers with us wherever we go as if she was your pet teddy bear.'

'Then why do we go?'

Martha bent down to her in surprise. 'Do you mind so much? You haven't said anything.'

'Why should I? I don't mind.' She dipped her head over the carpet and the short dark hair swung forward across the corners of her eyes.

Two nights later, Bernadette had a nightmare. 'What was it about?' Martha asked, but Bernadette would not talk. She cried herself to sleep in Martha's bed, and in the morning she was gone, not only from the bed, but from the house.

She had run away before. She had been running away off and on ever since she could walk, but since she never got farther than the second corner before she found some excuse to come back without losing face, her brief disappearances excited nobody. If she threatened to run when thwarted or in trouble, Theresa was told to watch her. That was all.

But this was different. Martha and Guy and Terry spent two hours walking the streets in the rain and telephoning or visiting every house or shop where Bernadette had friends. Then Guy went to the police station and then he got into the car and widened his search, while Martha took Terry in a taxi through the back streets of the Rise in a mounting panic of dread for what could happen to her here.

In the taxi, they sat apart, looking out of opposite windows. 'Why did she do it? Why did she have to do it?' Martha kept asking the futile question as they drove hopelessly through the squalor and the dangerous streets.

Terry was silent, but after a while when they were on the slope of West Hill where the vegetable market was, she said: 'I think I know.' She was looking out of the window, as they both were, raking the busy Saturday streets for Bernadette. 'I think it was because she – well, she was upset about leaving our house, you know.'

'I didn't know!' Martha turned from the window and put out her hand to grip Theresa's arm. 'Why didn't you tell me?'

'Oh . . . I don't know. You'd both made up your minds to go. What was the point of us saying we didn't want to? I made Bernie promise not to fuss, under threats. I thought it would spoil it for you.'

'Spoil it! But look what's happened. If I'd only known how she felt, I could have talked to her, and she wouldn't have run away.'

'Oh yes, she would. She made up her mind quite a long time ago, after she heard you and Daddy talking, and you cried.'

'You knew?' Martha was terrified by the impenetrable mystery of children's secrecy. 'You knew, and you didn't tell me?'

'Well, I didn't believe it.' Theresa's eyes were frightened too, seeing her mother's face. 'She's always saying crazy stuff like that. Things she's going to do. I don't pay any notice.'

'But you know where she's gone.' Martha gripped her arm tightly.

'No I don't.'

'You're lying!' Martha cried in anguish.

'I'm not. Honestly, I'm not. I don't know where she's gone. I wish I did. You're hurting me!'

'I'm sorry.' Martha dropped her hand and turned back to stare out of the window at the barricaded street and the broken archway beyond which what was left of Armstrong Mews lay huddled under the rain. 'I do believe you. It's all right, darling. I do believe you.'

For two days they lived in a nightmare from which there was no waking. The police had advised them to talk to the newspapers, since any publicity might help to find Bernadette. All day long the telephone rang, and Martha or Guy or Terry jumped to it, for this time it would be someone saying: 'I have your little girl here'; but it was only a reporter, or a detective checking, or a friend saying in distress: 'I've just heard about Bernadette. Is there anything I can do?'

And then quite late on the evening of the third day, when Guy was still out in the car and Martha and Terry were sitting together half stupid with fatigue, for Terry would not go to bed, and Martha had not slept since Bernie vanished, someone rang the bell. When Martha opened the door, Uncle James Donahue stood on the step, red in the face, with the unceasing curtain of rain behind him, shaking water from his sloppy hat.

'Oh. I'm sorry. I can't see you now. It's nice of you to come, but . . .' Martha was not surprised that he had come, for he had loved Bernadette, but she could not let him in to sit and condole with her sentimentally about his little angel.

'I know where Bernadette is,' he said, and Martha opened the door wider and he stepped into the hall, wiping his feet very thoroughly and looking at her with the sort of innocent delight of a child offering a birthday gift.

'How can you know?' Drugged with exhaustion and misery, Martha could not believe him. There had already been two cruel telephone hoaxers and one attempt at extortion.

'Because I saw her.' James Donahue let his statement go up into the quirk of a question mark. 'Mind if I take off my coat? The thing is wet clear through. She's with Bessie, at the new flat in Marylebone.'

'With Bessie –' Martha swayed and put a hand out to his short thick arm. 'My God, I'll kill her.'

'I wouldn't blame you,' Uncle James said calmly. 'She's trying to get even with you, I suppose, for putting her out. As you know, she won't have anything to do with me since my little bit of trouble, but I knew where she was, because I met her old lady in the street and she told me. So I'm walking by this evening to see what kind of a joint she has now, and who do I see going up the steps and into the block of flats – like a jail, it is; she was much better off here – but Miss Bessie Myers and me little Bernadette.

'That child should be in bed was my first thought. Which shows you how creeping the mind can get, for I'd seen the papers and been half out of my mind with worrying about the child. But it wasn't till my second thought that I realized what I had seen. I came straight here.'

'Oh, thank you. I don't know how to thank you . . .'

'Don't cry, my dear. It was my pleasure.' Uncle James bent his thick waistless trunk in a clumsy bow and looked up with his pre-fabricated roguish twinkle. 'Miss Bessie Myers turned her back on me when I needed her help. Why shouldn't I be glad to pay off such a bitter score?'

'I had a good time with old Bessie,' Bernadette said about a week later when the hysteria and emotion had died down and it seemed safe to speak above the muted, apologetic voice she had brought home with her to ward off retribution. 'We ate all the time and she never made me go to bed. Perhaps I could go and visit there again?'

'Have you absolutely no shame?' Terry rounded on her. 'If your father was here, he'd whip you.'

'If he was going to do any whipping, he'd have done it when I first came back. I was surprised he didn't though, weren't you, Mum?'

Martha said dutifully: 'Yes,' but she had not been surprised. After what Bernadette had said, clinging to her in the car after the unspeakably ugly fight with Bessie, neither of them could have punished her. Punishment was for them. They had suffered their punishment in three days of agony, but it was not over. It would be a long time, if ever, before Martha ceased to remember every note of her child's tired, hysterical voice. *I know what moving means. It means that one of you is moving out. We shall never be happy again – never!*

Half asleep in the back seat, Theresa said with surprising perception: 'She thinks you want to move because the house has made you quarrel. But it isn't fair to blame it on the house. People can fight anywhere, even in the middle of a desert, I suppose.'

'We aren't going to fight any more,' Guy said quietly.

'Then perhaps we could stay?'

Afterwards Martha could not remember which child said that, but she remembered that Guy had said: 'I don't know,' and did not look at her, and when Terry leaned forward to put her chin on her mother's shoulder, Martha had said: 'I don't know,' and did not look at Guy.

There was a man coming to see the house. A Mr Slessinger. He was coming at four o'clock, and the house agent seemed to think he would not quarrel about the price. 'With the basement already a separate flat and not too much required to convert the rest into rentable apartments, this is a handy little property, Mr Banning. We'll have no difficulty, I think.'

'Even with the new road spoiling the neighbourhood?'

'Oh that.' The house agent had been here for many years. 'Cottingham Park has been here for a long time. If you're willing to accept that it wasn't irretrievably spoiled a hundred years ago when the houses were crammed in, a little thing like an Expressway shouldn't bother you.'

Guy was to come home early to see Mr Slessinger. Martha was supposed to hurry home, but she was not hurrying. When she came out of the makeshift Underground station, she walked slowly, and walked on past the West Hill turning to take a longer way home.

She walked down a small back street with trees in thick leaf, stubbornly flourishing out of the meagre soil below the pavement. She walked through what used to be a gloomy yard until the warehouses on one side of it had been knocked down to expose the poor terrace houses on the other side openly to the sun for the first time in their lives.

Anywhere else but Cottingham Park, they would have knocked down both sides of the yard while they were at it. But here the shabby terrace where the scavenging cats were far cleaner than the children would drag out its retrograde span cheek by jowl with the swift new highway, the concrete pillars of the fly-over rising soon to black out its brief love affair with the sun and put it back in the familiar shadows. The uncaring traffic would flow over and away above the smoking roofs, and after a while the people in the houses below would never even look up to see the top of a red bus or the roof of a silver truck bound for Scotland speed disembodied by above the parapet.

She turned a corner into a street of little shops where people who lived nearby could buy everything they needed for life without going farther afield. This end was barricaded, for the demolition was nicking off one corner, but you could walk through on planks where the paving stones were gone, and the rest of the street was as busy as usual in its small way, with the green raffia mats spread under the polished apples, and the piles of cheap china bowls with dust in them and bits of straw set out on the pavement in front of the shop that reeked of paraffin and firewood.

One of the shops was being done over. It used to sell old paintings and books bought by the sackful, but the man with the lump over one side of his collar had died, and now the empty windows were scrawled with whitewash and two men on a painter's scaffold were fixing up a signboard over the door.

It was a long board. It ran the whole length of the shop, with too many words, too small to be effective. If Martha had not stood there and seen it herself, she would have found it hard to believe; but seeing it now, as the men juggled with the long board and set one end down and tried to bolt the other in place first, and then lowered that and tried the other end again, the surprise was that it was not surprising. The fact that the board going up over the newly decorated shop said: 'Second Hand Clothes. Misfits. Uniforms. Waiters. Weddings. Riding Clothes Bought and Sold' was merely part of the pattern. It was not surprising at all.

With a lightness in her heart that carried her swiftly, she hurried home. Mr Slessinger had not yet come. He had telephoned to say he would be late.

'I wish I'd been here,' Martha said breathlessly. 'I'd have told him not to come.'

'Oh now, look here,' Guy said. 'What is it you want, Martha? What is it you want us to do? God knows, I don't want the trouble and expense of finding another house and the nightmare of travelling into town and out every day if you don't even want it.'

'I'm not sure yet,' Martha said slowly. 'I want what everybody wants, but I think we should talk about it some more and not hurry to do anything. Why can't we wait and see?' She put her arms round Guy and looked into his face. 'We've been so happy here. Why can't it go on? I have a curious feeling that nothing is really going to change.'

When Mr Slessinger came, they hid upstairs like four children, and heard the door bell ring again and again. From the bedroom window of their fortress, they watched his narrow seemly back walk down the steps and out through the front gate.

But then, because it seemed unfair to let him walk away like that when they were suddenly all so happy, Martha ran downstairs and out of the door and down the steps and after him along the street to catch him and explain to him. To try to explain the unexplainable.

*Some other Penguins by Monica Dickens are
described on the following pages*

THURSDAY AFTERNOONS

For the background of this book Miss Dickens returns to the hospital life which she portrayed so successfully in her autobiographical *One Pair of Feet*. *Thursday Afternoons* is an extremely attractive novel – a tale of human relationships, in which she describes simply and shrewdly some of the events in the day-to-day life of a young doctor.

'A novelist who has all the airs and graces a reader can wish. She can tell a story, she is funny, observant, tender, interested in the people she describes. She can etch a character in a single sentence' – John Betjeman in the *Daily Herald*

'Monica Dickens is beyond the stage of reviewers recalling patronizingly that she is a great-granddaughter of the great Charles. She is, in her own right, the authoress of *One Pair of Feet*, the portrayer of a nurse's life, perhaps the best woman novelist in Britain – just Monica Dickens' – *Evening News*

MARIANA

They say that when a man is drowning he sees as in a flash the whole of his past life pass before him. No one can say if this is really so. Yet at great crises we sometimes see life in retrospect, things forgotten, things loved and unimportant. So it was with Mary when she heard that her husband's ship had been mined. As she lay in bed that sleepless night waiting for the moment to find out whether he had survived, her mind went back over the years. She remembered perfect holidays in Dorset at her grandfather's house, the rides and parties, her schoolgirl adoration of her cousin; the drab routine of lessons, duty visits to her other grandmother, her feckless but genial uncle. She remembered her first serious love affair, with its bewilderment, delight, and disappointment; then the startling joy of meeting Sam, how on that day after their engagement they had visited the now deserted house in Dorset, and how much smaller it seemed.

Those who have read *Thursday Afternoons* will remember Monica Dickens' skill in writing with sympathy and understanding about ordinary people.

ONE PAIR OF FEET

'A brilliantly funny account of the first and only year of her training to be a nurse. . . . Her funniness on the subject she chooses is far from being facile or irresponsible. She is shrewd, and she shows not only a quick eye, but an excellent heart. . . . Her character sketches of sisters, nurses, public-ward patients, the grandees of the private wards, and the grandees of the town are little masterpieces' – Elizabeth Bowen in the *Tatler*

'Is this as good a book as *One Pair of Hands*? The answer is that it is much better. The cheerful impudence is still there. The power of observation and the family eye for a comic character are in better form than in her early work. And there are occasional touches of genuine and unforced pathos' – J. B. Priestley

'The most striking thing about the book is, that for all the emphasis on trivial irritations, monotony, hardship, mental stultification and lack of appreciation, Miss Dickens succeeds, almost in spite of herself, in conveying the essential nobility of the profession and the supreme satisfaction of a life saved' – *Listener*

JOY AND JOSEPHINE

Of this story of a foundling and her search for her own life the reviewers said:

'She presents a hilarious variety of character types, all seen with an accurate and deadly eye ... with the brilliant but pitiless verve that is particularly her own' – Pamela Hansford Johnson in the *Sunday Chronicle*

'Altogether delightful ... She has the supreme gift of producing living and lovable human beings. ... It is the stuff of life as most of us see and feel it for three-quarters of our waking existence. And it is the sort of novel which will keep you from doing a thousand more important things till you have finished it' – Rupert Croft-Cooke in the *Sketch*

'Miss Monica Dickens has a good idea in her novel, and she makes the most of it. ... *Joy and Josephine* is neatly conceived and almost consistently amusing; Miss Dickens is observant and has a sharp sense of the ridiculous' – *The Times Literary Supplement*

NOT FOR SALE IN THE U.S.A.

THE HAPPY PRISONER

'Miss Monica Dickens gets better and better. It is a pleasure to record such steady and admirable progress in a world in which so much gets worse and worse. . . . A long but light novel that nearly every kind of reader will be able to enjoy. We congratulate Miss Dickens on her skill and invention and continued liveliness' – J. B. Priestley in the *Bookman*

'It is quite certainly her best book to date and puts her in a very short list of the lighter novelists who are also true literary artists, with sureness of touch and facility for brilliant character sketching' – *Birmingham Mail*

'Miss Monica Dickens is unfailingly entertaining: she has as sharp an eye for the amusing trifle as the ace reporter for news, and a genius for the humours of the commonplace . . . what a lively comedy it is' – Pamela Hansford Johnson in *John O'London's*

NOT FOR SALE IN THE U.S.A.

THE ANGEL IN THE CORNER

This absorbing novel is set in London: in Bloomsbury, St John's Wood, the West End, and the tenement buildings near Paddington. The central character, Virginia, an ambitious young journalist, longs for the love she has never had from her sophisticated, divorced mother, the successful editor of a fashion magazine. So she makes an impulsive marriage, and a new world engulfs her, a world of cruelty and smells and drunkenness, and endless worry about money. But Virginia's courage, and the Angel in the Corner whom her old nurse taught her to believe in, are with her through poverty and suffering and tragedy, until she gains a new peace. Spenser, the successful American businessman, the kindly Benbergs, Feliz the clever young specialist, blowsy Mrs Batey, valiant little Lennie, and a host of other characters make the story vividly alive.

ONE PAIR OF HANDS

Tired of the life of a debutante Monica Dickens decided to be a cook-general. This uproarious backstairs view of the English upper classes in moments of comedy, drama, selfishness, and childish pique holds the reader's attention from first page to last with that 'exuberant vitality' which Compton Mackenzie finds in the work both of Charles Dickens and his great-granddaughter, Here is fun, wit, malice and – in the face of the tartars who rule on both sides of the Green Baize door – courage. You can also discover how to cook a *crème brulée*.

'There must have been some dull patches in Miss Dickens' kitchen career, but there is none in her book. The high spirits which first made her think of getting a cap and apron infect its pages, and she has an appreciation of character which may well be inherited. Nearly everyone will want to read this irreverent chronicle from below stairs' – *Time and Tide*

'Glorious entertainment' – *Daily Mail*

'Riotously amusing as the book is in parts, Miss Dickens' also manages to make it a social document' – *The Times*

MY TURN TO MAKE THE TEA

As a cook-general Monica Dickens irreverently recounted how other people's crockery came to pieces in *One Pair of Hands*, and as a nurse how the hospital wards thundered under *One Pair of Feet*. In *My Turn to Make the Tea* she rounds off the record with an account of those glorious months when she helped, as a cub reporter, to put the *Downingham Post* to bed each week.

'Anyone who has a junior reporter will recognize the truthfulness of the picture the author paints ... I take off my hat to Miss Dickens as the most entertaining junior reporter ever to enter a newspaper office' – Howard Spring in *Country Life*

'Vivacious ... wherever her eye falls, it finds the exact, significant detail, and her ear for dialogue is unerring ... All in all, Miss Dickens is bringing the word Dickensian up to date' – *Observer*

'It is a book which will be read, as it has been written, with enthusiasm and with pleasure' – *The Times Literary Supplement*

MAN OVERBOARD

'Axed': a brutal word for a brutal action! When Ben, the Lieuten-
ant-Commander hero of this book, was retired from the Navy, at
thirty-six, it was neither Ben's, nor England's, finest hour. For, like
so many of his kind, Ben was not at all well-equipped for the rigours
of civilian life. How could he be, considering that his knowledge and
experience were largely confined to submarines and Gosport? A
widower with a small daughter, he had some very delicate first steps
to take on the alien dry land. You'll laugh a lot at his adventures,
but with no malice in the laughter, for Monica Dickens blends
sympathy with humour in this account of Ben's struggle to find a
new way of earning his living.

'The best novel by Monica Dickens since her autobiographical days.
Hurrah for a real sense of comedy!' – *Oxford Mail*

'Full of zest, as always, and full of those sure descriptions of people
and places which make all her stories a pleasure to read' – *Book of
the Month*

THE WINDS OF HEAVEN

The predicament of Louise Bickford was not uncommon. When her husband died, leaving her to struggle along on a shoestring, she became dependent on the hospitality of each of her three daughters in turn. But efficient Miriam was preoccupied with the cares of a house, husband, and three children, whilst Eva, the actress, lived in her London flat a life verging on the Bohemian, and slovenly Anne could hardly care less. Our hearts go out to Louise as she jolts uncomfortably from one to the next, with occasional visits to a friend's hotel in the Isle of Wight. Yet her ability to laugh at herself stands her in good stead, and due to one Gordon Disher – alias Lester Drage, author of *The Girl in the Bloodstained Bikini* – her fortunes take an unexpected twist.

The Winds of Heaven is related with all the humour, tenderness, and perception for which the author of *One Pair of Hands* is justly praised.

For a complete list of books available please write to Penguin Books whose address can be found on the back of the title page